roaming WILD

TRACEY DEVLYN

STEELE RIDGE
www.SteeleRidgeSeries.com

TEAM STEELE RIDGE
Edited by Deborah Nemeth
Copyedited by Martha Trachtenberg
Beta Reads by Amy Remus, April Renn, Cricket McGraw and
Isabel Seligstein Hofmann
Cover Design by Killion Group, Inc.
Interior Formatting by Author E.M.S.
Author Photo by Lisa Kaman Kenning, Mezzaluna Photography

Print Edition, June 2017, ISBN: 978-1-944898-15-1
For more information contact: tracey@traceydevlyn.com

roaming WILD

TRACEY
DEVLYN

CHAPTER ONE

July 28, 11:37 a.m.
Bamford, Western North Carolina

DEKE CROUCHED BEHIND A LARGE tree, his AR15 at the ready while he waited for his team members to get into position.

Eleven months. That's how long it had taken him to get to this point.

Eleven months living as Dan Wimberly, a gun store clerk looking to make a quick buck.

Eleven months currying favor with a greedy lowlife who cared nothing for the things Deke had dedicated his life to for the past decade.

Eleven months away from family and friends. Away from Evie.

He sensed more than heard his second-in-command, Keone Akana, move into position twenty yards away. "Team check," Deke whispered into his mic.

Voices from the other five members of his team chimed in his ear.

"All appears quiet inside," Keone said.

"Too quiet." Deke flipped his night goggles in place. Everything turned into shades of green and shadow. He searched the area around the large red barn and two outbuildings. Nothing stirred. Not even an insect.

"Are you sure you got the right night?" Keone asked.

Forty-eight hours ago, his confidential informant had warned him that the Distributor would be moving his inventory from this location at midnight. Deke assessed the barn. It had to be at least five thousand square feet. A lot of space to store illegal contraband. A lot of senseless deaths.

The muscle in Deke's jaw tightened. No matter how many of these busts he made, he would never get used to walking into a room full of animal pelts and parts. Never.

Had his CI screwed up the date or time? Had Deke's cover been blown?

"We'll soon find out." Deke squashed the coil of uncertainty in his gut. "Move in, on my mark. Three…two…one. Move."

His unit advanced as one toward the barn. Deke didn't need visual confirmation to know it. They had trained together for a year in a half before their first mission. Their tactics came to them second nature, though each man and woman brought their own expertise to the table and acted accordingly. As long as each member achieved their individual missions, Deke left it to them to determine the best method.

Deke and Keone flanked a door on the east side of the building. Trying the latch, the door creaked open. Their gazes met, grim.

With a hand gesture, Deke gave his partner the *go* signal.

Keone eased through the opening and entered the barn. Deke closed in behind him.

They'd barely cleared the door when Keone yelled, "Get down!"

A *whish* followed by a *thrump* split the air.

The force of the arrow spun Deke around, throwing him off-balance and buckling his knees. Steel ripped through muscle and tendons. Searing pain stole his breath. Blood pounded in his ears, deafening him to the outside world. For several precious seconds, he lay on his back, disoriented.

"You okay?" Keone pulled him clear and propped him against a stack of empty crates.

"Fine," Deke panted, holding his injured arm against his body. "Warn the team."

"Shooter!" Keone fired back in his mic. "Stay sharp—"

"Fuck!" someone roared into Deke's earpiece.

"Matteo's down," Wes said in his usual can't-rattle-me tone. "Arrow to the leg."

"I'm on my way," Raelyn said.

"Rae's the best. She'll patch the new kid up." As usual, Keone could sense Deke's turmoil before he could. The Hawaiian had a deep connection to the entire team's inner workings. It was damn uncomfortable at times.

"Have you located the bastard?" Deke peered through the slats in the crate.

"No, but I see a spent crossbow mounted against a support beam."

"Sonofabitch." He spoke to his team. "The entrances are booby-trapped. Team check."

Everyone's voice came over the mic, including Matteo's, though the engineer's was strained.

"Commander," a more distant female voice called through Deke's earpiece.

"Go ahead, ComOne."

Intelligence analyst Marisol Vega continued, "Satellite imagery is picking up some activity about a half mile south of your location."

"What kind of activity?"

"Two large trucks and nine subjects." Typing echoed in the background. "No buildings in the area, though there appears to be…"

"What're you seeing?"

"Sorry, sir. The image is unclear."

"Taj, Jax, check it out."

"10-4," Taj said.

Deke got to his feet. "Let's continue our sweep."

"Hang on a second," Keone said. "I'll get Rae over here to take a look at your injury."

Deke glanced down at the arrow protruding from his shoulder. Bad idea. Sweat broke out on his forehead. "Leave her with Matteo."

"But—"

Not in the mood to argue, he brushed past his second, but within minutes Deke knew the mission was a bust. The barn sat empty, except for some wooden crates and metal shelving units.

Frustration burned through his veins. Eleven months' worth of work vaporized before his eyes.

"Loft and perimeter empty. Entrances clear," Keone said, rejoining him. "We've got a damn rat in our midst."

Deke lifted his goggles and rubbed his eyes, the exhaustion he'd been holding at bay finally breaking through. "Appears so."

"Any ideas?"

"Not offhand."

"Any chance the new kid made a mistake? Maybe he inadvertently passed on intel?"

Although each team member came to SONR with a specialization, everyone had to put in field time. Which meant undercover work. Some were naturals, some stuck out like a red M&M in a peanut bowl.

"Anything's possible. But from what I've observed, Matteo can hold his own." Into his mic, he asked, "Matteo's status?"

Raelyn replied, "The arrow's lodged deep in his thigh. He's going to need surgery."

"Load him up. I'll be there in a few minutes."

"The Distributor got wind of our arrival somehow," Keone pressed. "And our circle of trust is damn small."

Distributor. Not very original, but it was the name the team had adopted for the elusive mastermind behind a multimillion-dollar wildlife and plant trafficking scheme. The U.S. Fish and Wildlife Service established his elite team, SONR—Special Operations for Natural Resources—for the sole purpose of taking down empires like the Distributor's. The problem was, no one knew the guy's identity, and Deke had only found one who would dare cross him.

Could someone within SONR have betrayed the team? He'd trained, eaten, slept, trained, shot, killed, and trained with these agents. How much money would it take to turn comrade against comrade?

"You think one of us tipped him off?" The words scraped along Deke's throat like slivers of glass.

"No—yes—maybe. Damned if I know." Keone's brown eyes passed over a few members of the team filtering into the main room of the barn. "We've got enough shit to sift through. The last thing we need is a dirty agent."

"Commander," Taj said in his ear.

"What'd you got?"

"We're too late. All that's left is a set of large tire tracks leading out of the woods."

Dammit. "Head back. We'll return tomorrow for a better look."

"Tire tracks aren't all that's left," Jax said, snapping her gum.

"What's she talking about, Taj?"

A mountain of silence followed.

"Someone talk to me."

"Looks like the Distributor left a message for you," Taj said.

"What?"

"Probably your CI," Jax interjected.

"Bald, scruffy beard, reeks of stale smoke?"

"You got it."

"I'll be right there," Deke said. "He's got some explaining to do."

"Not gonna happen, boss," Jax said around another bubble. "His throat's slit."

Chapter Two

July 31
Steele Ridge, Western North Carolina

DEKE PUSHED THROUGH THE DOOR of Blues, Brews, and Books—or, as the locals liked to say, Triple B. It was good to be back in Steele Ridge, which had formerly been named Canyon Ridge. His family had moved here right before he entered the fourth grade and stayed through his junior year before returning to their hometown of Rockton.

For him, Steele Ridge would always be his true home. He'd made lifelong friends here, and it was the place where he'd become a man.

His eyes took a moment to adjust before settling on the lone figure stationed at the bar. Zigzagging his way around islands of low and high tables, he slapped his friend's broad shoulder. "Hello, shit for brains."

Rather than be startled by such an abrupt greeting, Britt Steele angled his lumberjack body around and held out his hand. "You're late." He shook Deke's hand before bellying up to the bar again. "Some of us have to return to work, you know."

Deke slid onto the barstool kiddie corner to his friend's. "Can't even work up an ounce of sympathy." He nodded to the bartender, Grady. "My last vacation was over a year ago. I'm going to enjoy every second of the next fourteen days."

Britt eyed the sling cradling his arm. "What happened? Keyboard attack you?"

Deke did his damnedest not to lie to those he cared about. As far as his friends and family knew, he worked for the U.S. Fish and Wildlife Service's Office of External Affairs, traveling all over the Southeast Region in search of his next story. Or he could be found cooped up at the Asheville field office banging out articles for the Service's quarterly newsletter. All true—but not the whole truth.

"You have no idea how threatening the office environment can be."

"And I hope I never do. How are you healing?"

The dull, throbbing pain in his shoulder served as a constant reminder of how quickly a mission could go wrong, even with hours of careful planning. Matteo had gotten the worst of it, though. SONR's engineer had spent three days in the hospital after the surgeon had dug the arrow out of his leg. The damned thing had gone so deep that the tip had embedded in bone.

Clenching his jaw, Deke flexed his fingers and lifted his elbow until the action caused an involuntary wince. Better than yesterday, but he wouldn't be playing basketball anytime soon.

"Getting there."

"What do you have planned, besides lunch with a friend you've blown off for months?"

"Not a damn thing."

"You're going to stare at your apartment walls for the next two weeks?"

"Maybe. If the mood strikes."

"Don't see it. I've never known you to be idle, in over twenty-five years."

"I'm hoping to sleep away the first two days." Deke rubbed his tired eyes. "I'll see where things go from there."

"Tough assignment?"

He chose his words carefully. "They get more complicated every time."

"Complicated how? Don't you just go into an area, interview people, take some pictures and then write up an article?"

"I wish it were that simple."

"What can I get you?" Grady asked.

"Surprise me." He glanced at Britt. "You order food yet?"

"Yeah. Hope you're in the mood for a burger."

"Do you order for Randi?"

"Not a chance," a new voice said.

Randi Shepherd cuddled against Britt's side and kissed him. Although she kept it short, Deke could feel the power of their intimacy from two feet away. A pang of envy clutched his chest, and he shifted his attention to Grady's nimble hands. What he wouldn't give to have a woman love him as Randi loves Britt. It was a notion that had filtered through his thoughts a lot lately.

"He knows better." Randi wrapped Deke in a warm hug. "Seems like forever since we saw you last. You gonna hang around Steele Ridge for a while?"

"I'd planned to. Mind if I rent the loft above the bar for a few days?"

"Of course. I'll have someone run up there to see if it's habitable."

"Thought you didn't have a plan," Britt said.

"My plan is not to have a plan."

Randi laughed. "Let me go check on your food."

He watched his friend's gaze follow Randi from the room. "How's domestic life treating you?"

"Bit of an adjustment at first, but we've settled into a groove now."

"A good one?"

"The best."

"How's the Center?"

Thanks to a hefty investment from Britt's younger

brother, he was running a Wildlife Research Center on the outskirts of town.

"I hired a botanist to study the red wolves' habitat and the surrounding conservation area."

"Is that trepidation or skepticism I hear in your voice?"

"Fear." Britt lifted a beer mug to his lips. "She's my cousin."

He searched his memory for another conservationist in the Steele family. "Not Riley."

"Ding, ding, ding."

"The Kingston menace?"

Britt smiled.

"What the hell were you thinking? She used to plant shit bombs in our sleeping bags."

"She just got back from a research expedition in Costa Rica and needed a job. The Center needed a botanist, so everyone's happy."

"Can't wait to see how long that lasts."

A gust of air signaled the arrival of a newcomer to Triple B. Even before Deke turned, a buzz of awareness sprinted down his spine. Only one person had ever had that effect on him.

The last person who should.

Evie Steele.

Even though he'd known her since she'd toddled around on chubby legs, he'd first noticed her crystal blue eyes, silken black hair, and long, long legs right after she turned sixteen. He'd come upon her sunbathing in a gut-socking white bikini. The sight had stopped him cold. Then the heat had come. Scorching, blood-searing heat.

When she'd glanced at him over her bare shoulder and thrown out her sweet Evie smile, he could only stare at the way the triangle of white material molded her firm ass. She'd twisted around, and his attention had torn from her rounded bottom to mouthwatering breasts that would fit his hand perfectly.

Somewhere between fifteen and sixteen, his Squirt

had...*developed*. And he'd stirred. For her. *Evie*. The girl who, up to that point, had been like a sister to him. Guilt had consumed him.

For years afterwards, he'd done everything he could to avoid her.

Avoidance hadn't stopped his thoughts. His vivid dreams. His comparing every woman he looked at to Evie's perfection.

Evie Steele had squirmed her way into every conscious thought and desire he possessed. No amount of cursing, women, or distance had managed to shake her hold.

At one point, when she'd cleared high school, he'd considered braving Britt's big brother wrath and asking her out. But she'd plunged into college and nursing school at the same time he'd been invited to join a newly formed black ops unit with the Service.

Now, four years later, their journeys were still worlds apart. With a degree under her belt, Evie would be starting a career. Whereas kids, family, and settling down had begun visiting his thoughts, as of late.

Britt had found soul-searing happiness with Randi. She smoothed his edges, cared for him in a way no one else ever had. And he'd almost lost the love of his life to a greed-driven trophy hunter.

The power of that kind of love struck fear in Deke's heart and warmed it, at the same time. Problem was, he didn't have a wife, fiancée, or even a girlfriend. Not one viable candidate.

His gaze locked on Evie's across the bar, and the pressure on his chest intensified, became crushing. Time had passed, and his lecherous guilt had faded. They were both adults now. If not for the twelve years separating their ages, Evie might have been the one.

But he could never ask her to put her career on hold to be with him and start a family. What if she did and then couldn't stomach the demands of his career? She would've given up so much, for what?

Heartbreak.

Resentment.

Anger.

Hate.

He swallowed back his longing and returned to his beer, allowing the familiar mask to drop in place.

Forcing away the memory of last year's stolen kiss.

Evie Steele spotted her brother the moment she entered Triple B. Over two hundred pounds of muscle and shaggy blond hair was hard to miss, even in this lunch crowd.

Her big brother held her attention for about a half a second before her Deke radar blared.

There he was. Every bit as tall as Britt, but with the sleek, muscled planes of a leopard rather than the thick sturdiness of a tiger. Deke's coloring was even darker, deeper. As if he'd spent all the hours of his days outside. Curly ebony hair shaved close at the sides and back and tamed at the top by a hint of hair product.

What she wouldn't do to see that beautiful mane grow wild, to run her fingers through his thick curls. To feel their softness whisper against her bare breast. Evie shook off the erotic fantasy before she made a fool of herself in front of the good residents of Steele Ridge.

Instead, she braced herself for their reunion. At the moment, she was quite unhappy with him. But Deke Conrad could charm the cantankerous out of any farmer and he had every woman in town holding their breath for one of his lopsided grins to float their way.

Deke was a dangerous man.

Especially to her. She'd crushed on him since before she'd known what the word meant. Then her young girl's worship transformed into something deeper, hotter, more stirring than a simple attraction. She *ached* to draw imaginary lines over his broad, bare back, to trace her lips down the center of his glistening chest, to inhale his musky, masculine scent as her tongue explored his most intimate parts.

Gah! She had to stop with the naked, entwined images.

The big lug refused to see her as a beddable woman. Scratch that. He'd noticed. She'd caught him looking at her behind a time or two. The most memorable moment, the time that had given her the most hope, was when she'd been sitting in front of the picture window in her mom's front room.

At that time of the day, silhouettes from inside the house reflected onto the glass, giving her fair warning should any of her brothers try to sneak up from behind. But her brothers hadn't filled the picture window that day. Deke had.

He'd stopped by to pick up Britt for some outing or other and spotted her reading. He hadn't announced his presence. He'd just stood there, watching her.

Even now, years later, her flesh heated, her breasted tightened, her center dampened at the memory. All for a guy who couldn't get beyond the fact that she was his best friend's little sister.

Sometimes she'd like to flick his ears. Knock the fog from his eyes. Last year, at the groundbreaking ceremony for Britt's wildlife research center, she'd thought he'd set aside the ridiculous barrier he'd erected and decided to see where their mutual attraction led. But the next morning, the scaredy-cat had disappeared.

For eleven months, eight days, and…never mind. It was a long frickin' time.

His dark gaze honed in on her across the bar. A spin top tore across her chest, then idled on her stomach, burrowing deep. She slapped the damn thing away.

Who disappeared after a first kiss? Caveman Conrad, that's who. When he'd vanished without a word of goodbye, he'd lost his chance with her. Not that he was rolling any dice in that direction, but if he were, he'd hit snake eyes. Too many loved ones had ditched her over the years. She wasn't about to get tangled up with a guy who couldn't see past her last name to the woman she'd become.

At least that's what she told herself. One come hither-glance from those iridescent eyes, and all her hard lines would go limp like a spaghetti noodle. No getting around it. She was a hot mess when it came to her feelings for Deke Conrad. "Evie-girl, what are you up to today?" asked a woman with a thick salt-and-pepper braid resting over one shoulder.

"Here to pester my brother before I set off for another MedTour. Speaking of which, how's your knee? Still painful when you bend it?"

"Nah. Those exercises you gave me did the trick."

"Happy to hear it. Have a nice afternoon, Mrs. Grossman."

As she wove her way to the bar, several diners gave her quick waves, big smiles, and warm hellos. She mustered a half-hearted acknowledgment. She didn't stop to chat like normal. She couldn't. No words could get past her air-locked throat.

Deke was in her midst.

Damn the man!

"Hey, Squirt," Deke said when she neared.

The nickname was like a palm to the forehead. Blunt. Hard. Crushing.

She met his gaze. Held it long enough to determine whether or not he remembered their kiss. Those ice-blue eyes held the same warm friendship they always had. No longing. No passion. No glimmer of hope. "Hey, Deke."

Britt turned around on his barstool, and she hugged him before sitting on his opposite side.

"What? No squeeze for me?"

Somehow she produced her most mischievous smile. "I don't hug strangers."

"Ouch. It hasn't been that long."

"Guess that depends on your perspective."

Britt eyed the two of them, big brother suspicion creasing the area between his brows.

Time for a subject change.

"Thanks for the lunch invite," she said. "I'm glad we could get together before I head out."

"Need anything?" Britt asked.

"I'm good, thanks." She nudged her shoulder against his. "I have a job now, you know."

"I know."

She let the issue alone. Britt would always look out for his younger brothers and sisters. No matter their age or economic status. Heck, Jonah was a billionaire and Britt still tried to buy his lunch.

"Taking a trip?" Deke asked.

"Yep."

He waited for her to explain. She didn't. She was that annoyed with him.

"Here you go." Kris McKay slid plates in front of Britt and Deke. "Can I get you boys anything else?"

"Not in front of the kid," Deke said, winking at Kris.

"What in the world are you talking about, Deke Conrad?" Kris asked, throwing a conspiratorial grin her way. "Evie's my age."

Deke glanced between Kris and Evie.

"That way lies trouble, my friend," Britt said, biting into his burger.

Evie raised a brow in Deke's direction, waiting.

He grabbed the ketchup bottle and squirted a blob next to his steak-cut fries.

Noticing his sling, pressure squeezed her chest. "What happened to your arm?"

"Hunting accident." He popped a ketchup-coated fry in his mouth. "I'll be rid of it in a couple weeks."

"How'd it happen?"

"A second of inattention."

She wanted far more detail, but his expression closed like an iron gate protecting the castle.

"Want something to eat?" Britt asked, forcing her attention away from Deke's injury.

"I've been thinking about Randi's bruschetta all the way here."

"What about your meal?"

"That will be my meal."

Smiling, Kris said, "I'll put your order in."

Britt scooted his plate over to her. "Have some fries."

"Afraid I'll waste away?"

"No chance of that."

She smacked his shoulder. "Rude."

"Do you have a job lined up now that you're done with college?" Deke asked.

"I'm not done yet."

He glanced a Britt. "Didn't you tell me she graduated?"

"She did. Evie's starting a Master's degree."

"Master's." Deke's flat tone drew her gaze. His expression remained neutral, but his eyes...his eyes revealed...loss.

Her throat closed at the small tell of his feelings. Why loss? Why wouldn't he be happy for her?

Breaking eye contact, he lifted his beer bottle to his lips. "Is that why you're taking a trip? A little me time before classes start up?"

"No me time." She stared at the tray of quartered limes and lemons. A strange hollowness filled the area where her heart used to be. Why couldn't she figure him out? Why did he persist in ignoring this thing between them? Why did she let him?

The bartender set a glass of ice water in front of her.

"Thanks, Grady."

"MedTour," Britt said.

Evie sipped her drink, wishing her brother would've let the subject drop.

"MedTour?"

"She's going to travel around the mountains in an

RV, patching up patients who don't have health care or reliable transportation."

"By yourself?"

"I'll be working under the direction of a Nurse Practitioner. Lisa Frye. She went to school with you and Britt."

"I remember her. She's an old friend."

The softening around Deke's mouth and eyes lanced her insides. She reached for her water again. "Then you've heard of her MedTours."

"I knew she went to different towns to offer up her services, but I didn't realize it was so structured. Definitely didn't know about the RV."

"One serving of Randi's bruschetta." Kris set a rectangular dish in front of her. "Let me know if you need anything else."

"Thanks, this should be more than enough." Evie picked up a piece of toasted bread piled high with tiny cubed tomatoes, herbs, onions, garlic, and balsamic vinegar. She bit into the mound, and the mixture of flavors burst into her mouth. She closed her eyes, chewing slowly, appreciatively. Enjoying something besides yogurt and Ramen noodles, for a change.

"Good?"

She opened her eyes to find Britt smiling down at her. She grinned back until she caught Deke staring at her mouth. She licked her bottom lip, hoping like hell she didn't have basil stuck in her teeth.

His focus intensified, burned, until his gaze lifted to hers.

Blink. And the fire disappeared.

Deke cleared his throat. "How does this MedTour thing work? Are people scheduling appointments? Or do you make house calls?"

Evie released a painful breath, wishing she could blink away emotion as easily as he. "Every month the MedTour visits impoverished communities all over the Smokies."

"Residents come to expect you, then."

"Yes, Lisa has set up a regular route. Every once in a while she'll veer off-course because of an emergency or something. But the whole thing runs like clockwork. Takes two weeks to complete the route, barring anything crazy coming up."

"Two weeks on tour, two weeks off?"

"Yep."

"What towns are you hitting?"

"I don't recall the entire schedule, but I know Haden's Hollow, Niles, and Creede are on the list."

"Creede?" His gaze sharpened on her. "Isn't that close to Bamford?"

"I have no idea."

"Just to the north of Bamford," Britt interjected.

"When are you headed out?" Deke asked.

"Three days from now."

Deke took several bites of his burger, throwing them all into a thoughtful silence. Then he asked, "Do you enjoy the work?"

She nodded. "After four years of nursing school, I'm glad to finally put what I've learned into practice. Everyone we treat is so grateful. It's an amazing program." She aimed another mound of bruschetta toward her mouth. "This is only my second tour. I live in fear I'll screw something up and cause someone more harm than good."

"If you treat enough people, the odds are good that you'll screw up something," Britt said in his most pragmatic voice. "The important part is what you do afterwards."

"Are you trying to terrify me?"

"No." His eyebrows pushed together. "All I'm saying is when you mess up don't dwell on the mistake. Figure out how to fix it and how not to do it again."

Deke chuckled. "I think your sister needs a peppier talk. Something like, 'You're doing great. I'm proud of you.'"

"Of course I'm proud of her. But no one's perfect, especially not when starting a new job. Mistakes happen."

"It's okay, Britt," she said. "I knew what you meant." Britt didn't waste words, nor was he one for chitchat. For him to say as much as he had on the topic told her that he was as nervous about this new adventure as she.

"I'm proud of her, too," Deke said.

Startled by Deke's quiet statement, Evie stared him.

"Many people talk. They empathize with their neighbor about the poor in Appalachia, while enjoying lattes at the local coffee shop. But they don't act. The poor have no impact on their daily lives, so their empathy wanes with the next weighty topic." He lopsided smile appeared, the one that always, always melted her heart. "You're a doer, Evie Steele. Always have been."

Needles stung her nose and the backs of her eyes. Words of thanks clogged her throat, refusing to emerge for fear of their inadequacy.

He tossed his napkin onto the bar and drew a twenty-dollar bill from his wallet. "Gotta go."

"You just got here," Britt said.

"Just remembered I need to follow up on something for work."

"I thought you were taking some time off."

"I am. Or will be." He shook Britt's hand and hesitated a second before nodding to her. "See y'all later."

"Hey," Britt called, angling around. "If you're free this Sunday, give me a call. Found a new fishing spot with bluegills the size of your hand."

"Sounds like my kind a hole."

She followed Deke's departure until his dark head was no longer visible. A familiar ache of loss filled in her chest.

"What was all that about?" Britt asked.

"All what?"

"The tension between the two of you was so thick I nearly suffocated."

"So melodramatic."

"I'm waiting."

"We've always teased each other."

"Exactly. Tease." Britt rubbed a hand over his face and released a harsh breath. "Listen, I recognize when a man—"

"There's nothing going on between us. All I did was call him out on staying away for so long."

He regarded her for several uncomfortable seconds, disbelief storming in his eyes. But he didn't press her. Simply dipped a fry into his ketchup and handed it to her.

Gratitude made her smile. How could she tell her brother that the tension he sensed might have been sexual on her side, but avoidance on Deke's? One humiliation per day was more than enough. Thank the sweet Lord she wouldn't see Deke Conrad again anytime soon.

CHAPTER THREE

July 31
Creede, Western North Carolina

"I'VE FOUND A NEW LOCATION to store our product. The first shipment will be ready to go within a few days."

Blaze Harwood lifted his gaze from his workbench to his eldest son Caleb. "First shipment?"

"Our sellers are promising larger than expected quantities. I'd rather make several smaller shipments than one large shipment. It's not safe to keep too much in one place—as proven by the Bamford raid."

Blaze lowered his attention back to the block of basswood, concentrating on running his gouge in the right direction and at the right depth. With only one eye, he struggled with depth perception. But like everything else he attempted, he conquered the weakness.

Slowing his breathing to match his strokes, he asked, "You made the decision to increase our number of shipments? On your own?"

Silence dropped into the air like a front-end loader dumping a bucket of boulders.

"N-no, sir," Caleb stuttered out. "The increase in shipments was a recommendation."

"Increased shipments mean an increase in my costs. Increased costs cut into my profit. Decreased profits mean less money to put towards your mother's dinner table." His one-eyed black gaze met his son's. "How would I explain that to your mama?"

Caleb's shoulders slumped and he ducked his head. "Sorry, Daddy. I didn't mean to overstep."

Pleased by his son's submission, he set his carving tool to the wood again. "Your heart was in the right place. But don't ever forget this is my business and I make the decisions."

"Yes, sir."

"Rather than more shipments, we'll store our product in smaller quantities at numerous locations. Once we have enough to transport, you'll combine the product and send it off."

"I'll search for new locations right away."

"They must be secure, out-of-sight, and climate-controlled."

"Of course."

The door burst open, and Blaze tore his sidearm from his hip holster.

"Granddaddy, look what I made!"

He slid his Glock back into place and noted Caleb doing the same. His five-year-old grandson leaped, and Blaze caught him midair before settling him on his lap.

"Tobias," Caleb scolded. "I told you to knock before coming into Granddaddy's shop." He held out his hands to take the child. "Sorry, Daddy. Let me get him back to his mama."

Waving Caleb off, he said, "The boy can stay." To his grandson, he said, "What have you got there?"

"A boat!"

"Why, yes. I see it now."

"I'm going to sail to Disney World."

"Why not let your parents drive you? Or better yet, fly."

"Mama said we're never getting out of his hellhole."

His gaze rose up to Caleb's once again. "Did she?"

"Yeah," Tobias said, oblivious to the tension. "She doesn't like it here much."

"Florida's quite a distance. You might need some food."

Tobias stared at his paper boat, no doubt devising a plan to get himself and his provisions aboard his creation. His young mind never stopped. Unlike Caleb at that age, when all he'd focused on was making mud pies.

"What's that?" Tobias pointed to the block of rough-carved basswood.

"A duck." He drew the carving closer so his grandson could rub a grimy finger across the woodgrains. "Can you see it?"

Tobias tilted his head. His finger stopped where the head would soon appear. "Wing."

"Smart boy." To Caleb, he said, "Leave him with me."

"Yes, sir."

When the workshop door opened, he warned his eldest, "Search quietly. My contact at the Service said they're more determined than ever to locate the owner of the barn warehouse."

"It's good you buried your connection behind a wall of shell companies."

"Yes, I did my part." He allowed three heartbeats to pass. "Did you?"

"They won't find anything. The only thing we left behind was a betrayer."

"I hope your confidence is warranted." He brushed a hand over Tobias's blond head. "I truly do."

CHAPTER FOUR

EVIE SLUNG HER BULGING LOUIS Vuitton handbag—a birthday gift from her brother, Grif—over her shoulder and retrieved her carryon suitcase and snack bag from the trunk of her Nissan Rogue. Given the space limitations in the RV, she'd packed light knowing that if she ran out of clean clothes she could stop at a local Laundromat.

She trudged toward the RVs idling in the Blue Valley Medical Clinic's parking lot. To get the most use out of their two-week tour, they traveled in two RVs. One for staff to use as sleeping quarters and a bigger one for treating patients.

Although the space within the Med Mobile was limited, they had everything they needed to treat common ailments and injuries for up to two patients at a time. The RV held two small but private exam rooms, each containing a comfortable table, otoscope and ophthalmoscope to check eyes, ears, nose and throat, a blood pressure cuff and thermometer, plus scalpels for incisions and abscess drainage and forceps to remove foreign bodies.

Each room had a strong light source for suturing wounds and an array of syringes and needles for local anesthesia, blood draws, and vaccines. The RV even had a defibrillator and gowns for women who came in for their annual physicals.

About halfway to her destination, Evie's suitcase rollers stopped working and began dragging across the asphalt.

Setting her bags down, she crouched to have a look. "Oh, for Pete's sake." One of the rollers had hit a wad of blue bubblegum, which had snagged a large rock. Rock and gum were now wedged in the metal well between the roller and suitcase.

Perfect. "Lord, if you have any mercy, you won't let this be the tone of our entire tour."

Standing, she glanced around for a stick, discarded paper cup, anything she could use to dig out the crap lodged against the roller. Nothing. Not even a straw or oversized stone.

She laid the suitcase on its side and pulled her favorite pen out of her bag. Regret speared through her, but she pushed it aside and got to work. The wheel hollow was so deep and the angles so sharp that her pen could only stab tiny holes in the gum. She couldn't reach the rock, at all.

Dropping the pen back into her purse, she stared at the gummy gob, dreading what she would have to do. If her finger slipped into the gum...she shuddered. Lord only knew whose mouth that had been in. She could do this. The RV had plenty of soap and sanitizer. If all went well, the gum would come out with the stone.

Before she talked herself out of it, Evie plunged her fingers behind the roller to hook around the rock. The damn thing was stuck good. She pulled and pushed and pulled and pushed. When she'd made up her mind to just carry the damn suitcase, her fingers slipped into the gum.

"Ugh!" Out of reflex, she jerked her hand away and three long lines of blue bubblegum followed. She flicked her hand and only managed to fling the gum against her leg. She tried lifting it off with her other hand and the gum acted like a frickin' stalactite, clinging to her flesh as if its life depended upon it.

"This can't be happening."

"Evie?"

She froze. Her brain recognized the voice but shied away from tying it to a name. To do so would lead to mortification. Full-on red-cheeked mortification. She tried to remove the gum from her fingers, but it kept fighting for superior position.

A pair of worn cowboy boots entered her line of vision. She refused to lift her head. Refused to look into the pair of iridescent blue eyes that had haunted her dreams since their conversation at Triple B.

"Looks like you've got a mess on your hands."

She closed her eyes against the amusement lacing his words. "Yep."

"Dare I ask why you're playing with gum in the middle of the parking lot?"

"Go away, Deke. Or I'll be tempted to rake my gummy fingers through your hair."

He kneeled next to her and reached for her hands.

"Don't touch me, or you'll end up tangled in raspberry bubblegum, too."

"I've had my fingers stuck in worse."

She raised a brow.

"Don't ask." He motioned for her hands. "Give over, Evie."

Presenting her blue fingers to him, she asked, "What are you going to do?"

He produced a bandana and proceeded to wipe her fingers clean. "The rest you can remove by dousing it in hairspray or peanut butter." He eyed her jeans. "Got a microwave or freezer in that RV?"

"Both."

"Throw your pants in the freezer until the gum is frozen. Should be able to scrape it off then."

"How is it that you're so knowledgeable about gum?"

"My kid brother." His gaze roamed over her. "What happened? Did it get stuck to your shoe?"

She pointed to her suitcase. "My roller. The rock's still in there."

Using his good arm, he lifted her carry-on as if it weighed nothing, analyzing the stubborn rock. He wiggled the roller, then whammed his palm against it a couple times. The rock dropped to the ground.

"Where were you ten minutes ago?"

"Over there. Talking to Lisa."

Peering over his shoulder, she saw the nurse practitioner loading supplies into the staff RV. "I should get over there. I've wasted enough time on this goofy thing."

After helping her to her feet, Deke grabbed her bag.

"You don't have to carry my suitcase. I doubt God would put me through an ordeal like that twice in one day."

"I don't mind."

Deke entered the staff RV and set Evie's suitcase near one of the two sleeper sofas. A large brown canvas bag sat next to the other sofa. The bag didn't belong to Lisa, who had a zebra print suitcase. Besides, as team leader, Lisa enjoyed the queen-sized bed in the back of the RV.

"What's going on?" Evie asked.

"Hey, Evie," Lisa said, entering the RV. "I didn't get a chance to call you. Deke's going to join us on this tour."

"What?" she asked, a little bit shriller than she'd intended. "Why?"

"He's going to write an article about the MedTour."

"I don't understand. Aren't you still recuperating?"

"In my spare time, I like to freelance for different magazines in the area. Traveling around the mountain while observing two talented—and beautiful—women seemed a much better way to spend my time off."

"Our tours have nothing to do with wildlife."

"Exactly why I'm here. I'm spreading my writing wings. Health care's a big issue these days."

"This makes no sense."

"When you spoke about your tour at lunch the other day, I became intrigued. I contacted Lisa to see if she minded me hovering around, asking questions, interviewing patients, and taking pictures."

"And I said yes. Getting some free press can't hurt. We're always in need of sponsors and supplies."

She glanced between Lisa and Deke, trying to decipher Lisa's comment about sponsors, while still reeling over Deke's presence. "You'll be traveling with us the entire two weeks?"

"That's the plan."

"Sleeping in here?"

Concern crinkled the corner of Lisa's eyes. "Is that okay? Deke said the two of you have known each other for years. I thought you'd enjoy his company, especially since I'm such a loner at times."

Her thoughts collided like molecules, sparking into a flame. She wanted nothing more than to spend two weeks hovering in Deke Conrad's orbit. But she'd sworn off the damned man. How would she survive such close quarters while pining for a guy who didn't see *her*?

Being the youngest Steele, she'd learned a number of survival techniques, including how to brace herself against any storm. But sharing sleeping quarters with Deke might require a Herculean strength of will she didn't possess. *Dammit, she wasn't prepared for this.*

"If you're concerned about your modesty, I promise not to peek." Deke produced his lopsided grin, though he held her gaze, challenging.

She glared at him simply because it felt good. "I doubt I have anything you haven't seen before." *Or anything you want to see.*

Lisa laughed. "What do you say, Evie? Won't it be fun having a token male around? Someone who can carry all our heavy equipment?" She sent him a flirtatious, teasing smile. "Someone to do our bidding?"

"Does he do laundry?"

"Only if it includes your underwear," he said.

Out of nowhere, a thought occurred to her. "You're not here to spy on me, are you?"

"Why would I spy on you?"

"Did Britt, or one of my other brothers, put you up to this?"

"Hell, no. They wouldn't do that to you—and neither would I."

"Are you kidding? They track my every movement. During my first few years at college, my brothers would take turns popping into my dorm, or wherever I was living, unannounced."

"Sounds like they were worried about you."

"That's one theory."

"What's another?"

Her gaze flicked between him and Lisa, suddenly uncomfortable with the topic.

"Doesn't matter. If I find out you're sending updates about me to my brothers, I'll kick you out. I don't care if we're maneuvering a four-thousand-foot switchback at midnight." She made an ass-kickin' motion with her foot. "Out you go. Are we clear?"

"I think I got it, yes."

"O-okay." Trepidation tinged Lisa's voice. "Now that we have that settled, why don't you unpack. We'll roll out of here in ten minutes." She focused on Deke. "Ride with me in the Med Mobile."

"I'll be there in a few minutes."

Lisa nodded and left.

A tsunami of silence followed in her wake.

"What's going on, Evie?"

She unzipped her suitcase, refusing to look at him. "Nothing."

When she made to open her bag, a large hand held it down.

"Don't feed me bullshit."

Instinctively, she met his gaze. Big mistake. He was too close, too gorgeous, too everything that was dangerous to her. She broke eye contact and stepped away.

"Give it up. You've been itchin' for a fight since lunch

the other day. Get off whatever's on your chest so we can move on."

Bile burned its way out of her liver and idled in the back of her throat. Anger like nothing she'd ever felt before made her see a kaleidoscope of colors before it finally landed on red. How could he not know what was bothering her? Was this some kind of male denial? Could he have forgotten already?

Or was she making too much of their kiss?

Sweet Mary, he was driving her insane.

She blew out a hard, decisive breath. "There's nothing on my chest. As long as you're not here at my family's request, I have no problem with you joining us."

"You're avoiding the issue."

"There's no issue to avoid." She put on her best Evie smile, dimple and all. "We're cool."

He stared at her, suspicious. The way she was acting around him today, and at Triple B, was completely out of character. They both knew it. For the first time since she'd survived puberty, she didn't have control over her emotions.

But he had to have made the link as to why. Surely he couldn't be that dense.

"All right, then." He scraped a hand along the back of his neck. "I'll unpack tonight." An engine roared in the distance. "Sounds like Lisa's ready to go."

"Better hurry up, or you'll be forced to ride shotgun with me, instead."

His features hardened. "Wouldn't want that now, would we?"

"Not today." She turned back to her suitcase. "See you on the other side of Weaverville."

Once the RV's door closed, she collapsed onto the sofa. Her heart raced a million miles an hour and her face throbbed from the sudden rush of blood. *No, no, no. Not now.* She sat up, trying to get control of her breathing, concentrating on each inhalation. *I'm not suffocating, I'm not. Just get through the next ten seconds. You're fine.*

She talked herself through the panic attack until her body began to calm into its normal rhythm. No one knew about her attacks, not even her mom. They had started when she showed up for her first day of college.

Freshman move-in day. Nothing in her life had prepared her for the organized chaos. Hundreds of wide-eyed freshmen unloading their belongings from their parents' vehicles, rolling carts full of colorful possessions, crying, hugging, laughing. Scared out of their wits.

When Mom and Britt had hugged her goodbye, she'd held tight, afraid to let them go. She'd made it to her room before the attack hit. The episode had been terrifying. She'd been certain that her first day of college would be her last.

Her new roommate found her sprawled on the floor, stabbing ineffectually at the keypad on her phone. As luck would have it, her roomie Karen had an aunt who suffered from panic attacks. Karen knew exactly what to do and, before long, Evie could breathe again.

When her mom had called later that night, she'd said nothing. The last thing she'd wanted was to worry her—and Britt. They would have hightailed it back to campus and taken her to the doctor. Mortifying.

Karen had explained that there was little she could do to prevent panic attacks from coming on, but a strong, calm mind would reduce their severity.

Suddenly thirsty, she pushed to her feet at the same time her phone vibrated. A text from Lisa. *Ready?*

Give me 5 min. Nature's calling.

Shuffling over to the small fridge, she retrieved a bottle of water and downed a third of it before dropping trou and stuffing her gum-stained jeans in the even smaller freezer. She shoved her legs into a pair of backup jeans, then cleaned the gum off her hands. Slipping into the driver's seat, she forced her trembling fingers to wrap around the steering wheel. She closed her eyes, willing tranquility into her mind.

Having Deke so close for such an extended period of time wouldn't reduce her to rubble. She'd known him most of her life. He was gorgeous and charming and funny as hell, but not so special as to tie her in knots and make her lose control.

No siree, Bob. She would admire him and that was it. No more what-ifs, maybes, or hopes for this Steele girl. She had better things than Deke Conrad to fill her brain cells. She had people to treat, kids to help, diseases to kill.

To hell with Deke.

To hell with her dreams.

Chapter Five

"YOU DIDN'T TELL ME YOU and Evie weren't cool," Lisa said, maneuvering the Med Mobile onto the road.

Deke was still fuming about his encounter with Evie. "I didn't know myself."

"Think. You did something to piss her off." Lisa snapped on her turn signal. "Not much rattles Evie, but you did back there."

"Maybe if you'd given her a head's-up, she wouldn't have been so surprised."

"It slipped my mind. Evie's used to my absent-mindedness. Besides, she loves people and hanging with friends. Under normal circumstances, she would have been happy about the situation. I'm sure of it. There's something going on."

"I've got nothing. A few days ago, I saw her for the first time in several months. She seemed like she wanted to pick a fight with me then, too. Kept talking about me being gone." He rubbed his fingers over his left eyebrow a couple times. "I don't know why it bothered her. I've been off-the-grid several times over the last five years."

"Did anything happen between the two of you before you left?"

"I don't recall an argument."

"But did anything *happen*?"

He frowned. "Romantically?"

"Yes, you clod."

A familiar image surfaced. One where he'd walked Evie to her car, and she'd flung herself into his arms. She'd kissed him with enthusiasm that he would later recognize as liquid courage. But that night, he'd accepted her passion, devoured it. He'd waited years to caress her soft lips with his, to burrow his hands beneath the thick fan of her hair, to match his heartbeat to hers.

When he ended the kiss, he'd stared into wide, shocked eyes and knew she would regret her impulsiveness the next morning. So he'd left for his next assignment a day earlier than scheduled, saving her from an apology that neither of them would find comfortable.

Could that be the reason for her anger? Because he'd left without giving her a chance to apologize?

"If you have to think about your answer that long, you're either hiding something or clueless."

"I'm not hiding anything." Telling Lisa about Evie's drunken kiss was out of the question. "I'd certainly remember if anything had *happened* with Evie." Maybe Evie didn't even remember kissing him. Maybe she was upset about something else. He raked his mind for another possibility. "Before I left, she and I attended a ceremony for Britt's research center. We ate, we talked, we danced, and we might have had a little too much to drink. Everyone over-imbibed that day."

"Did you insinuate something? Make fun of her hair? Cop a feel?"

"No, no, and hell no."

"You said you drank too much. Maybe you forgot."

"Not likely." He surveyed his surroundings. "Where are we going again?"

"To a little community not far from Weaverville."

"Have you heard anything about the grant?"

"Not yet. I've never applied for this particular grant before. The dollar amount is significant, so the application process was much more intense than usual."

"How many more days of operating funds do you have?"

"Enough to complete this tour."

"Then what?"

"I don't know."

"You don't have any more funding options?"

"Not right now."

"What about your supervisor at the clinic? What's he doing to help?"

"Not everyone's as attached to this program as I am. However, Dr. Muir's doing what he can to protect the funding that the clinic provides. I couldn't ask for more."

They both fell victim to their own thoughts for several winding miles. What would Evie do if the MedTour lost its funding?

"Are you sure it's a good idea to keep the real reason behind your presence from Evie?"

He clenched his teeth, regretting that he'd let the grant conversation wane. "The less she knows the better."

"I can see that you care for her. If she ever finds out about your deception, she might not be able to forgive you."

He glanced out the side window. Instead of rolling tree-covered hills, he saw an image of Evie's smiling, beautiful features collapsing into a pool of betrayal and mistrust.

"I'm already regretting my decision to bring you into the fold."

"Even if you hadn't, I would've guessed you were investigating something." She caught his skeptical expression. "You forget that I spent over a year navigating your half-truths and vague answers before calling it quits."

Halfway through graduate school, he and Lisa had taken their friendship a step farther, becoming lovers. They'd celebrated his first job with the U.S. Fish and Wildlife Service tangled together near a campfire in the Smokies. When he'd completed the training to become a special agent, she'd made him a pot of spaghetti before heading off to work. After his third long absence and inability to answer her questions, they'd shared a beer and decided they made better friends.

"Evie doesn't have a deceptive bone in her body. If someone started poking around, she wouldn't be able to pull off ignorance."

"You're underestimating Evie. She's fiercely loyal to her family—and I assume she'd be the same with her friends. Plus, I've seen her navigate some pretty tricky situations with patients."

"I can't chance it."

"What if she finds out?"

"I'll have a lot of apologizing to do."

"An apology might not be enough."

"Maybe not, but it's the best I can offer." He drew his iPad from his backpack. "Look, I know what I'm about to say will sound cold. Evie's disappointment in me isn't my main concern right now. Successfully completing this assignment is." He wiped at a smudge on the screen and only managed to make it worse. "If what I'm about to embark on winds up hurting her, no one will rip me apart more than myself."

"At least try to keep your lies to a minimum, then. She'll have less to forgive when the truth comes out."

CHAPTER SIX

THE MED CARAVAN PULLED INTO Tanner Pharmacy's parking lot, and Lisa went inside to say hello. Partnering with local pharmacies had proven beneficial for everyone. Lisa didn't have to keep a large stock of medications, the pharmacy got some extra business, and patients received their prescriptions at a discounted price.

Evie threw on a set of light pink scrubs and memory foam shoes before heading next door to the Med Mobile. Normally, she'd be wearing a mile-wide smile right now. She loved spending time with patients and puzzling out their symptoms. But today her every step seemed weighted with wet sand.

Would Deke watch her every move? Log everything she said on a recorder or notepad? Would he stand too close, smell too good? Could she keep her eyes on her patients with him in the same room? Would her hands tremble under his scrutiny?

Sweet baby Jesus. This was going to be the longest two weeks of her life.

The door to the Med Mobile swung open as she approached, and Deke stuck his head out. Almost as if he'd been watching for her out the window. *Don't go there.*

"I'm riding with you next time. Lisa took ten years off my life on those switchbacks."

"She's been maneuvering these roads for years."

He studied her a moment. "Has the shock worn off yet?"

For a split second, her attention shifted away, but she forced her gaze up to his. "I enjoy your company, Deke."

"Why such a negative reaction to my joining you?"

"I need to focus on my patients."

Closing the door, he descended the two stairs to stand before her. "You can't do that with me nearby?"

The answer adhered to her throat like molasses.

Inches separated them now. His shadow engulfed her, chilled her.

"It's the kiss, isn't it?"

He remembered.

"If my leaving the next day upset you, I'm sorry. I wanted to spare both of us the awkwardness."

"Awkward?"

"Too much alcohol. An intimate moment." The blue in his eyes intensified. "Regrets and next-day apologies. Or worse, oblivion." He shrugged. "It happens."

Did he really think she'd been that tanked? Tipsy, yes. But drunk to the point of amnesia? She was beginning to wish her mind *had* failed.

"I remember everything about that night." Her eyes sparked. "And the next day."

"Then my decision to leave had been the right one."

"How do you figure?"

"When I ended the kiss, your wide-eyed expression made your feelings clear."

"What is it that you think my eyes revealed?"

"I know regret when I see it." He tapped the tip of her nose with his finger. "You're still my Squirt."

Frustration churned at a nauseating speed in the pit of her stomach. She didn't want to be his Squirt. Well, she did, but she craved far more. And she was damn tired of hiding the fact.

"You missed the mark on this one, big guy. What you saw was shock."

"Shock." He said the word as if testing the arrangement of letters on his tongue.

Moving into the small space between them, she angled her face up, beneath his. "I didn't handle last year well. Nerves and alcohol made me clumsy and unsophisticated. My inept attempt at seduction ended in embarrassment. But more than that, I couldn't believe you'd kissed me back. With such passion."

She breathed in his scent, his heat, and her voice lowered. "I've wanted you longer than I can remember. I want to feel you inside me, over me, behind me—not brotherly nose taps. I've been waiting for your Neanderthal brain to catch up and realize I'm a grown woman—with a woman's needs."

He stared at her for several clock-ticking seconds. Enough time for her to start analyzing her words and deciding she'd lost her flipping mind. Then he blinked, and his shadow heated around her.

"Neanderthal brain?"

"I know you're attracted to me," she whispered. "I've seen the way you look at me, sometimes."

"Yes." His index finger slid along the ridge of her nose, over her lips, down her chin. "But I've got a dozen years on you. Almost a lifetime."

"Is that why you've never acted on your interest?"

"I thought about it a few times."

"But?"

His features hardened. "You were too damn young."

"Are you saying you don't care that I'm Britt's sister?"

"No, I'm not saying that. If we got together and things didn't work out, I could potentially lose your friendship and Britt's. Both of which are important to me."

Invisible arms curled around her chest and squeezed until it became difficult for her to inhale. "Do you still think I'm too young?"

"Yes." The one word emerged flat, yet unyielding.

"A dozen years isn't a lifetime. Nine years separate my mom and dad, and they still managed to produce six kids."

"How did her career play into their relationship?"

"Mama never went to college."

"Why's that?"

"Money was tight."

"Couldn't her parents afford to help with tuition?"

The onset of fear stabbed her heart. "No."

"Why?"

"Our situation's different than my parents."

"They married young, right?"

She couldn't answer. Couldn't travel the path he wanted to lead her down.

"I recall Miss Joan saying once that if she couldn't teach the kids, she'd do the next best thing."

Although her mom never complained about her lot, she'd at one time dreamed of being a math teacher. She loved numbers and analyzing things and children. But she and Eddy Steele started having babies not long after they married, and all thoughts of higher education and classrooms disappeared. Instead, Joan Steele took a part-time office position at the elementary school, where she could be around the children and do a bit of tutoring on the side.

All in all, her mom appeared happy with her life. Now, thanks to Deke, Evie wondered if her mom had crafted a well-executed façade.

"Did she give up her dream of teaching to start a family?" Deke asked in a quiet voice.

Emotion burned the backs of her eyes. "I see where you're going with this and, the truth is, I don't know. Though I love her to death, I'm not my mom."

"But you've set your sights on a man whose thoughts have turned toward finding a wife and having kids."

"You want a family?"

"Watching Britt with Randi has made me realize there's much in this life that I'm missing." He stroked a skein of her hair between his fingers. "Are you ready to put your career on hold in order to marry and bear a few rugrats?"

She wanted to say yes, wanted to do whatever it would take to be with him. Wanted to tell him that women do it every…single…day. Yet all words of assurance clung to the tip of her tongue. The muscles in her throat tautened, and his image wavered, grew bleary.

"Babe, don't." He cradled her jaw and rested his forehead against hers. "You'll find someone more your age."

"I don't want—"

"Hear me out." He kissed her forehead. "Find someone who'll grow with you, someone who'll give you the time to continue your schooling or settle into a career. Someone who won't be making demands of you before you're ready."

"We can work something out. Figure out a compromise."

"I would never ask you to compromise your dream."

"Evie!" Lisa called from across the parking lot. "Is the Med Mobile prepped?"

"Not quite," she answered without turning around.

"We open for business in thirty minutes. I'm going to put on my scrubs."

Evie used Lisa's distraction to slip around Deke and climb onto the bottom step leading into the Med Mobile. With her five-foot-ten height, the new position brought her up even with Deke. She bent toward his ear, swallowing hard, forcing down the emotion. "You don't understand. I've already compromised my dream. For years."

She turned and went inside.

"I'm in Haden's Hollow," Deke said into his earbud

mic. He sat down on a curb facing the RVs and broke open his breakfast—a bag of Cool Ranch Doritos.

"Anything yet?" Keone asked.

"Nope, the ladies are preparing for their first patient. I'm staying out of the way." He snagged a triangle from the bag and shoved the whole chip into his mouth while keeping his attention on the Med Mobile's door.

"Smart."

"Got anything on who betrayed our mission and killed my source?"

"Are you eating in my ear?"

"I'm hungry."

"Could you at least cover the receiver?" Keone didn't wait for an answer. "The suspicious activity Marisol spotted south of the barn wound up being the exit side of an extensive escape route. The Distributor's men were loading the last of the contraband into trucks while we were descending on the barn."

"The Distributor must have been confident about the barn's concealment to invest in that kind of infrastructure."

"If not for your source, we would've never located it. Know anything about Gold Star?"

"No, what's that?"

"No clue. We found a reference to it in the barn."

"See if Jax can come up with anything."

"Is that a good idea, considering the whole team's under investigation?"

"Shit. I hate this." He rubbed his fingers tips over his right eyebrow. "How much more time do you need?"

"It's hard to say. I don't have the same technological resources as Jax and Taji."

"Do what you can to wrap up your investigation. I'd like the team cleared of any connection to the Distributor before I have to tap into our auxiliary support again."

His medical leave couldn't have come at a better time. By being part of the MedTour, he could scope out the area without having to request intel or travel arrangements or a dozen other necessities that went along with undercover work. The fewer people who knew what he was up to, the better.

"Will do."

"I'll be in touch."

"Roger that."

He pulled the buds from his ears and stuffed them into his jeans pocket.

Some townsfolk milled around the outside of the RV emblazoned with *Med Mobile - Bringing Quality Health Care to Your Hometown.*

A chip got stuck in the back of his throat, and he snatched up his water bottle lying in the grass behind him. Opening it, he took a large swallow.

To anyone's eye, he would appear a bored, thirty-something guy with not much to do. But those who knew him would recognize the rhythmic sweeps he made over the growing crowd, analyzing, calculating, memorizing. A middle-aged woman with large, swollen ankles, using a walker to get around; a preteen boy throwing rocks across the parking lot and ignoring his mother's hellfire warnings to stop; an elderly man sitting limp in a wheelchair, his head tilted to the side while his rheumy eyes stared at the ground; a bearded guy idling in his decades-old truck, smoke billowing out the driver's side window.

They all needed medical attention, for one reason or another. And they'd all traveled several miles to see Lisa and Evie, the only affordable health care around.

Evie.

She'd damned near made him blush with her bold talk of hot sex. In all the years he'd known her, he'd never heard her speak so *explicitly*.

The fact that she'd been aware of his interest bothered him. He'd tried damn hard to keep his inappropriate thoughts barricaded in a well-fortified compartment. When had he shown his hand? Had Britt picked up on it, too?

How the hell was he going to survive his craving for Evie? Especially now, knowing that she'd been as tangled up in knots for him as he'd been for her. Why couldn't he be six or seven years younger? Or someone who had no interest in building a big family? He'd always wanted a wife and kids, though that image had been a distant one, always in the future.

Who was he kidding? Even if they were closer in age, he couldn't see Evie—or any woman—putting up with his long absences or occupational secrets. Lisa was a perfect example. From the start, she understood the demands placed on a special agent. But all understanding flies out the window when the loneliness sets in and the secrets pile up, creating an immovable wedge.

Retiring from SONR wouldn't end either of those two conditions. He'd still be an agent working for the Service, tracking down poachers. By himself. No more team, no more immediate backup. Just him versus the bad guys.

He rapped his near empty water bottle against the pavement, realizing he hadn't thought through the whole settling down thing as well as he should. How did other agents do it? How did they make both career and family sync?

Now he had to decide what to do about Evie and her revelation. Knowing her, she wouldn't give up on them, no matter how compelling his argument. He might have given her some new things to think about, but it wouldn't be long before her beautiful mind found a way around it all.

While he sniffed out possible connections to the Distributor, he would have to keep a keen eye on his black-haired temptress. His attention drifted from the crowd to the Med Mobile door, waiting for her sweet smile to appear.

What a damn mess.

Rising, he smashed the empty Doritos bag and pitched it into a nearby garbage can.

Time to put aside his dismal love life and do some snooping.

Setting his sights on the nearest patient, he sidled up to a young mother with a toddler clamped around her waist.

"Here to get checked out?" he asked.

The woman moved her child to the opposite hip, away from him. "My baby has a fever."

Sure enough, moisture dampened the child's hair along the edges, and a rosy hue stained its cheeks. "Boy or girl?"

"Why, a boy, of course." She pinched the child's sleeve. "Don't you see Harry's blue T-shirt?"

Deke propped his mouth into a chagrined smile. "Sorry, color blind."

"Are you messing with me?"

"No, ma'am. Everything's in shades of gray."

"I can't even imagine."

"It's all I've ever known so it doesn't bother me much." He made a show of glancing around. "Not too many menfolk around. Must be at work."

She snorted. "More like off playing with their guns."

"As in shooting or collecting?"

"They sure as heck don't own anything so nice as to be considered a collector's item."

"Shooting, then."

Harry started to fuss, his eyes welling with tears.

The young mother glanced at the RV door, rubbing soothing strokes over her son's back. "Those boys spend hours and hours and hours putting bullets in paper villains. Or trying to." She lowered her voice. "None of them are all that great."

"Do they get much hunting done?"

"Enough to keep meat in the freezer."

The Med Mobile door opened, and Evie appeared. "My apologies for the wait, y'all. Who's first?"

"This young lady." Deke eased his new friend and her baby forward.

She dug in her heels. "Oh, no, sir. Three or four people arrived before me."

"Her baby's burning up with fever," he explained to Evie.

Evie glanced from Deke to the mother to Harry to the others trying to form a line, then back to the baby's rosy cheeks. Her features softened. "Y'all don't mind if we take the baby first, do you?"

A low murmur of agreement echoed through the group.

Stepping aside, Evie allowed her first patient to enter the Med Mobile. "Thank you." She studied him a moment. Her gaze thoughtful, yet warm. "Care to do that again?"

"Do what?"

"Ask each patient a few questions to determine their level of medical need."

Goldmine. He'd planned to pick and choose what patients he would interview in order to keep suspicions down. No one would think twice about a guy burning time by chatting up people.

But Evie presented him with a golden opportunity to speak with each patient. Britt liked to rib him about his ability to cajole even the crankiest into sharing their life history, by the end of a conversation.

"Happy to help."

She handed him five clipboards. "Have the patients fill out these forms. If you find someone who needs immediate attention, bounce them to the front of the line."

He read through the questions, feeling Evie's eyes on him. "Piece of cake, boss."

"Don't probe too deeply into their medical condition, or you'll violate HIPAA. Keep your questions surface level and out of earshot of the others."

He winked. "Yes, ma'am."

After Evie closed the door, he turned to address the closest patient and was surprised to see the crowd had swollen to over twenty—and more people were trickling into the parking lot.

The tactical part of his mind clicked into four-wheel-drive and he began developing a game plan.

He passed out the clipboards, then dug into his backpack for paper and pen. His attention landed on a twelve-ish-looking girl who leaned into a woman sitting next to her.

Cocking his most charming smile into place, he asked, "Are you a patient or moral support?"

The girl deferred to the woman, who smiled and said, "Amber's keeping me company today."

"Mind if I recruit Amber for a few minutes? I have a small task that requires good penmanship." He held up his sling. "Mine's not so good, right now."

"My daughter's handwriting is beautiful." She patted Amber's hand where it gripped her forearm in a white-knuckled grip. "Would you like to help Mr. —?"

"Conrad. Derek Conrad. Everyone calls me Deke. I'm assisting Miss Evie and Miss Lisa today."

"I guess," Amber said quietly.

"All I need is for you to tear this paper into fifty squares, then write a number on each one, from one to fifty. Easy enough?"

Amber nodded.

"When I send a patient over, give them the next number in line, okay?"

The worry weighing down her youthful features lifted. "Yes, sir."

"We're partners now. Call me Deke."

She blushed, and her mother's chin wobbled with emotion.

The mother's reaction puzzled him, but his tactical mind was fully engaged. He set off to organize and interview the other patients.

Not until his stomach growled did he realize the lateness of the hour. With one patient left, Deke knocked on the RV door.

Lisa answered. "What's up?"

"Looks like we're coming to the end. Can I take you ladies out for a bite to eat?"

"Not me, thanks. I've learned to give myself some downtime, or I'm useless the next day." She peered behind her. "Evie missed her afternoon snack. She's been holding back yawns for the last half hour."

"Can I bring you back anything?"

"I wouldn't turn down a milkshake from Bailey's."

"Vanilla with toffee pieces?"

"You remembered."

"How could I forget? Every Friday night, like clockwork."

A throat cleared. "Excuse me, Lisa." Evie stood a few feet away. "Mr. Lester is ready for you."

"Deke's buying dinner. Why don't you go with him. I'll finish up here."

"I'm not going to leave you to clean up—"

"I've got it, Evie," Lisa interrupted. "Once I take care of Mr. Lester, I'm off to find a quiet place to read."

Evie stared at her supervisor for a defiant moment before relenting. "I don't like leaving you with a mess."

"Just make sure our new assistant brings back my milkshake and we'll call it even."

"Come on, Steele," Deke said. "My blood sugar's dropping. If I faint, you'll have a helluva time dragging my two hundred pounds up those stairs."

Evie shouldered past Lisa before stopping next to him. "If you faint, I have a nice, cold bucket of water that will snap you back to life."

Lisa watched Evie march away. "Well, Deke, you managed to wake a sleeping tigress. I hope you're prepared for her bite."

Chapter Seven

CALEB HARWOOD UNLOCKED THE DOOR to one of six climate-controlled storage buildings he'd leased since his disastrous meeting with his father.

Humiliation still burned. Blaze Harwood gave and took in the same breath, preventing him from basking in his success.

Had his father forgotten how he'd emptied the barn and set booby traps in under two hours? Few could have pulled off such a feat. But he had saved their product and coordinated its shipment. All while maintaining the appearance of having a day job. His source at the hospital had even confirmed that his traps had wounded two agents.

An image of Tobias sitting on his granddaddy's lap surfaced. Many saw Blaze Harwood as a somewhat reclusive war hero, a self-made scholar, an artist, and a loving family man. They didn't see his ruthlessness, his coldness, his inhumane tendencies. Those who knew him as a devoted family man would never believe him capable of killing a child to incent his own son to do his bidding.

But he knew the depths of evil that writhed in his daddy's chest. The whole family did, except trusting Tobias, who adored his granddad.

"Ready for us to unload?" Eli Harwood asked.

He pivoted to find his younger brother framed in the doorway.

"Yes. Quickly."

He supervised the transfer of the product, though he needn't have bothered. For a number of years, Eli had been lost in a world of vice and drugs. But Caleb had rescued him—in squalor and skin and bones.

It had taken weeks to remove the stench of addiction from his brother. To look at Eli now, no one would ever guess how close he'd come to standing before the gates of hell.

He'd given his brother a second chance at life. Something Eli thanked him for every day, in small ways, meaningful ways.

"Daddy asked about the alarm systems again," Eli said.

"Walter said the first two would be done by this weekend." Being down three technicians, their cousin hadn't been able to install the building alarms before the product started arriving. Not an ideal situation, but Walter—and anyone who worked for him—knew better than to betray Blaze Harwood.

The transfer took less than an hour. Eli strode next to Caleb as he checked the wall-to-wall storage containers, ensuring the product was stored to their father's exact specifications. The old man was known to make surprise visits.

He tested the lids to make sure they were airtight. The next shelf held large square glass units filled with foreign delicacies. He didn't understand the demand for them, but his family had made a fortune supplying the items.

"Well done, Eli. Everything is as it should be."

His brother waved a muscular arm through the air to encompass tonight's work. "This is the last of what we had on hand. More should be coming in daily, though." To keep his mind off drugs, Eli had focused his energy on honing his body into a perfect example of masculine power.

"Prepare the other storage units as needed."

"Anything else?"

"Daddy's source said agents from the Service are still nosing around." He handed Eli a slip of paper. "Make them stop."

CHAPTER EIGHT

AFTER CHANGING INTO HER STREET clothes, Evie searched for her purse and phone, still not happy about leaving the day's mess to her boss. Toward the end of the day, she'd noticed Lisa rubbing her right temple. She'd been doing that a lot lately. Every time Evie would ask her about it, she would murmur something about a headache.

Despite Lisa's comment to Deke, she rarely read for pleasure. Most of her downtime was spent going over the current day's treatments and preparing for the next day.

On the last tour, Lisa had been preoccupied with administration matters, spending more hours than normal on the computer and pouring over documents. Evie'd only been able to manage a glimpse of the paperwork, but she saw enough to know they weren't patient-related. When she'd offered to help, Lisa had refused, citing her desire for Evie to concentrate on the patients.

Evie forced herself to set aside her worry for Lisa. In order to make it through the next two hours without embarrassment, she would need whatever end-of-the-day mental power she had left while dining with Deke.

Splaying her feelings at his feet had been one of the most liberating and frightening things she'd ever done.

But she wouldn't allow her inclination toward shyness—something she'd fought against her entire life—to send her running.

Few knew that she had to force herself to be outgoing and to talk to strangers. Confidence didn't come naturally to her like it did the rest of the Steele clan. Every day, she had to psych herself up for whatever challenge lay ahead. Succeeding at her part-time job and graduating college summa cum laude had helped a great deal.

The only time she didn't second-guess herself was while she worked with her patients. Every decision or recommendation she made seemed like second nature. Natural. Only after the patients had long departed did the questions and worry start.

As long as she didn't poison anyone, she could see kicking this lack of self-confidence thing, once and for all.

Dropping her phone inside her purse, she stepped out of the RV and searched for Deke. Halfway between the Med Mobile and staff RV, he stood in profile, a white earbud attached to the side of his head. His gaze strayed her way, and he gave her a wave of acknowledgment.

All these years she'd assumed he couldn't see beyond her connection with Britt. The sibling thing had been part of the issue, but not the grand banana. An age gap had kept him away. Had his fantasies of her made him feel like an old lecher?

She grinned. Not at his internal torment, but at the image of this big, strong, handsome-as-hell guy thinking he needed to protect her. From himself.

He turned, catching her smile. The moment drew out, intensified. Not backing down, she lifted a brow. He ended the call.

"Something funny?"

"Yep, but you wouldn't appreciate the humor. Are you up for a walk?"

"Lead the way."

They strolled down Main Street for a few blocks until they reached the downtown area. The hub of Haden's Hollow consisted of a bakery, restaurant, real estate agency, and bank. A gas station, park, grocery store, and church wrapped around the town's center.

A bell jingled when they entered Lantern Café, and the rich scent of mashed potatoes, coffee, fried chicken, grease, apple pie, and decades-old wood enveloped them.

"Hey, y'all," a fresh-faced young hostess said. "Two tonight?"

"Yes," Evie said. "Any booths left?"

"One just opened up." She showed them to a corner booth lit by a small hanging lamp with a shade made of amber glass.

"What's with family-owned, small-town restaurants and fake green plants?" Deke asked.

Evie scanned the dining room, spotting variegated ivy and philodendrons trailing along shelves. "Lower maintenance than the real deal."

"What's good here?"

"I'm fond of the chicken wrap. Lisa likes the Reuben."

He closed his menu. "Reuben it is."

Uncertainty burrowed into her chest. Did he value Lisa's opinion over hers? Or did he find Reubens manlier? A more insidious option scratched to the surface. Did he and Lisa have a history? She hadn't missed their exchange about milkshakes.

"How did things go today?" he asked.

"Pretty well. We had a couple of tough cases, though."

"Can you talk about them?"

"Not really."

"Will the baby Harry be all right?"

"Should be. Lisa will call his mom tomorrow to see if his treatment is working."

"The girl who helped me organize the crowd—is her mom very sick?"

She sipped her water. "Yes."

"Cancer?"

"I can't get into specifics. I'm already walking a thin line."

"Many of your patients quite freely told me about their issues."

"They're allowed to. I'm not."

He cocked his head, studying her. "Don't take this the wrong way…"

"Why do people always think that statement somehow lessens the blow?"

"I'm used to seeing you carefree and happy, as if nothing can dampen your spirit." The area around his eyes lifted in amusement. "Like the time I came over to pick up Britt before our high school graduation ceremony. It had rained the previous night. You came flying out of the house toward me, wearing a pretty blue dress. Your bare feet slipped on a patch of damp grass, and you went down."

"How could I forget such a mortifying time?"

"Most girls your age would've burst into tears or complained about the grass stain." His dimple deepened. "Not Evie Steele. You bounced up like a pogo stick and laughed about how your mama was going to kill you."

"My wild ways, Mama used to call them. It took me years to find the balance between my love of all things feminine and the need to run with my brothers." She rubbed her middle finger against the table. "You remember the color of my dress."

He broke eye contact. "Where the hell is our waiter?"

"That had to be sixteen or seventeen years ago."

"The point of my story," he said in a tone determined to change the subject, "was to highlight how nursing has brought out another side of you."

"Is that good or bad?"

"Neither, just different."

"Are you going to tell me how—or do I need to tickle the information from you?"

His attention slid down to her mouth, and her lips

parted of their own accord. Need darkened his features. Her pulse slammed against the side of her neck.

An eternity ticked by before a breath expanded his chest and his gaze lifted. "You're more serious, focused, though I detect some uncertainty. Does this work mean so much to you?"

"It's everything to me. If I don't nail this, I'm up a creek, because I don't have a Plan B."

"You won't need one. The Steele heart beats inside your chest."

"Steele heart?"

"Tough, unstoppable, take no shit. Not even from yourself."

She laid a hand against her chest. "All that's in there, is it?"

"And much more." A dimple appeared in his right cheek. "Those were the highlights."

She smiled.

"There you go."

"What?"

"Don't forget to enjoy the ride. No goal is worth achieving if you have to sacrifice your happiness."

"You know this by experience?"

"We all lose sight of what's important, from time to time."

Evie waited for him to elaborate. He didn't.

"Well," she said into the awkward silence, "I appreciate the reminder. But when a patient's health is in my hands, it's hard to think about anything other than 'Don't screw this up.'"

"Whereas, my worst worry is meeting a production deadline or navigating to the right location."

She nodded at his sling. "Are you sure?" Something about his attitude at Triple B still gnawed at her. When she'd asked about his injury, he'd shut down the conversation. Had he done something embarrassing to cause the accident? Or had he been protecting the truth? "Gonna tell me what really happened?"

"I already did. Hunting accident."

"I've known you for a long time and can tell when you're tweaking my nose about something."

He said nothing for a long while. "It's not something I'm proud to discuss."

The raw quality in his voice made her pause. She knew about regret. Knew its lasting effects. Before she could pull back her question, he glanced down at his injured arm and said, "It was a hunting accident. My shoulder got in the way of a crossbow arrow."

"An arrow?"

"A moment of inattention. Classic cliché, right?"

"I'm sorry for prying. I sensed you were keeping something from me…and I didn't like it."

"You dislike secrets in general—or those by me?"

"Both."

"What if the secret is for your protection?"

Evie huffed a breath and shook her head. "My brothers have used that excuse often. I love those egomaniacs, but 'protection' is a mask for control. No man's going to control my life again. From this point forward, I decide what's right and wrong for me."

"What if you have no experience with the situation?"

"Then I'll speak with someone who does before making a decision."

"My little Squirt has truly disappeared."

"She's been gone for a long time. The men in my life seem oblivious of the fact."

The rest of their dinner passed with the ease of two friends reminiscing over old times. They laughed, they conspired, they shared long stretches of contemplative silence. They even picked food off each other's plates.

Neither brought up the hairy gorilla eyeballing them from the corner of the room. Now that she knew the real crux of Deke's relationship avoidance, she needed time to devise a plan to crush it.

After paying the bill, they headed to Bailey's where they grabbed Lisa's toffee-chipped milkshake, Deke's three scoops of Rocky Road, and her vanilla ice cream cone dipped in chocolate.

They fell back into the silence of their own thoughts on the way to the Med Mobile. But this time, their lack of communication wasn't companionable. The air between churned thick with regret. Regret that the evening had come to an end.

Once they stepped inside the RV, they would have to share their conversation with Lisa. Evie didn't want to share Deke with anyone. Not now. Not when over a decade of clouds had finally lifted.

They paused at the staff RV's entrance, neither knowing how to end the evening.

"Thanks for dinner," she said.

"I enjoyed our time together."

"Me too." She cleared her throat. "Any ideas where we go from here?"

"Try like hell to forget today's revelations and settle back into friendship."

Not a chance, big guy.

"Then give me a hug goodnight."

Not one of his muscles moved. He didn't even blink, just peered down at her as if she'd give him a rash if he dared touch her.

"We've been hugging each other for years, Deke. Folks will notice if we suddenly stop. Think about Britt's suspicion at Triple B."

One hand bent the paper cup of Rocky Road nearly in half while the other remained at his side in a tight fist. The air crackled around them while he made his decision.

Temptation and fear roiled like a boiling kettle. Could they embrace without giving in to the heat? With knowing they each craved the other's touch?

For the love of God, one of them needed to break the tension, make the next move, prove that they could hug without shredding each other's clothing.

She took the two steps separating them and curled

her arms around his body like she'd done countless times before, only this time holding a milkshake and sugar cone. No one could blame her if she pushed the embrace further by pressing her body flush with his and resting her head against his broad chest.

Thrump-thrump-thrump-thrump-thrump.

The rapid pace of his heart brought her an odd comfort and a deep-seated excitement. Inhaling a long breath, she closed her eyes.

A strong arm enclosed her in a warm cocoon, though his body remained rigid. How long they stood in each other's arms she didn't know. Didn't care. She needed this small contact, this connection to the man she'd loved forever.

Soon his body loosened enough for him to bury his nose in her hair. His lips brushed the shell of her ear. "I will do the right thing by you, Evie Steele—" restraint shook his voice, "—even if it kills me."

He released her and strode into the night.

Cold ice cream dribbled over her knuckles. She ignored it, following Deke until the darkness consumed him.

She plopped down onto the top step, stunned by the power of one embrace. With absolutely no brainpower behind the action, she licked the dripping ice cream.

How to make a stubborn, honorable man to see that the best thing for her was to be wedded and bedded. Or bedded and wedded. She liked the sound of the latter better.

"Beware, Deke Conrad."

CHAPTER NINE

"WHERE ARE WE GOING?" DEKE asked, his muscles tensing.

Lisa turned the Med Mobile toward Rockton. The last place he wanted to visit.

"We're taking a slight detour. I got a call last night. There's a sick boy who needs our attention."

"Won't this screw up your schedule?"

"A little. I don't give the communities specific arrival dates—just a span of time. Something always comes up along the way. The night before, Evie sends out a targeted newsletter and calls the next location. Most of the pharmacies will put a sign out by the road that says, 'Med Mobile Today.' Everyone understands that if we're delayed it's for a good reason." Lisa glanced his way. "Everything okay?" When he said nothing, her eyes widened. "Visiting Rockton's not a problem for you, is it?"

How to answer her question? In the past several years, the only time he'd set foot in his hometown was to bail out his kid brother, Dylan, from his latest bad decision. He hadn't been to his parents' house since his father's ultimatum—family or a career with the U.S. Fish and Wildlife Service, aka the enemy.

Since before he'd been born, his dad and uncle had hunted and fished federal lands, snubbing their noses at the government's rules regarding public land use. The people's land. Their disgust and hatred grew with every citation, every discovered infraction.

As a boy, he hadn't understood any of their grumblings. All he'd cared about was spending time with his dad. Mitch Conrad taught him and Dylan how to shoot a bow, spear a fish, and build a fire. His dad had dubbed him Davey Crockett when he'd killed his first— and only—bear at nine years old.

Although his chest had expanded to the size of a gorilla's at his dad's compliment, he hadn't enjoyed the kill. The bear's intelligent brown eyes and the wheez of his last breath still haunted his thoughts.

He had no problem fishing or hunting birds and deer. But bears, bobcats, foxes, and coyotes paced behind an invisible threshold he couldn't cross.

As he grew older, his dad's comments became fanatic and made him uncomfortable. He'd started spending more time with his friends and less with his dad. From one year to the next, his dad's path was no longer his. When he'd announced his intention of accepting a position with the Service, he'd become the enemy in Mitch Conrad's eye.

"Your family's still being shitheads?"

"Still." Deke slumped into his seat.

"Thank goodness your mom hasn't adopted the all-or-nothing mentality."

He crossed his arms.

"Her, too?"

"She stopped answering my calls and texts a few weeks ago."

"Just like that? No more conversation?"

"Cold turkey."

"I'm sorry, Deke."

"My holidays are a lot less complicated these days. Sushi and a movie."

"What's the likelihood that you'll see any Conrads while in Rockton?"

He turned toward the passing landscape, cataloging a decade's worth of changes. Nick's Pizzeria sat empty, except the weeds overtaking the building. The only gas station in town now housed a mini mart, and the trees outside City Hall appeared taller and thicker.

Would his family come into town this morning? Possibly. Would they stop by the Med Mobile? His family was by no means well off, but his dad had finally pulled his shit together and got himself a stable job as a heavy equipment operator, a position that included health insurance.

"Not likely."

They rolled into a grocery-pharmacy parking lot and prepared for the boy and whoever else might stop by. He'd done his best not to think about Evie in his arms last night. Had even opted to ride with Lisa again in order to avoid her torturous scent. He'd gone rock hard with her pressed against him. Had he stayed another second, he would've given in to his primal need to kiss her, claim her, cherish her.

Grabbing his clipboards and other receptionist items, he fled the Med Mobile before Evie appeared, and began his own preparations.

He still couldn't believe how much she'd matured and become this career-driven woman. Where had the playful girl who'd flitted from one sparkling object to the next gone? Her wit and compassion had always been present, but the Evie he remembered lived in the moment. No cares or concerns—except for those she loved.

Responsibility.

It was one of God's greatest gifts and one of his most challenging tests. To be responsible for another's welfare made a person dig into the very core of their character. Some found a vast wealth from which to draw and others sifted through pennies.

Evie had hit the jackpot.

The RV door opened, and Evie appeared. "We're all

set in here." She glanced around, noting the lack of patients. "Odd. Even when we arrive unexpectedly, we always have a few people waiting. Did you say something to scare everyone off?"

"My fifty push-ups for admission campaign didn't go over so well."

She smiled, though it was not her normal bright Evie smile. "Try backing it down to twenty-five next time."

"On the way into town, I noticed a sign advertising an arts and crafts fair today. It's always a big draw."

"Does it feel good to be home?"

She had no idea about his estrangement from his family, and he had no wish to rehash the topic. "There's no other feeling quite like it."

"Are you going to drop by and see your family before we head out?"

"Depends on how hard my supervisor works me today."

Lisa appeared in the doorway. "Looks like our patient has arrived."

Evie frowned. "I don't see anyone."

"They parked around back. Deke, would you mind checking on them?"

"Sure thing."

Rounding the corner, he spotted a thirty-something woman helping a young boy out of a shiny new Chevy Malibu. Once on his feet, the boy seemed unable to stand fully erect, favoring his stomach. The boy tried to put on a brave face, but one eye cringed with each step. His mother kept peering around as if searching for someone.

Striding to their side, Deke introduced himself and handed the clipboard to the boy's mother. "Fill this out, and I'll get—"

She halted. "No one said anything about paperwork."

"It's just a few questions about your son's health so the ladies can provide the best treatment."

The woman hugged her son close.

"Is everything all right, ma'am?"

"No one can know we're here."

"We don't discuss our patients—"

"No paper trail. If my husband found out..."

"You can trust us to be discreet. I give you my word."

A moment later, she nodded. "Can we go inside?"

Deke ushered his charges into the Med Mobile. "I assured—" He glanced at the mother.

"Amy and Noah."

"I assured Amy and Noah that we would protect their privacy." He sent both ladies meaningful looks. "No paperwork."

Evie was the first to pop into action. "Noah, I have a place for you right over here."

"Amy, do you mind?" Lisa waved toward a sitting area. "I have a few questions before taking a look at Noah."

Deke cracked open the RV's door so he could see any newcomers. Then he braced his hip against a counter and observed.

From this vantage point, he could see Evie and Noah and could hear Lisa's conversation with the mother. The boy'd been experiencing intermittent, sharp cramping pain in his abdomen and running a high temperature. This morning, blood appeared in his stool—the reason for her frantic phone call to Lisa.

Deke's attention dropped to Noah's hands. He was worrying something between his fingers, over and over and over. The boy barely spoke and didn't make eye contact with Evie until she coaxed his chin up.

"What can you tell me about Noah's father's medical history?"

"Not much. His father passed away two years ago." Her voice lowered. "I remarried this past spring."

"Do you feel safe at home, Amy?" Lisa asked.

"W-what?"

"Safe. Do you feel safe at home? It's a standard question we ask all our patients."

"Is she asking Noah that question?"

"Yes."

"This was a mistake." She bolted from her seat. "I just wanted to get my boy some help, to make the pain stop. If you go nosing around into things that don't concern you, you'll stir up a whole lot of trouble."

"What sort of trouble?"

"We've got to go."

Lisa stepped in front of her. "No, wait. I'm sorry. I have enough information to examine your son."

"You'll take care of him?"

"I'll do my best to figure out what's wrong. Have a seat, and I'll go take a look."

Hands trembling, Amy sat on the edge of her chair, her hazel eyes following Lisa and Evie's every move.

He pushed away from the counter, intent on having a few words with Amy. Lisa asked Noah to shift a few inches to his right. When he did, Deke caught a clear view of what he'd been fingering.

A large claw.

A bear claw.

CHAPTER TEN

"NEXT," EVIE SAID AS SHE exited the tiny bathroom located just inside Lisa's bedroom. She wore a pale V-neck tee and gray shorts. Though she was modestly covered, she felt stark naked beneath the intensity of Deke's scrutiny.

Burrowing beneath the covers, she stretched hard and let out a satisfied groan.

"That's it for me." Lisa put her laptop away. "See you in the morning."

"Where're we headed tomorrow?" Deke set down his phone—a first since they'd finished cleaning up. For well over an hour, he'd had an ongoing text conversation with someone.

"Didn't you hear my announcement?"

He glanced between her and Lisa. "No."

"Maybe you stepped away when she spoke to the crowd." He'd done that often enough when there'd been a lull in new arrivals.

"Since we couldn't get to all those who came today, I decided to stay in Rockton tomorrow."

"All day?"

"Until we're no longer needed." Lisa frowned. "If my decision makes you uncomfortable, feel free to hang out in the staff RV or call a friend to rescue you."

"Don't worry about it. I'll be fine."

"I won't hold it against you, if you'd rather bug out tomorrow."

"I said I'll be fine. Goodnight."

"Goodnight, Lisa," Evie said, interjecting a friendlier tone. "I hope your headache goes away soon."

"After the meds I downed a while ago, I'll soon be oblivious to everything. Even your snores."

"Won't be so funny when I post a picture of you with drool caked to your cheek."

"Don't make me lock my door. You'll have to take your late night business out to the parking lot."

"Evil woman."

"Don't you know it." Lisa slid the bedroom door closed halfway—enough to give her some privacy and still leave room for Evie and Deke to enter the bathroom.

"What was all that about?" Evie asked in a low voice.

"I don't like surprises."

"She's got a lot going on." Like spending an inordinate amount of time on the computer again. "And obviously didn't realize you weren't present when she notified the patients."

"Because I'm so hard to miss."

His angry tone didn't match the situation. "I'd think you'd like to have more time in Rockton. Why don't you take the opportunity and go see your family?"

"I'm working a story." He scraped a hand down his face. "Everything's fine."

Staying in Rockton another day upset him. The most obvious reason would be something concerning his family or friends. She would love to learn more, but she could see it wouldn't be wise to press him with more questions.

"We've never stopped in Rockton before." Word of their arrival had buzzed around the town with superhero speed. At one point, over thirty people had lined up outside the Med Mobile, melting beneath the midday sun. This pharmacy had a connected grocery store. Deke had used his own money to buy several cartons of water. Then he'd straightened up the staff RV and invited some of the sicker and more heat-susceptible patients inside. His obvious care for the patients made his reaction all the more puzzling. "Lisa's incapable of ignoring such need."

He blew out a breath. "Which is why she's the perfect person to lead the tour." The tension lines between his brows disappeared. "Where did the two of you meet?"

"Through one of my instructors at UNC. I need clinic hours for graduate school, and Lisa needed a minion."

"So you're off to graduate school in the fall?"

"Yep. I hope to be a nurse practitioner, like Lisa."

"The two of you are a good team."

"She's great." She glanced toward Lisa's bedroom door. "I worry, though."

"Why?"

"Her headaches. They've been more frequent and more intense."

"Has she seen doctor?"

"Not that I know of. She thinks it's stress."

"The answer to all unknown evils."

Exhaustion moved through Evie's body, draining her strength. She yawned. "Well, I think that does it for me, too." She hiked up onto one elbow. "If ever you'd like to discuss whatever's bothering you about staying in Rockton, I'm a good listener."

"Hit the light, Evie."

Disappointment pinched her chest. She wanted to be there for him, give him reassurance or whatever he needed. But "back off" blazed in his luminous eyes.

"My offer still stands, even after you're done being a turd." A split second before she clicked the light off, Deke whipped off his T-shirt, revealing a ripped set of abs.

Her thumb slid off the switch, her mind and fingers disconnecting. One screamed, "Turn the light off!" The other fired back, "Stop—are you crazy?"

She shot Deke a look.

He lifted a brow. "Everything okay?"

Squeezing her eyes shut, she grappled for the switch and cast them into darkness.

The exhaustion numbing her muscles disappeared with one eye-popping glimpse of Deke Conrad's torso. How could she sleep with that image seared into her mind's eye? With all that raw testosterone lounging only four feet away?

What she wouldn't give to trace her fingers over the sculpted planes of his chest, the hard ridges of his abdomen, the tempting hairline trailing down beneath the sheet...

She rolled onto her back and stared up at the ceiling, following the shadowed lines from left to right, right to left, left to right, right to left. The mattress beneath her hardened into a slab of concrete—cold and unyielding. Lonely.

Turning onto her side, away from Deke, she prayed for Lisa's drugged oblivion. It didn't come. Finally, she gave up. "Deke?"

"Yeah?" he answered without an ounce of sleep in his voice.

"Would you please put your shirt back on?"

Silence blared through the RV.

"Are you serious?"

Lifting her head, she glanced over her shoulder to answer.

Big mistake.

Enough light from the lampposts filtered between the closed shades to illuminate his chest and face. He'd raised up on his elbows, the sheet pooled at his waist. Michelangelo or Giambologna would memorialize that body in marble, if they were alive.

Need swirled like a warm breeze between her legs. No other man had ever captured her attention like Deke. Lord knew she'd tried to find someone to sever his hold on her. But his grip was tight. Bone deep.

Her head dropped back to the pillow, and she slapped a hand against her forehead. "You're distracting me from sleep."

"Am I?" Humor edged his words.

"Not funny."

She heard rustling, then her bed dipped. Heat raced into every pore of her body. Lifting her hand, she found Deke looming over her. Torso bare. A roguish smile molding his lips.

Glancing at Lisa's door, she asked, "What are you doing?"

"Distracting you from sleep."

Closing her eyes against the sting of humiliation, she said, "I can't joke about this, Deke. Not this."

Her breath caught when a hand appeared at her shoulder. He shifted closer, his hip nudging hers. Heat from his body flowed into hers, flaming every nerve, every pulse point.

"I adore your honesty, Evie." The backs of his fingers caressed her cheek. "It's refreshing and makes me smile."

She didn't know where to put her hands. With all that naked flesh hovering over her, she knew where they itched to be.

What was he up to? Only yesterday, he'd made it clear that their age gap would prevent them from getting together. Now, his big bare body stretched above hers like a lover's.

His scent filled her nose and his heat... Oh, Lord, she wanted to burrow into his heat. But she wouldn't make the first move toward intimacy until she knew what he was about tonight.

The question still remained—what should she do with her damn hands? At her sides seemed too stiff. Off the bed seemed too weird. Across her chest seemed too angelic. Giving up, she allowed them to fall where they may. To her relief, they folded naturally against her shoulders.

"Enough to kiss me?" *How's that for honesty?*

"One would never be enough."

"I'm not opposed to a few more."

His grin deepened. "You give my control too much credit."

"Shouldn't you have your sling on?"

"Yes, Dr. Steele."

"Why don't you?"

"Because I'm a lousy patient."

She traced the edge of the taped gauze. "Does it still hurt?"

"Only when I cheat and use my arm."

Emboldened, she continued her exploration. Her fingertips caressed the ridge of his wide, smooth shoulders and thick biceps. An electric current sizzled beneath her touch, and her breaths became sharper, her legs restless. If she continued to touch him, she would make the mistake of wanting more. More than he was willing to give. Her fingers curled.

"Why are you here, Deke?" she asked in an aching whisper.

His eyes squeezed shut and his jaw hardened. "Breaking a promise. Screwing up a friendship."

"Never."

When he looked at her again, his eyes glowed in the dim light. "Touch me, again."

Surprise kept her immobile.

"Please."

The torment in his one-word plea sliced through her paralysis.

"Your wound?"

"Under control."

Afraid he'd change his mind, she smoothed her fingertips over his dark eyebrows and curved over his sculpted cheekbones. His eyes closed again, though not to fight some internal battle. Ecstasy deepened his breathing and relaxed his features.

She moved down his throat and onto his back, her touch deepening, seeking.

Lifting his head, his neck arched and a low moan rumbled through his chest.

Her splayed hands dipped into the hollow of his lower back and crept up the rise of his bottom, pausing at the waistband of his pajamas.

Desire lay heavy in his eyes as he lowered his gaze to hers. "Yes," he breathed, moving fully onto the bed, one leg nestled between both of hers.

Muscles deep in her womb clenched, forcing her legs together and her lips apart. Her harsh breaths mingled with his as her nails tunneled beneath his pajamas and scraped over his rounded ass.

She squeezed and massaged and caressed and pressed her center against his erection. This time, she groaned. Sought. Got lost in the moment.

Hungry lips covered hers, throwing Evie's body into a cauldron of desire. She gripped his scalp with both hands and angled her head for a more perfect fit.

His tongue slid into her mouth and curled around hers with an erotic thoroughness that made her head whirl and mind go blank. Instinct fueled by desperation took over.

With the backs of her fingers, she brushed over his hard nipples, enjoying his sharp inhalation at her touch. Her mouth watered for one taste, though they couldn't risk the noise of positioning and repositioning their bodies. So she toyed with the sensitive peaks until his head dropped into the crook of her neck, his labored breaths beating against her chest.

She slid her hand lower, and his muscles locked. His chest stopped rising. Taking that as a good sign, she didn't halt her downward momentum, though she did slow her progress.

Beneath his pajamas, heat scorched her flesh. His musky scent reached her nose. She took his mouth as her hand wrapped around his cock. Dear God, the size of him, the weight of him, the heat of him.

"Evie," he whispered against her mouth. "Sweet Evie."

Increasing the pressure of her grip, she slid down his length, then back up.

"This is wrong," he said through unsteady breaths.

"I can't think of anything that has felt more right."

She continued her ministrations, using their confinement to her advantage, pressing his hardness against her clit. Their breaths grew harder. Sweat slicked their skin. His back arched, her inner muscles contracted. Their cries of release were silent but no less explosive.

For a full minute, neither of them moved, as if they both feared a single twitch could shatter the ethereal world their lovemaking had created.

Tears pricked Evie's eyes. She'd waited so long for this moment, so long to create a deeper, more intimate connection with this man.

Deke's finger traced over her nose, making her smile. He kissed her forehead and rose.

Her eyes shot open, fear rising into her throat.

He shucked off his pajamas before slipping beneath her covers.

"Lisa?" she whispered.

"I'll be gone before she wakes." He wrapped his good arm around her, drawing her close. "Trust me."

She peered into his drowsy eyes. "Gone from my bed, or…me?"

"Never you, Evie. Never you." He coaxed her head onto his chest. "Sleep now. We'll figure us out later."

Though her body molded to his, hours passed before the worry gave over to sleep.

Chapter Eleven

CRUSHING GUILT ATE AT DEKE like a festering wound destroying his flesh one cell at a time.

He couldn't do anything by half measures. Instead of a straight-on frontal attack by his conscience for having broken his promise so easily, so fucking quickly, he also got slammed from behind for enjoying his fall.

Disentangling himself from Evie before dawn had been the hardest act of his life. At some point during the night, she'd lost her T-shirt and shorts. Having all that sweet, trusting warmth cuddled against him had been worth the sharp, burning ache in his injured shoulder.

For nearly an hour, he'd lain awake, listening to the rain and fighting an almost overpowering need to sink balls deep into her. He'd grown so hard and heavy that he hurt from lack of release.

Ripping away from her, he'd thrown on his clothes from the day before and left his beautiful temptation naked and untouched. The long walk in the rain had helped, but it hadn't taken the edge off. He was afraid only one person could right him again.

He slid a pen beneath the metal clamp of the clipboard, waiting for more patients to arrive. He'd been using pockets of downtime to check in with Keone. So far, he hadn't gathered much intelligence to convey to his second-in-command. The boy with the bear claw had been his most significant discovery, which wasn't all that impressive.

Two cars crept into the parking lot followed by a pickup with a rusted-out fender. Deke hovered near the Med Mobile, waiting to see who would reach him first.

An older woman with a head full of gray hair that grazed her shoulders, rail-thin body that disappeared in profile, and razor-sharp backbone that had the stamp of military exited an ancient Oldsmobile. The Taurus next to her swarmed with a disconcerting amount of small bodies and high-pitched screams.

The pickup backed into a stall, away from the other vehicles, a masculine silhouette its only occupant. Deke waited for the driver to emerge. He didn't. A plume of smoke crawled out the window and dissipated in the breeze.

The image reminded him of similar sighting at Haden's Hollow. Now that he thought about it, the bearded man hadn't approached the Med Mobile then either. Had he dropped someone off and waited in the truck? Had he been killing time? Waiting for a friend? Or had he been observing someone? Him?

Setting the clipboards down, he started for the truck. He got to within twenty feet of his quarry before the truck's engine roared to life and the guy sped away.

"What'd you want with Frank Cleamer?" the old woman asked when Deke returned.

Deke filed the name away. "Thought he might be shy about coming up to the Med Mobile."

She snorted. "That boy doesn't have a shy bone in that skinny little body."

He refrained from giving her toothpick-frame a once-over. "Why'd he take off?"

"You storming across the lot probably spooked him."

"I'm not that scary."

"Bobby, watch for cars! Willie, stop trying to trip your little brother."

The family from the Taurus had spilled into the lot

and the hive had dispersed in all directions. Deke tore his gaze away from the harassed mother back to the gray-haired spitfire who was eyeing him from head to toe.

"You could be one of those comic book characters what's on TV nowadays."

"The good guys aren't scary."

"But the villains are."

Deke smiled. "I'm going to have to warn the ladies that they have a handful coming their way."

"I'm not here as a patient."

"No? What can I do for you, then?"

"Our rainy night has given way to a beautiful day, and some folks from town have put together an impromptu get-together. As thanks for stopping here and fixing our sick, for nothing more than a thank-you, we'd like y'all to join us for a nice BBQ dinner tonight."

Shit.

He'd already come across a second cousin on his Mama's side, this morning. No doubt Sally had already told her mama about sighting the gov cuz, and Aunt Gertie's curiosity would've been piqued enough to ring up her sister.

If they'd left yesterday as planned, he could've avoided his family's looks of betrayal and questions he couldn't answer. But they hadn't left, and the Southern boy in him could never turn down genuine hospitality.

"That's real kind of you, but we never know when we'll finish up. We'd hate to keep y'all waiting."

"It's nothing fancy. City Hall gave us the Roundhouse pavilion for free, and most everything will be simmering in crock pots. Come when you're able."

"I'll speak to the ladies, but I doubt they'll refuse a home-cooked meal. We'll do our best to make it there by seven-thirty. How's that sound?"

"Whenever. I've got nothing better to do these days than wait for death. It'll do my heart good to keep an eye out for a full-bodied bourbon, like you."

He bent down to kiss the woman's cheek. "I don't even know your name."

"Rita Sampson."

"See you tonight, Mrs. Sampson."

"Rita. Never did like my husband, not even when he was alive. Now I'm stuck with the old goat's name."

She marched back to her vehicle and drove off. In many ways, she reminded him of his own tough-as-nails grandma. He missed her. Besides his mom and sister Dara, she'd been the only other one who'd been upset by his dad's ultimatum. Dylan had seemed unhappy about the situation at first, but his calls had dwindled to a semiannual come-bail-me-out-of-trouble.

If his cousin Sally hadn't managed to stir up enough interest about his presence, Rita's BBQ would finish it off. Nobody passed up a potluck in these parts. Except for his dad. The old man wasn't much for social gatherings on a good day. If he got wind his traitorous son would be in attendance, he'd for sure avoid the event. And where Mitch Conrad didn't go, his wife Iris didn't go.

A cannon-sized head plowed into his stomach, the impact knocking him off his feet and onto his back.

"Willie! I told you to stop tripping your brother." The woman from the Taurus kneeled beside him, a crusty-nosed infant in her arms. "Are you all right, sir?"

The Med Mobile door swung open, and Evie appeared, concern emblazoned her features. In one big sweep of her intelligent blue eyes, she assessed the situation. Concern faded to amusement.

He rolled to a sitting position, which put him eye-to-eye with the towhead who had rammed into him. Fear made the boy's eyes as big as baseballs. Not so with his older brother. The unrepentant Willie snickered behind his grimy, nail-bitten hand.

Ruffling the younger boy's blond head, he said, "I'm fine."

"Tell the man you're sorry, Bobby," the boy's mother said.

"Sorry, sir."

"Willie," she prompted.

The older boy stared at him a full five seconds before murmuring something under his breath. Could have been an apology, or a demand for Deke to go to hell. He couldn't be sure.

"Apology accepted." He got to his feet, and Bobby's eyes grew wide as he tilted his head back and back and back to take in his victim's full height. "Why don't you two be good boys and do your mama a favor by sitting down?"

The youngest scrambled over to the row of bag chairs Deke had set out to create an outdoor waiting room area. Willie crossed his arms.

Cooing to her infant, the woman was unaware of her eldest son's defiance.

He peered at Evie. She crossed her arms in perfect imitation of the boy's stance, her grin fighting to break free.

What the hell was he supposed to do? If he'd acted that way in front of his mama, he would've spent the next week cleaning toilets and brushing the dog. How did parents teach kids respect these days?

"Do you like to gamble, Willie?"

"Sure."

"Two out of three. Rock-paper-scissors. I win—you sit down over there and be quiet until your mama's ready to go. You win—?"

"I get a twelve-pack of beer."

"Try again."

"A gallon of cookie dough ice cream."

"Deal." He rested his fist in his palm. Willie followed suit. "On the count of three. Ready?"

Willie nodded.

"One, two—" they pounded their fists into their palms, "—three." He ended with his hand flat and Willie's fingers splayed into a V.

"I win!" Willie announced, bouncing on his toes.

"Not yet. We have two more to go."

This time, Willie did the count. "One, two, three."

He kept his hand fisted and Willie stayed with the scissors.

"One for one."

Willie scowled. The count came faster this time. Rock to rock. Tie.

Paper to paper. Tie.

Paper covers rock. Two to one. Game to Deke.

"Again," Willie demanded.

"That's not how it works, Sport."

Willie shoved his hands into his pockets, staring at the ground.

"Did you forget the terms of our deal?"

Silence.

"A man pays his debts—and honors his mother." When Willie's feet stayed planted in place, he pushed harder. "Of course, you're not quite a man yet. What are you? Ten?"

"Twelve!"

"Ahh. Not a boy, but not a man." He rubbed his chin, already hearing the sandpaper scratch of newborn whiskers. "I wonder what decision you'll make? The boy's or the man's?"

Willie glanced between him, his mom, and little brothers. Ego warred with honor. He left them in suspense a moment longer before shuffling over to a chair and plopping down.

His mother mouthed a "thank-you" as she accepted the clipboard.

"Bobby, Steve—go sit next to your brother. Behave yourselves while I take Clara inside to see the nurse."

The younger brothers dutifully sat on either side of Willie.

Evie stepped aside to allow the mother entrance, a soft, proud smile on her breath-stealing face. Her approval wrapped around his chest like a warm blanket. Already he wondered what he could do to make her smile at him like that again.

After the ladies went inside, he ignored the boys and turned his mind to the guy in the rusted truck. Frank Cleamer. The name didn't ring a bell, but he'd been away from Rockton for over a decade.

A few minutes later, the Med Mobile door opened, and the mother waved to her son. "Steve, you're next."

Willie continued to sit with his chin tucked into his chest and his hands stuffed into his pockets. The deal said nothing about not pouting. He gave the kid points for keeping up his end of the deal, though.

When the last boy was summoned into the RV, he jogged across the lot to the pharmacy-grocery store to purchase four quarts of cookie dough ice cream. He dropped the bounty into the passenger seat of the Taurus. With the vehicle parked beneath a tree, the kids' treat shouldn't melt too much before they finished up.

Out of all the things Willie could have asked for, he'd chosen ice cream, which told him little of it reached the boy's belly. A kid should be able to enjoy a scoop of cookie dough from time to time—no matter how much gray the punk added to his mom's hair.

Five minutes later, the brood left, but not before a chorus of cheers erupted from the vehicle. He kept his back to the commotion, a grin on his face.

"What's all that about?" Evie asked, stepping down beside him.

"Sounds like they're ready to go home. What'd you do to them?"

"The normal poking and prodding. Nothing that would create any excitement."

"We've been invited to dinner."

"By whom?"

"Rita Sampson and friends."

"Rita?"

"Spokeswoman for the good people of Rockton, who wish to thank you and Lisa for your generosity."

"Why? This is our job."

Did she really not understand the value of her work? "These are proud people, Evie. They might not be able to pay you, but they sure as hell can feed you."

"We're happy to help where we can. They needn't go through such trouble."

"They don't see it as trouble. They see it as a way of giving thanks."

"But I don't have a dish to take."

"We'll stop at the store." He moved close, framing her cheek in his palm. "What is it? Why are you making excuses not to go?"

Rather than answer, she nuzzled into his touch, and guilty need stabbed him in the gut.

"Tell me."

"I don't like to be in the spotlight."

"Aren't you the outgoing Steele? The one who flits around at all the social gatherings?"

"I'm the Steele who likes for everyone to be happy. Sometimes I have to step outside my comfort zone in order to make that happen. But I never like being the focus of everyone's attention."

"You won't be. Lisa and I'll be at your side."

"I had hoped that—" her gaze roamed the parking lot before resting on his again, "—you and I could have some more alone time."

"Evie, what happened last night—"

"Please don't tell me it was a mistake," she burst out. "I think I can handle almost anything but awful follow-up."

His mind scrambled for a new word. Giving in to his desire had been a mistake, one that caused him significant guilt and untold joy. No word existed for such conflicting emotions.

"I don't regret what we did, but things just got a whole lot more complicated."

"How?"

Sugarcoating the truth wouldn't make this situation any easier. It might get him off the hook for a few days, but the bite in the ass would eventually come. All the Steeles appreciated straight talk, no matter how unwelcome. Evie was no different.

"My uncontrolled actions planted a seed within your heart. A seed of hope. Hope where none should exist."

CHAPTER TWELVE

EVIE FOLLOWED THE CRUMBLING ASPHALT trail that led up to the Roundhouse pavilion. She could see how the structure got its name. Thick wooden beams rose from a concrete platform, reaching up to a green roof with a few missing shingles. The Roundhouse was just that—round. The twelve-sided pavilion easily held two hundred people, with enough room for serving tables and a podium, if need be.

All of this she viewed through Visine-laced eyes.

The eye drops might have eased the redness from her tear-burned eyes, but they'd done nothing to soothe the rupture in her heart.

After their bout of incredible lovemaking, how could Deke still believe they wouldn't be a good fit? That their age difference would create a crevasse too vast to bridge?

Out of the corner of her eye, she noticed Lisa massaging her temple.

"Another headache?"

"Just a little pressure behind my eye. I took something to knock it out before we left."

Evie peered over her shoulder at Deke and found him studying Lisa. Something unpleasant lanced her stomach. This wasn't the first time she'd detected something more to his and Lisa's relationship. She shoved aside her jealousy. Whatever had been between them was in the past. She couldn't let something like that eat at her. She couldn't. Not with everything else going on.

"I'm starting to worry," Evie said. "You've been getting headaches more and more often."

"You're a sweetheart, my friend. But I'm sure they're a reaction to our funding situation."

"What funding situation?"

Lisa's eyes widened. "N-nothing. I'm speaking nonsense."

Evie grasped her arm. "Is the Med Mobile's funding in danger?"

Her friend's stricken features told her all she needed to know.

In one smooth move, Deke pushed between them, linking his arms with theirs. "Let's discuss this tomorrow. Tonight, we're going to have fun." He nudged Evie. "Right?"

Questions clawed against Evie's throat.

"Right?" he coaxed with a little more force.

So many people depended on the MedTour—patients, Lisa, pharmacies...*her*. What would they all do without it?

"Of course," she said.

"Lisa, Evie," Deke said, "this is Rita Sampson, one of the BBQ organizers."

A tall, slender woman closing in on her late seventies stepped forward and gave her a warm smile followed by a big hug.

"Nice to meet you both. Glad you could squeeze in a bit of fun."

"This is incredibly kind of you," Lisa said.

"Nonsense. What y'all have done for us is far kinder than a bit of potato salad and pulled pork. We've been praying for your mobile to stop in Rockton, and now you have and we're right thankful." She waved them forward. "Come inside and say hello."

They spent the next hour eating and gossiping and dancing. After the initial introductions, Evie settled into a rhythm, one that felt more natural than she'd expected, less like a façade.

She loved these people. Not just the residents of Rockton, but small town folks, in general. They knew how to laugh, how to help their neighbors, and how to do right by their family.

Her gaze fell on Deke. He lounged next to one of the boys they'd treated that morning. The two spoke in low tones, their conversation punctuated by an occasional laugh.

The patience he displayed with the child surprised her. He rarely sat still long enough to eat, and his mind never stopped. But he appeared content just sitting there, chatting with the boy.

What kind of father would he be? Patient and mentoring? Annoyed and distant? Or the worst of all, absent? She'd never seen him shy away from kids over the years, and the attention he was giving her young patient now spoke volumes. Something close to pride warmed her insides.

Her attention jumped from one family unit to the next, paying particular notice to the mothers. What kind would she be? Caring, supportive, and nurturing, like her mama? Evie prayed that would be the case. Prayed she and Deke would one day find out their parental mettle together.

A couple in their middle-to-late sixties entered the pavilion. Standing at least six feet tall with a barrel chest, beer belly, and spindle legs, the man greeted some folks and flat-out ignored others. In contrast, the petite woman, with long black hair streaked with silver, doled out tentative hellos and short hugs as her husband split through the crowd ahead of her.

Rita approached the couple. "Good evening, Mitch. Iris. So glad you could join us."

Iris held out a metal pan covered in plastic. "I made Rice Crispies treats."

"They look delicious."

"Have you met our guests of honor?"

Iris looked to her husband, who stared at her and Lisa as if they'd interrupted his nap.

"This is Lisa Frye and Evie Steele."

"Steele?" Mitch asked, ignoring Lisa's outstretched hand. "Of Canyon Ridge?"

Steele Ridge now, but Evie didn't correct him. "Yes, sir."

"I hear your family's bought everyone out of house and home."

"Mitch!" Rita scolded. "What a thing to say to our guest."

Without thought, Evie's gaze sought Deke's. He caught it, his focus shooting between her and the jerk, whose head appeared ready to explode. Something sharp and menacing swiped down his features before his long strides tore across the pavilion.

"It's true," Mitch said. "Got friends over there. They ain't too happy about how that Steele boy's flinging his money around and changing names."

"I don't give two hoots about what's going on over there," Rita said. "This is Rockton, and we don't treat guests this way."

"Who died and left you boss of this town?"

Evie and Lisa moved to stand on each side of Rita.

"My mama told me once that if you don't have anything good to say, don't say anything at all."

Mitch whipped around to find Deke standing inches away. He took an involuntarily step back, the submissive action angering him further.

"What the hell are you doing here?"

"Hello, Daddy." Deke nodded to the woman, who now stood near Lisa. "Mama."

"Derek," Iris Conrad whispered, using his birth name.

"I asked you a question, boy."

"Enjoying some BBQ. What are you doing here? Besides making everyone uncomfortable?"

"Thought I told you not to come back."

"Mitch," Rita warned, "I told you—"

"Shut up, woman."

Deke got right up into his dad's face. "Don't ever speak to a woman like that again." His nostrils flared. "You drinking again?"

"Get the hell away from me." Mitch shoved against Deke's chest. His son didn't budge.

"Come on, Mitch." A blond-haired man in a plaid shirt and jeans clasped Mitch by the elbow. "Let's go see if the corn cobs are off the grill."

"Take your damn hands off me, Ray."

"What's going on over here?" a redheaded man with thick biceps asked. His dark brown eyes roamed down Evie's body before shifting to Deke. "Well, well. Look who decided to return. Fed man Deke Conrad."

"Prickett."

"*Sergeant* Prickett." He took a swig from of his beer bottle. "Things have changed around here since you turned traitor."

"*Sergeant*, don't you have some weights to lift or something," Iris Conrad piped up.

"Iris," her husband warned.

"I swear to bejesus," Rita said, throwing her hands up. "This is supposed to be a party. What do we have? A bunch of apes bumping their chests together. "Ray, Andy, get these boys a corn cob." She linked arms with Deke and Evie and motioned for Lisa to follow. "I need a shot of whisky. How about you?"

Deke watched his father refuse all attempts of appeasement. Stubborn old man.

He rubbed the ache at the center of his chest. The three shots of whisky that Rita had pressed on him had gone a long way to numb the pain. But he knew from experience that nothing could make it go away.

How had they come to this?

Why had they sacrificed family for ideology?

He swallowed back the lump, remembering the tears framing his mother's blue eyes—his eyes—before she'd shuffled after her husband. Now she sat a few feet away from her husband, alone. Not sending even one glance her son's way.

After a decade of his dad's cold shoulders, he'd gotten used to the old man's silence. But his mother's desertion hurt. She'd always been there when he'd needed her. Always had the right words to soothe any fear, any pain, any injustice.

Something had changed in the past few months. She'd cut off all contact with him. Not one word of explanation. Not a single whispered goodbye.

Did this sudden change have something to do with his dad drinking again? Where had his strong, loving mother gone?

The hollow ache in his chest sharpened.

A touch at his shoulder pulled his attention away from his parents.

"Are you okay?" Evie asked.

"I'm fine." He pushed the tension from his body and produced a smile. "Are you enjoying yourself?"

She studied his features a moment before turning to Rita and Lisa. "Will you excuse us?"

"Of course," they said in unison.

Evie slid her hand inside his and led him away from dozens of curious eyes. He didn't resist. When he'd accepted Rita's invitation, he'd known he might run into family—or, at least extended family.

She guided him into a cove of shrubs. In the center rose a large paint-chipped fountain that hadn't seen water in at least a decade. Sitting on the concrete ledge encircling the fountain, Evie patted the space beside her. "Join me."

He sat, feeling old and alone.

Except Evie was here.

It was enough for now.

"Do you want to talk about it?" she asked.

"Not really."

"Does that mean you *won't* talk about it?"

A corner of his mouth twisted. "Don't you have enough of your own family drama?"

"Makes me somewhat of an expert."

Deke raised a brow.

"Or maybe just a good listener."

He raked a hand through his hair, not wanting to analyze his screwed-up family.

"How long have you been estranged?"

"My dad hasn't spoken to me since I went to work for the federal government. My mom—that's new."

"Is your dad anti-government? Or does he have a beef with the U.S. Fish and Wildlife Service?"

"A little of both."

"But for your dad to turn his back on you, in such a public way, seems excessive."

"Conrads tend to hold grudges longer than most people, and my father doesn't care what others think."

"You really don't want to talk about this."

Deke pushed off the wall, no longer able to sit still. What little he'd divulged about his family had brought all the old, harsh feelings to the surface.

"There's no point in discussing it." He paced along the scrubby hedgerow. "Even if I were to quit my job, the damage is done. My dad won't welcome me back and I don't grovel well."

"What about your mom?"

"She's made her choice—to stand by her husband. I have to respect her decision. To do anything else would only upset her."

"You don't think she's being mistreated, do you?"

"My father's many things, but he's not a wife beater."

"Mental abuse can be as damaging as physical."

Deke closed his eyes. With his brother and sister now

grown, there was nothing keeping his mother with her husband. Why did she stay?

He listened to his breaths, focused on the stream of air moving through his body and nose. He worked to steady his heartbeat, calm the electricity sizzling in his veins.

When he finally opened his eyes, his mind shied away from all thoughts of Mitch and Iris Conrad. Over the unkempt shrubs, Deke spotted a winding trail leading down to the river.

"Up for a stroll?"

Evie glanced back at the pavilion. "They won't find us rude?"

"After the show my family and I just gave them, they're probably glad to be rid of me."

"You didn't cause that scene back there."

"I didn't end it, either." He held out a hand and she accepted it. The simple contact warmed parts of him that had gone cold at the sight of his parents.

"Where're your sister and brother these days?"

"Dara lives in Charlotte with her growing family. When she's not popping out babies, she's working as a landscape architect."

"How many kids does she have?"

"Four."

"That's hardly a brood."

"Maybe not from your perspective."

"True. Not many people have six kids anymore."

"Good thing Jonah bought himself a town. The Steele clan now has plenty of room to expand."

She smacked his good arm. "Not funny. Everyone in that town would've gone bankrupt trying to pay their property taxes. Jonah saved them, including my mom."

He squeezed her hand. "Didn't mean to hit on a sore spot."

Sighing, she said, "My family's constantly battling snide remarks, like your dad's."

"You know I meant only to make you smile, right? I'm in awe of your brother's generosity."

"What disturbed most people was changing the name from Canyon Ridge to Steele Ridge. But there would be no Canyon Ridge if not for Jonah's intervention."

"Jealousy's an unseen evil that eats away at a person's good sense. Ignore them."

"Easier said than done."

"Darwin's survival of the fittest will soon take care of the problem."

She eyed him suspiciously. "What are you talking about?"

"Now that Britt, Grif, Reid, and Micki have found their mates, the Steeles are going to breed out the rabble rousers."

"You're horrible!" She whacked again. "A little sympathy, please."

"Let me see if I can muster up a bit." He paused. "Hmm, perhaps I need proper motivation. Do you think Jonah would name a street after me?"

"Arghh! I'm not talking to you about this anymore." She dropped his hand and surged ahead.

Chuckling, he grasped her arm. "Okay, okay—"

In a move she could have only learned from her Green Beret brother Reid, she broke his hold and spun around with the speed of a Tasmanian Devil, using her momentum to climb—*climb*—his back. All without jarring his injury.

She wrapped her arms around his head like a monkey hunkered over a football—and squeezed. Within seconds, he struggled for breath. When he made to rip free her hold, she released him.

Whispering in his ear, she said, "Never provoke a Steele." She pulled his earlobe into the hot center of her mouth, taking away the sting of her action.

He hardened beneath her erotic assault. His hand smoothed over her thigh where it clung to his waist. He pressed closer, into her warmth.

The sun lowering behind the mountain did nothing to cool the temperature. In fact, the humid warmth of a moment ago now felt sultry and damn near perfect.

Just when he'd made up his mind to walk them down to the lake and peel Evie's clothes off, one by one, she stopped her sweet torture, kissing his neck before sliding off his back.

As they stared at each other, he knew he appeared as off balance as she looked. He held out his hand to her again. "Shall we continue? Before we're arrested for public indecency?"

"Are you going to behave yourself?"

"After that punishment, I'm not promising anything."

She smiled, and they lapsed into a comfortable silence.

A chorus of cicadas pulsed around them, and the rhythmic belch of bullfrogs punctuated the air. A don't-have-a-care-in-the-world peacefulness settled over him. A frame of mind he hadn't experienced in years.

"Should we turn back before it becomes too dark for us to see the path?"

"There's a historic schoolhouse right around the bend. Thought you might like to see it." He caressed his thumb over her knuckles. "I have excellent night vision."

"Lead on."

When they rounded the bend, his pace slowed and his heart bolted like a racehorse. The lighthouse wasn't the first thing they saw. It wasn't even the second.

The dead body took the number one spot.

His kid brother leaning over the corpse took number two.

A woman screamed, wrenching Evie's attention away from the man crouching next to an unconscious woman lying in the middle of the trail. The guy jerked around at the passerby's screech, spotting them at the trail's edge.

"What's going on?" Deke demanded.

The hysterical woman fumbled with her purse until she extracted her phone.

The man's features took on the appearance of a trapped animal. His instinct for flight was evident in the way his gaze darted around the area, though he remained in place. Something about his face seemed familiar. Had she seen him at the pavilion? Treated him in the Med Mobile?

"I didn't do this." He peered down at the blood on his hands. "I didn't."

The paralyzing effects of shock wore off, and Deke's long strides ate up the space between the trail and the victim. "Does she need an ambulance?"

Something in Deke's commanding tone—or his actual words—snapped the guy into action. He snatched something from the body and took off in the opposite direction.

"Dylan, wait!"

Dylan? Could he be Deke's younger brother? He had similar coloring, but she hadn't seen Deke's siblings in years, not since they moved away from Steele Ridge and returned to Rockton.

Deke gave chase, barked a command her way, leaving her alone with a hyperventilating woman—and a body. She approached the woman with caution, clicking on her phone's flashlight.

The victim lay on her side in a pair of tattered jean shorts and a peach tank top. One flip-flop on, one flip-flop off. Long blond hair obscured her face and fanned over her upper body.

Evie glanced at the bystander, who was holding her phone as if it were the only thing keeping her alive. "Is this your friend?"

The bun at the back of the terrified woman's head jiggled vigorously back and forth.

"I'm a nurse." Evie kept her voice low and calm, though her heart was sprinting toward the finish line. "Try to take deep, long breaths."

She circled the unconscious woman to kneel at her side. Blood drenched the woman's hair and pooled into the nooks and crannies of the old asphalt trail.

"Hello," she called. "I'm here to help."

The woman didn't move.

Slowly, as if sticking her hand into an animal hole, Evie peeled back a rope of bloody blond hair from the woman's face and throat. The woman's eyes stared into space, lifeless and cold. Bile raced up her throat, intent on making her look the fool. She caught it and forced it back. She'd seen death before. But never murder. Never such violence.

The victim's neck had been slashed so severely that little more than skin kept it attached to her body. Evie pressed two fingers to the woman's wrist, knowing her pulse would be silent, but unable to stop the confirming habit.

When no heartbeat met her touch, she sat back on her heels. Grief for the stranger pressed on her chest. Such a horrible, senseless death.

"She's dead, isn't she?"

"Yes."

The bystander went off on another bout of hysterics. Evie ignored her instinct to care for the distraught witness. Her mind had turned inward.

If the runner was Dylan, could he have done such a thing? The Conrad siblings Deke, Dara, and Dylan—the three Ds—were several years older than her and all bore the same coloring as their mother.

What had Dylan said before he ran?

I didn't do this.

So why did he take off?

Where was Deke?

Getting to her feet, she searched the shadows.

"Oh, my God," the bystander said. "Had I come through here a few minutes earlier, that could have been me! He could have murdered me, instead."

Any other time, Evie would've attempted to calm the

woman. But she couldn't see Deke anywhere. She spun in a half circle, worry building in her mind like a kettle of water on the verge of a boil.

No longer able to stand by and wait, Evie headed in the direction Deke had disappeared. The logical side of her mind pleaded with her to stay by the trail and wait for the authorities. But the part of her brain controlling her feet ignored all reason and set off to find Deke.

Within seconds of setting foot inside the woods, her stalker radar lit up. An overwhelming sense of being watched pushed down on her. The wind died down, the insects quieted, the leaves beneath her feet crackled.

Unlike many, she didn't fear hiking alone in the woods. She and her brothers had spent hours playing war games with paintball guns and whatever weapons they had on hand. So the prickling at the back of her neck had nothing to do with the darkening shadows or towering trees. No, the sensation forewarned her of the evil harbored within these forested walls.

A branch snapped.

She pointed her phone's flashlight toward the sound, searching.

What the hell was she doing? Time to get the hell out of here.

But Deke was still missing. She stood frozen with indecision until she finally pushed past her fear and barreled deeper into the unknown, following Deke's invisible trail. If her mother ever found out about this...

Her light shone on a man, and she nearly pissed herself.

"What are you doing out here?" Deke asked, sweaty and out of breath, but he appeared otherwise unharmed.

"Looking for you."

"Didn't I tell you to stay put?"

She recalled him barking out something before he took off. "Maybe. I was a little distracted by the dead body at my feet."

His voice softened. "Are you okay?"

"I'm fine. Did you catch up to Dylan?"

"No." He grasped her hand and marched toward the trail. "The little bugger's always been roadrunner fast."

"So it was your brother."

"Yes." A world of disappointment lay within that one word.

"The woman's throat—it's been cut."

"Cut?"

"Yeah. Whoever did it either wanted to make sure she was good and dead or had a severe grudge against her."

"That bad?"

She swallowed, nodding.

He paused, wrapping his arms around her. "I'm sorry you had to see that."

Her hold around him tightened. She absorbed his heat, his smell, his solidness. "What's going on?"

"Good question." He resumed their march. "One I'm going to figure out."

By the time they reached the corpse, streams of light bobbled along the trail. Authoritative shouts of "Mrs. Mullins, show yourself" filled the air.

"Here!" called the hysterical woman, aka Mrs. Mullins, waving her hands in the air. "Over here, officers!" When the newcomers drew nearer, the woman asked, "Is that you, Sergeant Prickett?"

At the sergeant's name, Deke groaned.

Following Mrs. Mullins' direction, Sergeant Prickett made a beeline for them.

The sergeant's attention dropped to the dead woman. "Looks like you got yourself into a whole heap of trouble, fed man."

She frowned. "Deke didn't kill her."

Deke gave her hand a warning squeeze.

"Is that right?" Sergeant Prickett asked, sarcasm dripped from every syllable. "Since you've figured everything out, why don't you tell me who murdered poor Gracie."

"You recognize her?"

"Gracie Gilbert. Waits tables at the Olde Town Pub & Grill." He bent down to get a closer look at her obvious wounds before pinning Evie with a nasty look. "Now tell me who killed her."

Deke nudged her half behind him. "We came upon the body at the same time."

"Did either of you see who slit her throat?"

She hesitated. The image of Dylan kneeling over the corpse didn't look good, though he might have found the woman seconds before they rounded the corner.

"No," she and Deke said in unison.

"What are you talking about?" Mrs. Mullins pointed at Deke. "He took off after a young man. Someone named Dylan."

The sergeant smiled. An oily one. One he greased often and with relish.

"Can only think of one Dylan in these parts. Wouldn't have pegged your lowlife, thieving brother as a murderer. But people disappoint all the time." Sergeant Prickett rested a hand on his sidearm. "Now tell me where I can find him."

CHAPTER THIRTEEN

"I'M ONLY GOING TO ASK you this one more time, son," Chief Middleton said. "Who did you see kneeling over Gracie Gilbert's body?"

They'd been through this a dozen times. Deke wasn't about to give up his brother's name. He'd find the mongrel first and get some answers.

"Same answer, Chief. It was too dark to identify the individual."

"Sally Mullins said she heard you call out the name Dylan."

"Not sure how she could've heard anything above all that caterwauling."

"So you deny seeing your brother?"

"My brother and I haven't been on speaking terms for a few years."

"That's not what I asked you."

"Look, Chief. I don't have anything for you. If something comes up, I'll be sure to give you a call."

"What do you know about the drugs we found on the victim?"

His attention sharpened on the chief. "Why would I know anything about a bit of marijuana?"

"Why do you assume it was marijuana?"

"Cocaine? Heroin? PCP?" He glanced at the scowling man standing to the right of the sheriff.

"Maybe Sergeant Prickett can answer your question."

The sergeant unwound his massive arms and took a step forward.

Holding up a hand, Chief Middleton said, "I could arrest you for obstructing justice."

"What am I obstructing? If you believe Mrs. Mullins, go find my brother."

"If I find out you've been lying to me, son, you won't like the consequences." The chief sat back. "Get him out of here, Sergeant."

Prickett grasped his upper arm, his fingertips digging into his flesh. Deke shrugged him off. "I'm pretty sure I'm capable of standing and walking without your assistance."

"Then get your ass out of here, fed man."

The sergeant led him from the interrogation room that was the size of a janitor's closet. He hoped Evie's interview had been less intense. Growing up with older brothers, she knew all about bluster and intimidation. He didn't think she'd buckle under either, though he did wonder what she'd told them about Dylan.

Prickett opened the door leading into the small lobby. "I know you're lying about your brother. With or without your help, I'm going to catch his drug-pimping ass."

"First a thief, now a dealer. Better make up your mind before you run off wasting your time and taxpayer's money." He plowed past the sergeant, wanting nothing more than to locate Evie and find a place where he could think.

Although his brother had never been an angel—except in his father's eyes—Dylan wasn't capable of murder. And Deke didn't think he'd gotten mixed up with drugs. Probably a bazillion other things, but not drugs and murder.

At the sound of his voice, Evie whirled around in her chair. Worry etched her features before a smile of relief swiped it away. He didn't give either of them an opportunity to indulge in an embrace. The less Prickett knew about their situation, the better.

"Outside," he said in a low voice.

She seemed to understand, allowing him to guide her from the police station.

Not until he'd put a block between them and the station did he ask, "Where's Lisa?"

"I sent her back to the RVs. Her headache had grown to the point of making her nauseous." Evie slipped her hand into his. "Something's not right. I wish she'd see a doctor."

"Lisa's tough. Whatever's wrong, she'll get through it."

"You have a lot of faith in her."

"I suppose I do." He glanced down at her. "You survived their interrogation?"

"Amateurs. They have nothing on my brothers."

"That's my girl."

"Why were you in there for so long?"

"They thought asking the same question a hundred different ways would result in a different answer." He halted and faced her. "I need to ask you something. The answer itself isn't important—other than giving me a heads-up."

She placed a hand on his chest. "It was too dark. I didn't see the person's face. And I couldn't hear what you said over Mrs. Mullins's screaming."

Deke released a breath that had been trapped in his chest. "Why?"

Shrugging, she said, "He's family."

He cradled her face in his hands. "Thank you."

She rose up on tiptoes and kissed him. "You're welcome."

The ease with which she kissed him sent a shiver tripping down his spine. She'd kept the intimate contact simple and reassuring—exactly what he'd needed.

"What do we do now?" she asked.

"Check on Lisa. See if we need to strong-arm her into

seeking medical attention. Then I'm off to track down my brother, which means I'll need to drop out of the MedTour."

She seemed on the verge of arguing but gave him a wan smile instead. "The tour won't be quite the same without you."

"I'd much rather stay with you than be chasing down Dylan."

When they entered the staff RV, Deke spotted Lisa lying on the floor in the fetal position, her face carved by agony.

Evie ran to her side. "Lisa, are you okay? Where do you hurt?"

Lisa tried to cover her eyes. "Head," she whispered.

"Help me get her into bed," Evie said to Deke.

"Stomach." Lisa crossed her arms over her middle.

"We'll take it slow," Evie promised.

Lifting a hundred and twenty pounds off the floor with one arm proved challenging, but with Evie's help, he managed it.

"Have you taken anything?" Evie asked Lisa once they had her settled in bed.

"Couple acetaminophen."

"How long ago?"

Lisa's face contorted and she shoved it into the pillow, withdrawing.

Recognizing the signs of a debilitating migraine, he held a washcloth beneath the faucet, wrung it out and then folded it into thirds. He approached from the opposite side of the bed and smoothed Lisa's hair away from her cheek.

"Let me see your forehead, Lisa."

He heard her swallow hard, no doubt bracing herself against the movement and light. Finally, she turned enough for him to drape the wet cloth over her forehead. She tensed at first, then pressed the cloth against her eye sockets.

Evie readjusted the cloth. "It's cold."

"One of my good friends suffers from migraines. He swears by cold compresses, darkness, sleep, and a cool room.

He caught Evie's eye and motioned her toward the door. Clicking off the light, he closed Lisa inside the cavelike room.

"How long did it take your friend to recover?"

"Depended on the severity and the medication."

"She never indicated that the pain was at the level of migraine."

"I'm only speculating based on my experience. It might just be a bad headache."

"I'll see how she's feeling tomorrow. If there's no change, I'm taking her to urgent care."

"What about your patients?"

"Lisa's supervisor at the Blue Valley Medical Clinic will know what to do. Maybe he'll send a replacement nurse practitioner. In the meantime, I'll do what I can for them."

"Extreme on-the-job training."

"I can handle it. I think."

He brought her face up to his. "If anyone can handle this situation, it's you."

She curled her arms around his waist. "I don't want you to go."

"Why not?"

"I've gotten used to you being underfoot."

He squeezed her, hard.

"What if you're wrong about your brother? You could get stuck in the middle of something dangerous."

He chucked her under the chin. "I have a big brother obligation to make sure he's not in over his head."

"Ugh." She rolled her eyes and plopped down in a chair. "Lord save me from big brothers." Her gaze climbed up to his and held there for several seconds. "What's with you and Lisa?"

He tensed. "What do you mean? She's a friend."

"Perhaps more than a friend, at some point?"

Torn, he scrambled for the right response. If he lied, she would eventually find out and he'd lose her trust. If he confirmed her suspicion, she would constantly be analyzing his every word, every look, every gesture. Which hell should he pick?

"It was a long time ago, Evie."

"Did you love her?"

He anchored his hands on his waist, staring at the floor, wishing he'd had a third option. "I cared for her."

"You never loved her?"

"I suppose I did on some level. We were together for two years."

"Why did you break up?"

He couldn't tell her the real reason. That Lisa hated his long absences. Hated not knowing if he'd return home alive or stuffed in a body bag. If he gave Evie some vague reference to his work, she would pelt him with questions. And when he stopped answering, she would become suspicious or, worse, curious about his career. Evie Steele was the last person he needed sniffing around that area of his life. He couldn't think of a more tenacious person.

"We grew apart."

"You grew apart." She repeated his words in a dull, disappointed tone.

"Expecting something more messy?"

"Something more, yes."

"We're friends, Evie. Nothing more."

She gave him a tentative smile. "Have I ever told you that I'm territorial? It seems to be a Steele trait."

"I'm a one-woman guy." *Where did that come from?*

"I hope to be the one woman someday."

The vulnerability in her beautiful eyes nearly forced him to his knees. "Evie—"

She held up a hand. "Don't. Please. Let's get through the migraines and murder case first." Her eyes darkened to a deeper, more determined shade of blue. "I'm not giving up on you. On us."

If anyone else had said those same words to him, he'd be running to the opposite side of the county. They would've sounded clingy and desperate. But not with Evie. Her quiet statement sent an inappropriate heat down his spine. Never before had a woman staked such a claim on him.

Evie was a force of nature.

One he hoped didn't explode around them.

CHAPTER FOURTEEN

THE NEXT DAY, LISA FELT well enough to see the handful of patients lined up outside the Med Mobile. Afterwards, Evie—with Deke's help—managed to talk her into postponing the rest of the tour so she could go see a doctor about her headaches.

Evie spent the afternoon updating their website and drafting a notification to their newsletter subscribers. Lisa insisted on calling each of the host locations to deliver the bad news and to assure them the tour would resume soon. Deke had been making his own phone calls, though she couldn't discern their nature.

She thought he was trying to arrange a pickup, but he wound up driving back with them to Steele Ridge, only to leave as soon as they arrived. After he loaded her luggage into the back of her Rogue, he tangled his fingers with hers. An uncertain silence descended between them.

"Are you headed back to Asheville?" she asked, trying to find a clever way of asking when he'd return—and failing.

"Not for another week." He opened her driver's side door. "Enough time to find my brother and ring his neck."

"Be gentle. He might have stumbled upon Gracie Gilbert seconds before we did."

"Why did he run from me?"

"Maybe because he'd just seen the inside of a dead woman's neck."

"Gallows humor, already?"

"All I meant by my comment was that there's no way to prepare yourself for such a sight. And there's not a right or wrong way to react."

His lopsided grin appeared. "When did you get so smart?"

"Around three years old, I think." She squeezed his fingers. "I'm going to miss you."

He tucked a few strands of wayward hair behind her ear. "I won't be gone long."

"You won't?"

"We have more talking to do."

She tried to smile, but it came across wobbly. "We do?"

Nodding, he whispered, "I'm about to do something contradictory and foolish and so damn necessary." He drew her against his body and covered her mouth with his. The kiss was gentle, tender. More so than any other before it. An ache formed in her throat. She couldn't shake the feeling, despite his assurances, that it would be months before she saw him again.

He pulled away, and her anxiety trebled. The words "call me" clung to her lips, clawing for escape. Too desperate, too needy.

Instead, she sent him off with an even more inane parting. "Stay safe."

When she made her way down Tupelo Hill's long drive, she noticed several familiar vehicles parked outside her mother's most prized possession—a large white farmhouse with a beautiful wraparound porch. A place her six children could always call home, even though the house they grew up in was about a quarter of the Hill's size.

The screen door leading into the kitchen slammed behind her, forcing five pair of eyes in her direction.

"Evie!" her mom exclaimed, casting the other occupants a nervous look before giving her youngest a kiss and hug. "You're home early."

Her smile faded as she took in Britt and Randi and Reid and Brynne. They all wore the same "caught me" expressions. She could hear others in the dining room.

"Lisa got sick. What's going on?"

Britt strode over, bussed her cheek, and relieved her of her carry-on bag. "Hello, Squirt. Welcome back."

"What am I interrupting?"

"You're not interrupting anything. Boring family reunion talk," her brother Reid said, hooking his arm around her neck and pecking a kiss on her head. "Mom's feeding us. Come sit down. Food's almost ready."

Reid guided—or rather dragged—her into the dining room where she found the rest of the gang—Grif, Carlie Beth, Aubrey, Micki, and Gage. They were playing some kind of card Q&A game.

"Aunt Evie!" Aubrey bolted forward, all arms and legs and budding breasts.

Squeezing her niece tight, she asked, "Are you stomping the adults?"

"Everyone but Micki. No one can beat her."

Micki, wearing a black tank top and jeans, waggled her eyebrows. "Hello, sis."

Although she'd gotten over feeling abandoned by her sister, she still had a hard time doing the whole sista-love thing. She'd idolized Micki. Her big sister was crazy smart and kick-ass. No one had ever messed with her when Micki had been around.

But then Micki had run off and gone to Vegas, leaving Evie to deal with all the snotty, cruel kids. Those days still had the power to sting if she dwelled on the memories too long.

"Hey, Mick. You gonna tell me what this get-together's really about?"

"Nope. Drop it so everyone can go back to pretending."

She smiled. *This* was the Mikayla Steele she

remembered and loved. Outspoken and never lip-glossed anything.

"I can go to my room and let everyone continue conspiring against me. I'm dog tired, anyway."

A wiry, muscled arm curled around her middle, holding her steady. A hand shot out in front of her, and a jittery image of her and her brother appeared.

"Say 'I'm a party pooper.'" Jonah crossed his eyes, then snapped a shot.

She tried to elbow him in the ribs, but he jumped away, laughing.

"That's enough," Joan Steele said, placing a large dish of lasagna on the table. "Evie, take your place."

Grif's lips twitched. "Got a spot right here."

Randi, Britt, Reid, and Brynne brought in the rest of the dishes. To her amazement, Britt didn't take the seat at the head of the table. A place he'd assumed not long after their father had crawled in the woods and never returned. Instead, he took the place to their mother's right, with Randi moving to his other side. Evie slid next to Grif and waited to see who would take the head chair. The answer shocked her more than Britt's decision not to sit there.

Busy uploading their selfie to God knew where, Jonah hadn't yet realized the dynamic going on around him. When he finally dropped his phone into his pocket, he frowned, glancing between the head chair, Britt, and Mama—who raised a brow.

Britt said, "Food's not getting any warmer, bro." A look passed between the eldest and youngest brother. An understanding.

Tears stung her eyes. Britt had been the head of the household for over a decade. Tonight, he released the reins to Jonah—the only unattached male Steele.

Jonah looked supremely uncomfortable when he eased into the seat next to her.

She placed a hand on his arm. "You brought us all back together. The spot looks good on you."

"Don't get used to it," Reid said. "If you ever join the ball and chain club, I'm busting your ass out of that chair. Always wanted to see the view from there."

"Ball and chain?" Brynne repeated.

Reid winked. "Just an expression, Brynnie. You know you're more like my anchor."

"Not much better," Grif warned, passing the breadbasket.

"I caught a glimpse of your new house on the drive in," she said to Jonah. "They've made a lot of progress."

"That monstrosity's going to block out the sun and kill all of Mama's flowers," Reid said.

"Hardly," Carlie Beth said. "The sun will flow right through all those big, beautiful windows."

"The river stones were delivered today," Jonah said. "I'm most looking forward to seeing the fireplace done."

"Something you've always wanted," Micki added, knowing her twin better than anyone else, despite their decade-long separation.

"The lasagna smells amazing, Mama," Evie said.

A chorus of agreement wove around the table.

Mama smiled. "What happened to Lisa?"

Evie plopped a spoonful of cottage cheese next to a square of lasagna and a pool of her mom's homemade applesauce on her plate. "She got a really bad headache. One that had her in the fetal position last night. Deke thinks she suffered a migraine."

"Deke?" Britt asked.

"After you talked up the MedTour at Triple B the other day, he decided to spend his recuperation writing an article about us."

"He joined the tour?"

"Yep."

"Where's he sleeping?"

"Right next to me."

Granite solidified beneath Britt's features. She glanced around. All her brothers wore the same I'm-going-to-kill-Conrad expression. Even Gage joined the mob.

Oh, crap. She could tease her brothers about a lot of things, but they would never find the sullying of her honor funny.

"He's in the spare sleeper sofa." Her clarification did little to soften their concerns, though Gage backed off a bit. Since he'd never seen the inside of the RV, he didn't realize how close the sleepers were to each other. "Might I remind you all that Lisa slept only a feet away?"

One-by-one, her brothers' attention returned to cleaning their plates. Micki's mouth quirked into a sideways "You survived that one" smile.

"How cool that Deke's writing about your good work," Brynne said into the silence. "You'll soon be a local celebrity."

She released a tension-ridding snort-laugh. "I don't think his literary reach goes that far." She took a drink of water. "Besides, with the tour cut short, I doubt he got enough information to complete the article."

"Where's Deke now?" Britt asked.

She narrowed her eyes on her brother. "Why?"

"I want to see if he's still up for some fishing."

And a man-to-man chat, no doubt.

"Something came up with his brother. He returned to Steele Ridge only long enough to make sure Lisa was settled."

"What's going on with his brother?" Randi asked.

She hesitated. Only she and Deke knew for certain that Dylan was at the crime scene. The more people in the know, the more vulnerable Dylan would become. She had to give Deke a chance to sort out his brother's involvement in Gracie Gilbert's death.

"I'm not sure," she said, settling on the truth.

"Dylan's been in and out of trouble since they moved back to Rockton. Shoplifting, reckless driving, fights, the list goes on. Deke's been cleaning up after him for years."

"I've never heard him complain about Dylan," she said.

"Have you heard Deke complain about anything?" Britt asked. "He's like you. Lets all the negative stuff slide off his back."

"Negativity solves nothing."

Although Britt's explanation about Dylan seemed to put the brakes on the any further questions, she decided to drive the conversation down a lane that wouldn't catch fire.

"I've been thinking." She caught Gage's eye. "The training center needs a yogi."

"Yogi?" Reid cut in, his face a mass of horrified wariness.

"To teach your participants yoga. It's a complete mind-body workout that combines stretching and strengthening poses for the body with meditation exercises to focus the mind."

"Sounds like a great idea," Micki said.

"I agree," Carlie Beth added.

"You want a bunch of cops and special ops guys doing the downward dog? In bike shorts?"

"Yes," all the women chimed in, including Aubrey and Mama.

Gage smiled. "We're outnumbered." He contemplated Evie, his right eye scrunched. Although she'd used the workshop to redirect her brothers, the yoga concept was something she'd been toying with for several weeks. She had assumed Reid would pooh-pooh the notion as too metaphysical or something, so she hadn't made any attempts to persuade him about yoga's benefits.

Gage's next comment was slow and thoughtful, as though he were working through the idea in a logical, systematic fashion. "Might be the thing that sets our training center apart from all the others. Wouldn't hurt to strengthen more than our trainees' instincts."

"Dear God." Reid sat back, glaring at his friend and president of the training center. "Are you siding with these lunatics?"

Resting his arm over the back of Micki's chair, Gage

caressed her bare shoulder. "Lunatics make for good company."

"Evie, since you're free for several days," Mama said, swerving the conversation into yet another direction, "can you help me go through the attic? There's so much up there that could go to charity."

A cold sweat broke out all over Evie's body as images of a dusty, dark, insect-filled shed overwhelmed her mind.

Everyone at the table became very interested in their food again, avoiding eye contact with Mama in order to dodge recruitment. Cowards.

For three decades, the Steele clan had accumulated *stuff*, like every other American family. All that stuff had lived in a shed behind their tiny house for years. When Jonah purchased Tupelo Hill for Mama, their stuff had traveled with them. Mama had not been ready to part with her children's poorly drawn artwork or their third grade report cards or their first pair of shoes. Nor had she been prepared to trash her husband's old grill or his rusted-out handsaw.

The clearing project would take days to complete. Days of battling old fears. Under normal circumstances, she would have jumped at the opportunity to sort through the memories and trash the junk. She loved to organize. Her clothes hung in her closet by color, not by season or style.

But she couldn't organize the attic. No matter how much she loved her mother and wanted to help. Especially not right now. Right now, she needed to be moving, doing. She needed Deke, dammit.

Never in her wildest dreams would she have considered herself the clingy type. She wanted Deke here, beside her, joking with her family. Or she wanted to be with him, helping track down his brother, offering up a hug if he learned Dylan's involvement in Gracie's murder wasn't incidental.

She rubbed her sweaty palms over the napkin in her

lap. "Sorry, Mama. We'll have to clean out the beast another time." Holding back a shudder, she cut a bite of lasagna with her fork. "I'm headed out of town tomorrow."

"Where're you going?"

"I intend to finish the MedTour."

"By yourself?"

"How are you going to treat patients without Lisa's supervision?" Jonah asked. "Doesn't that violate some health care rule?"

"I'll work out a plan with Lisa's supervisor, Dr. Muir. There will definitely be some things I can't do, but lots of other things I can do."

She caught Randi glancing at Carlie Beth, whose lips twitched before she caught Brynne's gaze.

What were those three smirking about? She peered at her sister in confusion. Micki wore a knowing grin and one brow hitched into a you-can't-be-that-dense arch.

Rather than call them out on whatever crazy notion they floated around to each other, she mixed her cottage cheese with her applesauce before spooning the combo into her mouth. She ignored the whisper of understanding that crackled in the back of her mind.

Deke had nothing to do with her resuming the MedTour.

Nothing at all.

CHAPTER FIFTEEN

DEKE REACHED SONR'S BUNKER AT the summit of one of many mountain ridges surrounding Asheville. Unlike a lot of the natural areas in this region of Western North Carolina, this pocket of wilderness had never been timbered or destroyed by fire. Tulip trees thicker than the widest SUV thrived here. Abundant populations of ginseng covered the hills, and black bear, bobcats, and elk roamed the valleys.

What made the location perfect for SONR's headquarters was the absence of humans. No trails zigzagged the ridges, no campsites dotted the landscape, and no engines pierced the air.

When he approached the entrance, an armed figure broke away from the shadows. "Commander."

Outside his wide-brimmed cowboy hat and handlebar mustache, Wes Crawley appeared ready for combat.

He nodded toward his weapons specialist's AR15. "Expecting trouble?"

"Taj's surveillance cameras picked up a drone on our southern border. Thought I'd keep an eye on things for a while."

"Probably a hobby aircraft that got away from its owner. Good to take extra precaution, though."

Wes rapped out a series of knocks. Not that he

needed to with Taj watching their every move through the entrance cam.

It didn't take long for the telltale sound of sliding deadbolts. The door squeaked open, and Keone appeared.

"Welcome back." Keone stepped aside for him to enter.

Looking at the bunker from the outside, no one would guess at the vastness within. Matteo designed the structure to nestle into the mountain, be a living, breathing part of it, leaving only the south-facing side vulnerable to detection, though not the only way out. Once past the double entrance barrier, a dozen pods snaked off a large circular area known as the Status Room. The epicenter of SONR. Or, as Jax like to say— where the magic happened.

Dropping his backpack on the floor next to a well-used brown leather couch, Deke took in his team one more time, still unable to believe that any of them would betray their mission or each other. Even though Keone hadn't been able to identify the leak yet, Deke had taken a leap of faith last night.

He'd brought the team up-to-speed on the MedTour and Distributor and shared what little facts he had on the murder case involving his brother. Every single team member had offered their assistance with his personal situation. Though he'd expected no less of them, their unblinking support had left him tight-throated for several minutes. When he'd warned them about using SONR's resources to ferret out information on Dylan's case, they'd all smirked, and Wes had murmured something about family coming first.

"What's the latest?" he asked. "Anything on the kid with the bear claw?"

"Not much dirt on the stepfather," Jax said. "Successful real estate agent and well-respected family man. The only blot on his record was a DUI conviction, five years ago."

"Came across some folks reporting the family as odd," Keone added.

"In what way?" he asked.

"They're somewhat social, but mostly tend to stay to themselves. No one could recall ever getting an invite to their home."

"Is he a hunter?"

"Every chance he can get."

"Dig deeper. I got the distinct impression that Amy was scared of her husband."

"What about Noah's biological father? Did Amy's story pan out?"

"Yep," Jax said. "He died two years ago from complications after an appendectomy. By all reports, Kyle McMann had been a loving husband and terrific father."

He paced in front of the couch. Ever since he and Evie'd parted, he'd felt...*restless*. Like he'd left something undone, left a part of himself behind. "Rae, anything on Gracie Gilbert's autopsy yet?"

"Medical Examiner hasn't released his report yet." Rae broke open the cap on her water bottle. "My contact saw the body arrive. He said the sheet slid off the corpse's foot, revealing discoloration around the toes."

"What kind of discoloration?"

"He only saw it for split second, but he said the area was dark, like a severe contusion."

"Maybe it got stepped on during the assault."

"I'm not sure her foot could have gained that level of discoloration before she died."

"Could've gotten the contusion a hundred different ways," Keone said.

"Or it's not a contusion at all," Deke added. "Any luck locating my brother, Taji?"

"If he turns on his phone, uses his credit cards, or withdrawals money from his bank, I'll have him pegged within seconds. Matteo's keeping an eye on his apartment."

"Matteo? What's he doing back to work?"

"Same could be asked about you."

"What about your kid brother's friends?" Wes asked, joining the group. He secured his AR into a long gun cabinet by the door. "Should we be talking to any of them?"

"I have a few names, but I don't know if he's even hanging out with them anymore."

"Worth a shot."

"We'll have to tread carefully. There's a sergeant—Prickett—who would love to see me in jail for interfering with his investigation."

"What's the matter? Did you destroy his sand castle?"

"Worse. His high school girlfriend decided she liked the looks of me more."

"Was that before or after alcohol?"

"You do realize I'm doling out assignments, right?"

"Some things are worth the punishment."

"Speaking of girlfriends," Jax said. "Does Dylan have one?"

"Damned if I know." Deke recalled the gregarious blonde his brother had been seeing when they were still on speaking terms. "He used to date a Leah."

"Got a last name?"

"Brunner? Brewster? Brist—Bristow. That's it. Leah Bristow."

Jax tapped on her keyboard for several seconds. "Looks like she's still in the area. 567 Fulton Road, Rockton."

"I know the place." Deke jotted down a couple names and handed them off to Jax. "Once you have those addresses, pass them on to Keone and Wes. I'll pay the girlfriend a call." He checked his handgun before sliding it back into his chest holster. "Rae, I want the results of that autopsy. If you still can't get it, find out from your contact if Gracie Gilbert had any controlled substances in her system."

"I'm on it."

"Check on the police report, while you're at it." He caught Taji's eye. "Anything from Matteo?"

"Just got a text. All's quiet at your brother's apartment."

"Tell Matteo to hang tight. I'll join him after my interview with Leah."

"Haven't the police already swept the place?" Keone asked.

"Yes, which is why I want to take a look. Even though I haven't seen Dylan in months, I still know my brother and can spot his screwups a mile away."

"Heed your own advice," Keone warned. "The cops are almost certainly surveilling his apartment. Stay sharp."

He swung his pack onto his back, snapping it into place at his waist. After exiting the bunker, he stretched his legs into a steady jog. In order to avoid detection, they parked their vehicles near the bottom of the mountain, though they had an ATV available to cart up equipment.

As much as he'd like to rail at Dylan for getting himself mixed up in a murder, the Gracie piece wasn't adding up. Why would a well-liked mom, with two kids, who'd never been involved with controlled substances, all of a sudden turn to drugs?

He couldn't see Dylan as a murderer either. Not because of the family connection. Slitting someone's throat took a lot of balls and a steady hand. It was far more intimate than shooting a person from twenty yards away. The act was up close, personal. The killer might have even held Gracie in his arms as he drew the knife through flesh, muscle, and tendons.

No sign of false starts was evident on Gracie's neck. The killer had made one, clean, swift slice, and that was it.

Dylan had been one of those quirky boys who removed worms from the driveway so they wouldn't get squashed. One time, he'd cried until their mom agreed to use live mousetraps instead of the spine-crushing ones. Then he'd cajoled her into driving him to the nearby national forest to set the rodent free. All these years later, the conservationist in him cringed at the thought of his family introducing new strains of disease into the national forest through their vermin rescue efforts.

No matter how hard he tried, he couldn't reconcile that the gentle-spirited kid had become a coldhearted killer. But people changed.

Dylan had been a sweet kid before he'd become the family terror at thirteen. A hardcore thrill-seeking hooligan who never seemed to be aware of the destruction he always left in his wake.

Had he run through his repertoire of physical and chemical stimuli and now sought something more psychological?

Primeval?

CHAPTER SIXTEEN

EVIE LEARNED SOMETHING ABOUT HERSELF. She might not possess the required amount of patience for the health care world.

When Dr. Muir mentioned that a replacement nurse practitioner wouldn't be available until the following day, she'd cajoled—okay begged—the kind old man into allowing her to drive the Med Mobile to their next scheduled stop in Niles. She'd reasoned that she could have the clinic ready to go by the time the nurse practitioner arrived.

The doctor had relented, and she'd hightailed it out of town before he changed his mind. But not before she checked in on Lisa and recruited Britt to help her hook up her Rogue to the back of the RV. No way was she going to be stranded in the Med Mobile for the rest of the day. Not with Deke so close by. She used her bit of downtime to locate Deke and see how things were going with his brother's case.

All the way to Niles, she'd texted Deke, but he never answered. Anxiety chipped away at her excitement of seeing him again. She unhooked her vehicle from the Med Mobile and prepped the clinic for the next day.

Still no response from Deke.

Should she be worried? Or ticked off? She didn't like the idea of him getting in the middle of a murder case.

What if he'd learned something important and the killer had gone after him? What if he lay somewhere, bleeding and helpless, even now?

What if he was ignoring her texts?

After another hour of pacing and silence, she took matters into her own hands and called Rita Sampson.

"Hey Rita, it's Evie Steele."

"How are y'all doing after our BBQ bungle?"

"Thanks again for organizing the BBQ. We're doing fine. Lisa saw her doctor and he prescribed her some migraine medicine."

"What about Deke? I could've whopped Mitch Conrad's hide for how he'd treated his son."

"Deke's fine. Unfortunately, he's somewhat used to his daddy's abuse."

"I'm sorry to hear that." A long sigh passed through the receiver. "Did you call to give me an update, or is there something I can do for you?"

"A little of both. I've been trying to get a hold of Deke with no luck." She sent up a plea of forgiveness. "He was headed to see his brother Dylan. Deke left something in the Med Mobile, and I'm in the area and thought I'd drop it off." Her fingers rubbed at the tightness in her chest. "I wondered if you knew where Dylan lived."

"Last I heard, he had an apartment on the corner of Western and Peck. You can probably Google his name and get an exact address."

Evie blinked. Why hadn't she thought about searching the Internet first?

"Be careful," Rita continued. "His apartment building's near a park that houses troublemakers once the sun sets."

"Thanks for the warning. My plan's not to be there that late."

"If you don't have any luck at Dylan's place, he might be at the yellow house on Fulton. He used to spend quite a bit of time there. Not sure if he still does, though."

"You're an absolute gem, Rita. I owe you one."

"Just make sure that Med Mobile passes through Rockton again, in the near future."

"You got it."

It took her about forty minutes to get from Niles to Rockton. Every minute rolled into one eternity after another. When she finally located Dylan's apartment building, she saw no sign of Deke's truck. Disappointment knifed through her.

She idled outside the building for another fifteen minutes before giving up on Deke's arrival. Armed with her GPS, she pulled away from the curb and followed the directions to Fulton Street.

As she approached the intersection of Fulton and Peregrine, a familiar black Ram 1500 roared by. Her eyes strained to see inside.

Deke!

Her foot stomped the gas, and the force slammed her against the seat. She didn't realize her small crossover had *that* much power. When she swung onto Fulton, she accelerated to intercept him before he made it to the house.

But he was too far ahead. His truck pulled into the driveway of a small yellow one-story house. Deke strolled to the front door, and a beautiful blonde appeared. A welcoming smile played across her generous mouth. At this distance, she appeared to be in her late twenties.

She embraced Deke.

The hug went on for an eternity before Deke followed her inside.

The door shut.

While she followed the tableau playing out in front of the yellow house, her vehicle had parked itself a few doors down. Was Dylan inside? No other cars lined the road or driveway. Had he hiked in from another street?

Or was Deke alone inside with the blonde?

Heat crawled up her neck, and her heart tried to ram its way out of her chest. She was *spying* on him.

Why, for goodness sake?

Her intention had been to intercept him before he knocked on the door. Perhaps he and the woman were old friends or cousins...or lovers.

The heat intensified, burning into Evie's ears and steaming the backs of her eyes.

Minutes turned into a quarter hour, a quarter hour turned into a half hour, a half hour became an hour. Just when she thought she couldn't stand the unknown any longer, he emerged. The pretty blonde lounged in the doorframe, a kitten-and-cream smile on her face.

He paused to say something, and the blonde wrapped her lean body around him again. Evie closed her eyes, unable to watch the next part.

When she peeled her eyelids open, Deke's truck was backing out of the drive. Tears threatened. She shoved them away. He'd warned her. Warned her not to hope.

Much to her amazement and unparalleled mortification, she followed the Ram.

Chapter Seventeen

DEKE SLID ONTO THE PICNIC table bench next to a large Italian man eating carrots and humus and reading a small paperback featuring a bare-chested man holding a long gun. "Good book?"

"Your timing sucks," Matteo said. "Come back in five minutes."

He nodded toward the agent's side. "How's the injury?"

"Eighty percent."

"Do you have clearance to be at work?"

"Modified duty. No bending, no lifting, no sitting for long periods of time. Lots of reading."

"Sounds like you've already blown your doctor's orders."

"Only if I get caught."

Deke raised a who-the-frick-am-I eyebrow.

"You don't count. You're one of us."

"And responsible for your well-being." He slid his thumbnail beneath a loose piece of green paint and it chipped free. "Just take it easy. SONR can't afford to lose you." He nodded toward the apartment building. "Any movement?"

"Nothing."

"Signs of other surveillance?"

"Don't think so."

"Think or know?"

"A brunette sat in her vehicle outside the building for a quarter hour, then took off. Haven't seen her back." He flipped a page. "Probably waiting for someone and the person never showed up."

"Can you pull yourself away from—" he nudged Matteo's book up so he could read the title, "—*Darkest Secret.*"

"Don't knock it." Matteo dog-eared his spot. "Are we going in?"

"There's got to be something inside Dylan's apartment that'll shed some light on what's going on."

Instead of leaving the book on the table, Matteo tucked it into the back of his jeans.

"You're kidding, right?"

"Told you, your timing sucks."

They took the stairs two at a time until they reached the third floor. Deke led the way to apartment 307 and bent to pick the lock. The mechanism was so old that he managed the feat in less than five seconds.

He half expected to be hit by a wave of rotting food and poor plumbing. But all that wafted through the opening was stale air. A scent normally associated with homes that have been abandoned for weeks instead of days.

"You take the kitchen," he said. "I'll start in the bedroom."

At the entrance to his brother's bedroom, he paused to scan the square space. No clothes littered the floor, and smooth sheets graced the bed. He opened the closet and found a half dozen T-shirts, two pair of jeans, a jacket, and a set of running shoes. A scarce amount of clothes for a thirty-year-old.

He pulled down a shoebox and found it full of old baseball cards, some in protective sleeves, most tossed around haphazardly. He pushed on the walls and stomped on the floor.

Finding nothing, he strolled the room, looking for

forgotten slips of paper, receipts, anything unusual or out-of-place. He scoured the area. Nothing.

"Come on, Dylan. Talk to me."

Moving on to the bathroom, he found signs of the brother he knew. Toothpaste tube left open on the sink, toilet paper roll empty, towels on the floor... Deke gave the bathroom the same thorough search.

Still nothing.

He stood on the threshold, peering between the pristine bedroom and sloppy bathroom. Something besides stale air made his nose twitch with distaste.

He stomped his way into the front room, where he found Matteo methodically searching. The same neat cleanliness existed here.

"Does this place seem oddly tidy for a bachelor, especially one who'd just been caught hovering over a dead woman?" Matteo asked. "Items in the kitchen cabinets are in perfect alignment and even though the fridge is near empty it's cleaner than a surgeon's hands."

"The bathroom's the only place that looks lived in."

"Might be worth taking a second glance."

He retraced his footsteps. Once again, he paused in the doorway and scanned the ten-by-six space. An old memory surfaced. His attention sliced to the shower. He opened the glass door and flipped on the hot water.

"What are doing?" Matteo asked.

"Years ago, when we were kids—" he closed the door and waited, "—my brother and I used to communicate through secret messages."

"In the bathroom?"

"Where else?"

"Oh, I don't know. Maybe a piece of paper hidden in the closet?"

"Not as much fun."

Steam filled the shower, coating the glass enclosure. Letters began to emerge.

"I'll be damned," Matteo said. "How'd he do that?"

"Soap."

"You shittin' me?"

"Give it a try, sometime."

Curves and straight lines formed into three words. "Gold Star. Lean-to."

"Gold Star. Coincidental?"

"Could be, but I doubt it. This has to be linked to the Gold Star reference we found at the Bamford raid."

"An odd pairing of words. Any idea of what Dylan's trying to tell us?"

"No clue. But Dylan went through a great deal of trouble to make sure I found it."

"He knew you'd come?"

"Despite our current estrangement, Dylan and I were close once." He tapped speed dial number three on his phone and clicked on the speaker.

"Hit me, boss," Jax said.

"Do you have anything on Gold Star yet?"

"Not yet—unless you want to hear about the history of the Chinese flag. Got something for me?"

"Nothing that will aid your search, I don't think. My brother left those two words for me to find."

"Ooh, a failure-ridden mysterious code. My favorite." Furious clicking echoed in the background. "Get anywhere with the girlfriend?"

Deke didn't want to go through that nightmare over the phone. "Yes and no. Let's focus on Gold Star right now."

"Kicked your ass, didn't she?" Jax chuckled. "Or maybe she wanted to do something else with your ass."

"Focus, Jax."

Feet shuffled behind him, and he reached for his gun.

Evie pressed into the doorframe, her startled gaze on his weapon.

"Jesus, Evie." He slid his Glock back into its holster. "Don't sneak up on me like that."

"Evie?" Jax asked. "Who's Evie?"

With a wary eye on Matteo, she straightened, though kept her distance. "What's going on, Deke?"

"Jax," he said, "call me back when you have something."

"Don't hang up now, this sounds interesting—"

He disconnected before Jax said anything more incriminating. How much had Evie heard of their conversation? Could he still salvage his cover?

"What girlfriend, Deke?" she asked.

Shhhit. A thousand excuses drove through his mind, with lightning speed. How could he give her enough of the truth and still protect the team? Though his brother's predicament had nothing to do with the Bamford case, he couldn't easily explain away Matteo and Jax or him breaking into Dylan's apartment.

His silence must have confirmed the heartbreak she'd feared. Without another word, Evie strode away. She didn't run or break into "How could you?" or curse him to hell.

She simply walked away.

Dread like nothing he'd experienced before kept him rooted in place.

An oarless boat drifting out to sea.

A hollow shell blistering in the sunlight.

A damn fool watching someone special walk out of his life.

CHAPTER EIGHTEEN

EVIE KEPT HER GAZE STRAIGHT ahead, hardly noticing the stairs she descended or the chipped wall paint she passed. The only thing that registered in her paralyzed mind was the absence of racing footsteps from behind.

Deke had allowed her to leave. No explanation or entreaties for her to understand. Just blaring silence and acceptance.

Why had she ignored the warning signs? Within hours of Deke joining the MedTour, something with him had seemed off. No, his unusual behavior went farther back than that—all the way to the moment he'd disappeared after their first kiss a year ago.

Why had he joined the tour?

Though he'd been interested in their patients, spending several minutes with each one, learning about their families and hobbies, she no longer believed he was writing an article. His attention hadn't been on the program or Lisa or her. His attention had been on the patients.

Why?

Why would a conservation writer question the local communities about such mundane subjects like the best hunting spots or recommended taxidermists or favorite hobbies or unusual animal sightings or the make of vehicle they drove? Any questions he'd asked about the actual tour seemed an afterthought.

Anger seared her chest. How dare he use the Med Mobile to disguise an ulterior motive. She and Lisa had trusted him. How had he repaid that trust? By lying to them.

A volatile mix of hurt, fury, disappointment, and shame had her pivoting on her heel and marching back up the stairs. She would get her answers, one way or another.

At the second floor landing, she swung around to climb the next flight and plowed into Deke.

"Whoa!" He grasped her shoulder, halting her momentum and preventing her from doing serious damage.

Without thinking, her hands arrowed between them, then her forearm slammed against his, breaking his hold. The violence in her move had him holding up his hands, a show of no harm meant.

"Deke, did you use me—the MedTour?"

His arms lowered to his sides but his steady gaze latched onto hers. In their depths, she saw regret before resolution hardened their edges.

"Did you?" she pressed. "Did you join the tour for reasons other than writing an article about our program?"

"Yes."

Her entire body contracted at his admission. "Why?"

A door above them closed, rocking the moment.

"Come with me," he said. "Please."

He didn't grab her arm and force her down the stairs like some guys would have. No, Deke Conrad descended, trusting she would follow.

And she did. No way was she going to let him ditch her before clarifying his mind-blowing answer. She couldn't even be mad at him anymore—not after such a blatant confirmation of her fears.

When they reached the sidewalk, he held out a hand to her. Her fingers slipped into the V of his, without hesitation. She should have made him work harder for her acquiescence, dammit.

They walked several blocks before ducking into a coffee shop.

"How can I help you?" a chipper barista asked.

"Two coffees. Black."

"I'd prefer tea," she said.

He collected their drinks and led her to a small table at the back of the shop. Like a cop, he sat with his back to the wall and seemed to keep one eye on her and one eye on the door.

"Enough cloak and dagger crap," she said, covering a bud of anxiety with a bit of bluster. "Tell me what you were doing in that apartment."

"Searching for anything that would lead me to my brother."

Again, he answered her question, throwing her off.

"Why do you have a gun?"

"For protection."

"From whom?"

"I don't know yet."

"Have you been carrying a gun while around the patients?"

Silence.

"What were you doing in the bathroom?"

"While growing up, my brother and I would write soapy messages on the shower glass to each other."

"Why?"

His brows folded together. "To defy our father, I suppose."

"I thought your relationship with your dad was fine until after college."

"The estrangement is new. My father's tyranny has existed for a lifetime."

"I'm sorry."

A glimpse of the old Deke crept along the edge of his mouth when he attempted a smile. "It's not your fault he's a prick."

She rotated her cup in circles, over and over and over again. "You should've told me about your girlfriend. I would never have—" she rolled her hand between them, unable to form the words, "—had I known." Round and round and round. "It all sort of makes sense now."

"What does?"

The cup turned so fast that the tea sloshed over the rim. He pressed his fingers to the back of her hand. The swirling stopped.

"What makes sense?"

"You go off and do whatever it is that you do, keeping a girlfriend at home and dreamy-eyed, willing me as a sidedish." She unlocked the muscles in her neck so she could meet his gaze. "Well, I'm not into sharing, Deke Conrad."

"You've got it wrong."

She stared at him for several seconds, waiting for more. "How? How do I have it wrong?"

His lips firmed.

"That's all you're gonna say?"

Something hard and unyielding locked onto his features.

If it had been any other day, she would've attempted to squeeze the information out of him. But today, her emotions rode too close to the surface, and she'd be damned if she'd allow herself to cry in front of him.

She was starting to see a pattern, though. When he felt comfortable answering her questions, he did. But he seemed opposed to out-and-out lying to her. Other times, she seemed to be on the right track, yet he refused to confirm it.

Something important, a revelation, an understanding, stood just out of her reach. She could sense it, almost feel it opening up to her.

Or maybe she was making crap up to soothe the sting of being played. Exhaustion melted into her bones and darkened her thoughts.

"I guess it doesn't m-matter." She cleared the lump

from her throat. "I know enough—about everything." She stood. "I won't speak of your betrayal to Lisa. I won't break her heart, too."

The stupid little girl that lurked in her chest waited two heartbeats for him to stop her. To ask her to sit back down so he could divulge all his secrets.

But he did none of those things. His secrets remained behind a vault of good looks and steely resolve.

For the second time in an hour, she walked away from Deke Conrad. This time he didn't follow.

CHAPTER NINETEEN

SMACK!

"What were you thinking?" Caleb stood over his quivering brother. Rage knifed through his veins, urging him to strike again and again and again.

"I did what you asked," Eli said, rubbing his cheek.

"Far from it, brother. I ordered you to redirect attention *away* from us—not drive it right up to our door."

"All the focus will be on keeping Dylan out of prison."

"How do you expect that feat to be accomplished?"

"That's the whole point. Nothing will stop Dylan's imprisonment."

Caleb released his fists and forced the tension from his back. "Go on."

"I selected Gracie as my target because there's a direct link between her and Dylan. Tina Armstrong."

Fire blurred Caleb's vision. "Armstrong? Your dealer?!"

Eli scrambled away. "I invited Tina to dinner in the guise of asking about her sister. The one diagnosed with leukemia. Despite her wicked ways, she loves her sister." His gaze turned inward. "I think that's why she deals drugs. To pay for her sister's treatment."

"Spare me your dealer's domestic issues. What's Dylan's link to the Armstrong woman?"

"They used to be lovers as well as *business* associates."

What was it about some women that made men lose all common sense? Caleb had never experienced such lust for the opposite sex. Women were tools. Why didn't other men see this? God placed them on earth to bear children, look after the household, and make their husband's lives comfortable.

If a man was lucky, like Caleb, he'd develop an affection for his wife. But his parents were a perfect example that love wasn't a requirement of a successful marriage.

"If Deke's the threat Daddy believes him to be, he'll eventually sniff out the connection and believe his brother was either dealing or using."

"And the link between the woman you murdered and Tina Armstrong?"

"They're childhood friends."

"What about you?"

"What about me?"

"What happens when Deke connects Gracie to Tina to you?"

"Won't happen."

"How can you be so sure?"

"For one thing, my association with Tina was discreet. And when I texted Gracie to set up the meeting with Dylan, I used Tina's phone."

Caleb lifted a brow.

"Everyone leaves their phone unattended for a few minutes, especially when they use the ladies room."

"Did you use a credit card at the restaurant?"

"No, and I met her at a dive outside of town where no one knows either one of us."

Respect for his brother's cunning replaced Caleb's rage. Although not a foolproof plan, his brother had meticulously worked through the details.

"Well done, Eli." He clasped his brother's shoulder. "Though next time I ask a favor, try to find a less public approach."

"I'll keep that in mind."

"Daddy mustn't be disappointed."

Eli dug his keys out of his pocket, preparing to leave. "I've got the Conrad situation under control."

"I hope so. Neither of us will like Daddy's response if you fail."

At the door, Eli half turned, peering at him out of the corner of his eye. "Caleb?"

"Yes?"

"Don't ever hit me again."

CHAPTER TWENTY

DYLAN CONRAD CROUCHED NEAR THE storage shed's ajar door, listening to the Harwood brothers' conversation. His heart fired in his chest like a rocket at takeoff.

He'd wondered many times over the past few weeks to what depths the Harwoods would fall in order to protect their empire.

Now he knew.

Murder.

He had walked straight into their trap. Deke's shocked features pulsed in his mind. Would his brother believe him capable of slitting a woman's throat? Would he remember the heart of the brother he'd left behind? Would Deke believe Deputy Dickhead's assertion that he was buying drugs through Gracie? *Gracie?*

Just thinking her name tore at his guts. She'd only been a month away from getting her associate's degree in accounting. He didn't know what she'd been looking forward to more—graduating or enrolling at the university. She'd wanted to be the first in her family to get a bachelor's degree.

Anyone who knew her would never accuse her of getting involved with drugs. She'd seen firsthand how they'd ruined her father's and brother's lives. Though she didn't like Tina's side job, she understood the desperation that compelled her best friend's actions.

Problem was Deke hadn't been around to know any of this, and he'd left thinking his entire family had turned their backs on him. Why would he give any of them the benefit of the doubt? Especially Dylan, who had been the loudest in his accusations. Not because he'd believed in any of his father's Big Brother paranoia, but because he hadn't wanted Deke to go. To leave him behind—in this life-sucking hellhole.

Sheesus, what a shit mess.

The sound of a boot scuffing against the floor reached into his consciousness and yanked him back to his current situation. He shot to the right, ducking around the corner just as the door squeaked open.

Pressing his back against the building, he strained to hear the telltale signs of detection. But no shouts or zinging bullets or violent attacks followed. He forced himself to count to ten before chancing a peek.

The youngest Harwood strode toward the bronze Ford F-150, keys in hand. His heart pounded in his ears while he waited for the older brother to emerge. Although it only took a few minutes, the time crawled by. When Caleb Harwood finally appeared and drove away, he sent a silent thank-you to the Almighty.

The windowless building only had one entrance/exit and it was located at the front. Exposed to anyone coming down the lane. He'd have to work fast. No telling how often deliveries were made to this facility.

Retrieving a nylon pouch from his back pocket, he selected two long metal instruments before returning the pouch. He inserted the tension wrench into the bottom lock and raked the pick back and forth until all the pins were set. Then he rotated the tension wrench until the dead bolt slid open.

The door swung open, and he slipped inside. He stayed near the entrance, giving his eyes time to adjust to the gloom and his emotions time to shut down.

When objects in the murky depths of the large room

began to materialize, he realized his emotions hadn't yet fully disengaged. His throat closed and bile seared his chest. Crate after crate after crate stacked high in the center of the room.

He moved closer, his steps sluggish. Knowing, dreading what he'd find. The same thing the last two buildings had held. Greed, death, and fear. Yet his body pushed forward, needing the macabre confirmation.

One row of containers stored jars of dried, dark brown tear-drop shaped bear gallbladders. Dozens and dozens of them. The row below held larger containers with black bear paws. Some of the paws were smaller than Dylan's palm.

"Sonsofbitches."

How many more of these storage units did Harwood own? Why were they stockpiling all of these bear parts? Who would buy all of…this?

He'd stumbled onto this trafficking ring after a feral-swine hunting trip with a small group of his friends. One of the guys'd had a bit too much to drink and bragged about the amount of money he'd made hunting bear out of season. By the end of the conversation, he'd extracted three vital parts from his drunken friend—bear parts, Harwood, and a codename, Gold Star.

He'd never liked Eli Harwood. Several of the grade schools in the smaller towns had merged into one high school. Even with the merge, their class size remained small. So everyone knew everyone.

Something about Eli had always put him on guard. He'd kept to himself—except at lunchtime, where he followed his older brother around like a lost puppy.

Whispers of animal cruelty had circulated around school, though he'd never heard of any specific incidents. Eli hadn't been the only oddball in his family. The Harwoods had built strong ties in their small town of Creede, through their involvement on the City Council, Development Committee, and School Board. However, their connections didn't stop them from being suspicious of anyone who didn't carry the Harwood name. Which made their trafficking enterprise all the more interesting.

Paranoia no doubt drove them to create an intricate network of hoops for their sellers to hurdle. His hunting buddy had only speculated that the Harwoods were behind the bear trafficking ring. All he'd been given was a codename and drop-off location.

Not long after his friend's speculation, he'd seen Caleb Harwood leaving a restaurant and decided to follow. When he looked back on that moment, he couldn't identify the exact reason for his pursuit. Boredom, maybe. Curiosity, possibly. An affinity for bears and anger at the Harwoods for their rumored part in an out-of-season poaching ring, more likely.

Whatever had spurred him to follow, he'd picked the right time to get nosey. Caleb had led him straight to one of their contraband storage sheds. To his surprise, they hadn't installed an alarm system on the building yet. Using his lock-pick set, he'd gained entrance and found a clipboard with all the other locations listed and which ones were unsecure.

What he still needed to discover was the final destination of all the illegal contraband. He'd hoped to find evidence in one of their storage buildings. But after overhearing the brothers' conversation, he'd have to set his curiosity aside and focus on proving the Harwoods had set him up for murder.

Why? Had they caught on to his quest to find their buyer? Why not just kill him, rather than Gracie? Why the elaborate scheme when they could have just dumped his body in a deep hole in the woods?

Unable to make out the crazy family's logic, he strode to the small metal desk shoved against the back wall. He rifled the drawers as quickly and thoroughly as possible, not bothering with stealth. He looked for something, anything that would explain Gold Star or a distribution network.

For all he knew, the name was a simple codename for

sellers and nothing else. However, his gut had told him that the reference had a deeper meaning to the Harwoods. He needed to find out what.

Had Deke figured out the clues he'd left in his apartment yet? Would he do anything with the information? Or had he finally flipped his little brother the bird and gone back to Asheville? No, Deke would never turn his back on family. If he'd been capable of doing so, he would've done it to him years ago.

All this he understood and even admired about Deke, yet he couldn't stop the resentment from eating at his thoughts.

Did his brother never screw up? Get in over his head? Make a bad decision?

How could they have the same parents and be so completely opposite? He and Deke had one thing in common—secrets.

Even though he'd been pissed about Deke leaving him behind, he'd also been proud of him for getting out of Rockton. So he'd kept tabs on his brother. Why would he get a Master's in Wildlife Biology and then become a conservation writer? Where did he go when he disappeared for long periods of time? His trips lasted too long for a writer investigating a story. And some of the people he hung out with were more intense than the Harwoods.

Deke had a secret, one he would unearth, but not until he dealt with the Harwoods' conspiracy.

Coming up empty in his search, he slammed the desk drawer closed.

"Who the hell are you selling this shit to, Harwood?"

"Hoping for a piece of the pie, Conrad?" a voice behind him asked.

Spinning around, he caught a glimpse of Eli Harwood's fist slicing through the air. His head snapped to the side, his legs buckled, and the ground lifted to meet his face.

Then nothing.

CHAPTER TWENTY-ONE

DEKE HAD BURIED HIMSELF IN a shit storm.

Seeing Evie at Dylan's place had thrown him off his game so badly that he was still trying to recover his wits.

Why had she returned to Rockton? How had she found him? What the hell was he going to do about her?

She'd caught enough of his conversation with Matteo to grasp that he was investigating Dylan's case. With Matteo and Jax. And she thought he had a girlfriend. Believed he could be intimate with her while being involved with someone else.

Shit. Storm.

If she were someone he barely knew, he'd write off the whole incident. But Evie was too enmeshed in his personal life. Sister to his best friend. One comment about this to Britt, and his friend would not only kick his ass, he'd shove his boot into his neck.

Britt's ability to hand him his ass wasn't what bothered him the most. The hurt he'd caused Evie sat on his chest like an anchor stuck in the sand. Knowing she'd left believing him capable of such heartless behavior stung.

Did she not understand how much he cared for her? Yearned for her?

He'd wanted nothing more than to kiss the pain from

her deep blue eyes. Ask her to trust him. Beg her to stay. The betrayal in her expression still haunted him.

He could have set her straight, but that would have required more explanation than he could afford. No matter his personal situation, he couldn't reveal details about SONR. Their work reached across the globe and left a lasting, positive impact on the environment. Every poaching ring they stopped meant thousands of plants and animals saved, which preserved ecological diversity and maintained healthy ecosystems, for everyone— humans, wildlife, and plants.

One word about SONR to the wrong person could sideline their efforts and derail their momentum. Not to mention the devastation that could happen to the wild populations they protected.

Lisa's warning about keeping his lies to a minimum bubbled to the surface. Staying true to his friendship with Evie while protecting SONR was a damn sight harder task than he'd envisioned.

"You gonna tell me where we're headed?" Keone asked, breaking through his self-recrimination.

After breakfast, he'd met up with Keone, who'd completed his interview with Scott Orin. Dylan's friend had proved as enlightening as his ex, which was to say not at all.

"My brother left me a message, at his apartment."

"What kind of message?"

"Gold Star and Lean-to."

"Since we're hiking in the woods, I take it you have a hunch."

"When things got bad at home, Dylan and I would hike to the far reaches of our parents' property, to a bluff that overlooked Swins Hollow."

"Sounds peaceful."

"It was. We erected a lean-to where the woods met the stone outcropping, so that we could hang there even in bad weather."

"How long has it been since you last visited?"

"Years. The structure's probably plummeted over the cliff by now."

"I'm bringing my internal investigation on the team to a close. I've been unable to find any evidence that a member of SONR leaked information to the Distributor."

"You've exhausted all possible scenarios, used every available resource?"

"Yes and yes."

Some of the tightness left his shoulders. "Then close it."

"You know what this means."

"I do." Someone at headquarters, with knowledge of SONR's activities, had to be colluding with the Distributor.

They hiked for another ten minutes before the woods thinned and limestone took the place of the forest floor. Pushing through a tangle of vines and brambles, Deke's chest clenched at the familiar view.

The bluff rose above the trees, revealing undulating waves of green that faded into a brilliant cerulean sky in the distance.

Up here, the wind whisked away every worry, every pain, every mistake. Up here, he could just be—no past, no present, no future. A man in the moment.

"Is that your lean-to?" Keone asked.

He glanced over his shoulder, surprised to find the wooden structure preserved and their sparse furnishings in pretty good shape.

"Looks like your brother still visits."

Ignoring the pressure building in his chest, he searched the small space with the same methodical precision he'd used in Dylan's apartment.

"What are we looking for?"

"Anything unusual."

Keone sent him a how-would-I-know look.

The confined space took only a few minutes to search.

"Got anything?" Keone asked.

"Nothing." He checked the exterior perimeter. Still

nothing. He waved Keone over. "Give me a boost up."

Keone clasped his hands together and he stepped into his second-in-command's grip. The extra two feet was enough for him to see the slanted roof was clear, too.

"Dammit." He hopped down. "I'm going to kill that little pecker."

"Hold on." Keone stared inside the scanty lean-to. "He sent you up here because only you would notice if something was out of place." His gaze caught Deke's. "So what's out of place?"

Frustration burned like hot coals beneath his skin. He couldn't see past the possibility that his brother had sent him on a wild goose chase. While images of him strangling Dylan surfaced, his gaze studied the wooden planks, plastic milk crate that served as a table, lidded plasticware bowl that held cards, dice, and matches, two lawn chairs, a blue one for him and a green one for Dylan, the—

He frowned and refocused on the chairs. Something wasn't right. Something about—

"They're switched."

"Come again?"

"I always sat on the right and Dylan on the left. The blue chair is mine, but it's been moved to the left side."

Picking up his chair, he scanned the rocky ground beneath. Keone did the same with the green one. He stomped the ground for good measure.

"What are you doing?" Deke asked.

"Making sure the ground's solid."

"Fifty feet solid would be my guess."

"Wait a second." Keone pointed to the underside of Deke's chair. "What's that?"

Beneath the seat, he found matching colored duct tape holding something in place. "Nice camouflage."

Separating the item from the chair, he tore away the tape to find the package wrapped in an oilcloth. He peeled back the layers to reveal a clear sealed container. Inside the container rested a smartphone.

"A phone?" Keone asked. "Why would Dylan leave you a phone?"

An image of his brother hovering over Gracie's body rose in his mind.

"When Evie and I stumbled across Dylan kneeling beside Gracie's corpse, he appeared to take something of hers before running off."

They both stared down at the phone.

"Maybe he knew something on this would exonerate him." He shook his head in frustration. "We won't know until Jax opens it up."

"What if Dylan took the phone out of desperation?"

"I don't know." He scraped a hand through his hair. "Let's hope I don't have to face that decision."

Before he could take a step, a beloved voice reached him. "Where's my son?"

He turned to find his mother with a shotgun balanced in her hands.

CHAPTER TWENTY-TWO

EVIE PLACED TWO FINGERS ON the patient's inner wrist, counting in her head while following the second hand on her watch. Never had sixty seconds taken so long.

The replacement nurse practitioner, Rachel Gardner, arrived in Niles the previous day as planned. Having worked with her for a day and a half now, Evie had come to like the new NP. Well into her thirties, Rachel stood a mere five feet two inches tall and sported short, spikey red hair. Freckles covered her face, and she wore a radiant smile all day long.

But it was her self-deprecating humor about her love for sweets and rounded middle that helped take Evie's mind off her embarrassing display with Deke, two days ago.

Rather than dig deeper into what he'd been doing in his fugitive brother's apartment, she'd allowed herself to get sidetracked by the possibility of another woman.

Idiot.

How had she let her jealousy overrule everything she'd come to love about Deke Conrad? If he'd been involved with the blonde in the yellow house, he would never have dishonored her by being with another woman.

I'm a one-woman guy.

Humiliation singed up her neck and into her ears.

"Heart rate's 79 and your blood pressure's sitting at a healthy 112 over 73." She transferred the numbers to sixty-year-old patient's chart. "Well done, Mr. Albany." Indicating a chair, she said, "Why don't you make yourself comfortable until Rachel's free."

A crack of thunder shook the ground.

"Got a big one coming in," Mr. Albany said.

"It's a good thing you're inside, then." She threw on her rain jacket. "I'm going to see who else might've braved the storm."

As it turned out, no one.

Other than Mr. Albany's van and the other patient's car, the only other vehicle in the parking lot was an old red truck tucked into a parking stall.

Standing outside the RV, wind whipped her hair into crazy circles around her head. The scent of rain drenched the thick air. Thunder rumbled in the distance.

Why would Deke be carrying a weapon? Who was the hot Italian? The perky techno-geek on the phone? From the tenor of their conversation, they knew each other well. They'd obviously done that sort of thing before.

Deke might not be a cheater, but he was definitely something more than a conservation writer. She needed to talk this through with someone who wouldn't try to ban her from seeing Deke again. Which pretty much ruled out a large portion of the Steele clan.

Sighing, she sifted through her options. Most of her friends were either vacationing or starting new jobs. Lisa seemed the most logical choice, though Evie couldn't spring this on her while she was trying to get her migraines under control. Mama would listen, sympathize, then tell her to follow her instincts. Not what Evie needed.

She couldn't bug Brynne, Carlie Beth, or Randi, because they might say something to her brothers. Britt would kill Deke or reject him for as long as his anger lasted. Grif would figure out a way to bankrupt the guy. Jonah would locate incriminating college pictures and blast them all over social media. Micki would—good grief, she didn't want to think about what kind of whoop-ass her sister would rain down on Deke.

That left her with Reid. Her Green Beret brother.

Dear God.

The more she considered Reid, the more the choice seemed right. He was trained to keep secrets. Of course, he'd bluster and come up with a dozen ways to cut off Deke's privates, but eventually his strategic mind would kick in and he'd help her figure this thing out with Deke.

She hoped.

She prayed.

Sweet baby Jesus, she was screwed.

CHAPTER TWENTY-THREE

DYLAN AWOKE IN A CAGE.

Awareness came to him by slow degrees, as if he were clawing his way out of a thick fog. His eyelids stuck to his eyeballs, clicking as he tried to keep them open for more than a second. His tongue felt like a raisin forgotten on the desert floor.

When he tried to move, excruciating pain shot through his head and neck. Nausea roiled in his gut. His arms and legs and back didn't want to move. Glancing down, he found his body contorted into inhuman angles in order to make him fit inside a four-by-five cell.

"What the hell?"

He tried to sit up, and his head swished back and forth like a dingy stranded in the middle of the ocean. Pain knifed through his skull.

"Shit!" he wheezed, turning on his side in time to vomit.

When he finished heaving, he slouched in his cage, brushing his fingertips over the source of his worst pain and found a large lump on the ridge below his eye. He sucked in a sharp breath at his light touch.

A few inches from his ear, something mewled. He made a sudden move and instantly regretted it. Nausea rolled over him, once again. Slowly, he angled his head around enough to find three black bear cubs hunched together in a cage similar in size to his.

"Hello, kiddos."

Given their small size, maybe thirty to thirty-five pounds, he guessed they'd been born later than normal. "Don't be afraid. I won't hurt you."

"How sweet," Eli Harwood said, coming into view. "You've already made friends with your cellmates."

Vague images wavered in his mind. Harwood standing above him, a rifle pointed at his torso. A sting to his thigh. Darkness. A mocking voice singing, "Nighty, night." Water streaming over his head, but not to quench his thirst.

"Let me out of here, Harwood."

"I don't think so."

"This is kidnapping."

"We see the situation quite differently."

"How so?"

"I'm detaining you until the authorities arrive." He levered himself up on the bear cage, making the cubs mewl louder and shrink away. "Breaking and entering's against the law."

More images surfaced of him picking a lock, seeing rows of animal parts, then nothing.

"So is wildlife trafficking." He squinted at all the crates and jars. "I'm more than happy to accept my punishment, are you?"

Eli's expression chilled. "You shouldn't have been nosing around."

He might not be able to remember what happened after he arrived here, but the reason for his visit sat crystal clear in his mind.

"Afraid I'll figure out what Gold Star means?"

"Gold Star?"

"You don't know anything about it." He laughed, holding back a wince. How could he not know the codename given to the sellers?

"Shut your mouth."

He laughed harder.

Eli jumped off his perch and slammed a boot heel

against the bars of his prison, catching the tips of his fingers.

He shook out his hand, not allowing his discomfort to overshadow the moment. "What's the matter? Family keeping secrets from you?"

"Shut up!"

"Why do you suppose Caleb's not entrusting you with Gold Star?"

"Last warning, Conrad." His breaths sawed through the air.

He should stop taunting the bastard. But the man's emotional wound was splintered wide open, and he couldn't stop salting it.

"Could it be that he doesn't trust his murderous little brother?"

Something hard, cold, and calculating formed in Harwood's eyes as his gaze swung from him to the cubs. Dylan's heart skittered to a halt. He straightened—or at least, tried to.

Unlocking the crate, Eli grasped one of the cubs by the scruff of the neck, dragging him out. The cub hung docile in his grip as if dangling from his mother's mouth. The sorrowful noises emanating from his small frame told the real story.

Eli produced a long-bladed knife and pressed it against the cub's side.

"Don't!"

"What's the matter, Conrad? Nothing funny now?"

"Put the cub back, Harwood. You've made your point."

"What's my point?"

"That you'll use every leverage available—even innocence—to force my compliance."

"I'm not after your compliance, though I'll take it."

"What'd you want from me?"

"Your respect."

The man was insane. When placed next to his towering dad and charismatic brother, Eli Harwood blended into the background, became invisible. Nonexistent. Evidently, the youngest Harwood was no longer content in his role as wallflower.

He couldn't watch the nutcase kill the cub, nor could he hand over total control. Guys like Eli fed off fear. Consumed it like a cold glass of water.

"The cub's better off dead. Whoever you're selling it to will either pen it, torture it, or slowly kill it."

A dam of unmitigated fury broke behind Eli's green eyes, though his expression remained disturbingly neutral. He threw the cub back into the crate. A high-pitched shriek pierced the air. Eli ignored it as he marched toward Dylan's cage.

As hard as he tried, he couldn't keep his fear in check. Death approached, and he had nowhere to run. The metal bars wouldn't stop the coming onslaught.

Eli's first stab glanced off his biceps. The next ripped through his jeans at the knee. Harwood didn't attack him with mindless fervor. He considered each hit with a physician's precision.

Dylan slid down to the floor of the cage, making himself as small as possible. The attack continued without pause, but Eli couldn't get his elbow through the narrow bars.

Still, he inflicted enough stinging wounds to make Dylan's blood flow freely and pool on the concrete floor, mixing with his vomit. His strength ebbed, making his defensive moves sluggish and ineffective.

Eli crouched next to his cage, waiting him out like a tiger watching its prey for any sign of weakness. When Dylan's eyelids fluttered, Eli raised the knife one final time.

Chapter Twenty-Four

DEKE HELD UP A HAND to keep Keone from shooting his mother.

"Mama, what are you doing here?"

"Waiting for your brother—or you."

"Me?"

She peered around his and Dylan's former hideaway. "Figured you'd come by here at some point."

"I didn't realize anyone but Dylan and I knew about this place."

"I've known about it for years. Used to follow you two hooligans to make sure you were safe." She peered into the valley, thoughtful. "Later, I came here to…get away."

"Did you used to clean up our mess?"

She nodded. "Couldn't stand the thought of my boys junkin' up such a pretty place."

"We always thought a raccoon or something carried the wrappers and cans away."

"Then you shouldn't have left them behind."

Spoken like a true mother. How had he missed her bent toward protecting the environment? Had he noticed it in subtle ways that'd worn off on him?

"Have you seen my baby boy?" she asked.

"Not since the night of the murder."

Worry wove deep groves in her forehead. "The darkness is upon me."

Deke's heart kicked against his chest. "How long?"

"Couple hours."

"Darkness?" Keone asked.

His mom sent Keone a wary look.

"This is Keone. You can trust him. He'll understand."

Over the years, his mom had learned to be careful with whom she shared her secret. Some folks in these parts had no tolerance for things they couldn't explain.

"Any time something awful is about to happen to a member of my family, a black cloud of sadness and fear surrounds me."

"There've been a dozen or so times in the last twenty years when Mama's premonition of danger has proven true. One notable moment was when I'd had a skiing accident and no one could locate me for seventeen hours."

"Does your gift come with the ability to track down the subject?" Keone asked, unfazed by psychic talk.

"Sometimes snapshots of the surrounding area accompany the darkness. They might include landmarks the locals would recognize."

"Have any surfaced for Dylan's location?" Deke asked

"Woods. Bars. Nothing identifiable."

"Bars?"

"Like a caged animal in a circus." His mom's attention dropped to his hand holding the smartphone. "Why are you here?"

A year ago, he would have shared the reason straightaway. But his mom had cut off all communication with him in recent months, without explanation.

"Don't trust me, son?"

Keone stirred. "I'll leave you two alone."

He handed off the phone. "Have it analyzed."

"Will do." Keone nodded to Deke's mom. "Nice to meet you, Mrs. Conrad. We'll find your son. Deke will make sure of it."

His mom watched Keone disappear into the woods. "Nice young man. Loyal."

"Why are you toting a gun?"

She glanced down at the weapon as if she'd forgotten about it.

"Do you know how to use it?"

"Of course."

"Since when?"

"Since you left."

Deke frowned. "Why did you need to learn how to use a gun?"

"Never you mind. You've got your own life to worry about. I'll take care of mine."

"Is that why you stopped answering my calls?"

Her attention drifted away. She said nothing, though she cradled her weapon tighter.

"Daddy's drinking again. Has he done something I need to address?"

"I told you, I'll take care of my own business."

He wanted to annihilate whatever or whoever threatened his mom. But her lapse into silence meant the subject was closed. Prodding at the issue would only manage to piss her off.

"Dylan left a message for me in his apartment."

Her eyes widened at his show of trust. "The phone?"

He nodded. "I think it might belong to the murder victim."

"Is your friend taking it to the police?"

"No."

"Why not? There could be something on it that would prove Dylan's innocence."

"It'll take too long. The phone is most likely password-protected. The authorities will have to go through legal channels to gain access. Even then, there's no guarantee."

"What if you find something? Won't the evidence be tainted?"

"Let's not worry about that unless the issue arises. I have resources."

She assessed him in the same way she used to when

trying to determine if he was being honest or attempting to avoid punishment.

"Will you keep me in the loop?"

"I don't know how far this stretches into the community. A wrong word to the wrong person—"

"I've no intention of discussing this with anyone," she interrupted, "including your father. He's already made up his mind about Dylan's innocence."

He didn't have to ask what side of the law Dylan came down on in his dad's eyes. His mom's tone said it all. Mitch Conrad never saw the good in people or the positive side of anything. He wrote people off faster than a roadrunner fleeing a coyote. His kids were no exception.

"How about we keep each other updated? I'll share new developments with you and you'll let me know if your snapshots reveal any landmarks we can use to locate Dylan."

"Don't call or text me. I pick up fresh eggs for your dad at the farmers market downtown every morning."

"When this is over, I'm getting you out of Rockton."

The smile she sent him was gentle, appreciative, before it disappeared.

"To where? I'm not good for much but cooking and cleaning. I have no fancy education, no dear friends, and no family besides you, Dylan, and Dara." She pointed a finger at him. "And I won't be a burden to my children." Her gaze hardened. "Find my son. Leave me to my life."

Chapter Twenty-Five

"STOP!" BLAZE HARWOOD YELLED.

Eli's knife halted mid-strike. His youngest son's head jerked around. A flash of fear raced across his features before he lowered his arm and stood.

Satisfaction drove away the tension that had surged into Blaze's spine. "Explain, son."

Eli stood mute, eyes averted, burning.

"Son."

"I found him snooping around in here."

Blaze forced his attention down to the man plastered to the back of the cage. A large bruise covered his swollen cheek, and bloody gashes scored his arms.

The guy shook off his shock and rattled the bars. "Get me out of here!"

Ignoring the captive, he asked Eli, "Who is he?"

"Dylan Conrad."

Unease crept beneath Blaze's flesh. "Did you kill the Gilbert girl?"

"Caleb told you."

"No. I connected the dots. You left many to follow."

"I figured if Conrad was stuck in jail, he wouldn't be bothering us."

"So you decided to kill an innocent?" the captive asked.

The knife in Eli's hand spasmed. "One less waitress. Who cares?"

"Her daughter, damn you!"

"Shut your mouth," Blaze commanded the captive. It wasn't wise to ignite his youngest son's volatile, often explosive, temper. Eli experienced neither remorse or empathy or fear. Only anger and frustration. And right now, he was frustrated with Blaze for interrupting his mutilation of the prisoner.

"We can't let him—" Eli pointed his knife at the captive, "—live."

"You're right. But now we have a bigger problem."

"What?"

"My source said his older brother came upon the scene you set up with the Gilbert girl."

"So?"

"Deke Conrad's even more dogmatic than this one." Blaze nodded toward the caged man. "He'll eventually make the connection, too."

"Then I'll kill him."

"Won't be that simple, son."

"Deke Conrad won't link me to the dead waitress. Like I told Caleb, she didn't know me."

"You and the younger Conrad have a mutual friend, right?"

Eli began smacking the side of the blade against his thigh. "Yes, but she doesn't know anything."

"Who are you talking about?" the captive asked, fear in his voice.

Ignoring him, Blaze said, "Conrad's resources are vast and they're pointed at finding his brother. We can't afford to have him nosing around, especially not before this next shipment. He could destroy us all."

"Leave my brother out of this. He writes boring conservation articles for an audience of like fifty people. He might search for me, but he'll be clueless about what else to do."

"Family's important," Blaze said. "You should get to know your brother better."

"What are you talking about?"

"Deke Conrad's a special agent with the U.S. Fish and Wildlife Service."

"He's a writer. I've read his articles."

"A cover for his true vocation." He smiled. "This isn't the first time we've had a run-in with your brother. Last time, he sported a beard, wig, and an assumed name. We gave him enough rope to ferret out any weak links in our organization, then we cut him off at the knees."

"If what you say is true, why would he need to hide being a special agent?"

"Because he's not just any special agent. He's part of a covert group—SONR—who specializes in infiltrating businesses like ours and busting them apart."

Silence dropped like a bomb in the shed.

The captive recovered from his shock. "If his group is so covert, how do you know about them?"

"I have eyes and ears, everywhere. Even within the Service."

The revelation extinguished his son's fixation on the captive. He raked a hand through his hair and asked, "What do you want me to do, Daddy?"

"Find Deke Conrad, remove the threat."

His son tapped his knife against the prisoner's cage. "What about him?"

"Keep him alive until you've dealt with his brother. Then we will stage his death to look like a suicide."

Eli's features puckered into a pre-tantrum collection. "But—"

"Who's in charge here?"

Silence.

He studied his son's vibrating body. Felt the rage boiling beneath his powerful frame. A wisp of fear crept along the edge of his consciousness. He shoved it away and set his jaw. No offspring of his would usurp his position in the family.

"Eli?" He waited for his son to acknowledge him. When he didn't, he unbuckled his belt. "Better look at me, boy."

Wary eyes swung his way.

"Don't fail me."

CHAPTER TWENTY-SIX

"DEKE'S A DEAD MAN."

Reid Steele released the arrow, hitting the sixty-yard target dead center.

Evie stared at her brother. Had she made the biggest mistake of her life by asking for his help? "You didn't let me finish."

"Don't have to. You came to me for advice. Either you're desperate or need my skill set. Or both."

Although he'd never provided details, she suspected her Green Beret brother knew how to kill a person a dozen different ways. Maybe even more.

"I don't need your special skill set. But I am desperate to unravel a mystery."

"Not buying it." He placed another arrow in his compound bow. "You would've gone to the twin brainiacs for puzzle solving."

"There's something...tactical about this mystery."

Lowering his bow, he said, "Now we're talking, Squirt."

They moved their conversation to his office in the training center. The state-of-the-art archery range contained target, field, and 3D settings to appeal to every skill level. Her brother had spent months on the design, and the final product couldn't have turned out more perfect, even to her untrained eye.

"Have a seat." He crashed into the depths of his leather chair. Propping his booted feet atop his desk, he picked up a pen and started rolling it, back and forth, between his thumb and forefingers. "Now that we're cozy, spill it."

Nerves held her mute. Not because she feared Reid's threat to Deke's life, but because of something deeper, more personal. Betrayal. If she divulged the details of their situation to her brother, would Deke consider it disloyal?

How did a simple desire to understand get so complicated?

"We're not getting any prettier." An eyebrow lift accompanied Reid's nudge.

Such a turd.

"Before I start, I want your promise that you won't share our conversation with anyone."

"You got it."

"Not even Brynne."

The pen rolled to a stop.

"I wouldn't ask it of you, but I already feel like I'm betraying Deke by seeking your help."

"Brynne won't say anything."

"She won't mean to do harm. But I know how this works. You'll swear her to secrecy and she'll swear someone she trusts to secrecy—probably Randi, who'll share it with one other person—probably Britt. Within a week, the whole family will be in the know."

"You got something going with this guy?"

"I hope to." He studied her with such intensity that she started to squirm. "What?"

"Trying to figure out how much to piss you off."

"Don't hold back now. You never have before."

"Stakes are higher." He blew out a screw-it breath. "Listen, Squirt. I'm your brother. It's my right to tell you I think the guy's too old for you. Knowing you, you'll do what you want. And if he makes you happy, then I won't kill him."

"Older, yes. But hardly crone material." She smiled. "Look at it this way. He's already worked through the pitfalls of his twenties and he's settled into a career." Her smile grew wider. "He'll know how much lead to give me."

"You said it, not me." Some of the tension drained from his shoulders. "I'll keep your secret. But it's going to cost you something big. TBD later."

"Deal." She straightened a stack of vendor catalogs on Reid's desk while she gathered her thoughts. "How much do you know about Deke?"

The pen rolling roared to life again. "Britt's best friend. Works for the U.S. Fish and Wildlife Service. Drinks craft beers. Ladies like him. A lot."

She pushed down the stab of jealousy. She'd witnessed the depth of his appeal to the opposite sex on many occasions at the Triple B. Nothing new. *Nothing new.*

"He's a conservation writer with the Service." She went on to explain about Deke's hunting accident, his leave from work, and reminded him about the MedTour and article.

"Why would he be doing a piece on health care? Not quite his area of expertise, is it?"

"I wondered the same thing. He said he liked to freelance in his spare time. Write about other things that interested him."

"So he joined the tour."

"Yep, everything was going great. He even assisted us with registration."

"But?"

"For some of our patients, he took a real interest in their personal lives—hobbies, hunting spots, favorite movie, etc." Evie's mind wandered over the first few days of the tour, wishing she could return and recapture the happiness.

"Deke's always been outgoing. Loves shooting the shit with people. How he and Tarzan became buddies is one hell of a mystery."

"I didn't think much about him socializing with the patients, until later."

"Are we about to get to the good part?"

Evie speared him with a knock-it-off look as she placed his spare pens in a wire mesh penholder.

"The Med Mobile made a stop in Deke's hometown and the residents coordinated a thank-you BBQ." Evie pushed out of her chair, no longer able to sit. She began adjusting the pictures and plaques on his walls. "Deke's parents arrived, unaware of their son's presence. He's been estranged from his family since he took the job at the Service."

"I don't get it."

"He's a federal employee with an agency that places restrictions on poaching, among other things."

"Ahh."

"After Mitch Conrad publicly shunned his son, Deke and I took a walk. That's when we discovered the body."

Reid tossed the pen onto the desk, straightening in his chair. "As in *dead* body?"

Nodding, she moved to the window. "Gracie Gilbert. She's a server at the local pub and a mom."

"You okay?" The soft understanding in his voice made her throat ache.

She tried to produce a convincing smile—but failed. "The worst part—for us, at least—was the identity of the person we caught kneeling next to the woman's body."

"Lisa?"

"No!"

Reid shrugged. "Just a guess. There's something about her that's always seemed off."

"You barely know her."

"Exactly."

She was certain her brother was losing his mind until she noticed how intently he studied her face. She did smile this time. "I'm okay, Reid." His expression didn't change. "Truly."

Several seconds passed before he nodded. "Who was it?"

"Dylan Conrad. Deke's younger brother."

He whistled. "Didn't see that one coming."

"When Deke called out to him, Dylan yelled, 'I didn't do this,' then he appeared to take something from the body before he ran off."

"You want me to help you figure out what he took?"

"No, I want you to help me figure out who Deke really is. He's much more than a conservation writer."

"What am I missing?"

"He's investigating the murder."

"So would I if I were in his shoes."

"You're ex-military. A warrior. Deke's a writer."

"Vocation doesn't stop a man from protecting his own."

She couldn't keep the skepticism from her face.

"Have you forgotten the lengths Britt and Grif went to last year to protect Randi and Carlie Beth?"

Britt had almost gotten killed trying to save Randi and a pack of red wolves from a trophy hunter. And Grif had stopped Carlie Beth's stalker from killing everyone she held dear.

"Those situations were more organic. They dealt with the onslaught with their brains and hands and whatever they had at their disposal—like paintball guns."

"You mentioned 'tactical' earlier. Explain."

"Jumping ahead—I followed Deke to his brother's apartment."

"'Followed' him?"

She waved off his comment. "He was there with another guy. They were talking with a woman on speakerphone, asking her to do some research. I got the impression she was a computer whiz." She rubbed her forehead, trying to match words to feelings. "It seemed like—"

"An operation?"

"Yes!" She played the scene through her mind again. "The conversation had structure, like they'd all done that sort of thing before." She turned to her brother. "He's not military or law enforcement. What *is* he?"

Reid peered over his shoulder to the landscape beyond the window. "There's one thing. Definitely a possibility."

"That is?"

"A U.S. Fish and Wildlife special agent."

"Special agent? Like the FBI?"

"Yeah, but for wildlife."

She plopped down in her chair. "Why would a wildlife agency be investigating a murder?"

"Because it involves his brother. Remember, Britt and Grif used everything at their disposal. Deke must be, too. The only difference is that your boyfriend's resources are far more vast."

"When I cornered him on his reason for joining the MedTour, he admitted it wasn't to write an article on us. But I couldn't get him to say more."

"Could be undercover."

"He lied to me. Used the tour."

"Nah. He kept quiet out of necessity. Probably to protect you. And his team. Undercover work is a puzzle with a frickin' billion pieces." He lowered his voice. "Sorry to say, Squirt, everything, including his feelings for you, comes in second to his job. Work's his priority and he can't share details of his mission. It would risk his integrity and the mission. He's gotta measure possible outcomes of any action he takes—or doesn't take. One screw-up could blow months of work and put people—or animals—in danger."

Her head spun like an out of control carousel.

"You think he was on a wildlife case, but got derailed by Dylan's situation?"

"It's the only thing that makes sense." He rubbed his

chin. "Based on the secrecy and number of players involved, I'm guessing he's black ops."

"That doesn't sound good."

"Depends on your perspective."

"What's yours?"

"He's the best of the best in his field."

CHAPTER TWENTY-SEVEN

"HOW'S YOUR SHOULDER HOLDING UP?" asked Luis Vasquez, director of SONR.

Deke rolled his shoulder. Grimacing at the twinge of pain but glad to be rid of the sling. He leaned back in the chair across from Vasquez's desk. "I won't be playing on the jungle gym anytime soon. The physical therapist set me up with some exercises. They're helping."

"What about Matteo?"

"Saw him yesterday. He's doing well."

"Did you see anyone else from the team?"

Now he knew the true reason behind the director's summons. "Briefly."

"I've received word about some unusual activity generated by your team."

"What sort of activity?"

"Jax and Taji seem to be quite interested in—" he lifted a sheet of paper from his desk, "—Dylan Conrad. Any relation?"

"Since when do your analysts keep tabs on my team?"

"Since Washington amped up its scrutiny. Personal agendas could put the whole SONR program at risk. I won't let that happen."

"He's my brother."

Vasquez nodded as though Deke's admission confirmed what he already knew. "Did he do it?"

"No."

"So certain?"

"Dylan can be an idiot at times, but he's not capable of murder."

"I can't authorize the use of Service resources for personal matters. Leave your brother's situation to local law enforcement and refocus SONR's energy on locating the origin of Gold Star."

"Yes, sir."

"I'm sorry, Deke," Vasquez said in a low voice. "Family's important. But SONR's success is my top priority."

"Understood."

"Anything new on that front?"

"The MedTour was cancelled due to the nurse practitioner getting sick. I have a couple leads to follow up on."

"Very good. Keep me up-to-date."

Closing the door behind him, Deke left the director's office with mixed feelings. He understood Vasquez's position. It had taken a lot of persuasion to establish SONR. His elite team of agents didn't come cheap. The cost of the equipment they used could feed a third world nation for an entire year.

But every cell in his body rebelled at the notion that Vasquez's analysts were following the team's actions. He pushed through the last door exiting SONR's private wing and nearly mowed over Colin Fisher—one of Vasquez's analysts.

"Deke, don't be pissed."

"I'm not." He kept walking. "Just trying to understand."

"Our employment agreement compels us to declare any unauthorized activity to the director. If we don't, we could lose our jobs."

Who was watching the analysts to make sure they were honoring their agreement?

"Don't worry about it. I'll figure it out."

"Good, good," he murmured to himself. "Marisol will be relieved."

"Marisol was the one who notified the director?"

Panic widened Colin's eyes and he stumbled through a set of words that made no sense. The only thing that Deke caught was "Gotta go."

He followed the analyst's retreat, shaking his head. Colin's bumbling attempt to placate him actually diffused some of the tension knotting his neck.

Now he had to figure out how to do the impossible with nothing more than his brains and determination. But first, he needed to speak with Evie and set things right between them. Too many days had passed since their fight. The whole thing weighed on his mind, gnawed at his conscience.

How he would make things right and still protect the team, he didn't know.

He had to figure out a way, though. Hurting her ate at him like an aggressive cancer. Silent, unseen, lethal.

CHAPTER TWENTY-EIGHT

EVIE'S BUTT WAS NUMB.

Uncrossing her legs, she straightened in the wooden chair she'd swiped from the bar below and flipped to the next page. She'd read the same five pages three times in the past hour.

Every floorboard creak or distant door slam or explosive laugh distracted her from the warrior-beast battle playing out on the pages. She loved fantasy romance novels. So much fodder for the imagination.

She stared at the white door leading into Deke's domain. According to Randi, Deke had been bunking in the spare apartment above Triple B since the MedTour had ended. Why stay in Steele Ridge? Why hadn't he rented a place closer to Rockton? Had he found Dylan?

She'd asked the same questions over and over again, another reason she hadn't finished a chapter. The natural light coming in from the fire escape window began to fade, and she had to hold up her book to continue reading. Pretty soon, she would have to go in search for a switch for the bare bulb outside Deke's door.

Or call it a day. No telling when he would return. If he returned at all.

If what Reid had surmised about Deke's true profession proved to be true, she doubted he had any normalcy to his life. She still couldn't believe it. In the span of a single conversation, she'd learned the guy she'd obsessed over for years wasn't who she thought.

Her cerebral conservation writer was a bullets-and-bones Jarhead. Okay, so he wasn't a Marine, or even in the military, but he was freaking black ops. His work was more like Reid's than Britt's. Did Britt know?

What would it be like to lead a double life? To have to lie—or prevaricate—all the time?

A door below squealed open, then clicked closed. This one sounded louder, not muffled by walls and people. Could it be the one leading up to Deke's apartment? She waited for telltale signs she was no longer alone.

After a few breath-stealing seconds, she caught the heavy weight of a man's step. Just one. The confirmation that Deke had arrived made the flock of hummingbirds in her stomach flare to life.

She stood, laying her book on her chair seat. Would he be surprised to see her? Angry? Indifferent? Please Lord, not the latter. She could work with any reaction except apathy.

Unable to wait him out, she strode to the top of the staircase. "Hello?" The light from the window only reached a third of the way down the stairwell. Deke remained in shadow. "I know this is a bit of a surprise, but we need to talk."

He paused, one boot in the light. The rest of him appeared as a gray silhouette against a black backdrop. She frowned. Her gaze traced the outline of his body. Her breath caught.

She'd spent years memorizing every angle, every plane, every perfection and imperfection of Deke Conrad. The man on the staircase wasn't her Deke.

"Sorry," she said with a self-conscious laugh. "I thought you were someone else."

The stranger said nothing. Just stood there, staring at her. Alarm bells skittered along her spine, awakening her to the precariousness of her situation. She had nowhere to go. Deke's locked apartment hovered behind her and the silent stranger loomed before her. The fire escape was her only viable option, but she'd have to fling herself out the window to have any chance of eluding danger.

Trapped.

"Can I help you?"

Rather than answer, he began climbing the stairs again. Methodical. *Predatory.*

She backed away. "Who are you?"

Creepy Guy continued his quiet ascent. His hand slid beneath his jacket.

Self-preservation kicked in, and she dove for her purse. Ripping it open, she searched the bottomless pit for the pepper spray Reid had insisted she carry after their discussion earlier.

The spray had been a concession, a compromise. Otherwise, her brother would have stuck to her like gorilla glue until the Rockton murder was solved.

She shoved aside wallet, makeup, deodorant, tampons, pens, notepad, and things she should have removed months ago, but couldn't locate the damn pepper spray.

"Shit! Shit. Shit, shit, shit!"

Her heart socked the wall of her chest. Once. Twice. Three-four-five times. Blood rushed to her head and breathing became a chore.

Not now!

She needed her wits. Couldn't afford to be debilitated by a panic attack.

A jean-clad leg appeared on the landing. Attached to the leg was a long, muscular body and a handsome, youthful face. Her attention riveted on his eyes. Long lashed, green, dead of emotion.

Her fingers wrapped around a cylindrical-shaped object and she aimed it at Creepy Guy. "Stop. Don't make me use this."

His gaze shifted to her hand. Unconcerned, he continued his slow stalk, a pistol menacing at his side.

Still struggling for every breath, she fought to stay

upright and conscious. She aimed the pepper spray at his face and pressed.

Nothing happened.

She tried again.

Nothing.

She opened her hand, palm up, confused. The fear faded long enough for her to realize she'd tried to defend herself with a tube of mascara.

It was her last rational thought before Creepy Guy lifted the arm holding the gun.

CHAPTER TWENTY-NINE

EVIE WASN'T ANSWERING HER PHONE.

After numerous phone calls, he discovered that she'd resumed the MedTour but after finishing up with the patients she'd returned to Steele Ridge. He stopped by all of her known haunts—Tupelo Hill, wildlife center, and a handful of other places.

He finally got a short-lived break after running into Reid at the training center. According to Reid, she'd planned on running into town to say hello to a few people before heading back to Niles. The whole time Deke was in her brother's company, he sensed the Green Beret had something sizzling beneath the surface.

Cutting the corner of the training center's drive too short, his tires chewed into the gravel shoulder before climbing onto Cloverdale Road and barreling toward Steele Ridge's downtown. He pushed back the panic burgeoning within his chest. Being off-the-grid didn't always equate to danger. Her phone battery could be dead. She might have left her phone at home. Maybe she was driving with the music too loud or the windows down. She could have made an unexpected trip to Charlotte.

Still, he called Jax. "I need you to track down someone."

"Shoot, boss."

"First, I should to tell you that the director has shut down our operation on Dylan."

"How the hell did he find out?"

"Headquarters is monitoring us."

"You're shittin' me."

"Nope."

"What do you need?"

"Evie Steele is missing. Or could be. No one has seen her for several hours. Can you ping her vehicle's GPS?"

"Sure thing."

"I want to reiterate—"

"This has nothing to do with Dylan, so we're in the clear."

The vice around his chest loosened. "Thanks, Jax."

"You got it."

"Be careful."

"I'll ping your girl and then track down who's spying on us at headquarters."

"Thatta nerd."

"Nerds rule. Give me five. Jax, out."

Taking up Reid's suggestion, he made his way into town. He'd make a quick stop at his apartment to grab his phone charger before heading to Brynne's.

As he passed Mad Batter Bakery, he read the chalkboard sign propped outside the entrance. His vehicle slowed to a halt. He read the baker's assistant's words again.

Life's too short to let the sweetest pastry slip away.

"Whoa." He'd heard folks swear that Jeanine Jennings's unusual sayings held prophetic meaning. But he'd never had one hit so close to home before. All in all, he didn't much care for the experience.

His phone rang, and he tapped the talk button on his steering wheel. "Deke Conrad."

"Found your girl."

He tore his gaze away from the bakery sign and let his foot off the brake. "Where?"

"Is there an alleyway behind your apartment?"

"Yes."

"Makes more sense now. That's where you'll find her vehicle."

"Great job. I'll check in later."

"Much later, I hope," she said in a sly voice. "Be bad, boss." Her laugh echoed through his vehicle before she cut the line.

Deke smiled at Jax's antics. His good humor lasted another block before questions started pelting him. Why would Evie park around back? Were all the stalls in the front filled?

Even in a small town like Steele Ridge, he didn't like her parking in an alley. Undesirables spent time in secluded, shadow-filled places. What if she'd been mugged? Or worse, rape—? Deke couldn't finish the thought.

He made it to Triple B in record time. Pulling down the alleyway, he spotted Evie's vehicle right away. He parked two doors down and checked his Glock before striding toward the back entrance to Triple B.

After scanning the area, he glanced inside Evie's vehicle and found a half-empty water bottle, phone cord snaking out of the console, and an umbrella in the back floorboard. Everything looked normal.

Testing the handle to Triple B's back door, he found it unlocked. It usually was until about ten o'clock at night. He'd accessed this entrance a few times when he wasn't in the mood for socializing.

All seemed quiet inside, though he could hear the drone of conversation coming from the common area. He stood still for a few seconds after the door closed to give his eyes time to refocus. He debated where to go first. To the bar? His apartment?

Randi's sudden appearance decided his next step for him. "Hey, Deke. Avoiding my customers?"

"Not this time." He nodded toward the alley. "Saw Evie's vehicle parked out back. Have you seen her?"

She sent him a knowing smile. "Try the landing."

He glanced upward as if he could see her camped out on the small five-by-five platform. "How long?"

"Awhile." She winked. "Good luck."

After Randi departed, he continued to stand near the door, staring in the direction of his apartment. Evie was safe—and here. Waiting for him to return home. Why? After their disastrous conversation at the coffee shop, he wouldn't have blamed her if she never spoke to him again.

Being alone had become an "other duties as assigned" requirement of his job. Few women could tolerate long absences or guys who feared revealing too much if they got too close. It was all damn exhausting and he'd given up on serious relationships after his split with Lisa.

But there were a few who would, and he only needed to find one.

He rolled his shoulders back and cracked his neck before snaking his way through the back halls of Triple B to the staircase leading to his apartment. When he turned the knob, voices above caught his attention.

Male. Female. Something about the woman's tone conveyed desperation. Anxiety.

He slipped around the door and ascended the stairs. Evie's voice reached him.

"You want money? Here, take my wallet."

Something cracked against the wall above him. He increased his speed, though he kept his approach quiet. If he had more time, he would go back outside and taken the fire escape stairs. At least then he could see what the hell was going on.

Material scraped against the floor. A *thwump* followed. "What is your connection with Deke Conrad?"

So the intruder wasn't interested in her money.

"Deke? What do you want with Deke?"

"Answer my question."

"Answer mine."

He shook his head. What was she doing provoking the guy? He edged farther up the stairs.

"How about I just kill you instead?"

"Then what? Wait for Deke to come home so you can kill him?"

"Maybe."

"I don't think so. The first gunshot would alert fifty people that a madman was in their midst."

"I've never strangled anyone before. You could be my first."

The calm quality in the intruder's voice shoved Deke's instincts into hyperdrive. This wasn't a burglary gone wrong. He was dealing with something far bigger. And he suspected his little brother was in the middle of the mess.

"I don't think so," Evie said, satisfaction ringing in her voice.

"Aaahck!" Staggering backward into Deke's line of sight, the intruder rubbed at eyes. "Fucking bi—"

Taking the final three stairs at a time, Deke bore down on the guy. Before he reached him, a feminine hurricane came out of nowhere and drove a chair right into the intruder's stomach, forcing him through the window.

"Evie!" Deke grabbed the tail of her sundress a split second before her momentum rocketed her over the edge, too.

Out on the fire escape, metal clanged several times.

After giving her a brief, hard hug, he commanded, "Get downstairs. Now!"

"I'm not going to leave you alone with that maniac. *He has a gun.*"

"Exactly! Go call 911."

"But—"

"Go!" When her eyes widened at his tone, he softened his words, even though adrenaline pumped through his body. "Please, Evie."

She nodded and stormed down the stairs. When he

peered out the shattered window, the intruder swung a leg over his motorcycle and zoomed away.

"Dammit." He slammed his palm against the window frame, causing jagged bits of glass to rain down.

Evie.

His feet barely touched the stairs in his rush to locate her. "Evie!"

She rushed out of Randi's office, a cordless phone in her hand. "The police are on their way."

"He's gone." He opened his arms, and she fell against his chest. "Are you okay?"

"I'm fine. Just shaken."

He kissed the crown of her head. "What happened?"

"I don't know. One second I was reading a book, waiting for you, and the next, I had a gun pointed at my head."

"So you decided to throw your wallet at him?"

"I thought he was a burglar!"

"And when he didn't take the bait? You challenged him?"

"How long were you listening?"

"Long enough for you to have shaved off a decade of my life."

"He knew you."

"I heard."

"Did you recognize him?"

"I didn't catch enough of his face."

"How about his voice? Familiar?"

"Afraid not."

"What are we going to do?"

"We aren't going to do anything."

She pushed out of his arms. "Don't you dare try to shut me out. Not after what just happened up there."

"I don't even know what we're up against. How do you expect me to protect you from what I don't understand?"

"In case you didn't notice, I did a pretty good job of taking care of myself."

"Evie—"

"No, Deke. Someone wants to hurt you. Don't ask me to sit back and do nothing. It would kill me."

"You getting hurt would kill *me*."

Her eyes rounded. "It would?"

"Of course." He frowned. "Why are you smiling?"

"There's absolutely no way you're getting rid of me now, Deke Conrad. You've got a thing for me, and I'm not going to let you forget it."

Chapter Thirty

"EVIE, DID YOU CALL THE police?" Randi asked, leading a deputy down the hallway.

"Sorry, Randi." She glanced at Deke. "Everything happened so fast."

"Super Nurse attacked an intruder," Deke said.

"What?"

Evie sent him a dirty look before whopping him in the stomach with the back of her hand.

"Where's the intruder?" Deputy Blaine asked.

"Gone," Deke said. "Evie threw him out the window on the second floor landing. It's possible that he's hurt."

"I'll have someone check the local hospitals." The deputy spoke into his shoulder mic. When he finished, he asked, "Can you walk me through what happened?"

Deke led their small group to the landing and detailed the incident as best he could. Evie added a few particulars that occurred before Deke's arrival. The detective asked a barrage of follow-up questions before requesting that she and Deke stop by the station later to give a formal statement.

After the deputy left, she said to Randi, "I suppose I can't persuade you not to tell Britt about this."

"Already done, sorry. Someone texted him about a sheriff's vehicle outside Triple B. Then he contacted me while you were going over the incident with Deputy Blaine."

Evie groaned.

"I'd better work on getting that window boarded up." She rubbed Evie's back. "You gonna be okay?"

"I'm fine. Try to hold Britt off as long as possible."

"Will do. I'll send someone to sweep up the glass."

"Thanks, Randi," Deke said. "I'll make sure whoever's responsible for this covers the damage."

Randi waved a hand in the air. "Don't worry about it." She squeezed Evie's hand. "Be careful."

Silence reigned on the landing. Evie wrapped her arms around her middle to ward off a sudden chill. A slow tremble started at her core and grew in intensity as it rumbled into her arms and legs. A cold sweat flushed her entire body.

Seeing her struggle, Deke asked, "What's wrong?"

"I'm not sure. Can't s-stop shaking."

He bent low to peer into her eyes before pressing a hand against her cheek. "Shock. I'm taking you to the hospital."

"No, p-please. I'll go home and take it easy for the rest of the day."

"That's not how shock works. You of all people should know."

"I can't stomach the thought of sitting in the ER, waiting forever for a doctor, only to be told I need to lie down for a while." All she wanted to do was curl into his arms and close her eyes.

His jaw hardened before he turned to unlock his apartment door.

"Thank you," she whispered.

"Don't. I already regret my decision." He lifted her in his arms and settled her onto his couch. The moment he released her, disappointment stabbed her heart.

He stashed a couple pillows beneath her feet, then drew a soft throw from the back of the couch to cover her from head to toe. Warmth penetrated the chill that had taken hold of her body. She burrowed deeper into her haven.

"How d-do you know so much about shock?"

"Lots of experience."

Sitting beside her, he rubbed her arms and legs until her shivering subsided.

"You're right," she said.

"Never doubted it." He gave her a lopsided grin. "About what?"

God, she loved that smile. "About me understanding shock." She tucked the blanket under her chin. "I've studied it. I've seen it. But I've never experienced it. I don't think I really understood the seriousness of shock until today. So odd. How it hit me after everything had settled down."

"Shock affects people in different ways. It took a while for it to penetrate that hard head of yours."

"Is that any way to speak to a sick person?"

"I noticed you're not denying it."

"Because I'm too sick to argue, muttonhead."

"Muttonhead?"

"Suits you, I think."

His playfulness vanished. "Feeling better?"

"Yes, thank you. Sorry for—" she waved her hand down her blanketed body, "—this."

"Don't be ridiculous. I should be apologizing to you."

"Don't be ridiculous."

They grinned at each other before he threw out the first salvo. "Why were you waiting for me?"

"I needed to talk."

"About what?"

"Something I discovered."

"Evie—"

"I'm not sure I'm in the right frame of mind to discuss such a heady topic."

"Would ice cream help?"

"Depends on the flavor."

"Butter pecan, of course." He strode to the kitchenette

and pulled out a quart of ice cream from the freezer. "How many scoops?"

"Two, please." She closed her eyes, finding her equilibrium and enjoying Deke's coddling. "I wouldn't have pegged you for butter pecan."

"Why not?"

"You seem more like the chocolate fudge or rocky road type."

"More manly?"

She chuckled. "I suppose."

He held out a coffee mug with a spoon sticking out of two mounds. "I suspect there's a lot of things about me that would surprise you."

"A day ago, I would have said nothing about you could surprise me."

"Am I that boring?"

"Hardly." She jammed her spoon into her ice cream, breaking it up. "I've been studying you for over a decade."

His spoon halted halfway out of his mouth while his piercing gaze roamed over her features. She'd learned a long time ago how to bury the emotional turmoil his presence often caused. Before she opened herself up to him again, she needed answers.

"I noticed you're not wearing your sling. Have you settled back in at the office?"

"Somewhat." He nodded toward her cup of ice cream. "You gonna eat that or play with it?"

The pivot. *Sorry, big guy, but I won't let you redirect my attention.*

"It's called foreplay." She swirled her spoon around, making the ice cream softer and softer. "What project are you working on?"

"Nothing new. Trying to get caught up on some admin stuff first."

She had to give him credit. He tried not to out-and-out lie. Some guys got off on crafting the most outlandish tales to make themselves look good. Deke did the opposite by downplaying the importance of his work.

Even with the rush of sugar in her veins, Evie found herself fighting off fatigue. She wanted to oust his secret, wanted him to confide in her. But the landing incident was sapping her strength, second by second.

Her eyes jerked open when he removed the cup from her lax fingers.

"Don't even think about eating my icth kweam."

"Wouldn't dream of it." He pressed a kiss to her forehead. "Sleep. I'll be here when you wake up."

Her body gave up its fight and floated down a stream of security and comfort.

CHAPTER THIRTY-ONE

DEKE STARED AT THE SLEEPING black-haired beauty who'd bewitched him years ago and wouldn't let go.

He couldn't stomach lying to her. At some point, she would back him into a corner and the wheel of destruction would start whirling between them.

Unable to sit still, he carried their cups into the small kitchen and stashed her ice cream soup in the freezer. When she woke, she'd have to start the mutilation process all over again.

Who the hell had come armed to his apartment?

This incident had to be connected to his brother's cluster or to the Distributor's case. He leaned against the counter, arms crossed, and stared at his warrior nurse. What would've happened had he not arrived when he did? She would've tumbled down the fire escape with the intruder. If the fall hadn't killed her, the intruder would have shot her for pushing him out the window.

If something happened to her because of him, he wouldn't survive the guilt. His gut urged him to tell Britt everything, when he arrived. The eldest Steele brother would lock his little sister at his side until her hair turned gray. It would be the safest option. The less stressful option. The easiest option.

But he couldn't cage her. She thrived on freedom. Loved her patients. The MedTour was a perfect fit. The program allowed her to roam wild through the mountains of North Carolina, doing what she loved best—helping people.

Her body lurched, and her hand shot out to grasp the back of the couch. She blinked awake.

He strode forward. "It's okay. You're safe."

She massaged the center of her forehead. "I must have dozed off."

"You've had an eventful evening." He sat on the coffee table next to her. "How are you feeling?"

"Better. The catnap helped." She glanced around. "Where's my ice cream?"

"I poured it down the drain."

"You didn't!"

"I should've. What you did to that dessert was un-American."

"Have you tried it?"

"Nope, and I don't plan to, either."

Pushing upright, she swung her legs over the side of the couch. Her new position put mere inches between their noses.

"This is cozy," she said

"Too bad we don't have a fire."

"We could make our own."

Desire speared straight to his groin. Her upturned face held not a hint of the earnest innocence of a year ago. Tonight, her passion and need and determination were clear. And if he didn't catch all of that in her expression, her fingers sliding beneath the strap of her sundress set the tone.

He couldn't force himself to stop her, so he tried to convince her with words. "You've got to think of your future, Evie. Don't squander it on the wrong guy."

"One day, I'll make you understand." The second strap drifted down her shoulder. "But right now, I want to feel you deep inside me."

An ache burrowed into his chest. "There's no room for us. Not with your career and not with mine."

"We're smart. We'll figure it out."

"Don't you think I've tried?" His hands fisted together between his knees. "Every night I stare up at the ceiling, devising ways for us to be together. But there's no path, without one of us making a sacrifice."

Her small hands cradled his jaw and her thumbs made soothing strokes over his cheeks.

"If we can't have forever, then let's steal tonight."

He squeezed his eyes shut, blocking out the temptation. *Stay strong, Conrad.* "Evie, this isn't—"

Warm lips angled over his, tentative at first, before becoming more demanding.

God help him, he managed not to respond for a full five seconds. The longest seconds of his life. But he'd wanted her for too long, wanted *this* too long. His hands began to tremble.

Why not give in to her sweet seduction? They were both consenting adults, who were attracted to each other. Why not accept this piece of heaven? Set aside reality for an hour and enjoy each other's bodies?

A small voice in the back of his head warned him of the emotional destruction that could come later. Later. He would worry about it later.

For now, he deepened the kiss. Gave himself over to his Evie.

He relished her control, her thorough understanding of her body's needs. He didn't fight his submissive role. He gave her three whole alpha minutes before turning the tide, nudging her back onto the couch, covering her with his body, devouring every inch of her responsive mouth.

A slender leg hooked over his hip, and he ran a hand down her bare thigh. *God, he loved sundresses.* He pressed into her welcoming V and soaked up the sound of her answering groan.

His lips followed a preordained path from the pulse

point at her neck to the hollow between her breasts. He breathed in her warm vanilla scent before revealing one perfect mound. A ruched nipple sat within a dusky rose ring.

Beautiful.

He laved the hard nub while guiding her other leg over his hip. "Hold on," he murmured. "I'll move us to the bedroom."

"No. Please." Her voice was husky, lust thick. "I don't want anything to break this moment."

"No complaints here."

She pushed the flimsy material of her sundress down her torso. In a move that could have only been done by a yoga master, she shimmied out of the dress without knocking him unconscious with those long, long legs.

His breath stuck to the back of his throat when he saw she wore no underwear. "Do you subscribe to Britt's commando philosophy?"

"For the love of God, don't bring my brother into this."

"You're right. Doesn't matter." He ran the back of his index finger down the inside of her thigh. Her musky scent filling his nose. "You're more beautiful than I dreamed."

"When did you dream about me, Deke Conrad?"

Wet. So damn wet. He pushed inside her slick passage, teasing, exploring, exciting them both. "Enough times to make me feel like a dirty old man."

"Time for you to remove your clothes, Grandpa."

"Not yet."

With his finger still inside her, he blazed a trail of kisses from the apex of her legs to one firm breast to the next.

"Oh, my God. Deke, I'm going to come."

"Hmmm," he groaned against her nipple. "We can't have that. Not until I'm inside you."

Slowly, he eased his manipulations between her legs while he kissed his way up to her mouth. Their tongues dueled for a spine-shattering minute before he got to his feet.

Evie thought her mind was either going to melt or explode when Deke began taking his clothes off, one piece at a time. He appeared to relish the suspense, her reaction. He studied her with an intensity that made her inner muscles coil and her spine curl.

He'd buffed up over the years. Wider shoulders, ripped abs, thicker biceps. He was magnificent. The Renaissance masters would have memorialized him into marble had they caught a glimpse of him centuries ago.

Propping herself up on one arm, she said, "You take my breath away. Always have." Her free hand roamed up the back of his thigh, over his rounded ass, and into the small of his back. She urged him closer.

He sucked in a sharp breath, guessing her intent.

The hard length of him seemed to expand before her eyes. She swallowed, trying to calm her racing heart. She'd anticipated this moment for so long and didn't want to muck it up.

Nuzzling his cock, she inhaled his scent, memorizing every detail. Her tongue stretched out to taste him, and a shiver trembled through her body into his. She explored him, inch by inch by inch, until she reached the summit. A pearl of liquid slid down the soft hood, tempting her.

She drew him inside her mouth…and sucked, moaning at the taste of him, feel of him, scent of him. Covering the crown of her head with his hand, his fingers tangled in her hair, holding her steady. His hips began a gentle thrust, meeting her demanding lips.

"Evie," he panted. "Inside you. Now."

After one last greedy swipe of her tongue, she laid back, allowed her legs to drift open. She beckoned him closer.

She half expected him to pounce on her and plunge inside. But Deke had never acted as she expected.

He kneeled on the couch, at her feet. Then he crawled toward her like a sleek jaguar on the prowl for his next meal. He paused only long enough to seat himself at her entrance before moving over her, covering her, claiming her.

Everything happened so seamlessly. In a blink, she was meeting him thrust for slow, thorough thrust. Her palms smoothed up and down his solid back, urging him faster and faster and faster. They were fused together from mouth to hips, everything in perfect synchronicity. Then the rhythm changed, became more urgent. Their lips broke apart and their bodies sought and sought and sought—until release hit them like a rocket blast.

Deke withdrew at the last second. They cried out in unison, their bodies frozen in time but for the vibrations that continued deep, deep, deep in her core.

Lowering onto his elbows, he kissed her cheek, her eyebrow, her nose. "You okay?"

"Lord, no."

He stiffened.

"'Okay' is too puny of a word for what I'm feeling right now. Heaven help me, I can't wait until we're able to do that again."

The grin that stretched across his face was all satisfied, cocksure male. Shaking her head, she covered her eyes, too sated to scold. "Get over yourself, Deke Conrad."

"Not possible with a naked Evie Steele beneath me."

To punctuate his comment, his flaccid member resting on her stomach kicked to life.

"Told you."

She cradled his head with both hands and drew him down for a kiss.

Knuckles rapped against his apartment door. "Deke, it's Britt."

Her heart skydived in her chest. She met Deke's gaze. "He will kill us both," she whispered.

After another hard knock, Deke's surprise turned to what looked like resignation. He pressed his lips to her forehead. "Get dressed."

"He'll figure out what we've been up to."

"I know. Leave him to me."

He threw on his T-shirt and jeans and then strode to the door.

"Hey," Britt said from the landing. "Randi said Evie had a run-in with an intruder. Is she still here?"

"She's fine. Experienced a little shock. She's resting now."

Thank goodness she'd worn a sundress. It took her no time to burrow back into the floral outfit, but her hair was a different story. Bedhead was a hard mess to fix.

"I'd like to see her."

She recognized the razor's edge that had entered her brother's voice. He already suspected they were keeping something from him. Probably because Deke was using his big body to block Britt's view inside.

Curling up in the corner of the couch, she pulled the throw over her. "It's okay, Deke."

He peered at her over his shoulder before stepping aside to allow Britt to enter. Her brother stopped short at the sight of her. Did she have "thoroughly screwed" written on her face? She gauged the distance between Britt and Deke, calculating whether or not Britt's fist could make contact with Deke's jaw.

But he didn't punch Deke. He stared at her, a mix of emotions torturing his beloved features. No matter how much her brothers insisted on babying her, they rarely saw her in a vulnerable position. Which was likely why Britt went ballistic.

"Why didn't you take her to the hospital?" Britt demanded. "Shock isn't something to dick around with."

"Because I refused to go." She sat up a little

straighter. "You know how I am when I set my mind to something."

"Did the bastard touch you?" Britt asked in a low, almost unintelligible voice.

At first she thought he was referring to Deke, which caused her to glance up at him. Britt caught her reaction.

"Don't keep something like that from me, Evie."

Deke stepped between them. "Chill, bro. The intruder didn't touch her in the way you're suggesting. But he had a gun."

"Thankfully, Reid gave me some pepper spray. So I shot him with a good dose of that before pushing him out the window."

"You pushed him out the window." Britt's studied her as if she were a foreign object that needed dissecting. "Why would you do such an idiotic thing?"

"Make yourself big and loud and go on the offensive. The bad guys don't ever expect us to fight back."

"Where did you hear that load of nonsense?"

"On one of the morning shows." She crossed her arms at his look of disgust. "Worked, didn't it?"

Britt looked to Deke for help.

Deke shrugged. "Can't say I'm any happier about the situation than you. But she kicked his ass without getting a single bruise."

Britt ran a hand through his shaggy blond hair and released a breath. And just like that, the tension evaporated in the room. "Randi said the guy knew you." Britt plopped down in a leather rocker-recliner.

Deke sat at the opposite end of the couch. Although she knew it was suicidal, she wished he would've sat closer so she could drape her legs over his lap.

"He asked Evie about her association with me."

"You didn't recognize him?"

"No."

"Any ideas of what this is about?"

"Nothing specific."

The two men stared at each other for a long,

uncomfortable minute, and she realized that Deke had kept his true profession from his best friend.

"Let me help."

She froze. Would Deke bring Britt—and her—into his confidence. Her body flushed with anticipation, hoping, praying he would voluntarily confide in her—them.

He didn't.

"You can't." Deke's attention shifted to her for a brief second. "I don't want your family anywhere near this." His expression hardened when he turned back to Britt. "Trust me."

It took a while for her brother to relent, but he finally nodded and stood. "Come on, Evie. I'll drive you home."

Anger simmered in her veins. She wouldn't be shuffled around like a child. "No, thanks. I have my own wheels."

"Not a good idea for you to drive."

"Says who? You, Dr. Steele?"

The tension in the room swelled again. Her brother's patience was never in abundance, especially when he was in protector mode. "Mama will want to see that you're safe."

She squeezed her eyes shut, defeated by familial obligation. In a small town like theirs, this sort of news would've already made it out to the Hill, and her mom would be worried. "Fine." Rising, she pinned Deke with a don't-you-dare-try-to-ditch-me look. "I'll be back in a snap."

He didn't acknowledge her comment, just studied her face as if it were for the last time. A shiver iced her spine.

Sensing her hesitation, he produced his rogue's smile and nudged her toward the door. "Later, Squirt."

Lead weighed down the soles of her feet, making her descent of the narrow staircase feel like she was traipsing through a bog. She glanced over her shoulder and found Deke following her progress.

Then he stepped back and closed the door. No encouraging smile or devilish wink to carry her through this separation.

Only the cold finality of goodbye.

CHAPTER THIRTY-TWO

ELI SHUT OFF THE ENGINE and let his Honda Shadow 750 coast beneath the crooked barn door. His haven.

Setting the kickstand, he tried to dismount, but a sharp pain shot across his lower back and down his leg, buckling his knee. He crashed to the hard-packed dirt floor. His breath whooshed out and didn't return for a good minute.

When he finally caught his breath and the pain subsided, he attempted to get to his feet, but his legs couldn't hold his weight. Keeping his eye on the horse stall, he used his forearm to pull-crawl himself into the familiar shelter. He collapsed onto a mound of rotting straw.

Closing his eyes, his mind wandered back to the hellcat that did this to him. Rage choked him. How could a girl have bested him? One by one, he began devising plans to make her pay for his humiliation. His breathing slowed and his body released its tension.

"Eli, wake up. Are you drunk, boy?"

Through a fevered fog, his bleary eyes focused on his mother, Greta Harwood. A solid, square-faced woman who ruled their home with the same authoritarianism as her husband ruled his business.

"No, Mama."

"Get out of there, then. It'll take me an hour to get the shit out of your clothes, as it is."

Knowing his mother wouldn't leave until he did as she demanded, he forced himself into a sitting position. But he could go no further.

"What'd you do to yourself now?"

"It's nothing. Go home. I'll be there in a few minutes."

"Don't you tell me what to do, young man." She pointed to his shirt. "Take it off. Let me have a look."

"Mama, there's no need to fuss—"

"Elijah Ezekiel Harwood, don't you dare back talk me. Take your damn shirt off, or I'll do it myself." She waved an arm toward the barn door. "Now, wouldn't that be a fine sight for our neighbors."

"We don't have any neighbors."

She stepped forward, and he held up his hand. "Okay, okay."

When he attempted to pull his T-shirt over his head, the material caught on something and a scream wrenched from his throat.

His mother turned him onto his stomach. "Lord have mercy. Why do you have a piece of glass sticking out of your back?"

Squeezing his eyes shut, he tried not to puke. He considered lying to his mother, but none of his attempts to evade her questions in the past had ever worked. "I fell through a window."

"Don't have to be a damn scientist to figure that much out. *What happened?*"

"Daddy had me run an errand, and I got into an altercation."

"Must have been some altercation." She prodded at the area. "Hope you showed the other guy what happens when he screws with a Harwood."

Swallowing back the bile searing his throat, he said nothing.

"Don't tell me you tucked tail."

"Hell, no."

"Language, boy." She yanked on his T-shirt. "Take that off now."

He carefully drew the piece of clothing over his head and handed it to her.

"Who did this to you?"

"You wouldn't know her."

"Her? A girl got the best of you?"

"She was a woman and a hellcat. Sprayed me in the face and body slammed me."

"God, forgive me. I've raised a pussy."

Fury flared in his chest. His mother had never been maternal and had always spoken her mind to the point of meanness. To him. She never served up her vitriol to Caleb.

His fingers curled into fists.

"Well, you can't go to a hospital. They'll be keeping an eye on those."

"What about Cousin Benjamin?"

"What could a damn animal doctor do for you?"

"He could stitch me up."

"How would you explain your injury to that goody two-shoes?"

"I don't know. I'll think of something."

"We can't take the chance, and I'm not paying your cousin to do something I can manage." She eyed his lower back. "Let's hope none of your organs have been punctured."

"Mama—"

"Hold still," she demanded. "I suspect this is going to hurt."

That was all the warning he got before she ripped the glass shard out of his back. He bit back another scream, not wanting to give his mother any more reason to insult his masculinity.

Wadding his T-shirt, she pressed it against his wound, putting her sturdy weight into the task. He couldn't breathe. Black spots formed before his eyes. He buried his face into the crook of his arm, hiding the gathering tears. Heaven help him if she saw such weakness.

She grasped his wrist and dragged his hand to his wound. "Push hard."

The position was so awkward that he had a hard time putting good pressure on the injury.

A shuffling noise caught his attention, and he angled around to find her at the stall's entrance.

"Where are you going?"

"To get a needle and thread."

"What if my kidney's been punctured?"

"Well, since kidneys contain a lot of blood, I suspect you'll be dead before I return."

His heart sank as he watched her walk away. Warm liquid trickled down his side. He scrambled to put more pressure on the hole in his back. Did it matter? Could he be bleeding out internally, even now?

His gaze fell on the bloody shard of glass before shifting to the stall opening. A muscle below his eye twitched. His trembling fingers walked across the dirt floor and enclosed the shard in his palm.

He waited for his mother's return.

CHAPTER THIRTY-THREE

"GOT SOME INFORMATION FROM MY contact at the Coroner's office," Raelyn said the moment Deke slammed through the bunker's door.

When he'd informed the team about Vasquez's edict regarding Dylan's case, every one of them had flipped headquarters the proverbial bird. He would never forget their loyalty.

"Better be good news," he said. "I've had my fill of the bad."

"Depends on your perspective."

Weariness crept into his bones. He made a bring-it-on hand gesture.

"Desomorphine was found in the victim's system."

"Desomorphine?" Wes murmured. "Never heard of it."

"It's an opioid derivative. Cheap. Home-brewed. Highly addictive. Deadly." Rae scrolled down her computer screen. "Began showing up in Russia around 2002. It hit the U.S. in 2013. Street name Krocodil."

"Why Krocodil?" Wes asked.

"Because the user's skin turns green, scaly, and bumpy."

"Doesn't make any sense," Jax said. "Gracie Gilbert's record was clean. No arrests. No prior drug or alcohol abuse. From all accounts, a good mother. Someone who was working hard to improve her lot—not washing it down the toilet. She was a semester away from graduating junior college." She flicked the end of her pencil against the glass surface of her desk. "Why would she suddenly become an idiot?"

"I agree with Jax," Keone said. "To go—"

"Exsqueeze me," Jax interrupted. "Could you say that again for the recording?" She shoved her smartphone in his direction, like a seasoned reporter.

Keone's eyes narrowed in warning before he continued. "To go from no drug use to Krocodil is extreme. Most people start with heroin and work their way down to Krocodil when they can no longer afford their drug of choice."

"Maybe she was stressing about school or finances or single motherhood—or all the above," Matteo said. "Gave in to temptation. She wouldn't be the first."

"If Matteo's right," Taji mused, "who introduced her to such a dangerous drug?"

"And why?" Deke added. He lifted his gaze to Rae. "Point of entry?"

"Between her toes. If you recall, my contact caught a glimpse of the victim's foot when she arrived. He thought it was a contusion. Turns out, the discoloration was the onset of gangrene, a common side effect when users miss their veins."

"Damn," Wes said. "That's some bad shit."

"You don't know the half of it," Rae said. "A heroin addict's average life span is four to seven years. Krocodil addicts? One to two."

"What else do we know?" he asked. "Taj, any sign of my brother?"

"Nothing, sorry. He's off the grid."

"Jax, did you gain access to the victim's phone?"

She sent him an are-you-serious look. "In the past five days, Gracie texted her daughter, someone named Tina, her mom, and a guy named Henry. She met Tina for dinner and swapped shifts with Henry." Jax held up the phone. "Would you like to see her social media pages?"

"Did your surfing unearth any new leads?"

"No, but I gotta try that new deli on Anderson Street now."

"What d'you have on Tina and Henry?"

"Henry Scoffield's a single white male, twenty-four years old, shares an apartment with two other guys, holds down three part-time jobs, and streams porn every Sunday night."

Matteo snorted. "Sounds like a typical twenty-something guy."

"Tina Armstrong's a single white female, twenty-seven, no kids. Childhood friend of the victim. She waits tables at the same pub as the victim and Henry, though she's transferred over five thousand dollars in the past two months to a bank account under the name of Belinda Armstrong."

"Mother? Sister?" he asked.

"Latter. Appears the sister's fighting leukemia."

"Where's a waitress getting that kind of money?" Keone asked.

"Sounds like an off-the-books job," Wes said.

"She has an arrest record for possession of narcotics."

They all shared a round-robin look, understanding dawning.

"Guess I need to pay Miss Armstrong a visit," he said. "Jax, I need the name of her supplier. Send her address and the name to my phone."

"On it, boss."

"Wes, Matteo, dig into the victim's personal life. Call me naive, but I doubt a childhood friend's going to introduce a virgin user to Krocodil. We're missing a link."

"What about me, Commander?" Taji asked.

"Technology has failed to find Dylan. Time for boots on the ground." He glanced between Taj and Keone. "You guys track him down."

"Rae, you're a runner on this one. Anything odd comes up—you handle it."

Everyone scattered, including Deke. He made it

halfway down the mountain before he realized he hadn't requested a status report on the Distributor's mole. His phone vibrated. Pausing, he checked Jax's information, but found a text from Evie instead.

Where are you?

He shoved the phone back into his pocket. He couldn't take on any more regrets. Watching Evie walkaway with her brother after their incredible bout of lovemaking nearly destroyed him. But he couldn't have her involved in this—at any level.

A few minutes later, his phone vibrated again.

Ignoring me? Really, Deke?

He clenched his teeth and picked up his pace.

Another vibration.

I guess I'll have to start my own investigation.

"The hell you will." He pounded a couple buttons on his phone. It rang four times before she picked up. "Don't you dare, Evie."

"Hello to you, too."

"This thing is growing before my eyes, and Dylan's still missing. I don't need another worry."

"I want to help, Deke. Not cause you stress."

"There's nothing you can do here. Stay where I know you'll be safe."

"So I can spend my time pacing and worrying about *you?*"

His descent slowed to a halt. "Don't worry about me. I have…resources that I can tap into."

She said nothing for the longest time. "I'd like to hear more about these resources."

Something in her tone kept his normal redirection behind his teeth. "Soon. Now's not a good time."

"Will it ever be a good time?"

He didn't know what to say. Since his split with Lisa, he'd never had the urge to share the work he did with SONR. But the desire to reveal that part of his life with Evie was strong. How could he open up to her and still protect the team? Was it even possible?

Dammit. No one could advise him on the issue either. Every member of SONR was single. And he sure as heck wasn't sharing his love life with Director Vasquez. That path would lead to expulsion from the team.

He'd remained silent too long, for Evie said, "I'm coming, Deke. Tell me where I can find you."

"Evie—"

"I'm coming."

The resolve in her voice thundered across the miles. No amount of persuasion would deter her.

Sonofabitch. "Meet me at the Roundhouse pavilion, two o'clock."

Evie rubbed her palms down her capris for the second time since exiting her vehicle and heading toward the pavilion. Seeing Deke for the first time since their lovemaking ripped at her nerves like a freshman experiencing her first out-of-control crush on the hottest sophomore in high school.

She shook her hands as if the action would break loose the tension. How upset would he be? Jalapeño hot? Or habanero?

Straightening her spine, she increased her speed. No sense dwelling on the storm ahead. She wouldn't change a single word of their conversation. Deke would soon learn—if he wasn't already aware—that she was no bystander. Not when those she loved were in trouble.

Love.

Yeah, she truly loved the big lug. It wasn't a silly crush or a case of wanting what you can't have. Deke had climbed beneath her skin, day by day, month by month, year by year, with every kindness he rendered, every joke he told, every touch he yielded.

Did he feel the same way? Sure, they'd made love, but that didn't equate to romantic love. Love that would bind them together for decades, help them through the dark patches.

She saw him the second she stepped inside the pavilion, sitting on top of a picnic table, staring at her.

"Hello," she said.

He said nothing. Habanero, then.

She strode forward, her orange Skechers silent against the concrete floor. Once she stood before him, she placed her hands on his knees. His features revealed neither anger or joy at seeing her.

Edging closer, she kissed his forehead before pressing hers to his. She tunneled her fingers through his hair, clasping the back of his head. "I've missed you."

He closed his eyes and hauled her close. Their lips an inch apart. "Beautiful, stubborn mule."

"Afraid so."

"It's too dangerous."

"We'll keep each other safe."

"You don't understand what we're up against."

"Then explain it to me, Special Agent Conrad."

His body hardened to granite. "What did you say?"

"You're not a conservation writer, are you?"

"Of course I am."

"But you're something more."

He nudged her away and stood, fingers digging into the back of his neck. After what seemed an eternity, he released a growl-sigh. "Dammit, Evie. I can't talk about this."

"I understand."

Facing her, his eyes narrowed in suspicion. "What are you up to?"

"Nothing."

"Close, but not convincing enough."

"I'm not up to anything." She shrugged. "Don't get me wrong. I would've rather you'd confided in me, but I get that work comes first."

"How?"

"The scene at your brother's apartment didn't ring true. I pieced it together from there."

"I'm doing my best to keep lies out of this. How about you do the same."

"After leaving you at the coffee shop, I realized you'd done an excellent job throwing me off the scent. Deep down, I knew you wouldn't get involved with me if there was someone else, but it took a while to cut through the distraction you threw my way. Then I recalled the weird vibe I picked up on between you and the hot Italian and the techno-geek on the phone."

"Hot Italian?"

"Just an observation. I didn't kiss him or anything."

"So you jumped from a weird vibe to special agent?"

She hesitated, not wanting to involve Reid.

"Who did you discuss this with?"

"I didn't know I was discussing *this* with anyone. Though I needed to talk through what I'd observed with someone.

"And that someone was?"

"Reid."

"Reid," he repeated in a flat voice.

"He was my best option, given the circumstances. As it turned out, I made the right choice."

"You're joking, right?"

"His tactical mind pieced everything together. He even suggested you were black ops."

He made a silencing sound and surveyed the area.

"Don't worry. He promised not to say anything. Not even to Brynne."

"People always talk." He let out a stream of F-bombs. "This could kill my career."

"He promised—"

"All it takes is one slip to the wrong person. My team's success is dependent on complete secrecy."

"If you'd confided in me at the coffee shop, I would never have gone to my brother."

"You don't understand. I could never reveal this part of my life to you—or anyone. Too much is riding on the organization's anonymity."

"Does Lisa know?" *Where did that come from? Of course, Lisa wouldn't know.*

When his silence stretched, her heart stuttered to a halt before slamming against her ribcage. "Oh my God, she does."

"Some of it," he admitted. "We were together when I became a special agent. She doesn't know about the other."

"Did your job cause the split? Or did something else?"

"A little of both."

"That's all you're going to give me? 'A little of both.'"

"I don't see how hearing the details of my breakup with Lisa is going to solve anything."

"It might not, but the information is important to me."

He released a harsh breath. "I became a special agent while Lisa and I were still together. She was there during the application process and weeks of specialized training. It was one of the happiest moments of my life, the culmination of years of hard work." He stretched the muscles in his neck, first one way then the other. "The job demanded—demands—that I be away from home a lot, which is tough on any relationship, but especially difficult on one that's already rocky."

"Rocky?"

"We were friends before crossing over to lovers. It proved to be a bad decision."

Although she found his and Lisa's story disturbing on a primal level, she didn't regret pushing him. She took an odd comfort from the fact that they didn't have the right chemistry to be intimate.

She pressed a hand against his back. "Thank you."

"Don't thank me for sharing something that had the power to hurt you."

"I admit that it was difficult to hear, but my mind's at peace on the subject now."

He faced her. "Does nothing make you mad?"

Smiling she said, "Brothers, broken fingernails,

animal cruelty." Her humor faded. "Threats to those I love."

He caressed the underside of her chin with his knuckle. "The Steele clan is lucky to have you."

"I wasn't talking about my family, you dope. Well, I was, but they're not the only ones."

"Did you just call the man you love a dope?"

Tears stung the backs of her eyes. "Not funny. This was a serious moment, and you ruined it." She cupped his face in her hands. "If you're not ready, don't say the words. I've waited half a lifetime. I can wait a while longer."

"Sweetheart." He brought their bodies closer together and whispered against her temple. "I adore everything about you. But this job destroys relationships. It's not unlike what happens to families of police officers and soldiers."

Her throat started to close. She wouldn't beg, but she still wasn't ready to give up. And it wasn't like her father or Micki. If he left her for long periods of time, he would return. She *knew* he would return. "Some couples have made it work and have spent decades loving each other and building families. What if we're one of the lucky ones?"

"What if we're not? I don't want to lose you."

"Haven't I proven my steadfastness? That what I feel for you is stronger than age, brothers, and long periods of separation? Don't we at least deserve a chance?"

His tortured gaze seemed to hang on her every word, as if they were a direct line to hope. Hope that he hadn't allowed himself to consider in a long, long time.

A burst of joy entered Evie's heart. Had she finally broken through the elusive barrier that had separated them for years? Would he finally set aside all his concerns and give *them* a try?

When he remained frozen in place, she closed her eyes a moment to push back the despair that threatened to turn her into a blathering, wild woman. "Can we take this one day at a time? Enjoy each other's company?"

He swallowed hard, and a new intensity shifted into his features. Heat radiated off his body, warming her, electrifying her. "I'm going to enjoy you a whole lot, Evie Steele. Are you prepared for that kind of company?"

"You don't scare me, Deke Conrad." She drew his bottom lip into her mouth and teased it with her tongue before releasing him. "And don't think you're going to keep me away from this case. That green-eyed creeper threatened you. I'm not going home until I find him. With or without you."

His hand cupped the side of her face. "Now I know why your brothers keep such a close eye on you."

"I ran circles around those egomaniacs." She melted against him. "If you're going to be a blockhead like them, I'll be forced to run around you, too."

He nuzzled the tender flesh behind her ear. "I've got a couple people I need to interview. You can tag along."

"Thank you—"

He squeezed her hip. "Don't thank me yet." A different kind of hardness entered his eyes. One Reid had warned her about. "I'll take you to my team, but they're the ones who'll decide whether or not you stay on the case."

"Why?"

"It's their lives I'm opening up to danger, and they should have a say in the matter."

She bit her lip. "What if they don't like me?"

"Then you're off the team."

CHAPTER Thirty-Four

INCH BY SLOW INCH, DYLAN scraped his cage across the concrete floor, ignoring the pitiful wails of the cubs he'd left behind and the stinging cuts on his arms and legs. He could no longer afford to rot away in his cell, hoping someone would find him.

Crazy ass Eli Harwood was hunting Deke. Time for action.

The mystery surrounding his brother's unusual lifestyle had been solved by people who wanted him dead. Black ops. Although Harwood's snide revelation had thrown him for a few minutes, the label fit. Deke had always been a protector. Fearless. Smart.

He hated bullies. When Peyton Collins and two of his friends started terrorizing kids in Dylan's grade school class, Deke had put a stop to it. To this day, Dylan still didn't know what his brother had used as leverage to get Peyton's cooperation.

When they used to hike to the lean-to, Deke would always point out and name the different shrubs, flowers, birds, insects, and anything else they passed. If he couldn't identify it, he'd pull out one of a bazillion field guides he kept in his backpack.

Glancing ahead, Dylan gauged the distance to the door and cursed. He fell back in exhaustion, sweat drenching his shirt. He gave himself a minute to recover, but no more. Who knew when one of the Harwoods would return. The last thing he needed was for them to find him trying to escape.

The cubs—Moe, Larry, and Curly—began another round of baleful mewling. Their chorus had a haunting quality to it that gripped his chest.

"I'm going to get us out of here, kiddos. Be brave."

Before leaving, Blaze Harwood had hung a set of keys in a gray metal box near the door. Dylan was banking on one of those silver beauties fitting the lock attached to his cage.

He stared up at the metal box.

Three feet above his head.

CHAPTER THIRTY-FIVE

"TINA ARMSTRONG?"

Suspicion carved the brunette's striking features. "Who's asking?"

Deke held up his Service badge, hoping she didn't demand a closer inspection. "My partner and I would like to ask you a few questions about Gracie Gilbert."

A shadow of sadness dimmed her bravado. "I don't know anything about Gracie's death."

"We won't take up much of your time. Ten minutes, and we're out of here."

Retrieving a bag of groceries, she shut her trunk and nodded toward the front of her house. "I'll meet you at the door."

"Wait—"

She pointed. "Front door, Mr.—"

"Conrad. Special Agent Conrad."

The garage door lowered.

"Do you think she just ditched us?" Evie asked.

"We'll soon find out." He slanted a glance her way. "I suppose I can't talk you into waiting in the car?"

"Nope."

"If she asks, I pulled you off vacation. That's why you're not appropriately dressed and don't have your badge—Special Agent Williams."

"Yes, sir."

The wait took far longer than a walk from the garage to the front door. He cursed his stupidity for letting her out of his sight. She'd either slipped out the back or contacted someone or flushed her stash. If ever he doubted bringing Evie along had been a bad idea, this situation proved it. Had he not been concerned about her, he would've kept the Armstrong woman in the garage or followed her inside.

He ripped the screen door open and raised his fist. A dead bolt slid home and the door opened. Standing to the side, Tina motioned them in.

"Thank you for speaking to us, Miss Armstrong." Evie glanced around. Family pictures dotted the walls and flat surfaces. Warm yet airy yellows, tans, and greens decorated the living room and small dining area beyond. "What a charming home you have."

"My sister gets all the credit. If it'd been left up to me, the walls would be bare and white."

"You're very lucky. I have four brothers and a tomboy sister."

Tina fixed her attention on a picture frame near the TV. "Belinda's special."

"Cancer's a hellish foe," he said. "I'm sorry for her struggle."

"How do you know about Belinda's illness?"

"There's little about you that I don't know." He prowled around the room. "When was the last time you had contact with Ms. Gilbert?"

"We worked together the night before she died."

"What about your dinner date with her the next day?"

"I didn't have dinner with Gracie."

"That's not what her phone indicated."

Confusion sliced across her features. "Did she have an appointment in her calendar?"

"A text conversation."

"With me?"

"Yes."

"When?"

"Three days ago."

"No way. I admit that I could've forgotten a pre-arranged get-together. But not a text message from a few days ago."

"Has anyone borrowed your phone?" Evie asked. "I learned a long time ago not to leave my phone sitting unattended around my brothers. They would send weird texts to my friends or leave goofy photos for me to find."

"No. My phone's never far from my side."

He cut in. "I'll need a list of your customers."

"Customers?"

He had to give her kudos for keeping it cool.

"The people who get their heroin from you."

"I don't deal in heroin."

"Not now, but you used to. Coke and ecstasy appear to be your product of choice nowadays."

"Whoever's feeding you information about me should double-check their facts."

"I have the utmost confidence in my analyst."

"What agency did you say you're with?"

"I didn't."

"We're not here to arrest you or shut you down," Evie interjected. "All we want to know is who killed Gracie." She dropped her voice. "You want that too, right?"

Tina closed her eyes. "Yes."

"Then help us. Please."

She nodded once, turning away a moment to collect herself. "I'll do what I can, but I can't give you a list of my customers. I-I need this job now more than ever."

"What you're doing for your sister is admirable—but dangerous."

"Most of my clients are either spoiled college kids, experiencing the dark side for the first time, or wealthy businessmen, escaping the realities of a life they've created. I can't think of one who'd be capable of murder."

He bent down to get a better view of a photo

containing three women—a brunette, a blonde, and a redhead. Lifting the picture from the wall, he focused on the blonde.

"How long have you known Leah Bristow?" he asked.

"Since grade school. Why?"

"Did she ever mention a guy by the name of Dylan?"

A ghost of a smile appeared. "She and Dylan used to be inseparable. He was sweet, though constantly seeking something."

"He's missing."

Her eyes widened. "For how long?"

"Since the evening of Ms. Gilbert's death."

"Dylan couldn't have done that to Gracie. He's misguided at times, but has a gentle soul." She studied him. "Special Agent Conrad. Dylan spoke highly of an older brother. Deke, I believe."

"Spoke highly?"

"With a few brotherly complaints mixed in." She glanced between him and Evie. "I'm beginning to understand why finding Gracie's killer is so important."

"You can think of no one who would wish Gracie or Dylan harm?" Evie asked.

Tina shook her head. "I have a few oddball clients. But capable of murder? Nothing comes to mind."

He held out a business card. "Call me if anything—*anything*—surfaces. My gut tells me you're the link."

At the door, Evie placed a hand on Tina's arm. "I hope your sister gets better soon."

Tears glistened in her eyes. "So do I."

"One other thing," he said. "Ms. Gilbert's autopsy report revealed signs of drug abuse."

"Gracie never touched the stuff. Not even in high school."

"You're sure?"

"Positive. Her father died from an overdose, and her brother's going to follow in his footsteps, especially now."

"Why now?"

"Because he started experimenting with Krocodile."

"What's Krocodile?" Evie asked after she and Deke got back on the road.

"A new drug. Worse than Meth."

He hit a button on his phone and his dashboard displayed *Calling Jax.*

"Worse?"

"Google it. Beware, though. The images are disturbing."

"Whatcha got, Boss?" A feminine voice piped through the speakers.

"I need you to run Gracie Gilbert's brother—Kevin Cassidy."

"Is that a scoop I smell?"

"Tina Armstrong said he's been a user for years, but now he's into Krocodil."

"Krocodil? He wouldn't do that to his sister, would he?"

Evie could hear furious tapping on the other side of the line. She recognized the woman's voice as the one she'd heard in Dylan's apartment.

"Anything's possible. You know that."

"I'm putting this guy in the SOB queue."

"Anything else?" Jax asked.

"Send what you find on Cassidy to Taj and Keone. I'm headed back to Fulton Road. Something she told me isn't adding up."

"The girlfriend? You never did share the skinny on your last convo."

"And I'm not going to now."

"Wait a second—"

He disconnected.

"What's her name?"

"Jax."

She gave him a dirty look. "The *girlfriend*."

"Leah Bristow."

"Tina's friend. The one in the picture."

"Yes."

"Dylan's girlfriend?"

He hooked an eyebrow in her direction. "Yes. Or was."

"Don't give me the challenging eyebrow. I already told you that I came to my senses after I got my emotions under control." She crossed her arms. "If you're going to live a life of lies and deception, you can't expect those around you to have a perfect response to every situation. We have to first weave through a bunch of crap."

He started to say something, stopped, resettled in his seat. "I've tried like hell not to lie to those I love."

"I know." She tunneled her fingers with his. "Was that a declaration?"

Lifting her hand, he kissed the backs of her fingers.

They said nothing more until Deke pulled into Leah Bristow's driveway.

"I'll stay here," she said. "It might seem weird for me to appear for a follow-up interview."

"Not a chance."

"Won't I be an unnecessary distraction?"

"A distraction, but not unnecessary."

He exited and came around to open her door.

"Why do I get the feeling I'm about to be a human shield?"

"Can't imagine."

When Leah opened the door, her smile could've spanned the width of a yardstick. Until she saw Evie.

"Hey, Deke. Back so soon?"

"Leah, do you have a minute? I'd like to ask you a few more questions about Dylan."

"Sure." She sized up Evie. "Who's your little friend?"

Little? At five-foot-ten, Evie could never be mistaken as little. However, Golden Girl had to be six foot in flats.

Wearing those sassy cork-heeled sandals added at least four more inches. *Dammit.* She refused to resent her favorite orange walking shoes.

Deke grasped her hand, giving it a quick, hard squeeze before hauling her inside. "A good friend."

"What's up?" Leah indicated an ivory sofa before melting into a plush, sage-colored chair. One long, bare leg crossed the other.

"When I was here last, you mentioned that Dylan had been distracted."

She began sliding the pad of her thumb over the nail of her middle finger. Back and forth. Back and forth. "Yeah, that's right."

"Distracted how? By work? By a new hobby?"

"By a new girlfriend?" Evie put in. Yeah, the "little" comment still stung.

The anxious finger rubbing stopped. "Dylan didn't fool around. He might have been a pain in the ass in other areas, but he wasn't a tomcat."

"Why do you think he was distracted?"

"I couldn't tell you. All I know is that there were days when I wouldn't see or hear from him."

"Did he ever mention anything about Gold Star?"

"No, what's that?"

"Not sure. I was hoping you could tell me."

"Sorry, sweetcakes."

"Did my brother have a journal or keep a paper calendar?"

Leah snorted. "Dylan wasn't the organizing type."

"What about a pad of paper? A voice recorder? Or a filing system?"

"You really don't know your brother at all, do you?"

"A man can change, given enough time."

"Or not at all." She flicked her fingers as if shooing away a fly. "Listen, if Dylan had a secret file or notebook, he probably kept it in his gun case."

"I didn't see a gun case at his apartment."

"That's because it's in storage."

"You never said anything about a storage unit last time."

"Didn't cross my mind." She sat forward. "You think he's hiding something important in there? He made it sound like the unit housed nothing but a bunch of guy toys."

"Do you have a key? Can you get into it?"

"Never had any reason to." She melted back into her chair. "Go talk to his friend Leo. He can get you inside."

"Where do I find this Leo?"

"Benetti's Storage in Canton."

Chapter Thirty-Six

"YOU WERE ALWAYS AN EVIL boy."

You were always a bitch.

Eli watched his mother's eyes widen, then glaze over as her chest rose one last time.

Blood pooled beneath her blue top, soaking the threads, inch-by-inch. It had taken a while to kill her with the glass shard. Not until he'd hit the carotid artery in her neck had he made any real progress.

He peered down at the bloody shard in his palm. Waited for shock to kick in. For his body to shudder from the impact of his actions.

Nothing.

No disgust or guilt or joy or relief.

Dropping the glass, he stared at his steady fingers.

Daddy wouldn't be happy about the closed casket. A break in Harwood tradition. Friends and family wouldn't be able to pay their proper respects to a polished wooden lid. Best to move the body to Daddy's basin, instead. The old man hadn't used it in a couple years. Time to start a new tradition.

But not right now.

Grasping the old woman's ankles, he dragged her into the corner of the stall. He found a pitchfork resting against one of the barn's thick support beams. Shoving the metal prongs into a stack of fetid, decaying straw, he lifted a hunk and tossed it onto the corpse. More followed until no sign of the woman remained.

Wiping the grit from his face, he studied the mound and decided it would do until he returned. Before he could take care of her properly and eliminate Conrad and his cronies, he had a score to settle with the hellcat who'd attacked him.

Evie, the man had yelled before Eli had flown out the window.

Not an everyday kind of name.

Unique.

Easily tracked down.

Ignoring the throbbing in his lower back, he strode from the barn, a whistle building behind his lips.

CHAPTER THIRTY-SEVEN

DYLAN STARED UP AT HIS lock-pick kit high above him. The pouch lay half on, half off the metal shelf, as if someone had carelessly dropped it there.

Rising on his knees, he pressed his shoulder against the bars overhead, giving him as much height as possible. He stuck his arm through the cage, reaching as far as he could.

Not enough.

Two inches still separated him from his kit. He tried several other positions—all attempts ended with the same result.

Failure.

A blast of disorientation forced him to stop. How long since he'd had food? Water? Not to mention blood loss.

Perspiration pebbled his forehead and upper lip. He blinked several times to right himself. He couldn't stay here much longer. The Harwoods could return any second.

A yellow box cutter and ink pen stood in a black pencil caddy on the desk. He judged the distance to his kit—hope had him surging forward. His arm threaded through the bars and he grappled for the caddy. The tip of his middle finger grazed the base. It wasn't enough to get a solid hold.

The muscles in his arm, shoulder, and back stretched to their limits. A cramp began to form in his upper arm.

Then the caddy moved. Not much, but enough to break the base's hold on the desk.

Closing his eyes, he concentrated on his finger's effort and the feel of the caddy drawing closer. The process took an eternity. Adrenaline poured into his body when he grasped the pen.

He shook off the pain screaming in his arm before attempting to retrieve his picks. All it took was one lift and pull maneuver with the pen, and his kit dropped to the floor. Satisfaction spiked through his veins. Time to get to work.

The awkward position forced him to take it slow and rely on his sense of touch alone. Sweat rolled down his temple, and his arms shook.

A good two minutes ticked by before the lock popped open.

He bolted from his prison on hands and knees. When he made to stand, every muscle in his body revolted. He wobbled on legs that had been too long locked in a ninety-degree angle.

Dizziness hit. He steadied himself against the desk until the black spots retreated from his vision.

"Now what?"

He had no phone or car keys.

A desolate mewling rose behind him, reminding him of his cellmates—Mo, Larry, and Curly.

"Hey, kiddos." He kneeled beside their crate. "How about we get the hell out of here?"

Mo and Larry paced the back of their prison, sending anxious looks Curly's way.

He laid a hand on Curly, and waited.

No heartbeat thumped against his palm, only an unmistakable stillness.

"Fucking Harwoods."

His outburst caused another round of pitiful sounds. "Sorry, kiddos." His mind raced with his various options—contact Deke, get the cubs to safety, notify the authorities, kill the Harwood clan.

With no means of transportation, he couldn't release the cubs. They would never survive these woods alone, without the protection of their mother.

He had only one option.

Leave the cubs behind.

Chapter Thirty-Eight

"WHAT DO YOU MEAN YOU can't let me into my brother's storage unit?"

"Can't say it any plainer," Leo Benetti said, his back to them while he replenished his stock of boxes, packing tape, and bubble wrap. "Customer's the only one with a key to the lock."

"I was told you're a friend of Dylan's."

"I am."

"Can't you help me out? I'm trying to find him."

"Wish I could. But I don't know you from Jack, and the law is the law."

"What happens if your customer dies?"

"I'd need a copy of his will."

"And if he doesn't have a will?"

"A small estate affidavit will do the deed." Benetti glanced over his shoulder. "Your brother missing or dead?"

"Which one's going to get me into his unit faster?"

"Depends on whether the rent's paid up."

He bit back a curse.

Benetti boomed out a laugh. "Don't matter none. I can't let you in without a key or legal documents." He went back to restocking. "You don't have either one."

Evie tangled her fingers with his and tugged, a silent

demand to leave. She waited until they got back to the truck before asking, "What do we do now?"

"We make our own key."

Evie stood in darkness. Her heart vibrated inside her chest, and a trickle of sweat meandered down the center of her back.

"Um, boss, who's this?"

The woman's voice sounded a lot like the techno-geek's. With a black hood covering her head, Evie couldn't see the other occupants. But their stares bore through the thin barrier.

Having run into a dead end, Deke needed to regroup with his team. Shock of all shockers, he invited her along—with one concession—the hood.

Since anonymity was a crucial element to the team's success, he wanted to give each member a chance to vote on her temporary acceptance into the group.

"Evie Steele," Deke said. "I'd like her to help us with the investigation."

"Commander," a deep male voice said, "can we speak in private?"

Commander? Did that mean Deke was their leader?

"Will you be okay for a few minutes?" Deke whispered in her ear.

"Of course."

He guided her to a comfortable chair and squeezed her shoulder before moving away. Several pair of boots shook the wooden floor as the team moved into another room. Although she couldn't make out their words, the tenor of their conversation sounded as though Deke had a lot of persuading to do.

Clenching her hands in her lap, she ached to yank off the stifling hood and have a peek. She wanted to see the people who got to spend so much time with him. People who placed their lives in his hands and vice versa.

She closed her eyes and prayed for his powers of persuasion to be on target today.

Boots filed back into the room. Chairs scraped against the floor. Fingers plucked her hood off.

An assortment of badass-looking men and women stared at her with a mixture of suspicion and curiosity.

Whiteboards and pegboards covered every available wall space of their mountaintop hideaway, each one littered with someone's scribble and a multitude of photographs. Cubicle-style desks, stacked with thick file folders and bankers boxes, filled the floor space. Time zone clocks lined up over a wide doorway leading deeper into their haven.

Swallowing, she said, "Hello."

Deke held out his hand. "I'll introduce you. Jax," he said, "meet Evie Steele."

A lanky redhead peered over her bank of monitors. "Steele? Any relation to that hunky Britt Steele?"

"My brother."

Someone snorted from the back of the room. Jax's intelligent brown eyes zipped between Evie and Deke. "Does he *know*?"

"Jax," Deke warned.

"Know what?" Evie asked.

The techno-geek's lips twitched and her expression shifted. "That I've been in love with him for years."

Somehow she didn't think that was what Jax had wanted to say.

"As you might have guessed, Jax is our resident computer genius, otherwise known as an analyst. Or nerd. Take your pick."

"Nerds rule," Jax muttered around a mechanical pencil now between her teeth.

Deke strode into the maze of desks, chairs, and scary pieces of equipment. He indicated a vertically challenged woman with short-cropped, curly black hair and flawless black-hued skin. "Raelyn's the best medic in the country. The Patch 'em Up Queen."

"Only if I like you." The medic shook her outstretched hand and gave her a sly, teasing—she hoped—smile.

"The two of you have a lot in common."

Raelyn raised a brow.

"He exaggerates. I'm a budding nurse."

"She travels around the hills in an RV, treating patients who can't afford the care otherwise."

"I *assist* a talented and experienced nurse practitioner."

Raelyn's expression warmed. "Welcome to the world of medicine, Evie Steele. May you save many lives."

"The wanna-be cowboy lounging in the back corner is Wes."

Wes tipped his Stetson in her direction. "I blow sh— stuff up."

She guessed him to be a few years older than her, but something about his mannerism screamed old soul. "Sounds handy."

Deke draped an arm over the shoulders of a large man with thick eyebrows and a to-die-for-tan. "This hunk of meat is Matteo, our engineer. He gets us to where we need to go and makes sure we have what we need when we get there."

Aka Hot Italian.

She held out her hand. "I remember you from Dylan's apartment."

"Good memory." Instead of clasping her hand, he waggled his eyebrows at Deke and wrapped her in a warm hug.

She smiled, returning the gesture.

"Back it off, loverboy."

Matteo released her, but not before kissing her cheek and whispering something in Italian.

"Pardon?"

"If he's crazy enough to let you get away, I'll claim you for my own."

"I might have something to say about the 'claiming' part."

Matteo laughed and went back to his charts.

"Taji gathers intelligence," Deke said. "He probably knows what you had for breakfast last Tuesday."

Evie sent the Daniel Dae Kim lookalike a tentative smile.

He nodded. "I am not so good as that. My knowledge of your background only extends to last Wednesday."

"Last but not least," Deke said, "I give you King Keone. He can track a gnat's flight pattern once he's on the scent."

The guy who rose to greet her had to be the biggest—most beautiful—man she'd ever seen. And that was saying a lot with Deke standing beside her.

"Keone. Hawaiian?"

"Astute." He produced a beautiful smile. "I like the smart ones."

In one visual sweep, Evie took in every detail of the room. "All of this to stop poachers?"

"Illicit wildlife and plant trade is a multibillion-dollar business," Keone said. "Many, many species are on the verge of extinction."

Deke chimed in. "It's our job to make sure that doesn't happen."

"How many cases do you work on at once?"

"Too many." Deke rubbed the back of his neck. "But we do the best we can."

"Is Dylan's disappearance somehow linked to poaching?" Every pair of eyes turned toward her, and panic surged through Evie's chest. Given SONR's conservation mission, her question seemed logical. Had Deke's supervisor authorized the use of government resources for an unconnected, personal case? "Did I say something wrong?"

Deke traded glances with several members of his team before answering. "You're wondering why an anti-poaching unit would be investigating a murder case."

"I suppose so. Your supervisor doesn't mind?"

"He minds."

"As long as we stay on top of our other cases," Raelyn said, "they don't have anything to bitch about."

"Family comes first," Wes added.

"I got a whiff of our headquarters spy a few minutes ago," Jax said.

"Marisol?"

"Just a whiff, boss."

"Don't do anything we'll regret," he warned. "Report before you act."

Jax pulled a pencil out of her ponytail and wrote something on a pad a paper. "Do they teach you that in Leadership Academy?"

"What?"

"How to ruin your team's fun. If so, I'm never attending."

"We call this area the Status Room." Deke pushed a roller chair toward her. "Make yourself comfortable." He pointed toward the wide corridor. "The fridge and restrooms are that way."

Heading to the restroom, Evie took the opportunity to check her phone for messages. Three missed phone calls from Lisa and six text messages—two from Lisa, one from her mom, and the rest from friends.

Why hadn't she felt her phone vibrate? She checked the settings and noticed it was set to Do Not Disturb. She'd toggled the feature before their interview with Tina. "Dammit." She read her text messages from Lisa.

Feeling much better. Will catch up to you in Niles.

She should have seen this coming. It'd taken quite a bit of time for her to convince Lisa to postpone the tour. Lisa being Lisa, she would've made a run for it the moment she got the doctor's consent.

After taking care of business, she returned to the Status Room in time to catch Deke's question to Matteo.

"You and Wes dig up anything on Gracie Gilbert?"

"One of her neighbors would watch over the victim's daughter when she'd get held up at work."

"How's that significant?"

"She would keep an eye on Gilbert's house even when the owner was home."

Deke sent Wes a save-me look. "Is there a shorter version?"

"The nosy neighbor spotted the brother visiting late at night. During the last week, another fella showed up an hour or so after the brother."

"Got any guesses?"

"Nope." Wes leaned way back in his chair and clasped his hands behind his neck. "We've got something better."

When both Wes and Matteo smirked at Deke, he growled, "Don't make me shoot you in front of our guest. What d'you have?"

"Fact," Matteo said, grinning.

"We paid Ms. Gilbert's brother a visit," Wes said. "He has a nasty habit he can't afford. Found himself a sugar daddy that doles out money in exchange for favors."

"He offered up this information?"

"My Italian friend can be downright charming—and convincing—when he sets his mind to a task."

"What was the favor?"

"Drug his sister and give his sponsor access to her for fifteen minutes."

Nausea churned in her stomach. "He allowed someone to rape his sister?" She couldn't even fathom such disgusting behavior. Her brothers protected her to the extreme. If a guy disrespected her in anyway, they made sure he never did so again. Steele style.

"Let's not jump to conclusions," Deke said, "even if the details point in that direction." He pinned Wes with a don't-give-me-any-bullshit look. "Did the brother give you a name?"

"Eli Harwood."

Sonofabitch. Deke recognized the name. Everyone in the room did—except for maybe Evie.

"Y'all look like a black cat just walked down your back," she said. "You know this Harwood guy."

"Not personally," Deke said. "Both boys were younger than me. Though I haven't heard anything in recent years, I recall some town gossip about the family being a good, God-faring bunch, if not a little odd."

"Odd how?" she asked.

"Dunno. Just odd." Deke's gaze skimmed across the room. "Anyone have more info?"

Everyone echoed the same sentiment. Odd. But no one could put a finger on anything specific.

Raelyn said, "The father, Blaze Harwood, is on the town council."

"If not for sex, why would Harwood want fifteen minutes of private time with Gracie Gilbert?" Deke asked.

"Compromising pictures. Blackmail," Raelyn offered.

Jax chimed in. "Money, money, mon-ey. Mon-ey."

"Can't think of anything else," Matteo said. "Everything that comes to mind revolves around sex."

"Big surprise," Jax murmured.

"Zip it, Red."

"Did the brother know anything about the Krocodil in Gracie's system?" Deke asked.

"Claimed he'd never heard of the drug," Wes said.

"What a croc," Jax threw out in a heavy Boston accent. When no one laughed, she prodded, "Get it? Krocodil. Croc."

Everyone stared at her. She turned back to her monitors, muttering "Stiffers" beneath her breath.

"Get anything from the Armstrong woman?" Raelyn asked.

"It's as we thought," Deke said. "She's dealing to pay her sister's doctor's bills."

Wanting to participate in the conversation, Evie said, "She denied texting Gracie Gilbert."

"Did a Gremlin get ahold of her phone and send prank texts?" Matteo asked.

"She swore she didn't see Gracie the day of her murder and has no idea about the text."

"We made two other discoveries."

With everyone's attention on her, including Deke's, she had to clear her throat before she was able to speak. "According to Tina, Gracie's brother uses Krocodile, and Deke found a picture of Leah Bristow, Gracie, and Tina together."

Wes whistled. "Thicker and thicker."

"The victim's brother uses Krocodil," Raelyn ticked off on her fingers. "He drugs his sister, leaves her alone with a stranger, and she dies a violent death with the disgusting narcotic in her system. We gotta take that guy down."

"We re-interviewed Leah. She told us about Dylan's storage unit."

"Sounds like we need to recruit Evie and make her our interrogation specialist," Wes said.

She smiled. "Can't claim the credit for that one, but thanks." The anxiety she'd been trying to hide for the past forty-five minutes ebbed away. "We tried to access the unit, but Leo wouldn't give us a key."

"Leo?" Wes asked.

"The owner of the storage unit. He said we needed a key, Dylan's will, or a small estate affidavit. None of which we have."

"Which brings me to an important question," Deke said.

Jax stopped typing. Wes righted his chair.

"How do y'all feel about breaking and entering?"

CHAPTER THIRTY-NINE

NIGHT WAS FALLING.

Dylan found it harder and harder to stay upright. He'd chosen to stick to the woods rather than hitting the highway. With his luck, the first car he'd flag down would be that bastard Eli.

In a little while, he'd break cover and take his chances.

That was if he didn't pass out first.

It'd been too long since he'd last eaten. His blood sugar was tanking by the minute. Blinking hard, he refocused on the large hickory tree ahead. That was how he'd made it this far. Chopping the miles of forest into smaller, achievable chunks. With the onset of night, his chunks got smaller and smaller.

A few feet.

He reached out to steady himself against the hickory, but his vision wavered, causing him to misjudge the distance. His face slammed into the rough, flaky bark. Something cracked, and his eyes teared up. His legs buckled. In the next second, he sprawled on his back, staring up at the darkened canopy.

Minutes passed without him moving. His dazed mind screamed for him to get to his feet. But his injured and dehydrated body began the slow process of shutting down.

He wanted to give into the temptation to rest, to sleep.

But Deke was in danger.

Rolling onto his side, he ignored the throbbing in his broken nose and braced himself for the physical challenge ahead. A large, oval yellow-brown pod lying a few feet away caught his attention. The near darkness made it hard to identify, though the sight triggered something in his subconscious. A memory. Faded with age. Dull around the edges. But there. Just there…out of…reach.

Saliva drenched his mouth as he caught a double-decade-old image of him, Deke, and Dara traipsing through the woodlands. Stopping to investigate the pint-size torpedoes, flinging them against tree trunks to reveal their fruity center.

He squinted at the branches, losing his equilibrium at the odd angle. He pinpointed the large, teardrop-shaped leaves clustered together in sets of six, hearing his big brother's long ago voice identifying the small understory tree.

Pawpaw.

Fruit. Food.

On hands and knees, he crawled to the energy-boosting pod. He attacked it like a dog that had gone too long without food. The sweet custardy flavors of banana, mango, and cantaloupe overwhelmed his taste buds. Bite by bite, his cells came back to life and his lightheadedness dissipated.

Licking the juice from his fingers, he scooped up more pawpaws and hiked another two miles before emerging from the woodland. The thick tree cover and lack of moon made the journey treacherous, even with a country road to guide him.

An hour later, he made it to a main intersection and veered toward town. The rumble of a vehicle in need of a new muffler approached him from behind. He moved to the edge of the shoulder, knowing the driver couldn't see him. An old rusted-out Ford F-150 toddled past him. Brake lights flashed, illuminating the road until the truck stopped.

He'd done a lot of stupid things in his lifetime, but hitchhiking wasn't one of his misdemeanors. He closed in on the truck, cautious.

"Need a lift?" asked a bearded young man, sporting a button-down plaid shirt and John Deere ball cap.

"Don't want to put you out. But if you have a cell phone, I'd appreciate using it to make a phone call."

"Can't help you there. All I can offer is a ride into town."

The driver's indifferent expression conveyed that he'd drive away without a second thought.

"Then I'll take the ride." He jumped into the passenger side, and the truck crept forward.

Crept.

After several miles of going ten below the speed limit, he began to wonder if he could've walked to civilization faster.

"Looks like you got into a bit of trouble."

His nose throbbed and his cheek hurt. Dried blood lined his arms, and his rumpled, dirty, cut-up clothing had seen better days. He finger combed his hair, though he doubted the gesture had much affect.

A dry chuckle escaped between his lips. "Yeah."

For a second, he considered sharing his ordeal with his escort. But everyone knew everyone—or, at least, knew of everyone—in this area. Harwoods enjoyed a lot of power in Creede. And that power extended to neighboring towns.

Would his driver relay every word back to one of the Harwoods? Or would he help him get to safety?

His escort hooked a thumb over his shoulder. "There's a cooler in the cab. Grab a water."

Every cell in his body clenched at the thought of water nearby. He twisted around and dug into the cooler. "Would you like one?"

"Nah."

Shifting back around, he broke the cap's seal with trembling fingers. Shooting a sidelong glance at his driver, he couldn't get a read on the guy. He appeared fresh out of high school, though the lines flaring out from the corner of his eyes indicated an age closer to his.

"You from around these parts?" the driver asked.

He took a long swallow of water. The cool liquid against his parched mouth created a pleasure-pain sensation. Not wanting to draw attention to how long it'd been since he'd had water, he forced the bottle away from his lips.

"Got lost in the woods for a few hours. Had a hard time seeing three feet in front of me once the sun dipped below the ridge."

"What business you got in them woods?"

"My vehicle broke down, and I thought cutting through the woods would save me some time."

"Guess that didn't work out too well, huh?"

Something about the driver's attitude sanded his nerves. Every question had a condescending quality that didn't set so well. But the driver gave him water when he didn't have to, so he did his best to let go of his irritation.

"Not really. You live around here?"

"Just passing through."

"I noticed your John Deere hat. You a farmer?"

"Hell, no."

"Don't care much for the profession, then?"

"My family's built a good living off the land. Not my path, though."

"What kind of work do you do?"

A heavy silence followed his question. He wished this pile of metal went faster than twenty-five miles per hour.

He waved his hand between them. "Didn't mean to pry. Just filling time with small talk."

"I take on odd jobs that need taking on."

Time to move their conversation to a less charged topic. "Town's much farther away than I realized. You saved me a good hour's hike, Mr. —"

His escort angled his head around to meet Dylan's gaze. "Cleamer. Frank Cleamer."

CHAPTER FORTY

"I DON'T LIKE THIS."

Rolling to a halt in the pharmacy parking lot, Deke brushed the fall of Evie's hair over her shoulder. "I can't take you with us."

"Aren't we a team now?"

He hated hearing the uncertainty in her voice. But taking her to the storage unit was out of the question. She would be safer at the Med Mobile. "Yes, though not to the extent that I'm willing to take you on a breaking and entering mission. If things go wrong, I don't want you anywhere near the heat."

"I could be your lookout."

"That's Matteo and Rae's job."

She drummed her fingers on her armrest. "I really want to know what's in Dylan's gun case."

"We don't know for sure that there is a gun case."

"Didn't Leah say—"

"Dylan's ex had little interest in helping us. She might have thrown out the storage unit just to get us to leave."

"Then why are you going?"

"Because it's the only active lead we have on Gold Star, at the moment." He traced the ridge of her jawline. "This is what I do, Evie. This is why relationships with my kind don't work." He cupped the back of her neck.

"Letting us go, day after day, night after night, to unknown destinations and into unfathomable danger, corrodes the mind and heart."

"So you're content to lead a life without passion, love, and family?"

"Not content, but I'm prepared to."

"You make my heart ache, Deke Conrad." She released a deep sigh and opened her door. The interior light blinked on. "But I'm not prepared to let you live such a dreary existence."

Something resembling hope melted the protective casing he'd constructed around his heart. He grasped her elbow before she slipped away.

"My happiness isn't your responsibility."

A wan smile made a brief appearance before her eyebrows clashed together. "You have the emotional intelligence of a lug nut."

She kissed him hard before stomping her way toward the Med Mobile.

"I found him."

Deke's pulse kicked into hyperdrive at his mom's breathless announcement. He turned up the volume on his truck's speakers. "Where?"

"I saw a red truck, a skinny, bearded man, and a sign for Creede."

Frank Cleamer. Had to be. No way could this be a coincidence.

"Deke? Did you hear me?"

"Just thinking, Mama." He shook off his surprise. "Could you tell if it was dark outside?"

"Like it is now. It's an active vision."

Her visions had a mind of their own. Sometimes they played out in the moment and sometimes they were delayed by several hours. She'd taught herself to focus on the light and shadow patterns in order to make a guesstimate on the time of day.

"I'm only twenty minutes away from Creede. Let me know if you see anything else useful."

"Be careful, son. I sensed your brother's anxiety."

"Will do." He hesitated a moment. "You did great, Mama."

"F-find my baby boy."

"I'll bring him home, and you can chain the little shi—him—to the nearest fence post."

Disconnecting, he called Jax.

"Yo, boss."

"Slight change of plans."

"If you're thinking I'm bored and need to mix it up, I'm not."

"I've got a good lead on my brother's location. I'm headed there now."

"Do you want me to send Keone and Taj?"

"No, I'll handle this."

"In all my spare time—" she made a loud hacking sound, "—I've been doing some digging into Harwood's background."

"The son or his old man?"

"All of them."

"What'd you find?"

"Blaze Harwood owns a trucking business, delivering a variety of products all over the southeast region of the States. He runs his business like a dictatorship, though both of his sons are involved."

"Sounds vanilla."

"In the last few weeks, he's rented several storage buildings and is in the process of having state-of-the-art security systems installed in all of them."

"Why does a trucking company need storage?"

"The million-dollar question."

"Maybe Harwood's transporting more than his clients' products."

"Like what?"

"Something worth setting up my brother for murder."

"You think Dylan came across Harwood's dirty business?"

"I have no idea. But it's the only thing that makes sense, right now."

"Ready to hear about the son?"

"Which one?"

"Take your pick. I got scoops on both."

"Oldest."

"He married a divorcée with a kid."

"Why's that a scoop?"

"The Harwoods are a bunch of holy rollers. Taking up with a divorced woman is a pretty big deal."

"I'm still not getting the significance."

"Do the names Amy and Noah ring a bell?"

"The bear claw boy and his mother?"

"One and the same."

Shit. He recalled how emphatic Amy had been about keeping her and Noah's visit to the Med Mobile quiet. How fearful she'd been.

"Now for the younger brother. Eli Harwood had a run-in with the police about a year ago."

"What was the issue?"

"I'll give you one guess."

"Drugs."

"Ding, ding, ding. Want the cherry?"

"Always."

"Many of the townsfolk are afraid of him. He's a loner and has been caught torturing animals. Sound familiar?"

"Textbook makings of a serial killer. When you get a chance, do a search for missing persons or unexplained deaths in the area."

"You're so yesterday. Haven't come across anything yet."

"Keep a scan on things. Something tells me that we're about to reach a breaking point."

"If anyone gets knocked off, you'll be the first to know. Well, I'll be the first. You'll be number two, for a change."

"Anything else?"

"Nada. Jax out."

Deke blasted into Creede five minutes later. The town was small, less than ten thousand people, and not a lot was happening at this time of night. He kept his search to the few places that stayed open past seven on a weekday night.

After checking two gas stations, an ice cream joint, and a fast food restaurant, he began to wonder if his mother's gift had failed her. No one he'd spoken to so far had noticed a thirty-year-old man with a skinny, bearded man in a red truck.

He turned down Ridgeview and noticed a convenience store at the edge of town. If he didn't find any trace of Dylan here, he would have to concede that his mom's vision had failed them. Maybe the gift dimmed with age. Whatever the reason, she would be devastated.

As he pulled into the parking lot, he spotted a red truck and a dark-haired man striding into the store. From this distance, Dylan appeared a bit disheveled but in one piece. Relief poured over him and he whispered a silent thank-you.

The Ford pulled away.

Deke hit the gas, maneuvering his vehicle to intercept Cleamer. He'd find out who this mystery man was once and for all. As least he hoped it was Cleamer, or he was about to make a fool of himself.

His wheels screeched to a halt, blocking the red truck. He peered through his passenger window into the windshield of the truck.

Cleamer.

The other man started to curse him—his eyes widened in recognition. He threw his vehicle in reverse, but there was nowhere for him to go. Another vehicle idled behind him.

Throwing his Ram into park, Deke hurried around to catch Cleamer in case he decided to bolt.

"Frank Cleamer?"

Mystery man stared at him, mute.

"Turn off your vehicle, Frank."

A muscle in his jaw flexed before he switched off the engine.

"Why are you following me?"

Cleamer's eyebrows slammed together. "I'm not."

"I've caught you watching me twice, in two different towns."

The vehicle honked behind Cleamer, and Deke motioned for it to go around.

When he turned back, Cleamer's features had settled into a good ol' boy's bored expression. "Ain't watching you."

Steel snaked up his back. "The ladies?"

Cleamer shrugged. "Yes and no."

Too many days of worry over his brother and heartache about his relationship with Evie had his control walking the edge. Cleamer's offhand attitude about stalking Evie snapped the thread of sanity holding his control in place.

He grasped a handful of Cleamer's plaid shirt and hauled him to the window. "I'm not jacking around. Who are you and what do you want?"

Fear flashed across his face, and he fought Deke's hold. "Let go of me!"

Releasing him, he demanded, "Talk."

"Doesn't matter," he mumbled as if reassuring himself. "My investigation's over."

"What investigation?"

He straightened his clothes. "I've been hired to observe the Med Mobile."

"Why?"

"Miss Frye applied for a grant. The grant sponsor wanted to ensure the Med Mobile was a worthy candidate."

Acid churned in his gut. "What have you determined?"

"They have some interesting practices."

"Like what?"

"You, for one." His sharp gaze roamed over Deke. "Where'd you come from? Why'd they give you access to the patients?"

"I'm a close family friend to Miss Steele and I went to school with Miss Frye."

"Still doesn't explain your role with the Med Mobile."

"I—"

Cleamer waved off any further explanation. "The complications caused by Miss Frye's medical condition were enough to disqualify her application. Cancelling the tour's serious business."

"Lisa didn't realize she had a condition. Her doctor prescribed medication to counteract the migraines."

"The sponsor's already made up her mind. Miss Frye can reapply next year."

"When will Lisa be notified?"

"Letter's in the mail." Cleamer's engine fired to life, and he backed away.

Astonishment kept him immobile a full minute after Cleamer's retreat. Evie and Lisa would be devastated by the news.

Guilt carved across his chest at the part he'd played in the grant denial. Would the Med Mobile be able to finish this tour?

A movement inside the convenience store snagged his attention.

Dylan.

Setting aside the Med Mobile for now, Deke went in search of his brother. He located him in the middle of an aisle, swigging down a large bottle of water and tapping on a phone.

His appearance was far worse up close. Swollen nose, bruised cheek, bloody cuts on his arms, clothes that hung on a too skinny body.

"Dylan?"

His brother didn't stop drinking, only his surprised eyes tracked over to Deke's location.

Moving closer, he noticed the hollow, blue-black circles beneath his brother's eyes and the pungent odor of stale body.

"What happened to you?"

Dylan handed the phone back to an older gentleman wearing a baseball cap with U.S. Army written across the front and a dozen pins decorating the bill. "Thank you, sir."

"Better get that nose looked at, young man."

"Yes, sir."

"Dylan—"

"You got any money?" Dylan interrupted.

Tension stabbed into Deke's shoulders. "I'm not your damn billfold—"

"Cash, credit card, anything?"

Dylan's voice carried an odd combination of fury and fear. He grabbed a gallon of milk, two oranges, a salami roll, bag of nuts, and another bottle of water.

Wrenching his wallet from his pocket, Deke pulled a twenty and held it out. "What's this stuff for?"

"I'll explain in your truck."

Deke's hand dropped to his side, still holding the cash, while he tracked his brother's unsteady stride toward the store's entrance.

"The boy's had a tough time," the veteran said. "Give him time to explain."

"Do I owe you for my brother's water?"

The veteran shook his head. "Glad to help."

"Thank you, sir. And thank you for your service."

"Remember what I said about your brother."

Deke kept an eye on Dylan while he paid the clerk. Where had he been holed up for the past five days? Had he been trying to call him?

In a blink, Dylan crashed to his knees in the parking lot, doubling over.

Deke shot out of the store. "What's the matter?" He removed the food from Dylan's arms.

"C-cramp."

"Where?"

"Stomach."

He sat back on his heels, calming his pulse. "How long has it been since you've eaten or drank anything?"

"Had some pawpaw not long ago."

"And before that?"

"I d-don't know. A few days."

"Take it easy on the water. Small sips only." He helped Dylan into his truck. When the cramps appeared to subside, he pushed his brother for answers. "What's going on?"

"Head west on Main Street. I'll fill you in on the way."

"Dylan, enough! I need some fucking answers."

"Drive, and you'll get them."

Dylan seemed altered. Hard, determined lines shaped his face, and his focus contained a laser's edge. If he had to put a finger on it, he would say his brother had been forced to grow up in a short period of time.

Once they were headed west on Main, Deke asked, "Where are we going?"

"A storage shed, five to seven miles outside town." Dylan clawed at the tough plastic wrapped around the salami. "Can this hunk of metal go any faster?"

Deke accelerated until the speedometer hit seventy. He held out his Leatherman tool.

"Thanks." Dylan snapped open the largest blade and sliced down the side of the package. He made to take a big bite.

"Keep 'em small, Dylan, or you'll regret it."

For once, his kid brother listened and cut a thin slice to eat. He chewed the meat slowly, watching the blackened landscape buzz by.

"Aren't you going to ask me if I killed Gracie Gilbert?"

"No."

"Why not?"

"You're a lot of things, Dylan, but not a murderer."

"Maybe I lost my head and did the unthinkable."

"Do you want me to believe you're a cold-blooded killer?"

"No!"

"Then why are you going down this stupid ass path?"

"I'm just surprised you don't think the worst."

"Don't put this on me. Decision after bad decision, you've thrown your life deeper into the toilet and then you wonder why people might think the worst. Own your own shit, Dylan."

"Forget it. Pull over and I'll walk the rest of the way."

"Another bad decision?"

Dylan huffed out a breath and threw another sliver of meat into his mouth.

"What's so important at this building that I have to break a dozen laws to get there?"

"Cubs."

"Are you really going to stretch out this conversation with one-word answers? I'm trying to go with the flow on this. But you seem determined to piss me off more than I already am."

"Bear cubs. They've been locked up as long as me. I want to put something into their bellies before I go kill the nutcase who caged me."

Rage burned through his veins. "Who caged you?"

His brother sent him a guarded look. "I'm not telling you."

"Why not?"

"Because you'll play big brother and get yourself thrown in jail. I won't have that eating at my conscience, too. I'll take care of this."

"Was it Eli Harwood?"

Dylan's eyes rounded.

"Rat-faced sonofabitch. I'm going to rip his arms off and shove 'em down his throat for dinner."

"No! I'll avenge myself in my own way. I don't need your help."

"I didn't mean that literally. Well, I did, but I know

better. I have resources that will make him regret laying a finger on you."

"The whole damn family traffics in wildlife," Dylan said. "The warehouse is full of animals and animal parts."

"What were you doing there?"

"Following their trail." Dylan gave him a sideways glance. "Harwood knows you're a special agent."

So Harwood's mole at headquarters had spewed everything to the poacher.

"What are you talking about?" He tried to cut a convincing tone.

"I've always suspected something was up with you. Always deflecting my questions. If not for your secrets, I might have been able to forgive you for leaving me— Rockton—behind."

After almost a decade of keeping the words behind his teeth, Deke's confession came out rusty and jagged and angry. "I hate what this job has done to my family. If y'all hadn't been so damn hardheaded about me working for the Service, I could've found a balance. But y'all disowned me like I was a fucking stranger. So I became one."

"Not so fast. The turn's coming up."

A slow burn crept up his neck at his brother's indifference. Years of bloody baggage strewn out in the open and now...nothing. Nada. Zip.

"Make a right turn."

He ignored the command and continued west.

"What are you doing? You should've turned back there."

As soon as the gravel drive came into view, a switch had flicked in his mind and all the emotional crud faded to the background. "Doing it right."

"But—"

Deke made a slashing motion with his hand. "Have I ever failed you?"

His brother's eyes narrowed.

"Let me rephrase." He made a u-ey at the next

intersection. "When it came to getting those I love out of trouble, have I ever failed?"

Dylan looked away. "No."

"You're gonna have to trust me not to this time." He tossed his phone to Dylan. "Call Mom. She's worried."

"Did she have a vision? Is that how you found me?"

"Yes."

"She must've been really worried to seek you out."

"Anything for her baby boy."

"At least someone loved me best."

"Everyone loved you best."

"Only after you went to work for the enemy."

"Oh, for the love of—"

"Chill. I was joking."

"What are we up against? Any of Harwood's people at the building? Or just starving cubs?"

"When I left, just the cubs. Fucking Eli killed one of them."

He pulled off the side of the road, not far from the gravel drive leading to the cubs. "Call Mom."

"What are you going to do?"

"Checking my supplies."

"What kind of supplies?"

"Make the damn call. I'll be back in a second."

He sorted through his keys until he found the one that unlocked the sideload cargo box. Locating the small flashlight he always kept inside, he shone the beam on his stash of weapons and ammo. In addition to the sidearm he already carried, he added an ankle gun, a forearm knife, and a flashbang, for kicks.

He stopped taking chances years ago. Just because something appeared or sounded benign, didn't mean it was.

Jumping back into his truck, he asked, "Did you get a hold of her?"

"Yeah." Dylan's attention dropped down to Deke's waist. "Expecting some kind of war?"

"I like to be prepared." He gave his brother a once-over. "How're you holding up?"

"My stomach no longer feels like it's trying to eat itself inside out."

His truck climbed onto the road again. Once he pulled onto the gravel drive, he flipped off the lights and waited for his night vision to kick in.

When they approached large metal building, all seemed quiet. Normal. From the outside, no one would suspect that a man had been caged and left to starve inside. The thought of Dylan being treated with such cruelty made his stomach convulse.

He drove around to the back, using the building as a shield. A fine sheen of sweat glistened on his brother's brow. His inclination was to order him to stay put, but something told him that Dylan needed to go back inside. To help the cubs, yes. Though he thought his brother's drive went much deeper. Down to his essence. The essence every man battles—to control his own destiny, no matter its size or breadth.

"You got this?" he asked.

"What's to worry about with a real life G.I. Joe by my side?"

"If any surprises meet us inside, I want you to get behind me. No arguments and no male pride. Agreed?"

"You gonna take a bullet for me?"

"Always, bro." He reached down between Dylan's legs and grabbed the milk, knowing his brother's strength still wasn't up to snuff. An eight-pound torpedo could drop the best of them. "Let's go."

Drawing his weapon, he followed Dylan to a side door and motioned for him to stand back.

Dylan held up a hand and whispered, "I overheard Caleb and Eli talking before they took me prisoner. Eli killed Gracie and arranged things to make it look like I was the murderer."

"Why?"

"I'll explain later. Wanted you to know these guys are more ruthless than an average trafficker."

Nodding, he slipped inside the building. The scent of

urine and excrement hit him first. Then a fainter, more pungent odor of death crept into his senses. He braced himself for the sight of the dead bear cub. He never got used to seeing the atrocities man inflicted on wildlife. He hoped he never did.

A soft keening cry emitted from the center of the building. He focused his beam in that direction and found two pair of glowing eyes staring back. "Be back in a second. Stay strong."

After making a sweep of the building, he returned for Dylan, happy to see he'd obeyed his command. He handed his brother a flashlight. "Keep the overhead lights off, in case your friends return."

Dylan once again took the lead, dropping to his knees by the too small crate housing the cubs. "Hey, Moe and Larry. I told you I'd return."

"Where's the dead cub?"

"There's a wooden crate in the back. I put Curly in there." Dylan peeled the oranges and tossed one to each of the cubs. "Find me something for the milk."

Sweeping his light beam back and forth, Deke searched for a container. Now that he wasn't hunting for bad guys, he allowed his gaze to explore the multitude of containers and jars on display. Gall bladders, paws, pelts, claws, antlers, snakes, salamanders, and more.

Disgust roiled in his stomach at the needless loss of life—and freedom.

He found an oval plastic bucket that would work for the milk.

"Remember, feed them a small amount at a time."

While Dylan took care of the cubs, he tried to call two different Service wildlife biologists, but neither answered their phones. So he called the next best thing.

"Hey, Britt. Sorry to call so late. If it wasn't an emergency, I wouldn't have bothered you."

"What do you need?"

"Are you able to transport and shelter two black bear cubs? Both are approximately six months old."

"Not a problem. Where are you?"

"Creede. I'll send you my GPS coordinates."

"On my way."

"Britt?"

"Yeah?"

"The cubs are in a poacher's storage shed. There's a possibility the owner might return."

"I'll grab Reid. We'll be there in an hour."

"Make it thirty minutes."

Chapter Forty-One

ELI READJUSTED HIS POSITION AGAINST the post. He'd been standing in the shadows for hours, waiting, watching, biding his time. Unlike his brother Caleb, Eli could stand in one place for hours and not get exhausted or lose patience.

Getting a lead on Evie Steele's whereabouts had taken more physical effort than he'd expected, and his injured body was rebelling against the exertion.

Rita Sampson had been a tough old tigress. When he'd started questioning her about the BBQ she'd organized for the Med Mobile, she'd sensed the danger he posed to Evie. Her intuition about his intentions was puzzling. But he didn't have time to work it out.

The old woman had finally cracked—Eli closed his eyes—quite a few times.

His attention resettled on the two RVs parked at the back of the pharmacy lot. A quick check on the Med Mobile's website was all it had taken to find Evie Steele.

He flinched as another searing flame shot up his spine. Sweat broke out, sheening his flesh. Evie would patch him up before he killed her. Then he'd burn her and her traveling clinic to the ground.

CHAPTER FORTY-TWO

EVIE BIT INTO THE COLD milk chocolate and released a contented sigh. After Deke had dumped her at the Med Mobile, she'd waited for him to leave before heading toward the only thing that could soothe her feelings at a time like this.

Vanilla ice cream cone dipped in chocolate.

The good Lord couldn't have made a more perfect treat. She jumped back as ice cream dribbled down the side of her cone, narrowly missing her leg. Her tongue lapped up the rogue ice cream, and she decided it was time to make short work of the remaining chocolate.

Quite a few other people'd had the same idea. It'd taken her nearly thirty minutes to get through the line, only to learn they were out of toffee pieces. She hoped Lisa liked the Chunky Monkey milkshake instead. If not, she could switch with Rachel's cup of cookie dough ice cream.

The moon cast a soft, silvery glow over the lot, lighting her way. Deke had better not find out about her little side trip. Like her overprotective brothers, he'd lecture her until his lips turned bloody for walking alone at night by herself.

The lot wasn't a big one, yet it wasn't small either. It took her a couple minutes to traverse the distance. About halfway across, the hair on the back of her neck prickled to life. She glanced around, checking the area for the source of her unease.

Nothing looked out of place, except one of the lot lamppost's had burned out. Unable to shake her unease, she quickened her pace.

Her senses sharpened with each step. Something *was* watching her. Maybe a feral cat or coyote that had wandered into town. She made another visual sweep, and her attention caught on the lamppost again.

The lower part, near the base, appeared misshapen. Her focus narrowed. Was that a bush? *No.* An animal? *N-nno.* A person? She squinted harder, and the shadow shifted. Rose. Moved toward her.

Her breath refused to exhale. Her feet stayed cemented to the ground. Not until cold ice cream dripped on her knuckles did everything start working. She didn't exactly run, but imagined her feet looked like one of those colorful pinwheels spinning in the wind.

Light radiated from both RVs. She made a quick decision and bolted toward the staff RV. Hooking the carry carton over her thumb, she pulled the latch. Locked.

Glancing behind her, she spotted the human shadow advancing her way. Faster. She tried the handle again. Door didn't budge.

She pounded the door. "Lisa, it's me, Evie. Open up."

Footsteps pounded within the RV. She peered over her shoulder. With a ball cap covering his hair and pulled low over his forehead, she couldn't make out the person's face. A strange familiarity crept along the edge of her memory.

The door opened, and she scrambled inside.

"What on earth is going on?" Lisa asked.

She pushed the carry carton into Lisa's hands and then flipped the lock. Pressing her ear against the door, she waited. Hearing anything over the pounding of her heart was impossible so she gave up and looked out the window.

The guy stood facing the RV, about thirty away, his body stone cold still.

She backed away, and the flimsy curtain swished into place.

"What's wrong with you?" Lisa asked.

She pointed her cone at the window. "Someone's following me."

"What?" Lisa marched over and glared outside. "Where is he? I don't see anyone."

Rushing to Lisa's side, she scanned the parking lot. Empty.

Had she imagined the spooky man? No way. He'd been real.

Maybe he'd needed medical attention. If so, why hadn't he called out to her?

No, something had been off with him. Familiar. She couldn't pinpoint what, but it was right there on the tip of her tongue, doing the macarena.

"He's gone." Straightening, she paced away. Her mind ran through dozens of images, contacts she'd made, searching for a name, a face, a place. Place. Place.

The landing. At Deke's apartment.

Creepy Guy equaled Spooky Guy. *Oh, Lord.*

"Let me have this." Lisa peeled the soggy cone from her hand and tossed it into the garbage. She ushered her over to the small utility sink and turned on the water. "Rinse."

She obeyed the command, her mind cataloging her next moves. Creepy Guy's appearance couldn't be a coincidence. What did he want with her? With Deke?

"I need to make a phone call."

"You're starting to scare me."

The tremble in Lisa's voice acted as a balm to her simmering fear. Nurse Evelyn Steele kicked into gear.

"I'm sorry, Lisa. It's probably nothing."

"A man following you isn't nothing."

"He might have just been cutting through the parking lot." An image of Creepy Guy standing outside the RV, watching them, sent her pulse racing again.

"Don't blow smoke up my scrubs. You know the difference between someone taking a shortcut and someone acting like a weirdo."

"Where's Rachel?"

"In the Med Mobile. She wanted to do a bit more prep. We're headed out early tomorrow."

"Headaches still under control?"

Lisa dug into her pant pocket and drew out a small, oval white pill. "As long as I take this little beauty at the onset of a migraine, I can function like a normal human being. It's been life-changing. I don't have to live in constant fear of debilitating pain, anymore."

"Can you tell the difference between the start of a regular headache and a migraine?"

"Oh, yeah. I can't describe it, but I definitely know one from the other."

"Glad to hear it." Evie adjusted the shoulder strap crossing her body in order to grab her phone. "I don't ever want you to go through something like that again."

"You and me both—"

A window shattered toward the front of the RV.

She hurried forward. Flames licked over the driver's seat. "Fire! Do we have an extinguisher?"

"In the back. I'll get it."

Whipping around, Evie searched for something to smother the flames. Desperate, she grabbed a sofa cushion and smacked it against the flames.

A blast of hot, ember-ridden air shot toward her, forcing her away.

More glass shattered in the back. "Lisa, are you okay?"

"Someone threw a fire bomb into the window."

"Can you get to the extinguisher?"

"Not anymore. Flames are inside."

"I'm calling 911." Evie put the phone to her ear and gave the emergency operator their location and told her about the fire bombs.

"Get to a safe location," the operator said. "Emergency personnel are on their way."

Evie coughed. A thick black-gray cloud billowed into the living area. "Come on, Lisa. The smoke's getting worse."

When Lisa didn't answer or appear, Evie barreled toward the back. She found Lisa holding a cloth over her lower face while frantically trying to save folders of paperwork, a large angry flame only a few feet away.

"What are you doing? We need to get out of here."

"Just…need…another minute." Lisa ducked her head to protect her face from the heat.

She grasped her friend's arm. "We don't have another minute. Come on!" Using all of her strength, she dragged Lisa from the burning RV and stumbled to a safe distance away.

Still holding the folders, Lisa dropped to her knees, overcome by a rib-cracking cough.

Sirens blared in the distance.

Every breath seared her lungs as she watched smoke and fire consume their beloved mobile home.

Rachel. "I need to check on Rachel." She lifted her gaze to the Med Mobile parked behind the staff RV. "Gotta back up the Med Mobile or it'll burn, too."

When Lisa didn't try to do it herself, she knew her friend was in bad shape. She hated leaving her, but she needed to get to Rachel.

Retrieving her phone, she scrolled through her Favorites and tapped Deke's name. She didn't even hear the phone ring before Deke's clipped voice cut through the receiver.

"Conrad."

"Hey, Deke. It's Evie."

"Everything okay?"

Where to start? She balked at telling him about her ice cream trip. But she couldn't think of a pliable way to start without confessing.

"Is that an emergency siren?"

"Um, yeah. They're responding to a fire." She stepped onto the first stair leading into the Med Mobile.

Silence.

"Spill it, Evie."

She grabbed the latch. "Someone set one of our RVs on fire."

"Are you okay?"

"We're fine." She sucked in a bracing breath. "I think it was Creepy Guy."

"The one you shoved out the window?"

"Yep. I didn't get a good look at him, but he gave me the same heebie-jeebies as the guy on your landing." She opened the door.

"Where are you now?"

"I'm checking on Rachel in the other RV." She stepped inside. "And I need to move the Med Mobile back before the fire jumps."

"Have you called the police?"

"Hang up the phone, Evie Steele."

Her head jerked around to find Creepy Guy sitting on an exam table, holding a gun to Rachel's temple.

Words coagulated in her throat like blood clotting an open wound, only this was no cool action her body had devised to save her life. In fact, her paralyzing fear might have just killed her—and Rachel.

"Evie, have you called the police?"

Creepy Guy cocked the hammer on his pistol.

Swallowing back her fear, she whispered into the phone, "I love you." And disconnected.

CHAPTER FORTY-THREE

"IT'S NOT LIKE YOUR MAMA to disappear." Blaze Harwood stepped into the kitchen. The screen door banged against the doorframe behind him.

Caleb's fingers froze over his laptop's keyboard, the mile-long spreadsheet forgotten in the wake of his father's foul mood. He shot a glance at his wife drying the last of the supper dishes.

"She probably got caught up in town," Caleb said. "I'm sure she would've called if she hadn't left her phone on the coffee table."

"Her car's outside."

"Maybe someone picked her up."

"Doesn't feel right."

"Are you still hungry? It won't take much for Amy to reheat the chicken casserole."

"I'm full enough. Don't think I could stomach more of that stuff, anyway."

Amy stood with her back to them, unmoving, for several seconds before resuming her dish drying.

He hated how Daddy picked at Amy and her son Noah. If he tried to defend her to the old man, the consequences would be far worse than a few hurt feelings. He always attempted to make it up to her afterwards, but he noticed his lovemaking no longer had the power to release the tension from her body anymore.

His eyes narrowed on his wife's back. At times like this, he wondered how he ever let a whore bewitch him.

"Let me have it," Noah growled. "That's mine."

"Can't make me! Can't make me!" Five-year-old Tobias barreled into the kitchen, holding a dark object in his small hand. Head down, his compact body snaked around the table and chairs.

"Tobias!" Amy scolded. "I've told you—no running in the house."

"Your son should stop chasing him," Blaze said.

Noah skidded to a halt at the sight of his step-grandad.

"Move, Granddaddy." Tobias tried to go around his grandfather, but Blaze had other ideas and hauled him into his arms.

"What do you have here?"

Noah's eyes widened, and fear cut across his narrow face.

"Rrrow!" Tobias made a striking motion with the item in his hand.

"A bear claw," Blaze said, his voice flat. "Where did you find it?"

"Under Noah's mattress." He lashed the air again. "Rrrow! Mine."

"No, it's not—"

"Noah." Caleb kept his warning low and his attention on his father. "Go back upstairs."

"Stay where you are, boy."

"Daddy—"

"Keep your mouth shut, Caleb. I've got a question that only Noah can answer."

Amy shuffled closer to her son.

Noah held his ground, though his gaze dropped to the tiled floor.

"Where'd you get the claw, Noah?"

He held his breath, hoping his stepson's answer wouldn't incite his father's vengeful side. A pair of dogs barked in the distance.

Noah shrugged.

"What kind of answer is that, boy?"

"I don't know."

"Sir."

"I don't know, sir."

"Are you, stupid?"

Noah's face pinched. "No."

Blaze stared hard at Noah.

"No, sir."

"Then tell me where you got the claw."

Tobias sucked on the curved, razor-sharp tip while watching his stepbrother fidget.

"From a bin," Noah murmured.

"Where was the bin?"

Noah peered at him out of the corner of his eye. Sweat broke out of Caleb's upper lip.

"In a building."

"One of my buildings?"

"Guess so."

"Who else was in the building with you?"

Again, Noah glanced at him.

Blaze noticed this time. "My son?"

Noah gave him one jerky nod.

"What do you know of this, Caleb?"

"Nothing, sir. This is the first time I've seen the claw."

"Did you take the boy into one of my buildings?"

"No—yes. I mean…I received a phone call from a client wanting to deliver some merchandise. Noah and I were headed into town for baseball practice. Rather than taking Noah to practice and then backtracking to meet our seller, I allowed Noah to tag along."

"What do you know of my business, boy?"

Another shrug. "Nothing much."

"'Nothing much' isn't nothing. What do you know?"

Amy placed an arm around her son's trembling shoulders. "That's enough, Mr. Harwood. My son meant no harm."

Blaze focused his one-eyed attention on Tobias. "Your Mama's telling me what to do in my own house." He wiggled his finger into his grandson's side. "Think I should let her get by with such disrespect?"

Tobias's eyes sparkled as if it were all a game. "No!"

The dogs' barking intensified.

Setting Tobias on his feet, Blaze patted his behind. "Run upstairs. Your mother will join you in a second."

A sliver of relief flaked off Caleb's chest as he watched his son toddle off. Once he was out of hearing distance, Blaze stormed across the room, grabbed a hank of Amy's hair, and bent her neck way back.

"Daddy, no!" He tried to loosen his father's grip on Amy's hair, but the old man was as strong as a mule. The back of his free hand slammed across Caleb's face, sending him stumbling into the sink. His head caught the corner of a cabinet and he slid to the floor, dazed. He tried to stand, but his knee buckled.

"I don't know what my son saw in a piece of white trash like you." Spittle flew from Blaze's white lips. "But I've tried to overlook your whoring ways."

"I've never betrayed my husband," Amy whispered, barely able to speak with her throat extended so far back.

"'For the woman which hath an husband is bound by the law to her husband so long as he liveth... So then if, while her husband liveth, she be married to another man, she shall be called an adulteress.'"

"Let go of my mama," Noah cried, pounding on Blaze's back with his fist. Tears tracked down his flushed cheeks.

Blaze shoved the boy away, throwing him against the wall. A decorative plate hanging above jostled and fell, cracking against Noah's head, knocking him out.

"Noah!" Amy screamed, clawing at Blaze's face. His free hand wrapped around her neck, squeezing.

Caleb scrabbled to his knees, then his feet. He hooked his arms under his father's, locking his fingers together behind the old man's neck. Blaze released Amy.

She gasped for breath as she crawled toward her son.

"Let go of me, Caleb, or you'll regret it."

"Not until you've calmed down."

"Don't tell me to calm down. Let. Me. Go."

The dogs outside went into a frenzy, catching both their attention. Without thought, he released his father. A boney fist slammed into his jaw. White spots blurred his vision for several seconds. Enough time for his dad to storm outside.

He followed, rubbing his jaw.

His father barked orders at the dogs. They scattered. Blaze stood over a large, misshapen form at the entrance to the barn.

Caleb's jog slowed to a hesitant walk until he stopped a few feet from his father.

The dogs had found Mama.

CHAPTER FORTY-FOUR

DEKE STARED DOWN AT HIS phone.

Disconnected.

He redialed. Evie's phone rang and rang and rang. He canceled and redialed again. Same result. He moved outside, thinking the metal building was blocking his signal. Still no Evie.

He scrolled his phone contacts. "Lisa?"

"Hey, Deke." A rack of coughs followed her greeting.

"Everything okay?"

"Did Evie tell you about the fire?" Her breathing sounded exaggerated and muffled, at the same time.

"Yeah, but we got disconnected and I can't get her back. Did you see who set it?"

"No, but Evie said someone was following her on the way back from the ice cream place."

"Following her?"

"I didn't see him. But a few minutes later the front and back of the RV l-lit up." Her voice broke. "Everything's burning."

"I'm sorry." He understood how shattering the loss was to her. Any other time, he would do what he could to lighten the blow. "Do you see Evie?"

"No, she went to move the Med Mobile and check on Rachel."

"Dammit."

"What's wrong?"

"Nothing. I don't know." He blew out a breath. "I've got a bad feeling, Lisa."

A second of silence past. "Oh, God. I didn't think. There was so much smoke. Couldn't breathe. She insisted I stay put—"

"Calm down, ma'am. You need to keep the mask on."

Lisa took another deep inhalation of oxygen. "Deke," she said, ignoring the EMT's orders. "The RV hasn't moved."

"Are the police there?"

"Yes."

"Have them check on Evie and Rachel." Deke returned inside. "I'm on my way."

"Britt," he called. "Will your staff be able to finish here and get the cubs back to Steele Ridge?"

"Shouldn't be a problem."

"Would they be able to drop off Dylan at the nearest urgent care?"

"Nobody's dropping me off anywhere. After what Harwood did to me, I deserve to see this through."

Deke ignored the urge to protect his brother. It was time they all let go of bad habits. Instead, he took off for his truck.

"Where are you going?" Reid demanded.

"To check on Evie," Deke said over his shoulder.

As the storage unit's door slammed shut, he heard Britt and Reid barking out orders. Dylan climbed into the extended cab and, before Deke could put his vehicle in drive, Britt slid into the passenger's seat.

"Drive and explain," Britt said, buckling up.

Deke punched the gas, and gravel spattered the undercarriage. They barreled down the narrow country drive and skidded out onto the highway, rocketing toward Niles…and Evie.

"The line disconnected while I was speaking to Evie."

"We're not driving like a bat out of hell for a disconnected line. What's got you spooked?"

I love you. Evie's whispered declaration spun through his head, over and over and over. "Someone lit up the RV with her and Lisa inside."

"What?" Britt burst out. "Are they okay?"

"Evie's fine. Lisa sucked down too much smoke, but she'll recover."

"Did they see who set the fire?"

"Evie thought she saw the guy who attacked her outside my apartment."

"Got a name?"

"Eli Harwood."

"The same guy who locked me in a cage."

Britt glanced over his shoulder at Dylan before staring out the front windshield. "What's going on, Deke?"

His grip tightened on the steering wheel.

"Explain," Britt ordered in a low voice.

"I can't. Not fully."

"You're family now. I'll protect your secret to my dying breath."

"Family," he repeated.

"We all knew it was only a matter of time before Evie nabbed you. And given her state of dishevelment in your apartment, I recommend that you propose to my sister sooner rather than later."

"I tried to do the right thing by her, Britt. I swear to you, I did."

"A decade of purgatory is enough, don't you think?"

The ache in Deke's throat worked its way up into the back of his eyes. "You don't mind?"

"Can't think of a better man for my little sister."

"My job. It'll be rough on the relationship."

"If you love her, don't let anything stand in your way." Britt held his fist between them. "She's worth whatever challenges you might face."

Don't we at least deserve a chance?

Evie's plea echoed in his mind, growing stronger on the tail of Britt's counsel. She was worth it. They were worth it. Why continue denying what they'd both craved for years?

He wouldn't. Not any longer. They did deserve a chance to see where this thing between them led.

Drawing in a shuddering breath, he bumped his fist against Britt's. "Thanks, bro."

Rolling his neck, he gave his passengers the Cliff Notes version of the past several days. By the time he'd finished, Britt and Dylan looked like they had a severe case of stomach flu.

"What's your plan?" Britt asked.

"My only solid plan right now is to get a visual on Evie."

A ringer blared through his truck's speakers.

He hit the telephone button on his steering wheel. "What'd you got, Jax?"

"Not good news, boss."

"Let me have it."

"Rita Sampson's dead."

"How?"

"Someone beat her to death."

Grief clamped around Deke's chest. "Suspects?"

"No names. A neighbor saw a man—white, approximately thirty years old, medium build—wearing a ball cap. He walked head down through the neighborhood about two hours ago."

"Harwood," Dylan said.

"Who's with you?" Jax asked.

"Britt Steele and Dylan."

"Maybe you should take me off speaker."

"Circumstances required me to bring them into the fold."

"How much into the fold?"

"Enough for you to talk freely."

"Britt, you don't need Randi Shepherd. I'm your girl."

"Not that freely, Jax."

"Be more specific next time. I've been waiting years to talk to your big friend."

He sent Britt an apologetic shrug. Jax was a damn good nerd, though her sensitivity chip shorted out on occasion.

"What else you got?"

Her voice turned solemn again. "Rae and Taj paid Gracie's brother another visit to see if he knew why Harwood wanted access to his sister."

"What'd they discover?"

"His tongue."

"Jax—"

"Pinky swear. Found it floating in the toilet."

"What kind of sick bastard would do that?" Dylan asked.

"The same one who slit Gracie's throat and beat Rita to death."

"Same one who might be with Evie." Britt's voice held a note of savagery.

Already clocking seventy-eight, Deke hit the accelerator, praying nothing entered his path. None of them would win that battle.

"Is the brother dead or alive?" he asked.

"Bullet to the head."

"Everything's pointing to Eli Harwood," Dylan said.

"Did they find anything at the brother's place to explain Cassidy's betrayal of his sister?"

"Nada."

"How many buildings did you say Harwood's leasing?"

"Six or eight. Why?"

"Dylan led us to a warehouse owned by the Harwoods in Creede. It was full of wildlife contraband."

"Let me pull up the list." Several mouse clicks later. "What the hell?"

"What'd you find?"

"I'm getting an error message. Hold on."

Deke peered at his brother in the back seat. "Now would be a good time to explain why the Harwoods set you up to take the fall for Gracie Gilbert's murder."

Dylan's gaze shifted and pain straddled his features. "They wanted to tie you up long enough for them to make their next shipment." He glanced at Britt. "They know about SONR."

"What's SONR?" Britt asked.

Ignoring Britt's question, Deke asked, "They told you this?"

"Blaze bragged about his *connection* at the Service and about how your secret's not a secret. The rest I heard from Eli and Caleb before they took me prisoner." Dylan pressed his fingers into his temples. "Eli asked Tina—a mutual friend of mine and Gracie's—out to dinner. When she went to the bathroom, she left her phone on the table and he used it to text Gracie about meeting with me."

"Why Gracie?"

"Eli thought you'd never be able to make the connection. His father set him straight in two seconds flat." Dylan met his gaze in the mirror. "That's when Blaze ordered him to eliminate you—and your teammates."

"Eli's the tool," Britt said. "Blaze is the machine."

"Boss, the gig is up," Jax said. "Headquarters has locked me out of the system. We're flying blind now."

Deke slammed his palm against the steering wheel. He couldn't believe Vasquez would shut them down without informing him first. The director could be a hard ass when it came to protecting SONR, but he also operated from a playbook that was steeped in honor and integrity.

"Sorry, Jax."

"Don't ever give up on the nerd, boss. I've got moves that'll blow headquarters away."

"First, contact the team. If they see any Harwood, they should consider them a threat. The storage unit op's a dead end. Call them off. Send Keone and his team to me in Niles."

"I'm on it."

"Then find the mole who's feeding Harwood intel."

"With pleasure. Jax out."

"Maybe Jonah can give her a hand," Britt said.

"He'd never find her location." He tapped his thumb against the steering wheel. "I learned a long time ago to never underestimate a pissed-off Jax."

"Sounds like Micki." Britt grasped the oh-shit handle. "What else do you know about Gold Star?"

"The term popped up on the Service's radar about a year ago. SONR began investigating and received a viable tip that a large inventory of illegal contraband would be moved from a remote location. By the time we got there, the barn was empty. I didn't hear the term again until this business with Gracie Gilbert." His gaze flicked to his rearview mirror. "Got anything to add, Dylan?"

"I learned about Harwood and Gold Star during a hunting trip. A friend of a friend bragged about the money he'd made hunting bear out of season. Piqued my interest." His eyes met Deke's in the mirror. "Not in a financial way."

"So you started following the family?"

"Yeah. I thought the Conrads were screwed up, but our family's not even in the same stratosphere as the Harwoods." He jabbed his thumb behind him. "That storage building back there. I broke into two others just like it. Same inventory."

"If Harwood has a half dozen of those buildings filled with animals and animal parts," he said, "I'd wager his business goes beyond the local Asian markets."

"International?" Dylan asked.

"Fits. A businessman would do much to protect an enterprise that size."

"Like murder," Britt said.

"He's employed the perfect weapon. Eli Harwood's got a taste of blood and now he can't stop."

Chapter Forty-Five

"RACHEL, ARE YOU ALL RIGHT?" Evie kept her attention on the shirtless, bandaged man who held a gun to the nurse practitioner's head with a steady hand.

"M-more or less."

"Who were you talking to?" Creepy Guy asked.

"What does it matter?"

"Because I asked."

Hollowness gripped his green eyes, as if nothing but air and darkness existed in their depths. What would he do if he knew she'd been talking to Deke? What did he want with him? How could she protect both Deke and Rachel?

She decided to stick to the truth. "Deke."

"Is he coming?"

"No, he's on his way to Rockton. Did you come here hoping to find Deke?"

"I came for you."

The pressure on her chest cinched tighter. "Have we met before?" His eyes narrowed. "I mean, before the incident at Triple B."

"No."

"What do you want from me?"

"To say you're sorry."

She glanced between him and Rachel, confused. "For what?"

He cracked the butt of the pistol against Rachel's temple. She dropped to the floor with a sickening thud.

A pitiful scream erupted from Evie's throat. She stared at the blood trail oozing over Rachel's eyelid, her nose, her cheek, before dripping onto the tile floor, pooling there. Her stomach tilted left, then right. It was the Gracie Gilbert scene all over again, but this time she got front row seating for the action.

He advanced on her.

"Who are you?"

"What does it matter?"

He used Evie's question against her.

"I'd like to know the name of the guy who's about to kill me."

That brought him up short. After a few seconds of indecision, he finally said, "Eli."

Eli. Eli. Eli...

Eli Harwood.

Gracie Gilbert.

Dylan Conrad.

Deke Conrad.

Evie.

The puzzle pieces aligned in her mind with terrifying, perfect clarity.

She scanned the small space, looking for something, anything to clobber the psycho with. Finding nothing, she decided to try and get some answers before she met her gruesome death.

"Why are—"

"You made me lose face with Mama."

"I did?"

It was then she caught the bead of sweat trickling down his temple.

His handgun tapped against his thigh.

Thrump, thrump, thrump.

Although she was no expert on mental illness, she could identify a lit fuse as well as anyone.

"Mama had to pull the glass shard out of my back."

"Oo-kay."

"Called me a pussy."

"Your *mother* called you that?"

The tapping got faster.

"She didn't give me time to explain, to tell her how you came out of nowhere, with your claws extended."

"I'm sorry if you were hurt, but you scared me."

"I meant to. Daddy sent me to kill Deke Conrad and you were in my way."

"Why does your dad want Deke dead?"

"He's meddling in our business."

"Did you kill Gracie Gilbert?" She held her breath, willing him to admit it.

He studied her, as if she were an insect he'd like to splay open so he could explore her innards. Then the corner of one eye crinkled. She supposed it was the closest he could get to a smile. The small sign of emotion was effective. It confirmed his responsibility in Gracie's death and conveyed his utter absence of regret.

"Are you the person who paid Gracie's brother to drug her, so that you could spend time alone with her?"

"How do you—" He slashed the gun through the air. "Never mind. I should have killed that spineless pecker when his usefulness ended. He won't be talking to anyone else."

"What were you doing with her? R-rape?"

His features scrunched into disgust. "I had to make her appear an addict. A few injections in the foot. I planted cocaine on her, when I bumped into her at the park. All false leads to keep the police—and special agent Deke Conrad—busy and out of our hair." The thrumping intensified. "All would have gone according to plan if Dylan hadn't stole Gracie's phone."

Foot injections? Krocodile.

A fist pounded on the door. "Miss Steele, it's Sergeant Prickett."

When she opened her mouth to scream, Eli aimed his

gun at Rachel's head. The dispassion in his features made her blood turn cold.

"Answer," Eli whispered. "Be convincing, or all three of you die."

"Everything okay in there?" the sergeant yelled, following another pounding.

The weight of her decision dug into her chest like the heel of a cowboy boot. Should she rush Creepy Guy again? Somehow she didn't think he'd fall for the tactic twice. Should she yell bloody murder and hope the cop reacted swiftly enough? She recalled his dislike of Deke and, by extension, her.

Drawing in a breath that caused her to cough, she strode to the door and opened. "Evening, Sergeant Prickett. What are you doing in Niles?"

"Interdepartment cooperation. Some of these small towns don't even have a police force, and it can take up to an hour for the sheriff's department to respond." He glanced beyond her shoulder. "Miss Frye asked me to check on things over here. She said you were going to move the Med Mobile."

She peered at the burning staff RV and her heart hurt all over. Such a loss. And for what? Throwing a maniac out a window? She caught Lisa's eye from across the parking lot. Her friend sat in the back of an ambulance, wearing an oxygen mask. She lifted her hand and waggled her fingers at her friend. Behind the mask, Lisa smiled.

Safe.

"Sorry to waste your time, sergeant. I was just getting ready to move the RV when you knocked."

"Miss Frye said someone followed you from the ice cream shop. Do you have a description?"

Damn Lisa for being such a good friend.

"Wish I could give you one, so you could hunt him down and make him pay for destroying our property. But he wore a baseball cap that obscured his features."

"Height, build, race, anything?"

"If I were to guess, I'd say Caucasian. Medium build, less than six feet tall. But I'm not sure any of that matters without a better physical description."

The sergeant snapped one more look over her shoulder. "It's a start." He nodded and turned away.

She started to close the door, and the sergeant paused.

"If I miss Deke Conrad when he shows up, tell him I have a few more questions about the Gilbert case."

"Last I heard, Deke's headed to Rockton."

"According to Miss Frye, he's on his way to Niles."

The sergeant's words paralyzed all thought, all movement, all awareness of her surroundings.

Deke was coming.

Here.

Where a psycho wanted him dead.

Fingers tugged at her shirt, forcing her back a step. The door closed. Locking out her saviors, enclosing her with death.

"Get into the driver's seat."

"Why?"

"Move the RV back."

She strode on numb legs to the front cabin. As she passed Rachel, she saw the familiar waterfall of blood on her neck.

"Oh, my God." She stumbled. "You killed her! While she was unconscious? What kind of monster are you?"

"The kind that will kill Deke if you don't get your ass upfront."

A tear crested her eyelid as she skirted around Rachel. She climbed into the driver's seat, the instruments blurring. Her fingers fished for the keys they kept beneath the seat. After three attempts, she latched onto the ring.

The engine rumbled to life. In front of her, emergency personnel were doing their best to minimize the damage, but Eli had made sure nothing would be left to save by lighting up the RV at both ends. Poor Lisa. This would be a tough loss for her.

"Nice and slow," Eli said from someplace behind her. "Back up twenty feet, then kill the engine."

She followed his instructions in a haze of fear and grief. The sight of Rachel's slit throat was frozen like jagged icicles in her mind.

Had she said something to the sergeant that had infuriated Eli? He hadn't seemed upset when he'd closed the door, but who knew with him. He showed neither happiness or anger, only frustration. A robot with a deadly weapon and warped programming.

Out of habit, she stashed the keys under the seat again. "Now what?"

He shrugged on his shirt. "Open the driver's side door and get out."

Hope leaped into her chest and, for a split second, she thought he would let her go.

"If you run or even try to run, I'll hunt down your boyfriend and make what I did to Rachel seem like a birthday party."

She didn't doubt for a second that Eli would torture Deke. The longer she was in his presence, the more she suspected he enjoyed the part he played in his father's business.

In exaggerated slow motion, she pulled the handle and pushed the door open with her forearm. Out of the corner of her eye, she saw a flame near Eli's hand before a sudden burst of glass at the back of the Med Mobile.

"What have you done?"

"Out. Now."

She jumped out and the acrid scent of smoke swooped up her nose, making her cough.

"Quiet!" Eli followed her out, shoving a hanky in her face before closing the door with a soft click. "Put it over your nose and mouth."

Holding the square of cloth between her fingertips, she tried to ascertain whether the thing was clean or not.

"If you cough and call attention to our location, I'll kill anyone who approaches."

"Do you have no care for human life?"

"Like anyone's given a damn about mine in the last twenty-six years. Now move." He pushed her toward a dumpster at the edge of the parking lot, the RV providing the perfect cover.

A shout split the air. "Fire!"

She choked back tears passing the dumpster and following his instructions to head west down an alley that bisected a row of ranch-style houses on each side. Would the firemen put out the flames before they reached Rachel? She couldn't stomach the thought of her friend's body being scorched as well as mutilated.

How long would it take the police to realize Evie wasn't among the ashes? Far too long.

When they were several blocks away from the pharmacy parking lot, she ventured a question. "Where are we going?"

"Someplace where I can think."

"Will anyone else be there?"

"No."

"Gracie Gilbert died the same way as Rachel. Did you kill Gracie?"

"Daddy wanted Dylan Conrad to stop snooping around. I gave Conrad something else to worry about."

"So you did try to frame Gracie's murder on Deke's brother."

"Would've worked if the little bastard hadn't stolen her phone."

"What are you talking about?"

"Don't play stupid. I watched the whole scene play out."

She recalled the overwhelming sense of being watched after she'd left the body and went in search of Deke. The same sensation she'd experienced in the pharmacy's lot. "The police would never have cracked her passcode."

"You give Gracie too much credit. She had a booklet in her purse that contained all her passwords."

As they approached a bronze-colored pickup, the lights flashed and she heard the telltale sound of locks gliding open.

"You drive." Eli tossed her the key fob. "Drive a few miles per hour over the speed limit."

Rather than start up the vehicle, she attempted to tap into whatever bit of humanity he might still possess, if any. "Why not end this now? Let me go and run. Deke's team has enough of the puzzle now to put you away for years."

"Not until I get my apology."

"I already said I was sorry for hurting you."

"I'm not doing all of this because of a damn cut."

"Then what am I apologizing for?"

"For making me kill my mother."

Chapter Forty-Six

DOZENS OF RED AND BLUE flashing lights lasered the night sky.

The sight confirmed Deke's worst fear.

Evie was in trouble.

Police vehicles from several different agencies littered the pharmacy parking lot and volunteer firemen rushed back and forth between the two RVs.

One engine sprayed the fire-consumed staff RV and another battled to tamp down a smaller flame at the back of the Med Mobile.

What the fuck?

Evie and Lisa were nowhere to be found.

"Dylan, stay in the truck."

"No way—"

"To that horde of officers out there, you're a person of interest for Gracie's murder. Somehow I don't think you popping up in their midst is going to be productive."

Dylan slouched in his seat and crossed his arms. "Still playing big brother."

"Be glad he has been," Britt said. "Or you'd be rotting in a prison cell by now."

Deke and Britt slammed their doors and took off at a run.

"There's Lisa," Britt said, pointing at an ambulance. "I'll see what she knows."

Another ambulance rolled into the parking lot, passing him. The vehicle stopped outside the smoldering Med Mobile. Two EMTs grabbed a gurney from the back and stationed it near the RV's side door, where smoke streamed upward from the corners. They went inside.

Thunderous pounding shook his chest as he sprinted toward the RV. A million scenarios streaked through his mind's eye—all of them gruesome, none of the good for Evie's well-being.

By the time he reached the crowd of milling officers and deputies, an EMT appeared in the doorway, coughing. Behind, a black body bag. He and his partner descended the stairs and placed the corpse on the gurney.

Deke lost his mind.

He shoved uniformed men and women out of his way like a bowling ball careening through a set of pins. Grabbing the nearest EMT, he demanded in a voice he didn't recognize, "Who's in the bag?"

When the EMT stared at him, he got into his face and yelled, "Who's in the fucking body bag?"

Rough hands yanked him back. He fought them off, throwing kicks and punches and elbows. Within seconds, he was on the ground, surrounded by a half dozen uniforms, hands cuffed behind his back. He craned his neck around to look at the black bag.

"Who's in the bag?"

"Well, well, well," an oily voice said, "if it isn't fed man Deke Conrad showing up at another crime scene."

"Prickett." He struggled against his restraints. "Who's in the bag?"

"Why don't you tell me, you sick bastard?"

Rage like nothing he'd felt before boiled to the surface. "Get these handcuffs off me and tell me who's in the bag!"

"What'd you do with the murder weapon, Conrad?"

"You're taking this high school feud too far, Prickett.

If you don't uncuff me in the next ten seconds, you're going to hear from my lawyer."

"I'm going to hear from your lawyer either way, so I might as well enjoy the sight while it lasts."

His burning gaze sought the bag again. The gurney was gone. Angling around as best he could with an officer kneeling on his back, he searched for the bag and found it at the back of the ambulance, about to be loaded. Beyond the ambulance, he caught sight of Dylan rushing toward him. He shook his head and shouted, "No!"

His brother halted, his chest heaving, his eyes stormy.

He shook his head.

"Who're you talking to, fed man?" Prickett strode forward.

"Who's in the goddamn bag, Prickett?" He began to fight in earnest again, giving Dylan time to disappear. "Is it Evie?"

Prickett smiled down at him. "Do you mean the delectable Evie Steele?"

"Britt!" he roared at the top of his lungs. *"Britt, stop them!"*

In a blink, his friend was at his side. "What's going on?"

"The bag," he panted. "Is it Evie? These bastards won't tell me."

Britt's spine straightened to its full, upright length. His shoulders widened to their impressive width. By anyone's standards, he was a big, big guy. When pissed? Damn threatening.

"I'm Britt Steele." He held out his driver's license. "Evelyn Steele's my youngest sister. My cousin, Maggie Kingston, is the sheriff in Haywood County." He nodded toward the bag. "If you believe that's my sister, open the fucking bag so I can identify her."

A muscle below Prickett's right eye twitched, and purple-red blotches appeared on his cheeks and chin, giving him a maniacal doll-like appearance. "The victim's name is Rachel Gardner."

Relief flooded the backs of his eyes. He blinked against the stinging sensation while some of the tension released its grip on his body.

Evie wasn't in the bag. Evie wasn't in the bag. Thank you, Lord.

Where was she? Not in the RV, or she would've come running when she heard the commotion outside.

Unless there was a second body bag inside.

"Why is Deke restrained?"

"He attacked several deputies."

"Before or after you refused to identify the body?"

"Doesn't matter. Assault is assault."

"Good luck finding a jury willing to convict a man who was out of his mind with grief."

"Is anyone else inside, Prickett?" he asked.

Prickett stared at him, a smirk on his face.

"Sergeant, is my sister inside?" Britt's voice was hard, deadly.

"No."

"Uncuff me, Prickett. Enough's enough."

"Not until you tell me your whereabouts for the last two hours."

"Britt can vouch for my whereabouts. I was with him and a small group of men near Creede when I got a call from Evie. She told me about the fire, and we came right away."

"I'm going to need the name and telephone numbers of all your alibis."

"Fine. Now the cuffs."

Prickett motioned for another officer to free him. When he jumped to his feet, Pricket backed up a step.

"Sergeant Prickett," a new voice said, "what's going on here?"

Prickett sent him a scorching glare before answering. "A misunderstanding, Chief. We mistook Conrad for the killer."

"Conrad?" Chief Middleton studied him more closely. "What are you doing here?"

"One of the Med Mobile nurses—Evie Steele—called me. I came right away."

"Ah, yes, Miss Steele. Your other partner-in-crime." The chief peered around. "Where's the victim?"

"Loaded in the ambulance," Prickett said. "Throat cut. Same as Gracie Gilbert."

Middleton eyed Deke. "Do you know anything about this, son?"

"I've got some ideas."

"Don't need any ideas. Got all those I can stomach."

"Can we talk about it inside the RV? I'd like to take a look around."

"So you can destroy the evidence?" Prickett asked. "Absolutely not."

Middleton turned his gray eyes on Prickett. "Last I heard, I held the chief's title and appear to be the highest-ranking member of law enforcement here, at the moment."

"He could be involved in this," Prickett said.

"Could be. Could be not." He motioned for Deke to follow him into the RV. "I'll wrangle up enough intelligence to make sure he doesn't move the evidence tape." He ascended the stairs. "Smoke's not too bad."

He peered at Britt. "You coming?"

"I'll do some digging out here."

When he entered the RV, the front cabin and exam room one appeared normal and untouched, but for a large pool of blood at the base of the exam table. The rear was a complete loss.

"What happened, Chief?"

"We have ourselves an open investigation. Wouldn't be right to share the details."

"Would you being willing to discuss them with a special agent with the U.S. Fish and Wildlife Service?"

"Depends."

"On what?"

"Is this special agent working the same case?"

"Yes, he is, but from a different angle."

"Then we have ourselves an interdepartmental cooperation."

"What do you know so far?"

"The arsonist used Molotovs to set both RVs on fire. One to the front and back of the staff RV and one to the rear of the Med Mobile."

Nodding toward the blood, he asked, "What happened?"

"According to Miss Frye, your Miss Steele decided to check on Miss Gardner and move this RV away from the fire. When the RV didn't move and Miss Steele didn't appear, Miss Frye asked an officer to check on her. Evidently, Miss Steele had thought a man was following her across the parking lot, earlier."

"Did your officer speak to Evie?"

"Sure did. Prickett said she appeared a little sad, but otherwise okay. She gave him a description of the stalker."

"Did Prickett ask to step inside, so he could verify the guy wasn't on the opposite side of the door, pointing a gun at Evie's head?"

"Can't say that he did."

"Is that protocol?"

"No, it's not." Chief clipped his thumbs inside his duty belt. "I'll be getting to the bottom of why." His fingers rubbed over the evening scruff growing on his chin. "Prickett checked on the women ten minutes later and found one dead and the other missing."

"Missing? How is it that none of the emergency personnel saw this guy take Evie?"

"We don't know that he did."

"What other conclusion's possible?"

"Maybe she ran."

The thought of Evie running for her life down the streets and alleyways, trying to evade her attacker, flipped his stomach.

"Why wouldn't she have doubled back and sought help?"

"There're more reasons than one for running."

He stared at the chief, uncomprehending. "Are you insinuating that she had something to do with her friend's murder?"

"The best of us are capable of the worst in us, with proper motivation."

"No, not Evie. Not for something like this." Deke circled the crime scene. "Did the body have any evidence of defensive wounds?"

"No."

"Hesitation marks?"

"None. He made one deep, clean cut."

"The stalker appears to be an old hand at slicing throats."

"Now there's a conclusion that doesn't sit well, does it?"

"No, sir." Rubbing the back of his neck, he pressed the chief again. "No one saw Evie or the guy exit the RV?"

"We suspect they used the driver's side door. I've dispatched deputies in all directions."

Striding to the front of the cabin, he maneuvered into the driver's seat. His hands ached to smooth over the steering wheel. The last place Evie'd likely touched. She must be so scared. Had the bastard hurt her? Was it Eli Harwood? Had to be. Everything's pointing to him with big, neon red arrows.

But he didn't have his mom's psychic ability, and her gift had only ever worked with her immediate family.

"In your investigation of Gracie Gilbert, have you come across any evidence related to Eli Harwood—or the Harwood clan?"

"Harwood," Chief repeated in a flat tone. "Is that the bright idea you spoke of earlier?"

Eyeing the sheriff, he wondered if he'd made a fatal mistake. Could the sheriff and Blaze Harwood be pals? They were of a similar age. Both elected officials. Worked together at the city.

"Any evidence of Harwood's involvement?" he asked again.

"Your brother's our only suspect, so far. Heard from him?"

"As I mentioned during my interrogation, my family and I are estranged. I know little of their comings and goings."

Chief Middleton's attention moved to a spot beyond Deke's shoulder. His eyes narrowed before sharpening on Deke once again. "Looks like your brother's got something he wants to share with you."

Angling around, he found Dylan crouching behind a dumpster, motioning for Deke to join him.

So much for staying put.

As he reached for the door handle, Prickett and a deputy emerged from the shadows and shoved his brother to the ground.

CHAPTER FORTY-SEVEN

EVIE'S TERROR INCREASED WITH EACH step she took through the cave-black woods. After driving his truck off the road and stuffing it into a dense web of trees and shrubs, they hiked deep into a blackened mountainous landscape, along an invisible path that only Eli could see.

After what seemed an eternity, she could stay quiet no longer. "Where are we going?"

Silence.

"Eli?"

"Keep your mouth shut."

The impact of his palm against her shoulder forced her to stumble and go down on one knee. Again.

Mr. Talkative used shoving as his means of navigation. Unseen vines and decaying logs littered the forest floor, which gave her a 50-50 chance of staying upright versus kissing dirt.

Using her scraped, bound hands to push off the ground, she rose and continued. Minutes later, the underbrush became thicker, and brambles caught onto her thin capris and tore into her bare calves.

She bit her lip, catching the cry before it emerged. She didn't stop. In fact, she increased her pace and plowed through, knowing the brambles meant sunlight. Sunlight meant the edge of the woods. Edge of the woods meant moonlight. Moonlight meant openness.

Like her Steele siblings, she'd spent years traipsing through the mountains and hiking miles of trails. Many people labeled her a city slicker, at first glance. She loved dresses, high heels, and dangly earrings.

However, she loved hanging with nature more.

Down she went, again. Raspberry thorns scraped her cheek and caught in her long hair. She sat back on her heels, trying to disentangle herself. Rough fingers curled into her hair and yanked her upright. Tears stung the backs of her eyes at leaving a good amount of her tresses behind.

Another push, and she bolted through the last of the brambles. The trees thinned and moonlight sprayed her face. She refused to look down at the damage to her legs and arms and hands. She had more serious things to worry about.

Eli grabbed the back of her shirt, hauling her to a stop. He came to stand beside her, his attention shifting from a dilapidated barn to their left and an old farmhouse with several more modern outbuildings farther in the distance.

The isolation pressed in on her, sucked the last breath from her lungs and killed the final dregs of her hope. No one would find her here. This place would become her tomb, her grave. A vacuum for her screams.

Poor Deke. When he found the carnage Eli left behind and discovered her missing, he'd be out of his mind with worry. He might not realize he loved her yet, but he cared about her.

If only she'd been smarter. Intelligent enough to alert Sergeant Prickett of the danger and save Rachel.

Rachel. Good God, Eli'd murdered her while she'd lain helpless and unconscious. The depravity of the act was beyond imagining.

"If you scream or try to escape, I'll stab you a thousand times. Then I'll hunt down your boyfriend and stab him a thousand times in front of his mama." He grabbed her forearm. "Step where I step."

As they neared the barn, three large dogs barreled toward them. Their vicious barks put her muscles on lockdown.

But only for a split second.

She nearly ripped her elbow out of socket trying to break free of Eli's hold. "Let me go! They're going to tear us to shreds."

Eli growled a low, firm command, and the dogs stopped. They didn't sit or stand or return from where they came. They paced. Tail tucked, ears down, head low.

Her captor continued toward the barn. His barn? Or rather, his father's? Could this be Harwoods' estate? Had they been walking on Harwood land since leaving his truck?

No wonder Eli knew the area so well. This was his home.

Once they reached the rear of the barn, Eli's confident steps became more stealth-like as he rounded the side. He paused at the next corner for so long that she bent forward to see what had him so transfixed.

His arm speared out, clotheslining her throat as he flattened her against the barn wall. Her head bounced off the weathered planks. Squeezing her eyes shut, she prayed for strength, courage, and the wits to outsmart this creep.

She had to find a way to escape.

To return to Deke.

Grabbing the knot between her wrists, he towed her along behind him, slithering into the barn like a feral cat sneaking in his evening meal.

The scent of decades-old dirt, fetid straw, and excrement filled her nostrils. She'd experienced the smell many times before, but something else, another more acrid, stomach-disturbing odor hovered around the edges.

He led her toward one of the half dozen horse stalls lining the wall. Moonlight didn't penetrate this deep into the building, and the stalls reminded her of gaping mouths ready to consume their visitors.

Once she stepped into the stall, blackness

overwhelmed her senses. She had no grasp of time or position. For all she knew, a dead body could be lying two feet away. A familiar hysteria began to bubble to the surface, taunting her mind, pushing her to flee.

A *click, click* reached her ears a moment before Eli's phone light flicked on. He shone the beam on a wooden ladder descending beneath the floor. "Go."

The sight blasted her back to her family's cluttered storage shed. *Spider webs, beetles, dust on everything. Locked door. Black night. Hot. Hungry. Scared. Urge to pee. Alone.*

Even though the incident had happened over fifteen years ago, the cold sweat and paralyzing fear was the same. Jonah wouldn't find her this time. No one would. Not in this creeper's hellhole.

She shook her head.

"Get down there, or I'll throw you down."

Backing away, she said, "I can't."

He stepped toward her, and she bolted. She didn't stop to think about the stab wounds he promised to inflict on her and Deke or of her hatred for running. In that moment, eight-year-old Evie gained control of her mind and body and had but one purpose.

Escape.

Every muscled churned, answering her demand for speed. She got as far as the opening, where a twelve-foot sliding door hung at a disturbing angle, before he tackled her to the ground. She let out one, piercing scream before he buried her face in the dirt.

"Shut up!" he demanded in her ear. "Shut up, you stupid hellcat."

She thrashed like a madwoman, knowing instinctively this was it. The End. But the Steele blood running through her veins refused to let her die without a fight. She wouldn't cower, cry, or beg. She'd become the hellcat he accused her of being.

Her courageous stand lasted only a few satisfying moments before his fist clocked the side of her head, throwing her world into darkness.

CHAPTER FORTY-EIGHT

"BOSS, REMEMBER WHEN I MADE that crack about Gold Star and China?"

"Jax," Deke readjusted his earpiece, "no jokes. We're ready to head over to Harwood's." A contingent of SONR and Steeles geared up all around the fountain located in the park where he and Evie'd stumbled upon Gracie Gilbert.

"You'd be nicer to me if you knew what montage of happiness I'm about to spin your way."

"Jax—"

"Fine. Call me just the facts Jax." A maelstrom of typing echoed through his earpiece. "Once I got us back online, Taj tapped into Harwood's trucking schedule. Every month, our little wildlife trafficker's company makes a trip to Wilmington."

"You've got my attention. Go on."

"Wilmington has an international seaport. So many ships come and go from these ports that it's impossible for Service agents to inspect every shipload."

"Interesting, but?"

"Next to each of Harwood's Wilmington entries is a 'GS' designation."

"Gold Star," he murmured. "Harwood's entered the illegal wildlife trafficking arena on a global scale."

"*Ding, ding, ding.* I'm placing my bet on China."

His phone vibrated.

Vasquez.

"Good job. Let me know if anything else pops up." He peered down at his phone's display again. "Any more leads on Harwood's mole?"

"I came across an ID number—70821. Need your permission to bust into the Service's HRIS system."

His phone stilled. "In and out, Jax. I don't want your digital footprint on anyone's personnel file, except 70821. Understood?" The display on his phone lit again—*Vasquez.*

"You wound me, boss."

"Kick in the nitro, nerd."

"Will do. Jax out."

Deke hit the Answer button. "Conrad."

"What the hell are you doing, Deke?" Director Vasquez said by way of greeting. "My analyst tells me that you're still investigating your brother's case."

"Yes, sir."

"Want to explain why you disobeyed an order?"

"Because Gold Star and my brother's case are linked."

"Where'd you get that intel?"

"Couple different places."

"Where?"

Deke rubbed his eyes. "My brother—"

"For the love of God, Conrad. What are you thinking—?"

"Harwood has a mole inside the Service," Deke interrupted.

"What? How do you know?"

"While my brother sat in a filthy, animal crate for five days, without food or water, Harwood bragged about his spy embedded in the Service." *Maybe even a SONR agent.* "He knows all about our team."

Silence.

"Who has ID number 70821?"

Paper shuffling scratched through the speaker.

"Colin Fisher," Vasquez said.

He took a precious second to whisper a silent thank-you. Although he'd already bet his career on the leak not being a SONR team member, the fact remained that he'd had no way of knowing with absolute certainty, until this moment.

"You're not suggesting Colin's a spy."

"That's where the trail has led us."

"He's one of my best analysts."

"Did you order someone to shut down our communications?"

"You would've been the first to know, if I had."

"Thought so. Find out who has the power or authority to make us go black, and you'll have your mole."

"I'll get you up and running ASAP."

"Jax already took care of it."

"What if I'd ordered the shut down? Would Jax have reversed it?"

"Since you didn't, let's concentrate on who did."

"I want regular updates, from this point forward. *That's* an order."

"Yes, sir." He pocketed his phone.

"Everything okay?" Britt asked.

He lifted his booted foot to the fountain's ledge. "I'm going to enjoy stripping Harwood of everything he owns."

"I had a similar feeling last year when dealing with those trophy hunters."

"Thanks for coming when I called."

Britt slapped his back. "Glad I could return the favor."

"You just let them take my boy?" a new voice demanded.

Deke jerked his pant leg down to cover the sheathed knife before lowering his foot to the ground. Pivoting, he faced his father. The old man's eyes appeared hard and unbending, even in the darkness. His chest heaved and his beer gut stood out beneath his light flannel shirt. As per usual, Iris Conrad stood several feet behind her husband, though this time she held her chin up, her shoulders squared.

Betrayal burned in his veins. Why had she brought Mitch Conrad here? Now? When he needed to concentrate on locating Evie.

This was all his damn fault. Not wanting his mom to hear of Dylan's incarceration through the normal gossip mill, he'd called to give her a heads-up. He'd also assured her that Dylan would be safer behind bars. What he hadn't told her was that Dylan had agreed to do what he could to keep the police busy while he dealt with the Harwoods.

"For now," he said. "It's the best place for him."

"You're deciding now what's best for my son?"

"I don't have time for your false bluster. I'll take care of this."

"Don't even think about bringing the feds into family business."

"I'll bring in the city, county, state, whatever it takes. There's a lot you don't understand, and I don't have the time—or desire—to explain it to you."

"How the hell is a newsletter writer going to stop a cold-blooded killer?"

"With friends." Britt and Reid moved to his side.

"Lots of them." Reid, Keone, Wes, Rae, and Matteo flanked him, creating a semicircle of protection. Each shoved a piece of clothing aside to reveal a weapon.

His dad eyed the row of men and women. "Y'all are here to help my boy?"

"Yes, sir," Keone said. "Deke won't let anything happen to Dylan—" he slid a glance toward the Steele brothers, "—or Evie."

"How're you gonna find this devil?"

"That's why we're here," he said. "To go over what we know and set up a search."

"Sounds like a tail chaser. Don't you have any leads?"

"Yes, we have a lead. A solid one."

"Then what're doing here?"

"Daddy, please. Leave us to it."

He picked up movement out of the corner of his eye. Three figures huddled together at the edge of the fountain's courtyard.

"Amy, Noah," he said, confused by their appearance. Did the whole damn town know they were here? "It's awful late for a walk in the park."

Neither said a word, though Amy's anxious gaze settled on his mom.

"Is everything okay?" he asked. "Are you looking for someone?"

"I asked her to come." Iris Conrad stepped out of the shadow of her husband and strode to Amy's side.

"What're you talking about, Iris?" his dad asked. "What's going on?"

"When I found out that Dylan was in jail, I called Chief Middleton. It took some doing, but I finally got Charlie to tell me about Eli Harwood and that poor nurse." Iris put her arm around Amy. "Amy's been helping me with my computer skills at the library." She drew in a deep breath. "We've been confiding in each other about…different things."

"You never told me about these meetings," Mitch accused.

"For good reason."

"Why do you need to learn how to use the computer?"

"So I can get a job."

"You don't need one. There's plenty to do around the house."

"I'm not arguing with you about this, Mitch. My mind's made up."

"Who's going to hire a fifty-three-year-old housewife with no skills?"

"Enough." Deke stepped between his parents. "Daddy, go home. You've become a distraction at a time when we need to focus all our energy on saving Dylan and Evie."

"A distraction." Mitch's flat tone carried an undercurrent of danger. "Fine. Come on, Iris."

"No," his mom said.

"So it's that way now, is it?" Mitch glared at his wife. "If you don't come with me now, don't bother coming later."

His mom's determination wavered under her husband's ultimatum. Deke resisted telling his dad to stick his offer up his ass. In order for his mom to break free of her husband's oppression, she would have to make the decision to go.

"Goodbye, Mitch."

His dad's eyes widened before narrowing into vengeful slits. "You'll be getting nothing. Everything in that house belongs to me, bought and paid for."

"I'm not interested in your junk, anyway."

Mitch snarled, "Junk—"

"Time to go." Keone and Britt moved to escort Mitch Conrad away.

The moment his dad cleared the area, the cloud of tension hovering over them dissipated.

Deke rested a hand on his mom's shoulder. "You okay?"

"I will be." She gathered herself, shucking off Iris the wife and drawing forth Iris the mom. "Enough about me. Let's find your Evie and free my boy."

The guys began shuffling around behind him, as if his mother's command released them from the horror of watching his family's drama play out.

"Why'd you ask Amy and Noah to come?" he asked.

"Because she can help you locate Eli."

"How?"

"I might know where he's hiding," Amy said. "Might."

"Might is more than we have."

"There's an old, dilapidated barn on my father-in-law's property." Amy peered down at her son. "Eli's been seen coming and going from the building, but it appears empty."

"Sounds like we have ourselves a secret room," Wes said.

He crouched to speak with Noah. He nodded to the small boy clutching Amy's leg. "Who's your friend?"

"My brother Tobias."

"He has a bear claw like yours."

Noah's face scrunched into anger, though he said nothing.

Amy caught Deke's gaze. "His granddad—"

"Step-granddad," Noah corrected.

"Mr. Harwood gave the claw to Tobias."

"Rrrow!" Tobias smiled, nearly taking out Deke's eye before his mother caught his arm.

Deke waggled his fingers against Tobias's ribs, causing the boy to giggle. Then he turned to Noah and whispered in the boy's ear. "Don't worry about the claw. Many believe it's bad luck to carry one." Not a complete lie. Several native tribes saw the claw as a symbol of strength and courage. He'd never seen any mention of luck.

To Amy, he asked, "Mind if I speak to Noah about the barn?"

Amy cast a worried look between her boys. "I'd rather you not in front of Tobias."

"How about I give the cub a ride on my shoulders?" Matteo offered and waited for Amy's nod. "Hello, Tobias. I'm Matteo. Do you want to go for a ride? You can see for miles up here."

Tobias raised his hands in the air. "Yes!"

"Let's leave this—" Matteo tugged the claw from the boy's grip, "—with your mama so you can hang on." He made a big show of scooping the boy up onto his shoulders before disappearing into the park.

"Noah, what can you tell us about your Uncle Eli and the barn?" he asked.

The boy shrugged. "He spends a lot of time there."

"Does he have a special place in the barn?"

"Dunno. I've seen him walk inside, then he vanishes."

"Ever see him carry anything in or out of the barn?"

"A few times. I think he goes there mostly at night."

"Can you describe what he's carried inside?"

Another shrug. "Blankets, grocery bags, jugs of liquid."

Amy caught his eye before addressing her son. "Noah, why don't you go find your brother." She pointed into the dark. "I hear him over there."

"I'm headed that way myself," Wes said. "Mind if I walk with you?"

"No, sir."

"Got any good fishing holes around here?" Wes asked, as the two wandered off.

"What'd you have?" he asked.

"My mother-in-law missed fixing the evening meal."

"Why is that significant?"

"She never has before." Amy's attention fixed on her clasped hands. "Caleb and my father-in-law found her a few hours ago."

"Where?"

"Just inside the abandoned barn." She swallowed. "The dogs found her body. She'd been stabbed dozens of times."

"Eli?" Rae asked.

"No way to tell, but Eli's not answering his phone. Caleb's searching for his brother now."

"Do you think Eli's capable of killing his own mom?" he asked.

"Eli's always been odd. It's difficult to explain—"

"Don't worry about it. We understand."

"Tell my son about the incident a couple weeks ago," Iris said, giving Amy an encouraging squeeze.

"I walked into the living room to wake my mother-in-law from her nap and found Eli standing over her. Just standing there, staring at his mother."

He shared a look with the Steele brothers.

"The dude's snapped," Reid said.

"Get everyone together." He prayed Evie didn't do anything to set off Eli again. If he could kill his mom, he wouldn't think twice about murdering the woman who kicked his ass out the window. "We'll target the barn."

CHAPTER FORTY-NINE

EVIE'S RISE TO CONSCIOUSNESS WAS slow and nauseating. Her stomach roiled with each small movement, and she was pretty certain someone had driven a spear through one temple and out the other.

Where was her right arm? She waggled her fingers, or at least thought she had. But nothing moved.

Why weren't her eyes adjusting to the light? She'd never seen anything so black, so bottomless.

Slowly, she levered herself up with one arm and something slid on the ground beneath her. She patted the area and found her lifeless right arm. How long had it been trapped beneath her?

Smoothing a hand over her face, she sought the cloth covering her eyes.

Nothing.

Then she remembered. The trap door. The pit.

Sweet baby Jesus, no. Not the pit. *"No, no, no!"*

A frigid sweat covered her body and her breaths carved icicles down her throat. Her heart clamored against her chest wall. Her mind refused to settle. This wasn't an imagined crisis, like the other times. This was the real deal, and her body knew it. Knew she would die in this rotting hellhole.

An image of Deke crowded into her mind. His sexy lopsided grin and teasing blue eyes warmed her insides, and her chaotic thoughts began to calm. Second by passing second, Deke grounded her, with nothing more than an illusionary smile.

She'd take it. Anything to get her through this nightmare.

Pinpricks attacked her right arm, confirming the thing was still alive. When she tested her fingers, only the tips curled on her command. It was a start.

Sticking out her good hand, she grappled for a wall, a chair, a hay bale, anything. She caught nothing but air. What was that rancid smell? She recognized it—part organic, part chemical—but her scrambled brains failed to identify the source.

With effort, she eased to her feet, checking the ceiling above to make sure it wasn't low enough to conk her head. The moment she stood upright, a wave of disorientation struck, and her arms spread wide for balance.

"Dammit, Evie. Snap out of it."

Her head hurt, but not so bad as to screw up her equilibrium. At least, she didn't think so. Perhaps she had a mild concussion. Or could the absolute darkness be playing tricks on more than her senses? Maybe this was the reaction inmates had to solitary confinement. She'd always assumed it was the lack of human contact. Now she would have to reassess her assumption.

Shuffling her feet forward, she once again spread her arms wide, searching, for anything that might lead the way out of here. The farther she traveled from her original location, the worse the stench. She'd finally figured out the odor.

Rotting flesh.

"Oh, good Lord, that's foul."

Had a rat gotten stuck between the walls and died? Or a raccoon? It happened, especially in old farmhouses, where mice can become trapped in the walls. You just gotta wait out the stink.

Her shin caught on something and all thoughts of

walls and rodents vanished. Reaching down, her fingertips probed the object. Long, narrow, and an odd combination of soft and hard.

Moving her hands to the right, she continued prodding at the object—until she reached a boot.

She screamed and would have shot backwards but for the hand that clasped around her arm.

"Hello, Evie Steele."

Eli Harwood. He'd been down here with her the whole time. Listening to her struggles? Watching her? How?

A bone-rattling shiver took hold of her entire body. What did he have in store for her? Nothing good. He'd killed his mother because she'd called him a terrible name. What would he do to the woman who'd started the chain of events?

"There's nowhere for you to go."

"Could you turn a light on, please?"

"Afraid of the dark?"

"I can't see anything."

"Just as well. I doubt you'd like the view."

"Please. It doesn't have to be much. A candle will do."

"Don't say I didn't warn you."

A match strike, followed by a blinding flare of light. It took a while for her eyes to readjust. When they did, she noticed Eli lighting a fat candle sitting on top of a short wooden table in the shape of a drum, with an intricately carved wildlife scene decorating the exterior. The beautiful piece of furniture looked out-of-place in this dank underground cave.

Eli sat on the dirt floor, his back to the wall. An elaborate pair of goggles in his lap. His posture appeared too relaxed, his eyes too satiated. Another man sat next to him. Head cocked. Mouth slack.

"Is h-he dead?"

"Yes."

The dead man carried some resemblance to Eli, though his features were more sleek, less bold. "Who is he?"

"Don't matter anymore."

She couldn't take her eyes off the man's neck. The severe angle didn't look natural. It looked...broken in half. *Dear Lord.*

"What are we doing down here?"

"Waiting."

"For what?"

"Maybe it's a whom."

"Deke?" she whispered.

A sickening excuse for a smile appeared. The predatory glint in her captor's eyes promised that her time was limited to however long it would take Deke to find her. Would he? Find her? How would he ever track them to this obscure location?

The pit was much more spacious than she'd expected, though she couldn't see the entire room due to the limitations of the candle's reach. A red and white cooler rested against one wall near a mattress with neat bedding. Clothes pegs dotted another wall, and at the opposite end of the pit stood a large rectangular table with thick iron cuffs on each side and at one end. Beyond the table dangled heavy chains and another, much smaller table housed bright objects gleaming in the candlelight.

She took an involuntary step backwards as her gaze surveyed the rest of the room. An enormous concrete basin was tucked into a deep, shadowy alcove. Sitting in front of the alcove rested a pair of women's sandals and a pile of clothes. Something about the basin and clothes made the hairs at the back of her neck prick to life. Lifting her nose, she sniffed the air, like a canine tracking a scent. She couldn't be sure, but the odor seemed to be emanating from the alcove. Again, she detected a strong chemical and something earthier.

"I warned you that the view wouldn't be pleasant."

Heavy footsteps above snapped her attention away from the basin. She didn't stop to think about the consequences or the identity of the stranger or even if the person could hear her through the floor. She acted on instinct. Pure self-preservation. She screamed. At a pitch she didn't even know she could attain.

Eli flew at her, covering her mouth, swinging her around. Before she could catch her breath, he had her back pinned flush against his front. The close proximity made her stomach crawl like a mass of worms.

"You shouldn't have done that." Eli's voice contained one part fury, one part fear.

The pit's hatch opened, and the hand covering her mouth grew damp.

A work boot appeared on the top rung of the wooden ladder followed by a pair of long legs covered in worn jeans. A lean torso wrapped in a red polo shirt emerged next. Sterling-gray hair cut military style glinted in the flickering light.

When the stranger faced her, she was struck by his resemblance to Eli. An older version, a harder version, a one-eyed version.

The moment he saw her, his hard features transformed into something unstable. He zeroed in on Eli. Then on the dead guy. "What have you done, son?"

Son? This was Blaze Harwood? Wildlife trafficker? City councilman?

Eli removed his hand from her mouth, but kept his arm secured around her middle.

"Don't make me ask you again. I sent you to take care of the agent and you bring me a woman."

"She's Conrad's girlfriend."

Blaze studied her. Roamed over her body like she was an unfamiliar species. "I'm not interested in Conrad's women. I'm interested in shutting him down before he ruins me and my business."

"He'll come for her."

"When?"

"Soon, I'm sure."

"Did you lay a trail? To my backyard?"

She could almost hear Eli's gears churning. If he said

yes, he'd win the old man's approval for his cleverness, but would lose points for leading a federal agent to their doorstep, removing any doubt of their involvement in the recent events.

"You didn't bring her here to catch Conrad, did you, son?"

Eli swallowed hard, though he said nothing.

"What're her transgressions?"

"She made me lose face in front of mama."

"How?"

Again, Eli retreated into himself.

"Is this why you killed your mama?"

Eli's eyes flickered.

At Blaze's blunt assessment, a small ray of hope ignited in her chest. He seemed to understand the volatility of the situation. Could he get her out of here?

"The dogs found her body," Blaze said. "All the damage they did still couldn't hide what caused her death. Your brother and I had to put her in the pot."

Eli's attention moved to the basin. "In a few days, all the evidence will be lost."

Bile crept into her throat as the meaning of their words sank in. She would never get out of here alive.

Blaze began a slow circuit of the pit. "Did Greta say something to upset you?" When Eli remained mute, Blaze slashed his hand through the air, connecting with Eli's cheek and the back of her head. Eli lost his grip on her waist and she stumbled away.

"You don't decide whether or not you'll answer me," Blaze yelled, getting into Eli's face. "I decide. Hear me? I decide."

"Yes, sir."

"How'd she make you lose face with your mama?"

"She threw me out a second story window and injured my back."

"What'd your mama say?"

Diamonds carved the contours of Eli's face. In his features, hatred burned. "She called me a pussy."

"You responded by stabbing her to death."

"Mama's always ripping on me."

He stopped near the dead man. "What about your brother? What'd he do?"

Brother? Her breath stopped.

"He tried to beat me for killing Mama. I warned him, Daddy. I warned him never to touch me again."

Blaze sighed. "How're you going to clean up this mess?"

Eli glanced between the table, the alcove, and her. "I'll wait for Conrad. Kill him, then this one."

Blaze canted his head, studying Evie. "What's your name?"

"Evie Steele."

"Are your people looking for you? Don't lie."

"I suspect so. They'll overturn every rock until they do."

Blaze chewed on his inner cheek before addressing his son. "Keep your shenanigans to a minimum. We can't take the chance of anyone finding her here."

Shenanigans?

Panic like nothing she'd experienced before rose up to suffocate her. She tried to bring Deke's image to mind, but fear was eating away at the edges of her sanity. This man was no savior and this place was no pit.

Blaze Harwood was a frigging enabler, and he'd just given his psychotic son permission to make her his next torture victim.

CHAPTER FIFTY

DEKE CROUCHED DOWN AT THE woodland's edge and waited for the rest of his team to get into position. To his right, Keone adjusted his night vision goggles and Rae checked her weapon one more time. Wes and Reid were making their way around to the rear of the old barn while Britt and Matteo kept an eye on the perimeter.

"All looks quiet back here," Wes said into Deke's earpiece.

"Same here," Matteo said.

"Unit One going in." He moved at a good clip across the hundred yards separating them and the barn. Keone on his six. Their movements were low and methodical. ARs at the ready. Rae remained at the tree line in case things went bad. The location allowed her to respond swiftly in any direction, if an emergency arose.

The open field was far from ideal, leaving them vulnerable to attack on all sides. Dylan had seen no evidence of a security force during his imprisonment. In fact, Blaze Harwood seemed content to trust the safekeeping of his product to an alarm system, alone. A system that could probably be disabled with nothing more than a pair of wire clippers.

Harwood was either ignorant of technology or frugal to the point of negligence.

Left, front, right—he swept the area in a constant rhythm, keeping the forest's edge, the barn, and the far away farmhouse constantly in his sights.

The large sliding door, marking the front entrance of the barn, hung at a dangerous angle. Keone, stationed on the opposite side of the opening, nodded his readiness.

He turned to slip inside.

A scream pierced his eardrum, halting his action.

His hand flew to his earpiece, intending to rip the thing out. He caught Wes's cursing and froze, pressing it deeper into the canal, instead.

"Report." He glanced around the barn, spotting empty stalls, antique equipment, and clumps of rotting hay.

Dogs barked in the distance.

Shit.

Reid said, "Wes got caught in a fucking bear trap."

"How bad is it?"

"Unknown. At least a broken ankle."

"On my way," Rae said.

"Get Wes back to the vehicles and call for an ambulance, if necessary."

"Leave me be," Wes said. "I can keep lookout."

"My order stands." If Wes found one of the old-style bear traps, he'd be lucky to still have full use of his foot. "Unit Three, report."

Neither Britt or Matteo responded. "Unit Three, come in?"

Silence.

"Matteo?"

Silence.

"Britt."

"We're here," Matteo said, out of breath. "Had a come-to-Jesus moment with a pack of dogs. What do you need?"

Angry canine snarls leapt through the engineer's mic.

"Stay sharp. Wes got caught in a bear trap. Where there's one, there're others." Deke glanced over his shoulder as if he could see Matteo's position. "Once you've made your sweep, send Britt to help Reid carry Wes to safety."

"I can take a shoulder, Commander," Rae said.

"Not for that long a distance." For her height, Rae was incredibly strong, but she wouldn't be able to support Wes's weight all the way back to the vehicles.

Once again, Keone signaled his readiness and Deke slipped beneath the awkward hanging barn door, careful of potential booby traps. With him in the lead, they cruised from stall to stall, searching for Evie, bracing for more of Harwood's surprises.

It didn't take him long to give the all-clear signal. He and Keone stood in the middle of the barn, neither one willing to vacate the building.

"Do you feel it?" he whispered.

"The barn's not empty."

"She's here."

He scanned the upper level. Not much still existed of the loft floor. At some point over the past couple decades, the Harwoods had either reclaimed the wood for other projects or used it for kindling.

If not up, then their search must go down.

After pointing at the barn floor, he made a swirling motion with his hand. Keone nodded and set off to find an entrance. Deke cut off in the opposite direction. A lot of abandoned machinery cluttered the barn. They didn't find an obvious door on their first sweep. The second time, they investigated every nook and cranny.

Nothing.

"Dammit." He couldn't shake the feeling that Evie was right under his nose. "We're going to have to make some noise."

"Where do you want to start?" Keone asked.

He peered to his right, where a large rusted wheelbarrow loaded with concrete blocks and fence posts resided. "This is as good as any."

After moving the wheelbarrow, they tested various sections of the floor.

Still nothing.

Matteo joined them, and they proceeded to look under every bit of machinery. When they came up empty-handed, he almost called a stop to the search. Why would Harwood have bear traps protecting this old barn, if nothing important were housed here? Made no sense.

"Is there something different about this stall?" Keone asked.

"Different how?"

"Can't put my finger on it." Keone pointed toward the next stall. "Stand in front of that one, then this one."

He did as instructed. "I see what you're talking about, but I'll be damned if I can figure out what's wrong."

"The depth is off," Matteo said, his engineer mind identifying what they couldn't. "The one in front of you has to be—" he stood by the partition separating them, studying one stall, then the other "—at least two feet shorter than this one."

Taking slow, careful steps, he entered the smaller stall. His boot slid over the floor, pressing down, here and there, searching for a hidden door. When nothing gave way, he paused near the back wall.

Nothing appeared out of place, though he might be missing a nuance with his night vision goggles on.

"See a latch or rope?" Matteo asked.

He shook his head. His gaze made methodical passes over the entire wall.

"Anything unusual?"

"Maybe. Can't say that I've studied many horse stalls before."

He splayed his hands over the wall and pushed. Nothing gave way. He moved to the left and tried again. Nada.

A mental clock ticked in his head. Evie'd been under Eli's power for almost two hours. Two hours with a murderer. If he didn't find her soon, the odds of him ever finding her became almost nonexistent.

Frustrated, he reared back and slammed his boot heel against the panels. The old planks splintered beneath the force, and his foot met air on the other side. When he jerked his leg back, the wall came with it.

"Damn," Matteo said. "Way to find a secret passage, Commander."

With their cover now blown for sure, his heart raced. Every second mattered. Every decision, life or death.

If he took the ladder, Harwood could pick them off, one by one, as they descended. The only way to get the upper hand would be through surprise.

Peering down the narrow opening, he gauged the distance from his location to the ground below to be about eight feet.

He secured his AR and straddled the opening. Glancing between Keone and Matteo, he mouthed, "Ready?"

Rather than drop straight down, he grasped the lip of the narrower side and used his body weight as momentum. Like a trapeze artist, he arched through the air and landed on the balls of his feet. The impact jarred every bone he possessed, from phalange to cranium.

With his AR set against his shoulder again, he stayed low and ran toward a thick support beam. Not a lot of protection, but good in a pinch.

In his three-sixty check, he realized several things at once. One—Evie and Harwood were nowhere in sight. Two—someone had spent a lot of time down here. Three—someone was rotting.

A man slumped against the wall. He approached him carefully. Using his boot, he kicked the man's foot. No response. He kicked it again. Nothing. Moving closer, he got a better look at the guy's features.

Caleb Harwood.

Even with night vision goggles, he could see the vacant stare, the slack mouth, the unnatural angle of his neck.

"Clear," he whispered into his mic. "One dead body."

Seconds later, Keone and Matteo dropped into the cellar-like room.

"Jesus," Matteo said. "Something reeks down here."

Too new to SONR, Matteo hadn't enough experience yet to recognize decomposing human flesh. Once an agent's olfactories identified the scent, they never forgot it.

If the stench didn't tell the story, the sturdy wooden table with the iron restraints told him all he needed to know about Harwood and what went on down here.

Dear God, had that maniac brought Evie into this pit of evil? She had to be frightened out of her mind. He sure as hell was.

"Sonofabitch." Matteo stumbled back from an alcove that held a large concrete-looking basin. Lined up before it, two piles of clothes. "Do you know what's floating in there?"

Deke stared at the yellow tee and capris stacked on top of a familiar pair of orange shoes.

His vision blurred and his legs grew rubbery.

No. No. Nooooo!

Rage boiled in his gut. His thoughts scrambled in a thousand directions before they narrowed to one.

Harwood did this. Harwood killed Evie. *Harwood's going to fucking* die.

"Found a tunnel." Keone shoved aside a wall, pegged with hooks. The hooks held clothing, rope, and a sundry of other items.

Hope sparked to life, dampening his fury. Evie might still be alive. He had to believe it. If he'd been uncertain of his feelings for her before now, he was no longer. He loved Evelyn Steele and he'd annihilate anyone who so much as breathed foul air her way.

"Remind you of anything?" Keone asked.

"The escape route from the Distributor's storage building," he said.

"The Bamford raid," Matteo added.

He nodded, as all the dots of his trafficking case

began to connect with Gracie Gilbert's murder. All the bits of intelligence converging into one explosive resolution. With Evie—innocent Evie—caught in the middle. He peered into the endless tunnel, vowing the Distributor—Harwood—wouldn't win this time.

"Let's finish this."

Evie held her restrained wrists close to her torso, hoping to retain as much body heat as possible. Her bra and panties were little protection against the tunnel's damp chill.

Would Deke recognize her clothes piled near the basin? Even if he didn't, would he assume one of the bundles could be hers?

When Blaze had caught a faint scrape on the floor above them, he'd ordered her to undress. As her trembling fingers had fumbled with the button of her capris, she'd been certain they were going to kill her and throw her in the basin of chemicals with Mrs. Harwood. Her only consolation had been that she wouldn't have to endure hours of torture.

How long had they been hiking through this underground path? It felt like hours, but more likely ten minutes. The rough-cut tunnel stood only five-and-a-half feet high and spanned a mere three-and-a-half feet wide.

It must have taken the Harwoods years to construct this escape route. But why such an elaborate getaway from an abandoned barn? Had they once used the barn to house illegal contraband? Maybe they'd outgrown the structure and moved the operation to a larger facility.

She did her best to keep her eyes on Blaze's back and her mind off the confining nature of the tunnel. Every time her panic surfaced, she envisioned Deke. His rogue's smile, his incredible abs, his caring nature. He kept her grounded when all she wanted to do was give in to her hysteria.

Her bare foot caught on another hard object, and she bit her lip to keep from crying out. Crumbled dirt and small stones littered the tunnel, making it impossible for her to avoid. By the time she reached the end, her feet would be shredded.

"Quiet," Eli commanded from behind.

All three of them stopped and canted their heads toward the direction they'd come. It took several seconds for her to key in on what had alerted Eli. A rhythmic swish of clothing against clothing echoing down the tunnel.

"Cut the light, Daddy."

The light flashed out, and she could no longer see her bound hands. "Help me!" she shouted, hoping her voice carried to her rescuers.

"Evie!" Deke shouted in the distance.

Eli's flashlight glanced off her cheek. Pain exploded in her head. Thank goodness his shot had been a blind one or he could have done some real damage.

"If you make another sound, I'll slice your throat and leave you to bleed out in front of your boyfriend."

Images of Gracie and Rachel crowded into her mind. She would never want Deke to see her that way.

The lack of light affected their speed but not their progress. Minutes later, she plowed into Blaze's back when he paused to scale a ladder. A circle of moonlight soon appeared above them, allowing a wave of August humidity to billow into the tunnel, knocking away the chill.

Once his father cleared the opening, Eli urged her up. The narrow metal rungs hurt like the dickens. No amount of readjusting her foothold could alleviate the discomfort, either. With her hands tied, she had to leap to grasp the next rung. It worked for her twice, but she missed the third one and crashed to the ground.

"Get up there!" Eli growled.

"My hands. I can't climb."

Cursing, Eli cut her restraints. He glanced behind them before pushing her toward the ladder. "Hurry."

When she surfaced on the other side, a large, strong hand grabbed her wrist. She waited until she had firm footing before she pinched the fleshy area beneath his arm and twisted with all her might. He released her on a cry of pain, and she slammed her foot into the back of his knee and smacked the palms of her hands against his ears.

She bolted.

Not an easy task, considering the grass reached her waist and tangled around her ankles. She had no idea where the tunnel had dumped out. All she comprehended was that this might be her best opportunity for escape.

Lord knew she'd had plenty of experience outrunning the opposite sex. With four older brothers, she'd perfected the art of strike, dodge, run—and hide.

"Get her!" Blaze yelled.

She pushed herself to go faster and faster and faster until she spotted a faint light twinkling to her left. She veered in that direction. Boots pounded behind her. The light turned into a door, the door into a house, the house into a refuge.

Bullets sprayed in the distance, and Evie's mad dash stumbled to a halt.

Deke.

A shadow barreled toward her, and she took off toward the house again. But those precious few seconds had cost her. She made it to the porch and shoved through the back door a mere second before Eli snatched a handful of her hair.

Inside the kitchen, a familiar face stared at the tableau with wide eyes and a hand over her heart. "Evie?" Amy asked.

"Go back to doing the dishes and forget this," Eli warned.

"What's going on, Eli?"

"I said mind your own business."

Evie's mind whipped through the connections and realized Amy must be married to one of the Harwoods, which meant Evie'd run to the least safe place on earth. No wonder Amy had been terrified that her husband would find out about her visit to the Med Mobile.

Noah.

He had to be in the house somewhere. Might even be creeping down the stairs right now to investigate the commotion.

She mustered a reassuring smile. "It's okay, Amy. Do as he said."

Amy's attention dropped down to Evie's half-naked body. "But—"

"Go to Noah," she said in her most commanding Steele voice.

Amy nodded her understanding, fear marring her pretty features.

Once Eli had her back outside, she knew that he would kill her for bringing his perversion into his family's home. What would he do to Amy and Noah? She couldn't allow one more person to suffer at this man's hands.

Sanity splintered in her head, and her body swung into motion. She forearmed Eli in the nose and kneed him in the nuts.

"Arghh, fucking hellcat!"

When he bent forward, she didn't take off. She climbed onto his back and wrapped one arm around his head and one around his neck. She squeezed the pressure points, ignoring his thrashing and cursing.

"Evie!" Deke called.

All her concentration remained on Eli. On bringing him down. On protecting Deke and Amy and Noah.

"Evie," Deke said, closer.

Eli's legs gave way. Still she held on.

"Evie, sweetheart. You can let go."

Deke gently pried her arms from her captor's neck

and lifted her from the ground. "You're safe now." He pulled her into his arms, held her tight. "You're safe now."

Not removing her face from the center of Deke's chest, she asked, "D-did I kill him?" She didn't know what answer would devastate her more—yes or no.

"Unfortunately, no," Keone replied.

A tremble started low in her stomach before spreading into each of her limbs.

"Here," a feminine voice said.

"Thank you, Amy." Deke covered her shoulders with something long and warm and soft. The breeze no longer touched her bare legs.

Feeling less vulnerable, she drew in a deep breath and backed out of Deke's arms. Keone had Eli's hands restrained behind his back, and Amy set a pair of flip-flops next to Evie's feet.

Tears of gratitude stung her eyes, then they widened when she found no sign of Blaze Harwood.

"The father." She gripped Deke's forearm. "Where's Blaze Harwood?" She remembered the gunfire and began searching Deke for wounds. "Did he shoot you?"

Deke clasped her hands between his, warming them, gentling them. "He tried to lock the tunnel's opening on us. We gave him a few reasons not to."

"He's dead?"

"The SOB's right here," Matteo said, leading a disheveled Blaze into the halo of porch light.

"You've all made a big mistake," Blaze said. "I'll be out of jail before morning."

"Fat chance of that, old man," Matteo said. "We've got you dead to rights on this one."

"What do you have? Me coming across a girl who was fleeing my deranged son?"

The tunnel was so dark that Deke and his men wouldn't have been able to see Blaze at the head of their line.

"We have Evie's side of the story."

"Who's going to believe an outsider over a city councilman?"

"It's true," Amy said. "Everyone falls in line with my father-in-law's wishes. He knows too many people. Has too much information on everyone."

Blaze smiled. "Let me go, and I'll forget about how this Italian used excessive force."

"We found your storage buildings," Deke said. "How're you going to explain away the illegal wildlife contraband?"

"I don't know what you're talking about."

"The buildings are in your name. Your son held my brother against his will. In a cage."

"What my son did in one of the storage buildings has nothing to do with me."

"My brother said you were there. That you ordered my death. How are you going to explain that one away?"

"Is this the brother that was in a relationship with a drug dealer? The one who fled a crime scene? The one who's been in and out of jail for petty crimes all his life—and even now sits in a cell?" Blaze chuckled. "Do you really think the good people of Creede are going to believe him over me?"

"You can have one bad mark against you," Deke said, "but I don't think there's a jury in the world who would believe a man who has that much bad luck in one lifetime, let alone one evening."

"Amy will swear that I've been home all night." Blaze's gray eyes sawed into his daughter-in-law. "Won't you, dear."

Amy dropped her gaze to the ground.

Evie pushed her hands through the robe's armholes and secured the sash at her waist before moving to stand by Amy's side. "This might be your only chance to shed yourself of this family. Don't let him bully you into lying for him."

"Haven't I provided for Tobias? Haven't I made sure

your boys have food and decent schooling? Haven't I paid for the clothes on your back and theirs?"

"My husband—"

"No! Caleb couldn't cover his ass in a rainstorm. I'm the one you owe your loyalty to. I'm the one who's taken care of you and your bastard."

Amy's head whipped up. "Noah's not a bastard."

"He sure as hell isn't my grandson."

"Then you won't mind if he leaves."

"No, I won't."

"We'll be out of your house by sunup."

"You're not going anywhere."

"That'll be hard for you to enforce while you're molding away in jail."

Blaze lunged forward. "You ungrateful whore!"

Deke stepped in front of Amy while Matteo got the older man back under control.

She held Amy close. "It's okay. Deke and the others won't allow him near you ever again." To Deke, she said, "Eli admitted to killing his mother."

"Is that true, boy?" Blaze demanded.

"You know it is," Evie said. "He told you so in the pit, and you didn't seem too choked up about it, either."

"What pit?"

Anger forced Evie to seek help in the least likely place. Glancing down, she found Eli's eyes open, staring straight ahead. How long had he been conscious?

When Eli said nothing, Blaze stretched out a foot to kick his son in the ribs, but Matteo's firm grip only allowed him to hit air.

Eli rolled over and popped up on his knees. "Deranged son?"

He'd been awake for most of the conversation. Waiting for his chance to escape? Or to see what depths his father would sink to survive?

"You're not exactly normal now, are you?"

"You dare criticize me after what you made me do as a child? Made me…watch? *You're* calling *me* deranged?"

Eli lunged, plowing a shoulder into his father's gut. They both went down, and Eli started head butting his father, over and over and over.

The violent action happened so fast, the only person in a position to help Blaze was Matteo, who half went down with the two Harwoods.

Within seconds, Deke and Keone had the younger Harwood on his feet. His forehead ripped open from numerous contacts with his dad's nose and teeth. Blaze didn't fare well, either. Blood covered his face, and Matteo had to roll him onto his side so he wouldn't choke on his own blood.

Red and blue lights bounced off the trees as three squads hurried up Harwood's long drive.

"Family reunion's over," Deke said.

"I haven't seen my husband Caleb for quite some time."

"We'll find him."

Evie noted the look Deke shared with Keone. So they'd noticed Caleb in the pit. It would appear no one wanted to be the bearer of bad news at the moment.

What a family. She would never take hers for granted again. Okay, she would. But she would always make sure they knew how much she loved them.

"Mama?" Noah stood with the screen door open, holding the hand of a smaller boy's.

Amy squeezed her hand. "Thank you."

"I'm the one who's grateful." She plucked at the robe. "You saved me from a great deal of embarrassment." She nodded toward the boys. "Go on. They need you now."

As she watched Amy bundle her kids back into the house, she wondered what would become of them. How would Amy explain the disappearance of their entire family to two young boys?

A light touch to her elbow drew her attention. "Are you okay?" Deke whispered.

"I think so."

"They didn't...hurt you, did they?"

"Not that way. But I don't think I'll ever be able to get that barn cellar out of my mind." She dug her fingers into her forehead. "There was a large basin…the smell…clothes on the ground…I c-couldn't tell Amy about her husband."

He drew her away from the activity around them and then folded her into his arms. She fought back the avalanche of tears that wanted to fall.

"Try not to think about what you saw or heard," he said. "I know from experience that following that kind of advice isn't always in your control. But do your best to focus on your family, your patients, your friends. Anything sunny and happy that has the power to push back the darkness."

"I already know what will help me forget."

"What's that?"

"You." She lifted her head from his shoulder. "When I started to have a panic attack—"

"Panic attack?"

"I've been getting them for years."

"Why don't I know this?"

"My family doesn't even know."

"Why keep it from them?"

"My first attack came on the same day Mom and Britt dropped me off at college. I didn't say anything, because I didn't want them making it a big deal. College is hard enough. I didn't want to add familial humiliation to the mix." She shrugged. "After that, it just never came up."

"You had an attack in the cellar."

"When I woke and realized Eli had thrown me in an underground pit, I grounded myself with images of you. You saved me."

He cupped her cheek and kissed her forehead. "I will always be there to ground you." His kisses moved down her nose and against each eyelid. "Always."

Despite the horrific events of the last several hours, she managed a smile. "Is that a declaration, Deke Conrad?"

"You tell me, my love." His mouth molded to hers. The gentleness of his kiss, the sweetness, enticed her. She slipped her tongue into his mouth, tangling with his, loving his delicious warmth, his taste.

Someone barked an order in the distance, and she reluctantly released him. "Tasted like a definite yes to me."

He kissed her forehead, her nose, her cheek. "I was so damn scared I'd be too late."

"You're weren't."

"If Amy hadn't come forward about the barn—"

She pressed her fingers against his lips. "You would have found me some other way."

"You can't know that."

"I do. You're unstoppable." She sent him a small smile. "Something we both have in common." Her attention drifted to his shoulder. "I've decided to postpone graduate school for a year or so." The declaration launched between her teeth, out of nowhere.

"What?"

Putting on her big Evie smile, she said, "I think I should practice my nursing skills for a while before moving on to a position with so much responsibility."

"What are you doing, Evie?" Even in the dark, anger illuminated his blue eyes.

"I'm working on a way for us to be together."

"Giving up graduate school's the best way?"

"To be honest, I haven't figured it all out yet."

"No."

"Maybe I could attend part-time, instead."

"No, Evie."

"It's a good compromise."

"I won't let you set aside your career. Not for the likes of me."

"Likes of you?" Sadness gripped her throat. "You make it sound like you're not worthy of—what? What aren't you worthy of?"

"Stealing your happiness."

A bomb of silence dropped between them.

"Oh, Deke. Don't you see?" She cupped his face in her hands. "My happiness depends on you. I love you. I would give up my life if I thought that's what it would take to finally be yours—and you to be mine."

"You'd give up your career, your dream for me?"

She rose up on her toes and kissed him. "Yes."

A tear dropped on her hand. "I can't let you do it."

Her heart tilted…then fell. She was out of ideas. Out of ways to win over Deke Conrad.

Out of hope.

She closed her eyes, and her fingers began to curl, letting him go.

Large hands skimmed up her back, trapping her against his body.

Her eyes flew open, and she found his solemn gaze on hers.

"I'm not letting you give up your career—and I'm not letting you go."

She blinked. "Okay."

One corner of his mouth hiked into his irresistible grin. "Is that all you've got to say?"

"Uh-huh. We'll figure it out." She traced every line of his beloved face. "As long as you love me."

"I've loved you half of my life, Evie Steele, and you know it."

The anxiety, the aches, the doubts flew out of her heart. She couldn't hold back her grin. "I suspected," she said in a singsong voice.

"You are going to be nothing but trouble."

"Don't pretend like it's a surprise. I haven't changed my stripes in years."

He laughed. "No you haven't."

"So it's settled?"

He drew a finger down her nose and over her lips. "It's settled."

She grinned. "Now, let's go find me some clothes."

EPILOGUE

Three Weeks Later, Tupelo Hill

DEKE STRODE AROUND THE PERIMETER of the crowd, searching for Evie. The Steeles had been planning this celebration for weeks, and he hoped they managed to pull off the big surprise after all of their hard work and behind-the-scenes scheming.

Judging by the number of people in attendance, he guessed half the town was milling around the vast grounds of Tupelo Hill—and then some. Lord knew it'd taken him a good fifteen minutes to hike his way up the long drive.

"'Bout time you made it, Conrad." Britt handed him a beer. "Brynne's been keeping Evie busy at her shop until she got word of your arrival."

"My arrival? Why?"

"Mom insisted on waiting. Seems you've won over the old girl's heart." Britt pointed to a pint-sized, salt-and-pepper-haired woman. "Here she comes."

Joan Steele made a beeline for Deke, giving him a big hug and kiss on the cheek. "Thank goodness you made it. Thought I was going to have to send one of my boys after you."

"Sorry, Miss Joan. I had to help my mom with something."

"Oh, well, think nothing more of it. Gotta take care of family." She waggled a finger over the partygoers. "Everyone's having too good of a time to even realize Evie's not here yet. Which reminds me, I'd better let Micki know it's time to retrieve her sister." She eyed Britt. "Is Jonah ready?"

"Yes, ma'am."

She smiled. "I knew he would be. I'm blessed with dependable kids." She slanted a sly look at Deke. "When's Evie going to add you to the Steele brood?"

"U-um."

Britt choked back a laugh.

Miss Joan patted Deke's arm. "You can't go wrong with my Evie." Then she scampered off to find her eldest daughter.

"Wish I could've caught your fish-eyed expression on camera," Britt said. "Special Agent Deke Conrad, able to level an elaborate trafficking ring, but buckled under Mama Steele's formidable, matchmaking eye."

"Shut it." He and Evie were still finding their footing after the Harwood family takedown. The incident had understandably shaken her net of safety, and he'd spent hours in interviews, doing paperwork, and getting his ass chewed by Director Vasquez.

Even with all that was going on, he and Evie had managed to spend all their evenings together. Sometimes talking, sometimes locked in a comforting embrace, sometimes bringing each other to passionate climax.

"Wes doing okay?"

"As salty as ever. Once his ankle's healed, he'll start several weeks of rehabilitation."

"Glad they managed to save his foot."

"Rae gets most of the credit. If not for her field triage, we'd be having a different discussion." Deke took a swallow of beer. "Thanks again for helping us relocate the live animals from Harwood's storage units."

"It's a damn shame about the cub."

"The good news is that the Harwood family business is dead and that Blaze and Eli are going to stand trial for their crimes."

"Amen. How'd things go today?"

"As expected." After thirty-seven years of marriage, Iris Conrad had given her husband the boot, with him and Dylan by her side. "Lots of bluster and 'this is my house,' but he packed up his necessities and left. Dylan and Dara are helping her box up the rest."

"Let's hope you and I will be better fathers than ours, when the time comes."

An image of Evie, heavy with his child, filled his mind. Although doubt still crept into his thoughts at odd times, he'd moved beyond worrying about the whatifs, couldbes, and ifonlys. Not age, brothers, education, or serial killers were going to keep him and Evie apart.

"Mama sent me over here to liven things up." Reid strode into their midst. "Said you two looked too serious."

He released a tight breath, thankful for the interruption.

"Any new news on the Harwood case?" Reid asked.

"We found another hidden compartment in the abandoned barn. In the cellar." The scent of rotting flesh still stained his nostrils. They'd found eleven skulls at the bottom of the basin. According to Eli, his father had been torturing "stray" people in the barn's cellar for years. Made his sons watch. "Blaze Harwood kept the bulk of his business records in the cellar. Didn't trust technology. He'd amassed a multimillion dollar business in seven short years."

"Anything on Gold Star?" Reid asked.

"A codename for an elaborate Chinese distribution network." Taj had tracked Harwood's recent shipment from Wilmington to China.

Britt shook his head. "Right here in our backyard."

"The Chinese have an insatiable appetite for black bear gallbladders—and other exotic animal parts—and they're willing to pay top dollar for what they want."

"At least Harwood won't be contributing to their demand any longer," Reid said. "Still can't figure out what the Chinese's attraction is to bear parts."

"Long-held beliefs about their medicinal properties. They believe the gallbladder cures illnesses like fever, diabetes, liver disease, and more."

"Did Vasquez confirm Colin Fisher as Harwood's spy?" Britt asked.

Deke nodded. "He's a cousin to the Harwood clan."

"Damn hillbillies," Reid said.

"I'm pretty sure we have as many relatives on this mountain as Harwood," Britt said.

"I hope you ladies aren't planning another family rescue mission without me." Grif Steele joined them. Though his words carried a teasing quality, the hard lines marring the corners of his eyes suggested he might never forgive his brothers. Ditto for Jonah and Micki.

"Instead of whining," Reid said, "you should be thanking us."

"Oh?"

"We saved your fancy shoes from smelling like cellar rot."

Grif stepped forward. "How about I shove my fancy shoes up your—"

Deke moved between them. "Your brothers kept mum about the operation out of respect for my situation. They weren't any happier about it than you are."

Grif's razor-sharp gaze landed on Deke. "I'm not happy with you, either. But Evie's safe, so we'll put this one behind us." He pointed his beer at Britt and Reid. "Jonah and I will settle this with the two of you later, in the woods. With guns."

Deke shot Britt a glance.

"Paintball." Britt cranked his lips into a smile. "Welcome to the family."

"Here comes the birthday girl," Reid said.

Four sets of male eyes followed Micki's vehicle as it

barreled up the gravel drive, with windows down. Three smiling females, hair whipping in the breeze, came to a jarring halt on the grass not far from where he and the Steele brothers stood.

All his tension floated away when a pair of warm blue sparkling eyes located him.

Evie.

"There's my baby girl." Mama wrapped Evie in a sweet, cookie-scented cocoon, forcing her to break eye contact with Deke.

"What is all this about?" Anxiety skittered beneath her skin.

"It's your birthday, of course."

"My *twenty-third* birthday. Not significant enough for—" she swept her hand over the crowd, "—all of this."

"That's why we decided to celebrate your graduation, too," Micki said, snuggling into Gage's embrace.

Overwhelmed didn't begin to describe the emotions running amok inside her. People filled her mom's front lawn and a large white tent erected on the side of the house. A steady stream of ladies banged in and out of the kitchen's screened door, and men milled near the large grills. Children chased each other with plastic water guns, reminding her of the many paintball gun battles she and her siblings had fought over the years.

As her gaze swept over the crowd, she began seeing familiar, yet non-family, non-Steele Ridge resident, faces. Many of them were patients that she and Lisa had treated. But she saw no sign of Lisa.

She clenched her shaking hands into fists and willed her heart to calm its frantic pace.

"Excuse me, everyone." Her mom's amplified voice echoed over the valley.

While she'd been gawking at the guests, the boys had

assisted her mom into the bed of Old Blue, Britt's beloved heap pile of a truck. She stood above them all, holding Grif's hand, like a general about to address her troops. Surprise twisted her stomach when she noticed her father leaning against the side of the truck, giving her a proud thumbs-up.

Good Lord, something must be wrong for Eddy Steele to crawl out of the woods to come to a large get-together.

"Gather round, y'all." Her mom waited a few more minutes while everyone formed a semicircle around Old Blue. "As y'all know, we're celebrating two momentous occasions in my youngest daughter's life."

A large hand slid over her lower back, warming her as it moved to rest on her hip. "I got you, Squirt," Deke whispered, enveloping one bloodless fist in his palm. "Lean into me. Breathe."

She followed his instructions, while concentrating on her mom's beaming face. She wouldn't ruin this moment with an attack. She wouldn't. Not with Deke by her side. Deke—her lifeline in the darkness.

"Today, we honor Evie's twenty-third birthday with a gathering of family, friends, and good food." Her mom began the birthday song. "'Happy birthday to you, happy birthday to you...'"

Splaying her fingers wide, she coaxed her body to melt into Deke's. Her breathing and heartbeat soon eased into a normal, rhythmic pattern.

Lifting her chin, she smiled into Deke's concerned blue eyes. "Thank you."

He kissed her. Right there in front of her entire family and friends and a few people she couldn't recall. It started off sweet, reassuring, measured. But when her fingers tunneled into his hair, the tenor changed. Became more demanding, intimate, raw.

A throat cleared behind them, and she broke away, embarrassed but not ashamed. She peered over her shoulder to find Britt, one blond brow raised high.

Grif and Reid wore the same guard-like expressions. Micki winked.

She giggled. Couldn't help it. She loved these big lugs, no matter how irritating they tried to be. Snuggling into Deke's arms, she closed her eyes as the last of her birthday song came to a close.

"'Happy birthday to Evie. Happy birthday to yooooou.'"

"Now, to mark this moment in my daughter's professional journey, the Steele Health Foundation, with the help of your generous donations, is proud to present Evie with a brand new Med Mobile to replace the one lost in a tragic fire."

"What?" she asked, not believing her ears. "What did she say?"

Deke's hold tightened as everyone's attention swung to the opening behind Britt's truck. An engine rumbled in the distance, and she took a tentative step forward. Then another. When she no longer sensed Deke's presence, she searched for him over her shoulder.

With his rogue's smile in place, he said, "You got this, Squirt."

She produced a wobbly grin before continuing toward the rumbling sound. Then she saw it—them. Lisa in the driver's seat of an enormous, shiny new RV. Jonah stuck his head out the passenger side window, pointing at her, knowing she was about to die of shock and loving every second of his surprise.

Tears blurred her vision and heat crept up her neck. *OhmygodOhmygodOhmygod.*

The RV rolled to a stop beside her, and she read the slogan emblazoned on the side.

The Dawn of a New EVE
Health Care for Everyone

She cupped her hands over her nose and mouth, unable to believe her eyes. She couldn't breathe for an entirely different reason.

A gentle hand smoothed down her hair. "Do you like your surprise, sweetheart?"

"Oh, Mama. It's too m-much."

"Never." Tears filled her mom's eyes. "Miracles are going to happen in that RV. And my baby girl's going to be at the helm." She swiped at Evie's tears. "I'm so proud of you, Evelyn Steele."

She threw her arms around her mom. "Thank you, Mama."

"Don't thank me. Thank your brother, Jonah, for setting up the foundation, and all these wonderful people for donating their hard-earned money."

"Everyone?"

"Everyone. From one dollar up to a hundred. Aubrey even contributed ten dollars." Her mom cradled her cheek. "Some of the money went to assisting with Rachel's and Rita's funerals."

An image of Rachel on the floor of the RV, her life's blood pooling beneath her. And poor Rita. Such a sweet, kind woman didn't deserve such a violent end.

"Go on." Her mom nudged her away. "Thank your brother properly. We both know this wouldn't have happened without his generosity."

Drawing in a breath and wiping her eyes, she made her way toward the RV. Toward Jonah. Her pace increased until she was running full tilt. She jumped into his arms. He hugged her back just as fiercely.

"How am I ever going to repay you?" she asked, her face buried in the crook of his neck.

"Help them. Help as many as you can."

"I'm not ready. I still have so much to learn."

He coaxed her chin up. "Sounds like you need a mentor to guide you." His eyes panned to the right, where Lisa stood talking to Deke.

"You've thought of everything."

"Not me. The whole family was in on the caper. We make a good team."

She slid out of his arms. "Thank you. The words are inadequate, I know."

"Your smile was more than enough. Now get over there and hire your first employee."

Grinning, she kissed his cheek and skidded to a stop in front of Deke and Lisa.

"How'd it feel to drive that big rig?" she asked her friend.

"It's a smooth ride, despite its size." Lisa squeezed her arm. "There's so much room inside. You have a proper waiting room and a little nook for kids to occupy themselves while their parents are being treated."

"I can't wait to look inside." She held her hand out to Deke, and he threaded his fingers through hers. "Lisa, I was wondering. What are your plans over the next few years?"

"Back to full-time at the clinic, I guess. They still haven't committed to replacing the Med Mobile. Even if they did, I don't have an operating budget."

After some coaxing, Lisa had finally confided in Evie about the Med Mobile's reduced funding and the grant application as well as its subsequent denial. Why her friend had believed she needed to bear that burden alone, she didn't know. No wonder she'd been having migraines.

"What do you think about operating my Med Mobile?"

"Your—" Lisa's attention darted between her and the RV "—mobile?"

"I still have so much to learn and can't think of a better mentor."

Lisa placed a trembling fingers against her lips. "Are you sure?"

"Of course. Why wouldn't I be?"

"I don't know what to say."

"How about yes?"

"Yes!" Lisa launched forward and threw her arms around Evie. "Yes, yes, yes! Thank you, thank you, thank you."

Evie laughed. "Just remember how happy you are right now, because I'm sure to annoy you later."

"Not possible." Lisa withdrew. "Now I need to start planning our next tour."

"Why am I not surprised?"

Lisa glanced between Evie and Deke, her smile warming. "I'll see you two later."

Feeling more content than ever before, Evie slid into Deke's arms. "That felt good."

"Good deeds always do. You have a sweet and generous soul."

"It wasn't entirely altruistic. I need her as much as she needs me."

"Then you made the right decision."

"Life's about to get very busy." She held his gaze. "It'll take a while for us to work out a rhythm."

"It'll be a beautiful melody when we're done."

She smiled. "Yes, it will."

He drew a line down her nose. "What do you think about kids?"

Her chest clinched. "Umm—"

"They're so cute, especially when they're small."

"Small—"

"Since you'll be busy with graduate school and squeezing in tours when you can, I'm thinking about adopting a couple kids."

She couldn't think of a time when she'd ever been struck speechless, but Deke had managed the feat.

"Two, maybe three, to start with. Of course, I'll need to get a house with a yard. Give them someplace to play and eat."

"I've heard the adoption process takes months, sometimes years."

"Shouldn't be an issue. There's a farm in Black Mountain that has a surplus."

Shaking her head, she asked, "Farm?"

His lips twitched.

Her eyes narrowed. "Kids. As in goats?"

"They make great lawnmowers, I hear."

She whacked his arm. "How about we get you a puppy or kitten, instead."

He kissed her softly. "I'll take one of all three."

"Good Lord," she nuzzled his nose, "we're going to wind up with a menagerie."

"Lots of animals need saving."

"People, too."

"Guess we'd better start with the two of us."

"Done."

Clasping her beneath the arms, he lifted her until her legs wrapped around his waist. "Ready for your birthday present?" His hands slid under her dress to cup her bottom.

"I already got it." She ran her fingers through his hair.

He started walking down the hill, away from the guests. "Not my special gift."

"Then let's go open it." She clenched her legs, bringing his erection into her center. "Together."

"Together."

Steele Ridge Series

Going HARD
Living FAST
Loving DEEP
Breaking FREE
Roaming WILD

Coming in 2017

Stripping BARE

www.SteeleRidgeSeries.com

Author's Note

While doing research for another series, I came across an interesting article in *OutdoorHub*. The author, James Swan, shared a story about a chance meeting he had with a U.S. Fish & Wildlife Service special agent.

Special agent? In the USFWS?

The gentleman went on to characterize this elite group of agents within the Service as the FBI of game wardens.

I was instantly captivated.

My author's mind began spinning for possibilities on how I could incorporate a USFWS special agent into my conservation corner of the Steele Ridge world. Luckily for me, Britt Steele had a biologist best friend—Derek "Deke" Conrad.

While writing *Loving DEEP*, I hadn't yet uncovered Deke's full professional potential. That changed in *Roaming WILD*.

Though USFWS special agents collaborate with many agencies, they seem, to me, to be loners. Now I know romance readers love a good brooding I-don't-need-anyone hero (I include myself in this category), but this didn't fit Deke's character.

Deke's a social guy. Loves people. He needed a team.

So I brainstormed ways to give him a support group. It didn't take me long to come up with an elite, black ops team hand selected from the ranks of special agents.

Thus, Special Operations for Natural Resources, aka SONR, was born.

I had a ton of fun getting to know Keone, Wes, Matteo, Raelyn, Taji, and let's not forget tell-it-like-it-is Jax.

I hope you enjoyed SONR, my fictional interpretation of a dedicated group of men and women who work hard to protect our precious natural resources, every day. A resourceful team willing to put their lives in danger for their beliefs, their passions.

Many readers might be wondering why all this species diversity stuff is important. It's not something many of us will notice as a part of our daily lives.

Unless...

We pause a moment in our backyard and inhale a deep clean breath of air, we glance over our shoulder while sitting at a stoplight to appreciate the swaying tallgrass in a local prairie, we brake to a stop on a bridge during our weekend bike ride to marvel at the clear flowing water in the creek below, or we travel to a national park, walk the trails, and soak in the sounds and scents of the wild things that call such a place home—and note how our minds grow calmer and how the white noise of our lives disappears, leaving us happier and healthier than when we started the journey.

Only then do we come to realize that everything on this beautiful earth is interconnected—from the speck of dust on a coffee table to an eagle soaring high above her nest perched on the cliff's edge.

It all matters.

Every. Single. Bit.

ACKNOWLEDGMENTS

A million thanks to my husband. His patience, love, and generosity makes it possible for me to write about the beauty of the human heart every day.

As always, I'm indebted to Adrienne Giordano and Kelsey Browning. Sisters of my heart, writers extraordinaire.

My editor, Deborah Nemeth and copy editor, Martha Trachtenberg, have my infinite gratitude for their wise counsel and eagle eye.

Kim Killion, I adore your talent. *Roaming WILD's* cover could not be more perfect.

As I have never written a military-style book before, I must give enormous thanks to Scott Silverii for helping me bring SONR to life. I love this group of wildlife warriors and hope to see more of them in the future.

Special thanks to my friend and Lady Jane's Salon-goer, Liz Semkiu, for helping me bring *Roaming WILD's* Med Mobile to life. The inside of the RV would have consisted of an exam table and a stethoscope, without your expert advice.

Sending a big hug to you, dear reader. Thank you for your continued enthusiasm and support of my stories. You're amazing!

TRACEY DEVLYN is a *USA Today* bestselling author of contemporary and historical romantic suspense, historical mysteries, and mainstream thrillers. An Illinois native, Tracey spends her evenings harassing her once-in-a-lifetime husband and her weekends torturing her characters.

www.TraceyDevlyn.com

CPSIA information can be obtained
at www.ICGtesting.com
Printed in the USA
LVOW13s1050190717
541880LV00023B/925/P